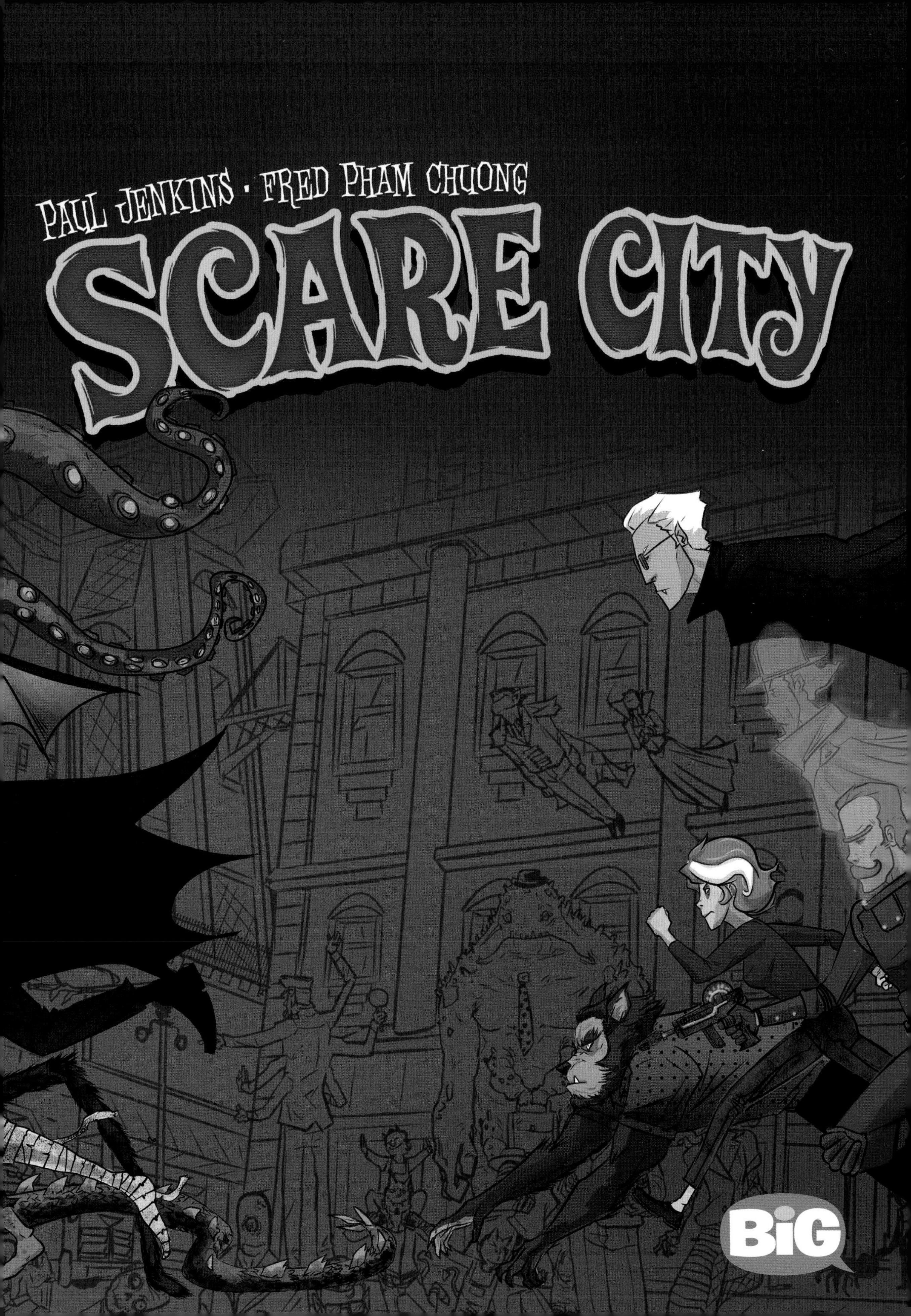
PAUL JENKINS · FRED PHAM CHUONG
SCARE CITY
BiG

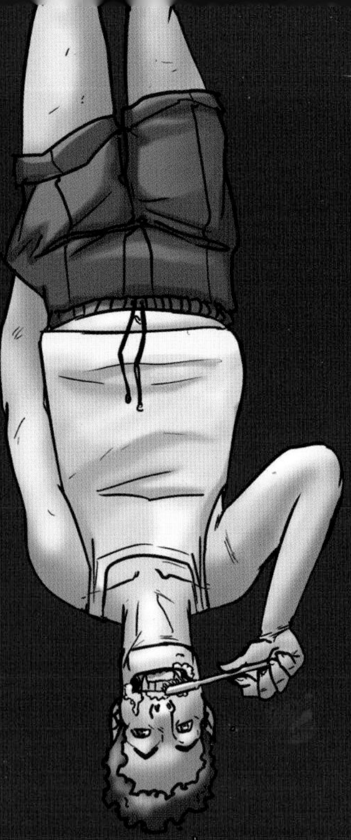

PAUL JENKINS
WRITER

FRED PHAM CHUONG
ARTIST

VERONICA R. LOPEZ
(COVER, P. 2–85)
CHRISTOPHE SONESAKSITH
(P. 86–116)
COLORISTS

A LARGER WORLD STUDIOS
LETTERING

FABRICE SAPOLSKY
SENIOR EDITOR

AMANDA LUCIDO
ASSISTANT EDITOR

JERRY FRISSEN
SENIOR ART DIRECTOR

FABRICE GIGER
PUBLISHER

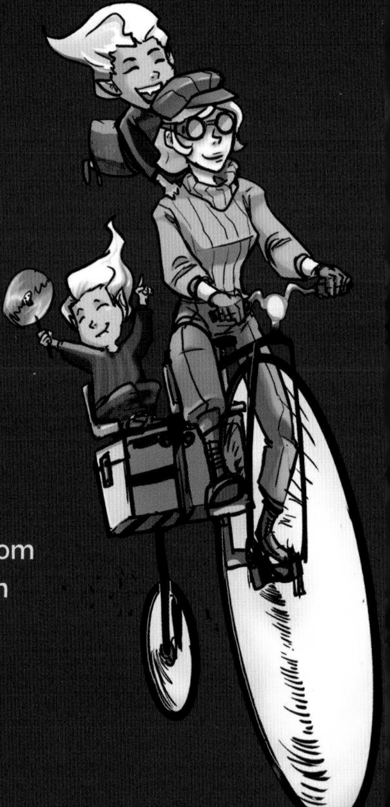

Rights and Licensing - licensing@humanoids.com
Press and Social Media - pr@humanoids.com

SCARE CITY. This title is a publication of Humanoids, Inc. 8033 Sunset Blvd. #628, Los Angeles, CA 90046.

Library of Congress Control Number: 2019930232

BIG is an imprint of Humanoids, Inc.

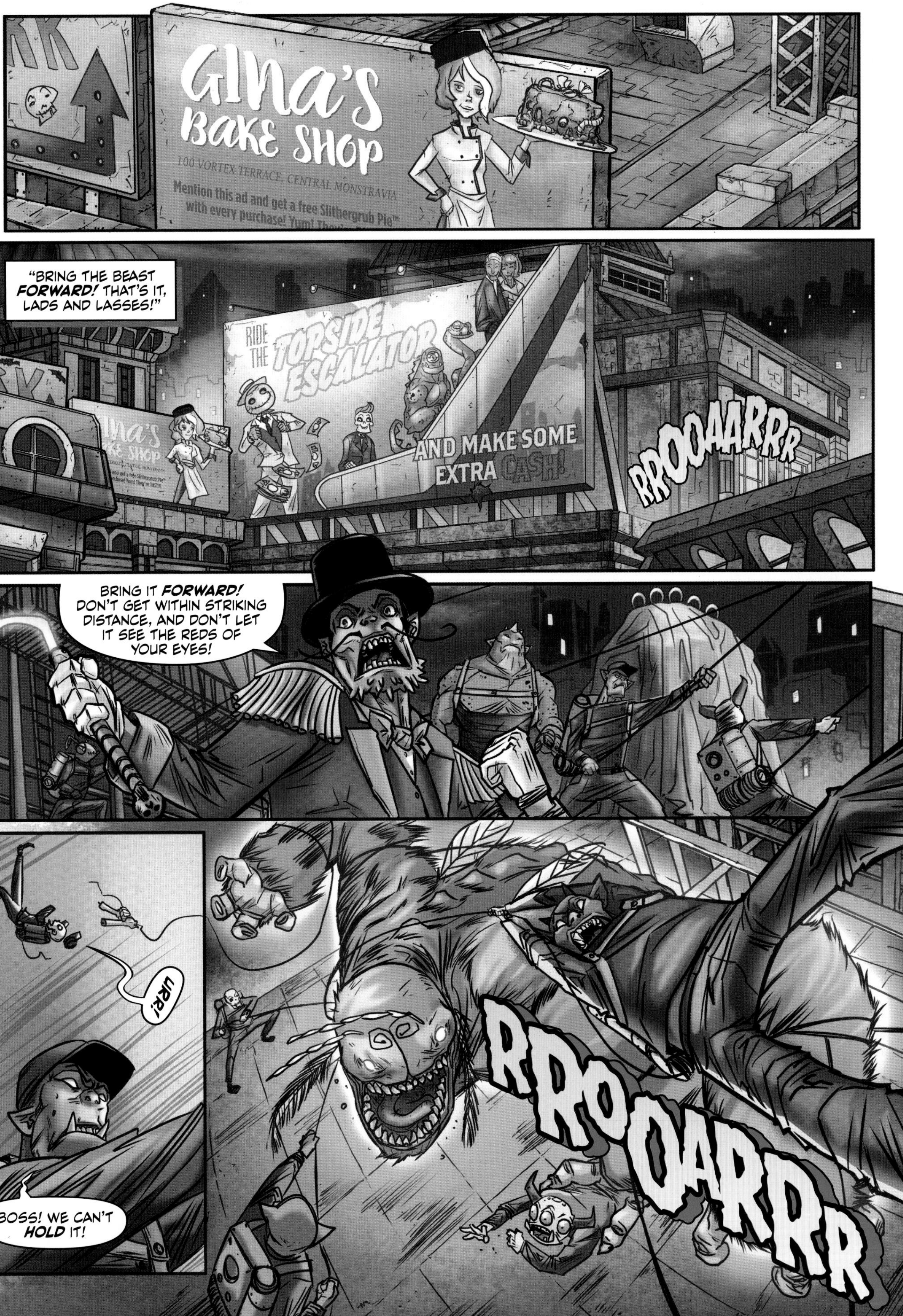
GINA'S BAKE SHOP
100 VORTEX TERRACE, CENTRAL MONSTRAVIA
Mention this ad and get a free Slithergrub Pie™ with every purchase! Yum!
"BRING THE BEAST *FORWARD!* THAT'S IT, LADS AND LASSES!"
RIDE THE TOPSIDE ESCALATOR
AND MAKE SOME EXTRA CASH!
RROOAARRRR
BRING IT *FORWARD!* DON'T GET WITHIN STRIKING DISTANCE, AND DON'T LET IT SEE THE REDS OF YOUR EYES!
URR!
BOSS! WE CAN'T *HOLD* IT!
RROOARRRR

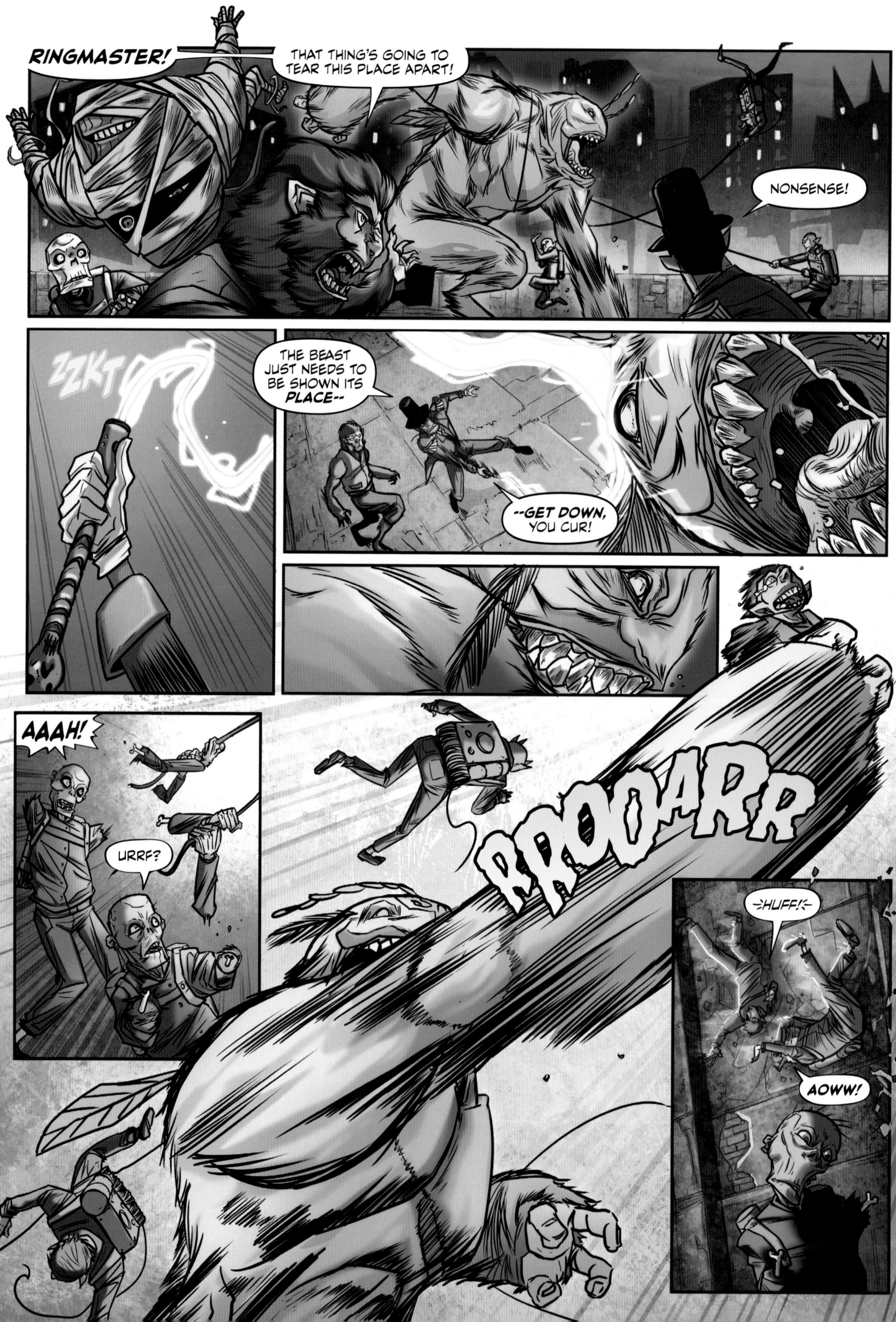
RINGMASTER!
THAT THING'S GOING TO TEAR THIS PLACE APART!
NONSENSE!
ZZKT
THE BEAST JUST NEEDS TO BE SHOWN ITS PLACE--
--GET DOWN, YOU CUR!
AAAH!
URRF?
RROOARR
HUFF!
AOWW!

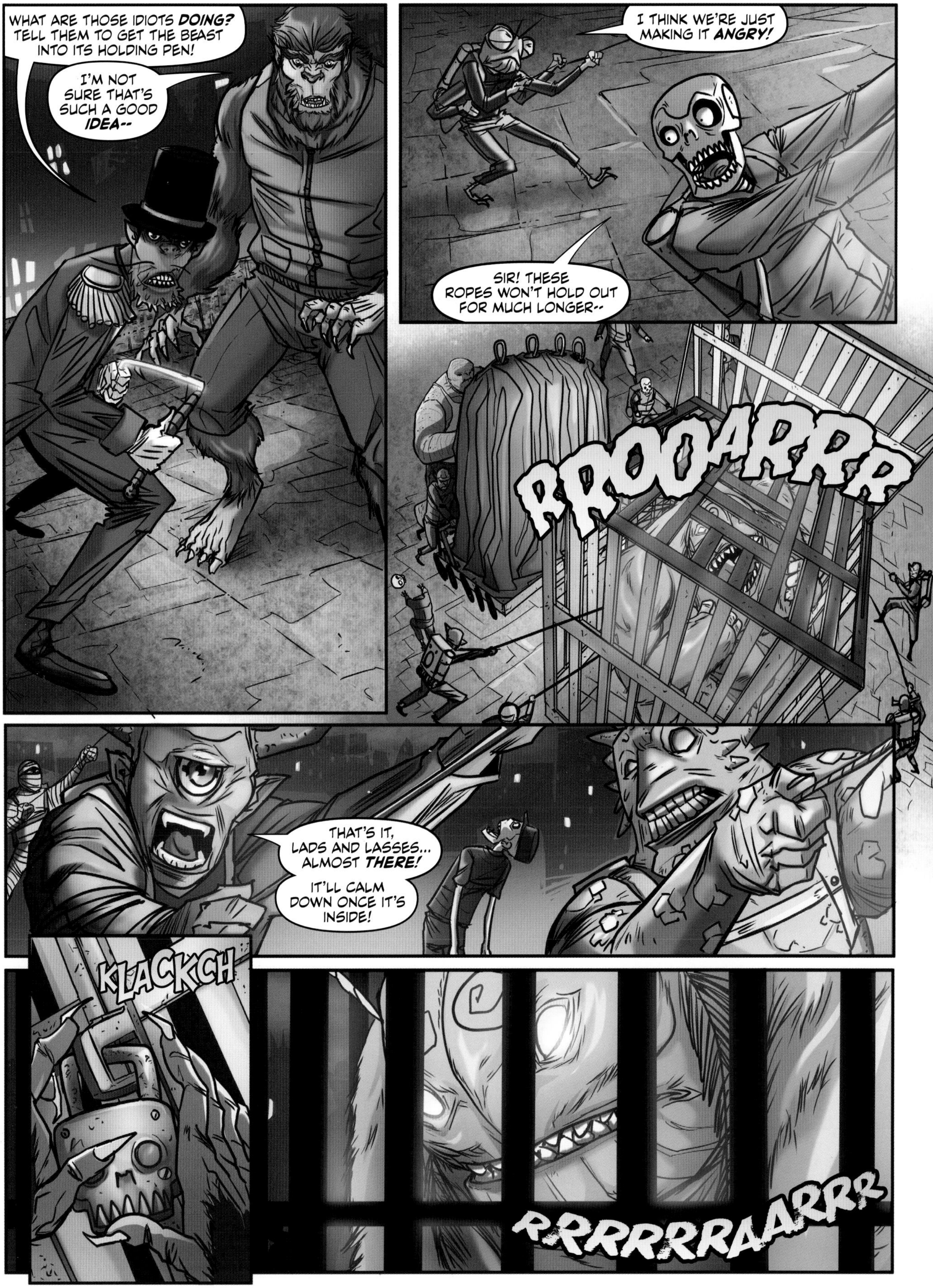
WHAT ARE THOSE IDIOTS DOING? TELL THEM TO GET THE BEAST INTO ITS HOLDING PEN!
I'M NOT SURE THAT'S SUCH A GOOD IDEA--
I THINK WE'RE JUST MAKING IT ANGRY!
SIR! THESE ROPES WON'T HOLD OUT FOR MUCH LONGER--
RROOARRR
THAT'S IT, LADS AND LASSES... ALMOST THERE!
IT'LL CALM DOWN ONCE IT'S INSIDE!
KLACKCH
RRRRRRAARRR

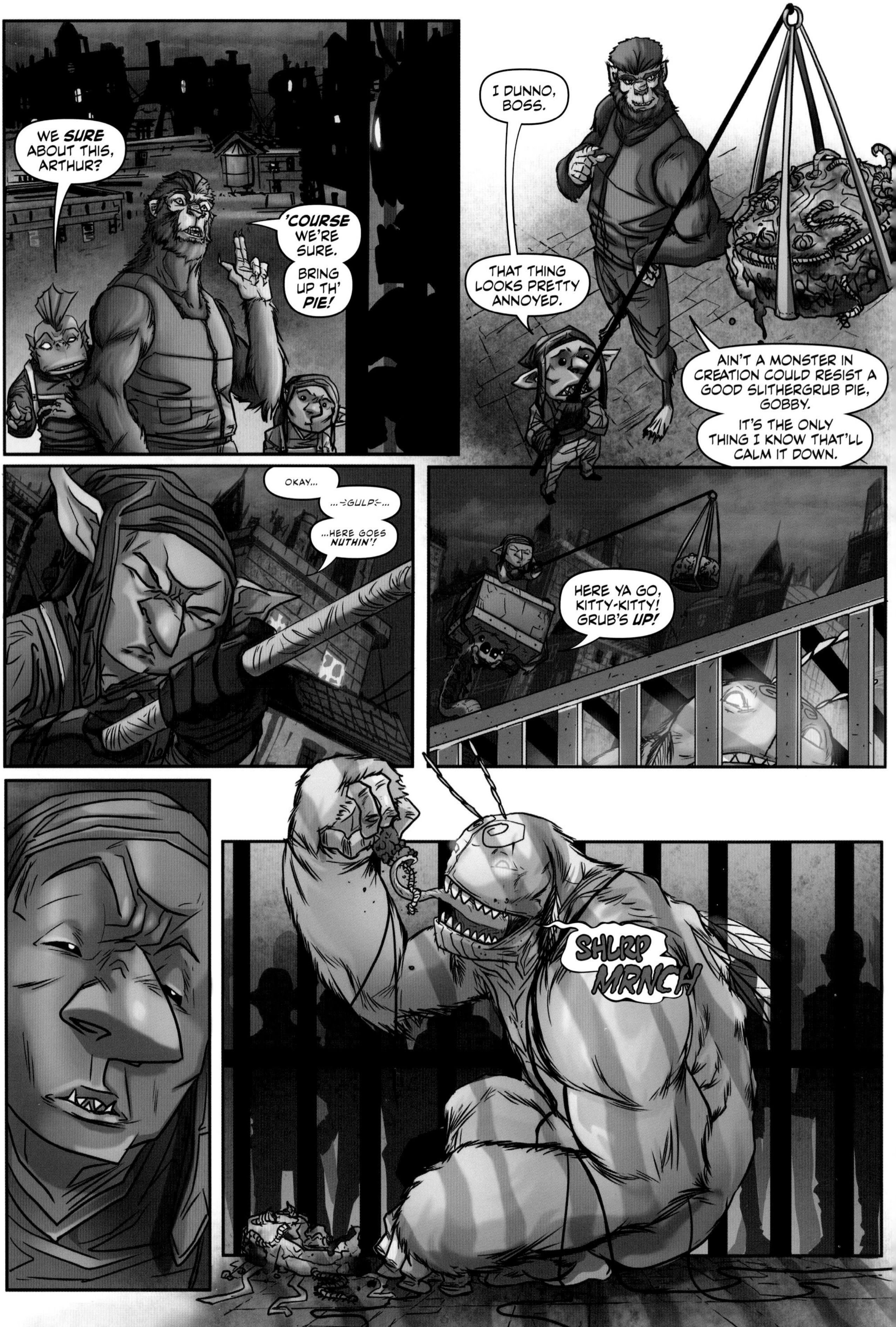
WE SURE ABOUT THIS, ARTHUR?
'COURSE WE'RE SURE.
BRING UP TH' PIE!
I DUNNO, BOSS.
THAT THING LOOKS PRETTY ANNOYED.
AIN'T A MONSTER IN CREATION COULD RESIST A GOOD SLITHERGRUB PIE, GOBBY.
IT'S THE ONLY THING I KNOW THAT'LL CALM IT DOWN.
OKAY...
...GULP...
...HERE GOES NUTHIN'!
HERE YA GO, KITTY-KITTY! GRUB'S UP!
SHLRP
MRNCH

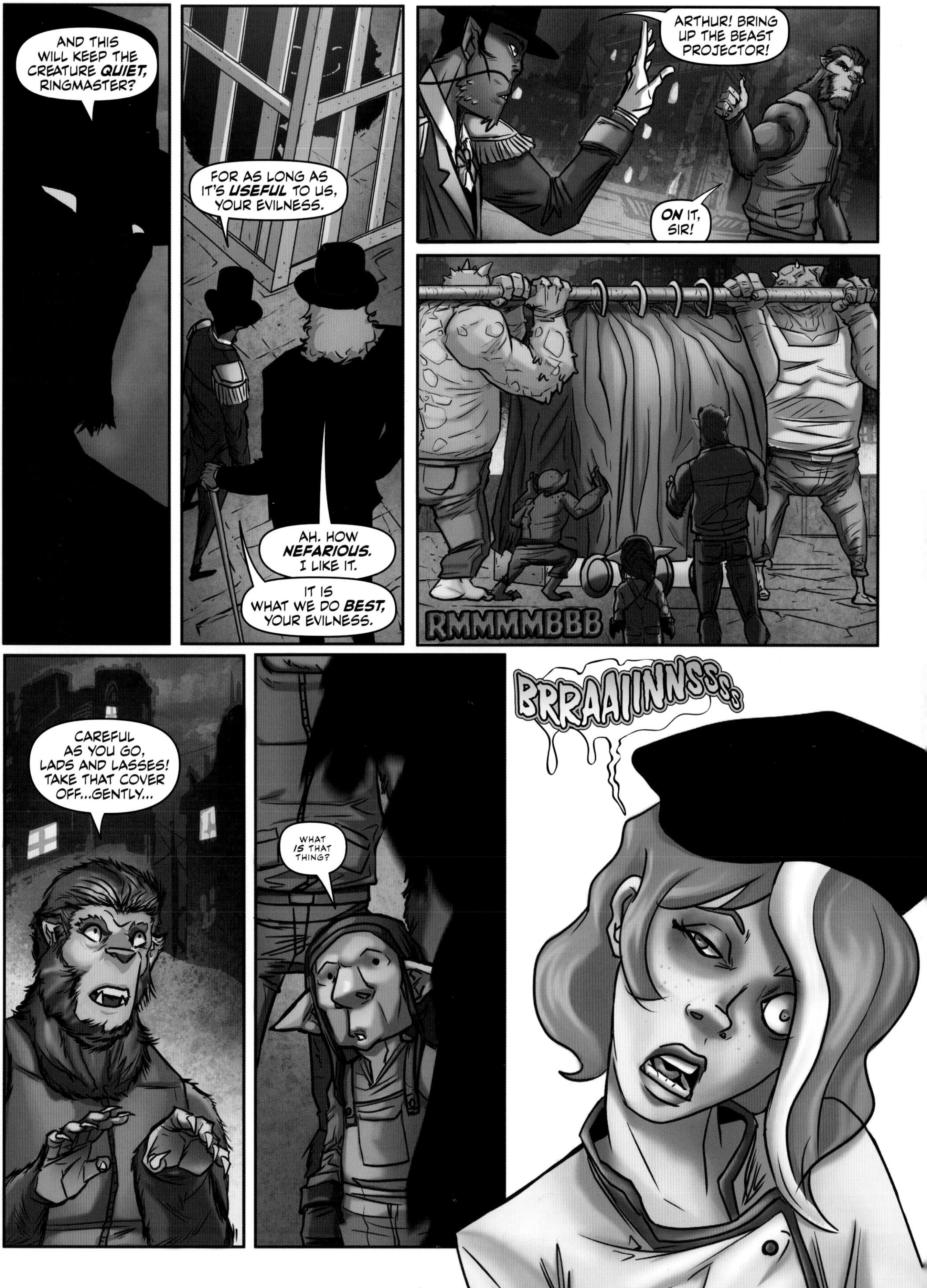
AND THIS WILL KEEP THE CREATURE QUIET, RINGMASTER?
FOR AS LONG AS IT'S USEFUL TO US, YOUR EVILNESS.
AH. HOW NEFARIOUS. I LIKE IT.
IT IS WHAT WE DO BEST, YOUR EVILNESS.
ARTHUR! BRING UP THE BEAST PROJECTOR!
ON IT, SIR!
RMMMMBBB
CAREFUL AS YOU GO, LADS AND LASSES! TAKE THAT COVER OFF...GENTLY...
WHAT IS THAT THING?
BRRAAIINNSSss

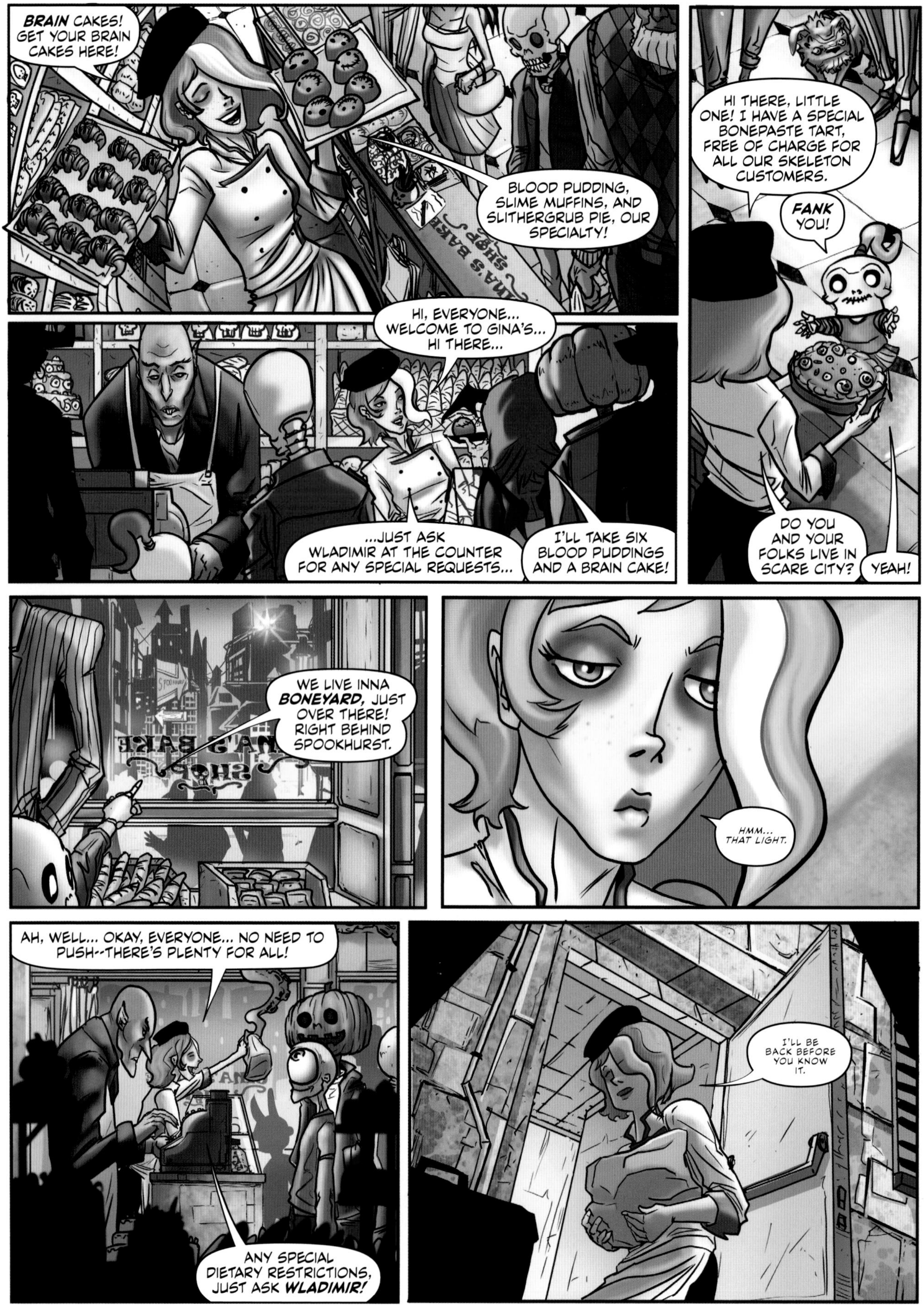

BRAIN CAKES! GET YOUR BRAIN CAKES HERE!
BLOOD PUDDING, SLIME MUFFINS, AND SLITHERGRUB PIE, OUR SPECIALTY!
HI THERE, LITTLE ONE! I HAVE A SPECIAL BONEPASTE TART, FREE OF CHARGE FOR ALL OUR SKELETON CUSTOMERS.
FANK YOU!
HI, EVERYONE... WELCOME TO GINA'S... HI THERE...
...JUST ASK WLADIMIR AT THE COUNTER FOR ANY SPECIAL REQUESTS...
I'LL TAKE SIX BLOOD PUDDINGS AND A BRAIN CAKE!
DO YOU AND YOUR FOLKS LIVE IN SCARE CITY?
YEAH!
WE LIVE INNA BONEYARD, JUST OVER THERE! RIGHT BEHIND SPOOKHURST.
HMM... THAT LIGHT.
AH, WELL... OKAY, EVERYONE... NO NEED TO PUSH--THERE'S PLENTY FOR ALL!
ANY SPECIAL DIETARY RESTRICTIONS, JUST ASK WLADIMIR!
I'LL BE BACK BEFORE YOU KNOW IT.

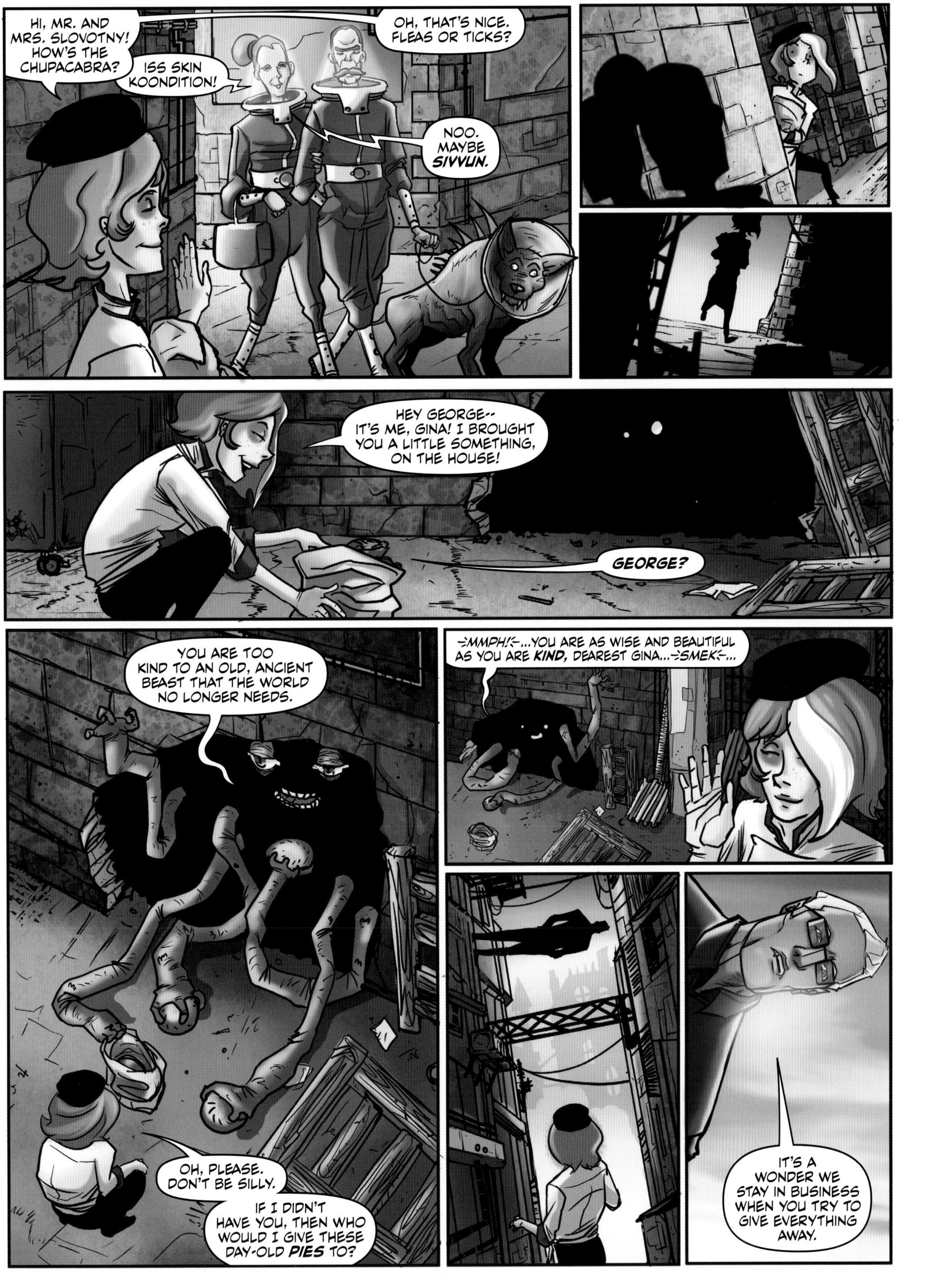
HI, MR. AND MRS. SLOVOTNY! HOW'S THE CHUPACABRA?
ISS SKIN KOONDITION!
OH, THAT'S NICE. FLEAS OR TICKS?
NOO. MAYBE SIVVUN.
HEY GEORGE-- IT'S ME, GINA! I BROUGHT YOU A LITTLE SOMETHING, ON THE HOUSE!
GEORGE?
YOU ARE TOO KIND TO AN OLD, ANCIENT BEAST THAT THE WORLD NO LONGER NEEDS.
OH, PLEASE. DON'T BE SILLY.
IF I DIDN'T HAVE YOU, THEN WHO WOULD I GIVE THESE DAY-OLD PIES TO?
=MMPH!=...YOU ARE AS WISE AND BEAUTIFUL AS YOU ARE KIND, DEAREST GINA...=SMEK=...
IT'S A WONDER WE STAY IN BUSINESS WHEN YOU TRY TO GIVE EVERYTHING AWAY.

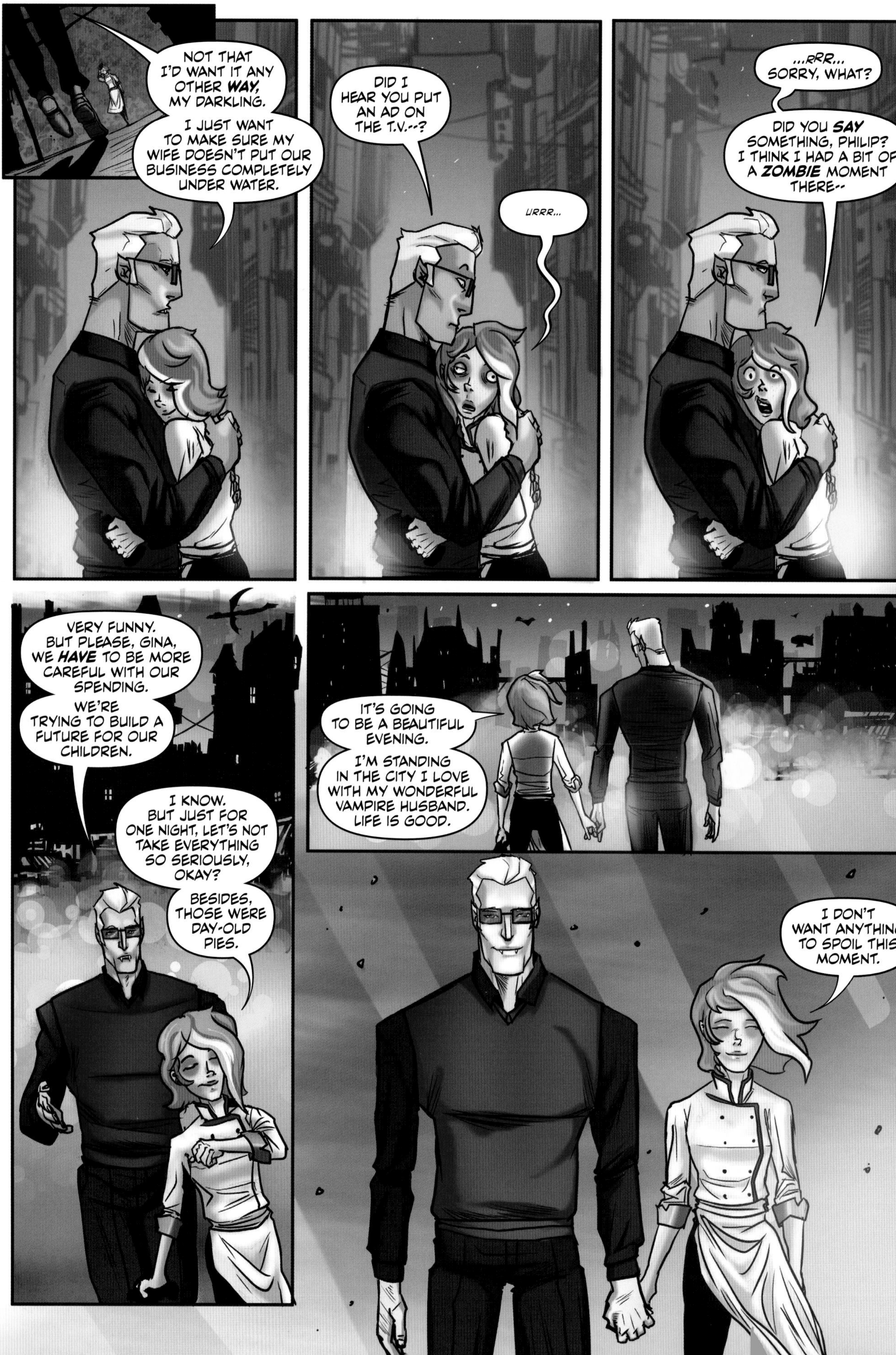
NOT THAT I'D WANT IT ANY OTHER WAY, MY DARKLING.
I JUST WANT TO MAKE SURE MY WIFE DOESN'T PUT OUR BUSINESS COMPLETELY UNDER WATER.
DID I HEAR YOU PUT AN AD ON THE T.V.--?
URRR...
...RRR... SORRY, WHAT?
DID YOU SAY SOMETHING, PHILIP? I THINK I HAD A BIT OF A ZOMBIE MOMENT THERE--
VERY FUNNY. BUT PLEASE, GINA, WE HAVE TO BE MORE CAREFUL WITH OUR SPENDING.
WE'RE TRYING TO BUILD A FUTURE FOR OUR CHILDREN.
I KNOW. BUT JUST FOR ONE NIGHT, LET'S NOT TAKE EVERYTHING SO SERIOUSLY, OKAY?
BESIDES, THOSE WERE DAY-OLD PIES.
IT'S GOING TO BE A BEAUTIFUL EVENING.
I'M STANDING IN THE CITY I LOVE WITH MY WONDERFUL VAMPIRE HUSBAND. LIFE IS GOOD.
I DON'T WANT ANYTHING TO SPOIL THIS MOMENT.

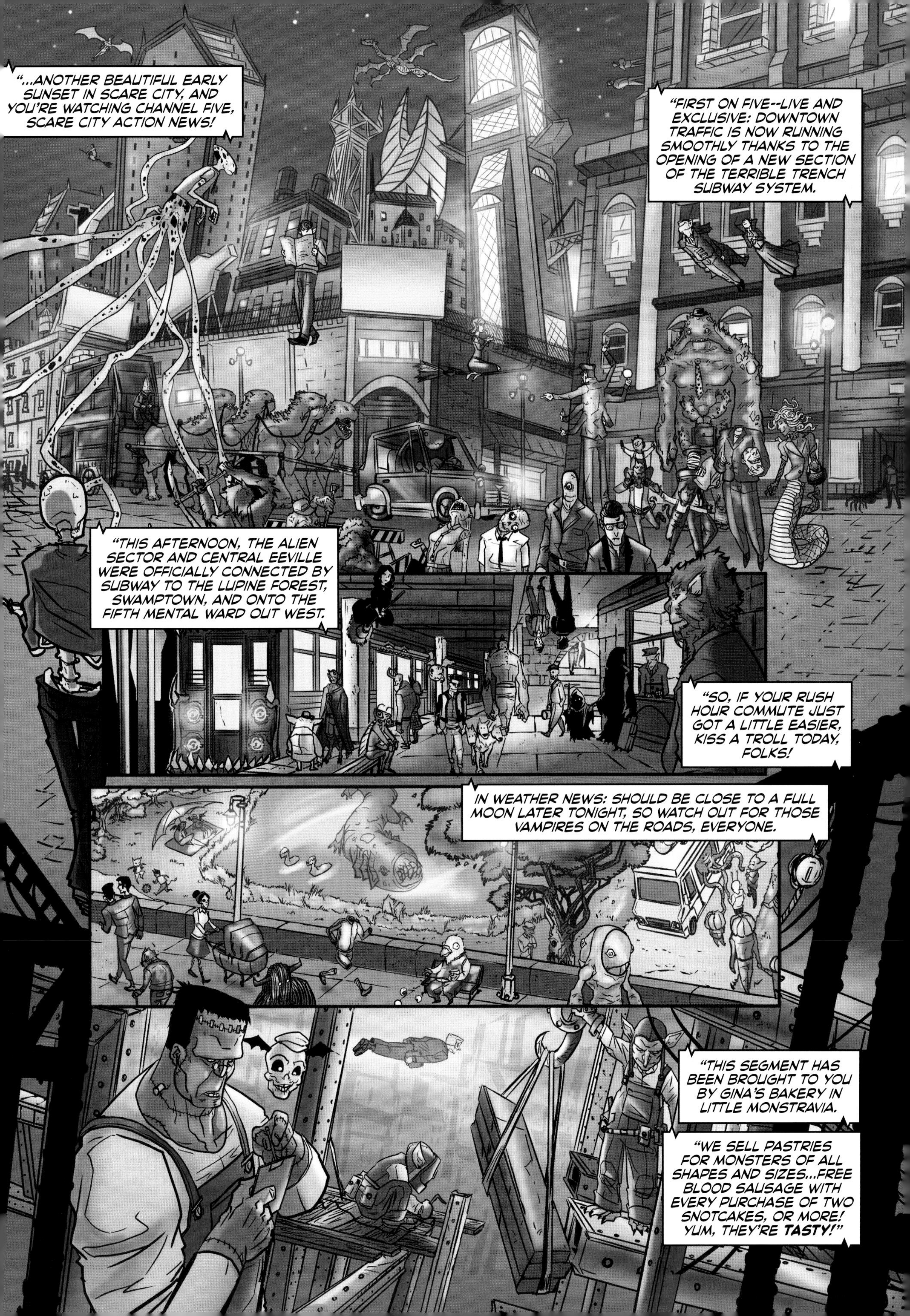
"...ANOTHER BEAUTIFUL EARLY SUNSET IN SCARE CITY, AND YOU'RE WATCHING CHANNEL FIVE, SCARE CITY ACTION NEWS!
"FIRST ON FIVE--LIVE AND EXCLUSIVE: DOWNTOWN TRAFFIC IS NOW RUNNING SMOOTHLY THANKS TO THE OPENING OF A NEW SECTION OF THE TERRIBLE TRENCH SUBWAY SYSTEM.
"THIS AFTERNOON, THE ALIEN SECTOR AND CENTRAL EEVILLE WERE OFFICIALLY CONNECTED BY SUBWAY TO THE LUPINE FOREST, SWAMPTOWN, AND ONTO THE FIFTH MENTAL WARD OUT WEST.
"SO, IF YOUR RUSH HOUR COMMUTE JUST GOT A LITTLE EASIER, KISS A TROLL TODAY, FOLKS!
IN WEATHER NEWS: SHOULD BE CLOSE TO A FULL MOON LATER TONIGHT, SO WATCH OUT FOR THOSE VAMPIRES ON THE ROADS, EVERYONE.
"THIS SEGMENT HAS BEEN BROUGHT TO YOU BY GINA'S BAKERY IN LITTLE MONSTRAVIA.
"WE SELL PASTRIES FOR MONSTERS OF ALL SHAPES AND SIZES...FREE BLOOD SAUSAGE WITH EVERY PURCHASE OF TWO SNOTCAKES, OR MORE! YUM, THEY'RE **TASTY!**"

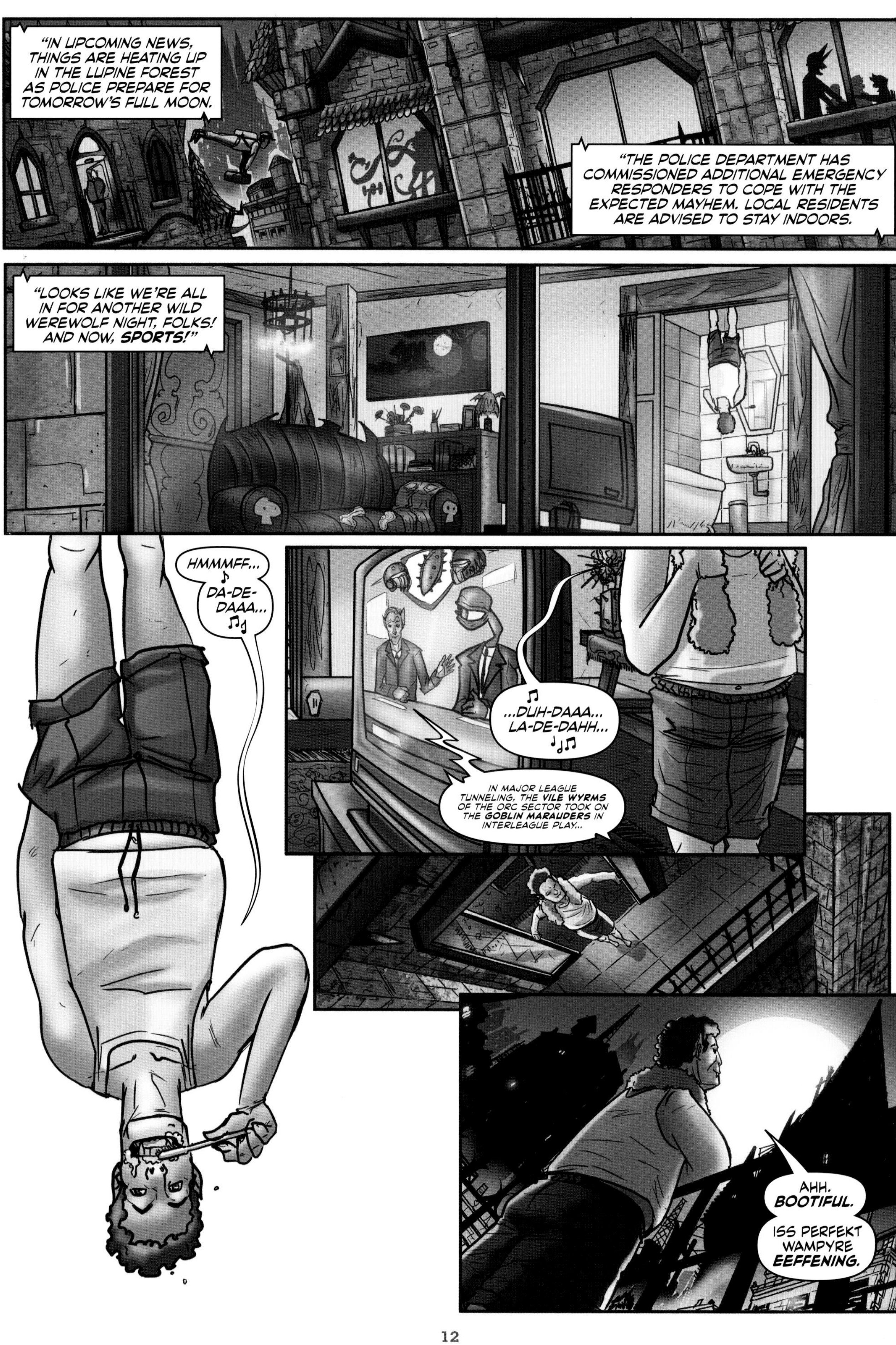
"IN UPCOMING NEWS, THINGS ARE HEATING UP IN THE LUPINE FOREST AS POLICE PREPARE FOR TOMORROW'S FULL MOON.
"THE POLICE DEPARTMENT HAS COMMISSIONED ADDITIONAL EMERGENCY RESPONDERS TO COPE WITH THE EXPECTED MAYHEM. LOCAL RESIDENTS ARE ADVISED TO STAY INDOORS.
"LOOKS LIKE WE'RE ALL IN FOR ANOTHER WILD WEREWOLF NIGHT, FOLKS! AND NOW, **SPORTS!**"
HMMMFF... ♪ DA-DE-DAAA... ♫♩
♫ ...DUH-DAAA... LA-DE-DAHH... ♩♩♫
IN MAJOR LEAGUE TUNNELING, THE **VILE WYRMS** OF THE ORC SECTOR TOOK ON THE **GOBLIN MARAUDERS** IN INTERLEAGUE PLAY...
AHH. **BOOTIFUL.**
ISS PERFEKT WAMPYRE **EEFFENING.**

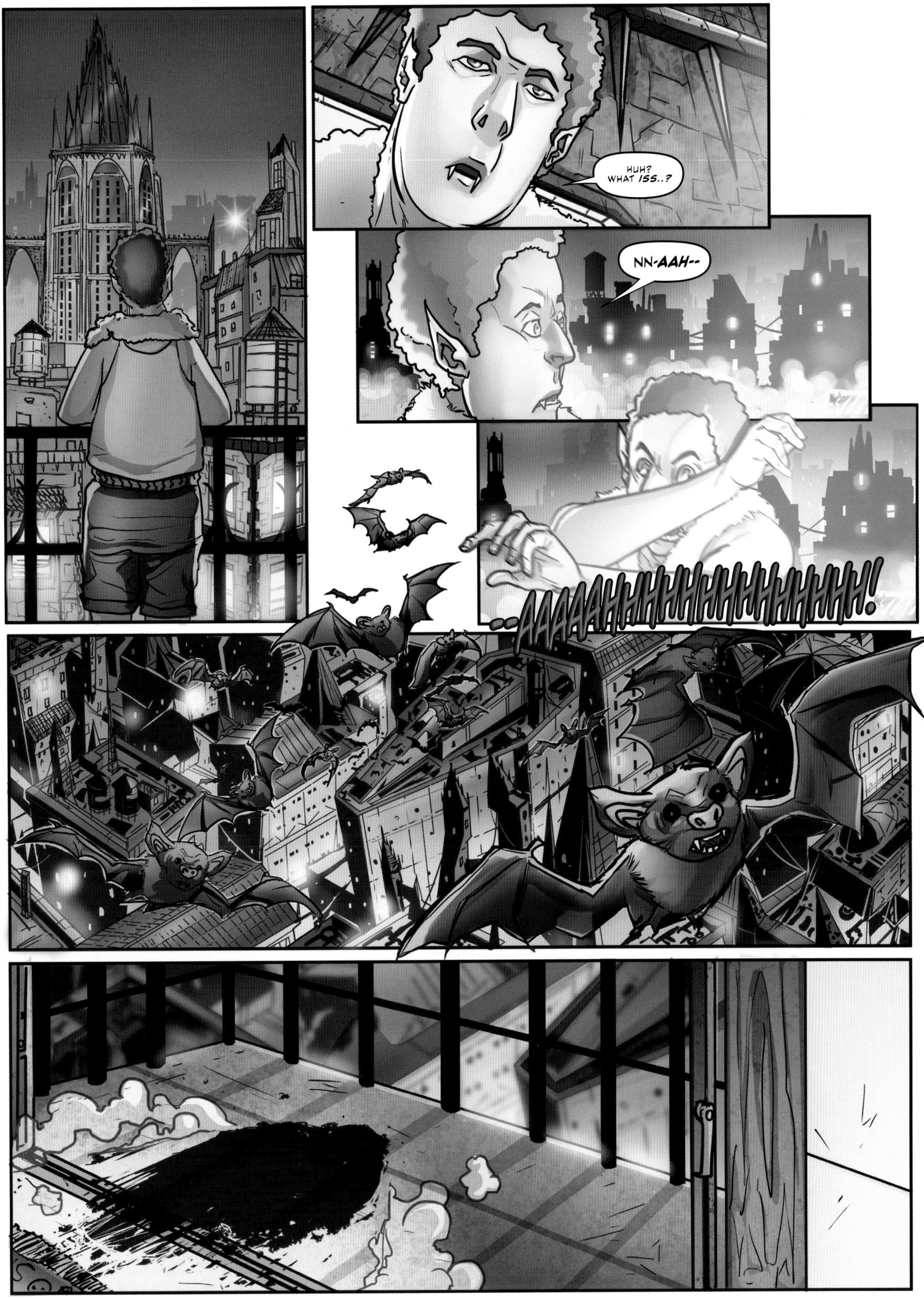
HUH? WHAT ISS..?
NN-AAH--
--AAAAAHHHHHHHHHHHHHHHH!

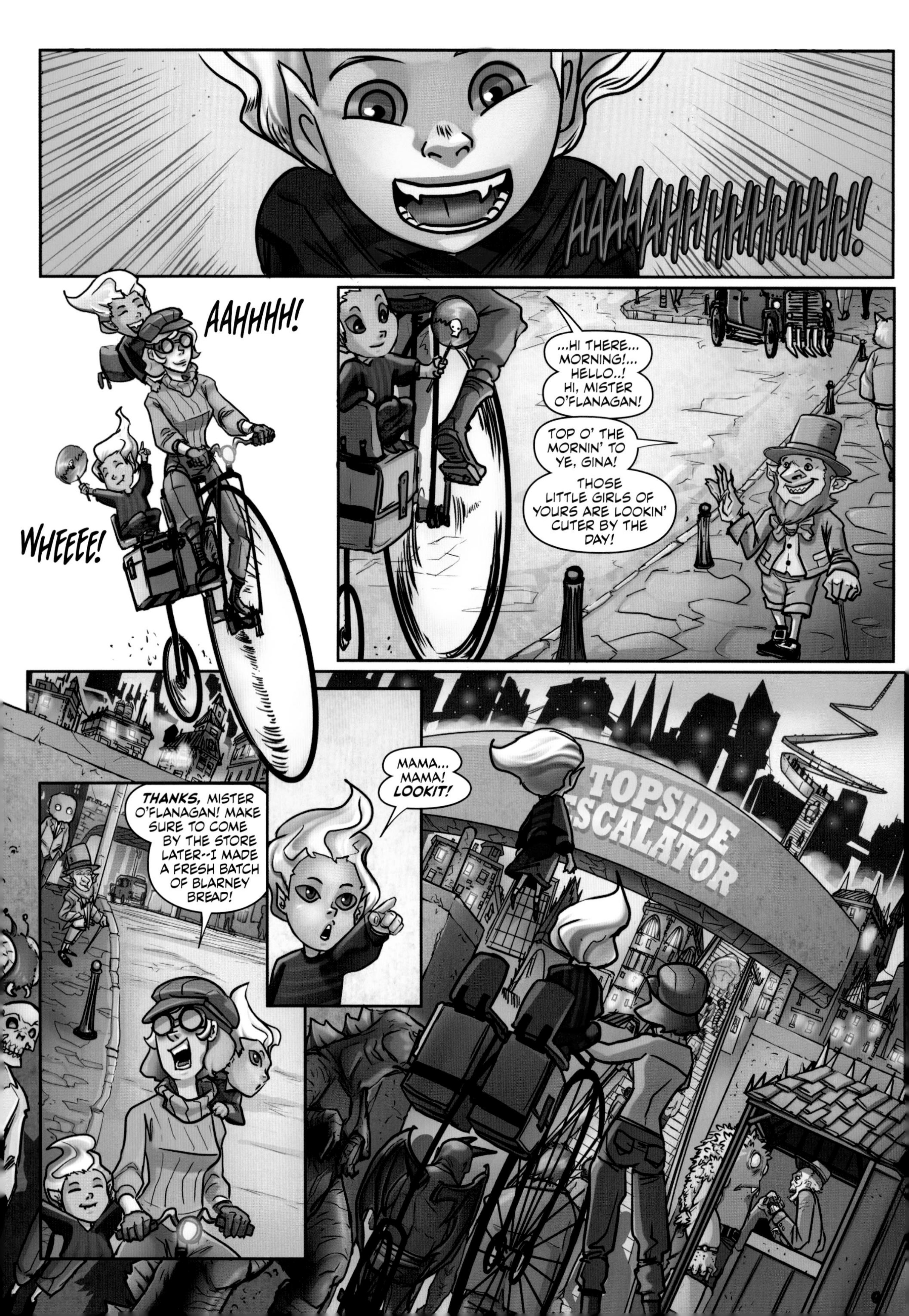
AAAAAHHHHHHHHH!
AAHHHH!
WHEEEEE!
...HI THERE... MORNING!... HELLO..! HI, MISTER O'FLANAGAN!
TOP O' THE MORNIN' TO YE, GINA!
THOSE LITTLE GIRLS OF YOURS ARE LOOKIN' CUTER BY THE DAY!
THANKS, MISTER O'FLANAGAN! MAKE SURE TO COME BY THE STORE LATER--I MADE A FRESH BATCH OF BLARNEY BREAD!
MAMA... MAMA! LOOKIT!
TOPSIDE ESCALATOR

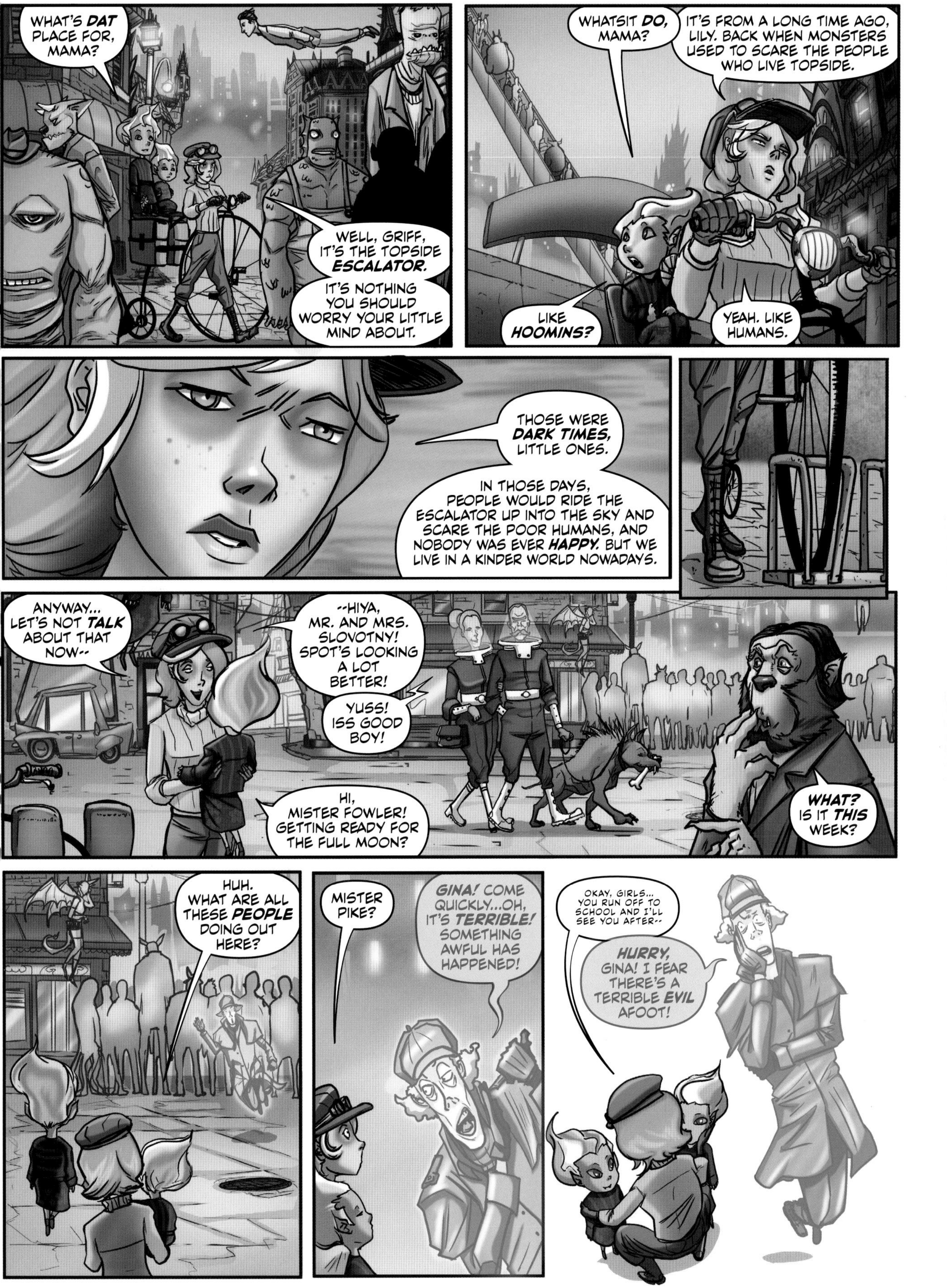
WHAT'S DAT PLACE FOR, MAMA?
WELL, GRIFF, IT'S THE TOPSIDE ESCALATOR.
IT'S NOTHING YOU SHOULD WORRY YOUR LITTLE MIND ABOUT.
WHATSIT DO, MAMA?
IT'S FROM A LONG TIME AGO, LILY. BACK WHEN MONSTERS USED TO SCARE THE PEOPLE WHO LIVE TOPSIDE.
LIKE HOOMINS?
YEAH. LIKE HUMANS.
THOSE WERE DARK TIMES, LITTLE ONES.
IN THOSE DAYS, PEOPLE WOULD RIDE THE ESCALATOR UP INTO THE SKY AND SCARE THE POOR HUMANS, AND NOBODY WAS EVER HAPPY. BUT WE LIVE IN A KINDER WORLD NOWADAYS.
ANYWAY... LET'S NOT TALK ABOUT THAT NOW--
--HIYA, MR. AND MRS. SLOVOTNY! SPOT'S LOOKING A LOT BETTER!
YUSS! ISS GOOD BOY!
HI, MISTER FOWLER! GETTING READY FOR THE FULL MOON?
WHAT? IS IT THIS WEEK?
HUH. WHAT ARE ALL THESE PEOPLE DOING OUT HERE?
MISTER PIKE?
GINA! COME QUICKLY...OH, IT'S TERRIBLE! SOMETHING AWFUL HAS HAPPENED!
OKAY, GIRLS... YOU RUN OFF TO SCHOOL AND I'LL SEE YOU AFTER--
HURRY, GINA! I FEAR THERE'S A TERRIBLE EVIL AFOOT!

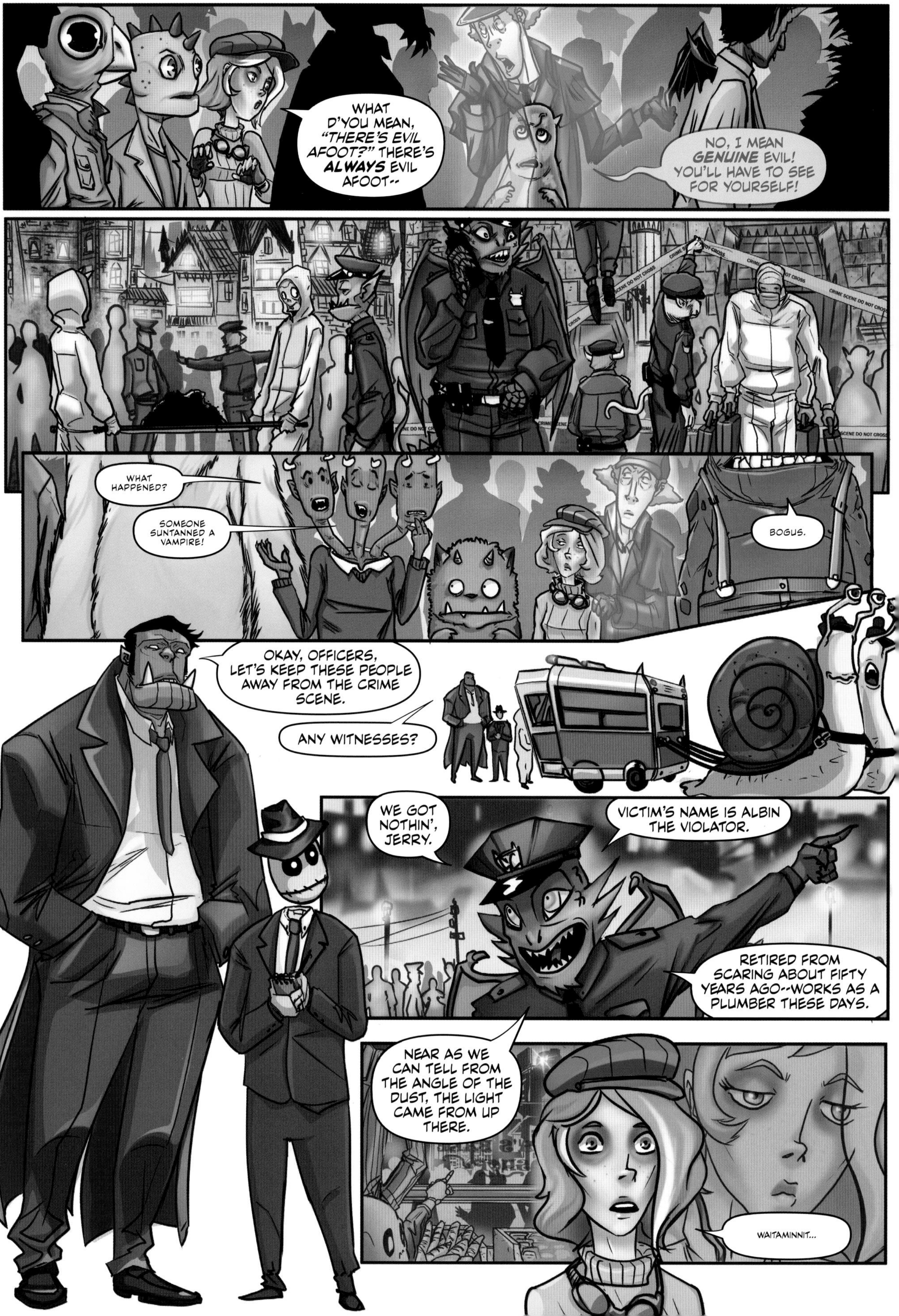

WHAT D'YOU MEAN, "THERE'S EVIL AFOOT?" THERE'S ALWAYS EVIL AFOOT--
NO, I MEAN GENUINE EVIL! YOU'LL HAVE TO SEE FOR YOURSELF!
CRIME SCENE DO NOT CROSS
WHAT HAPPENED?
SOMEONE SUNTANNED A VAMPIRE!
BOGUS.
OKAY, OFFICERS, LET'S KEEP THESE PEOPLE AWAY FROM THE CRIME SCENE.
ANY WITNESSES?
WE GOT NOTHIN', JERRY.
VICTIM'S NAME IS ALBIN THE VIOLATOR.
RETIRED FROM SCARING ABOUT FIFTY YEARS AGO--WORKS AS A PLUMBER THESE DAYS.
NEAR AS WE CAN TELL FROM THE ANGLE OF THE DUST, THE LIGHT CAME FROM UP THERE.
WAITAMINNIT...

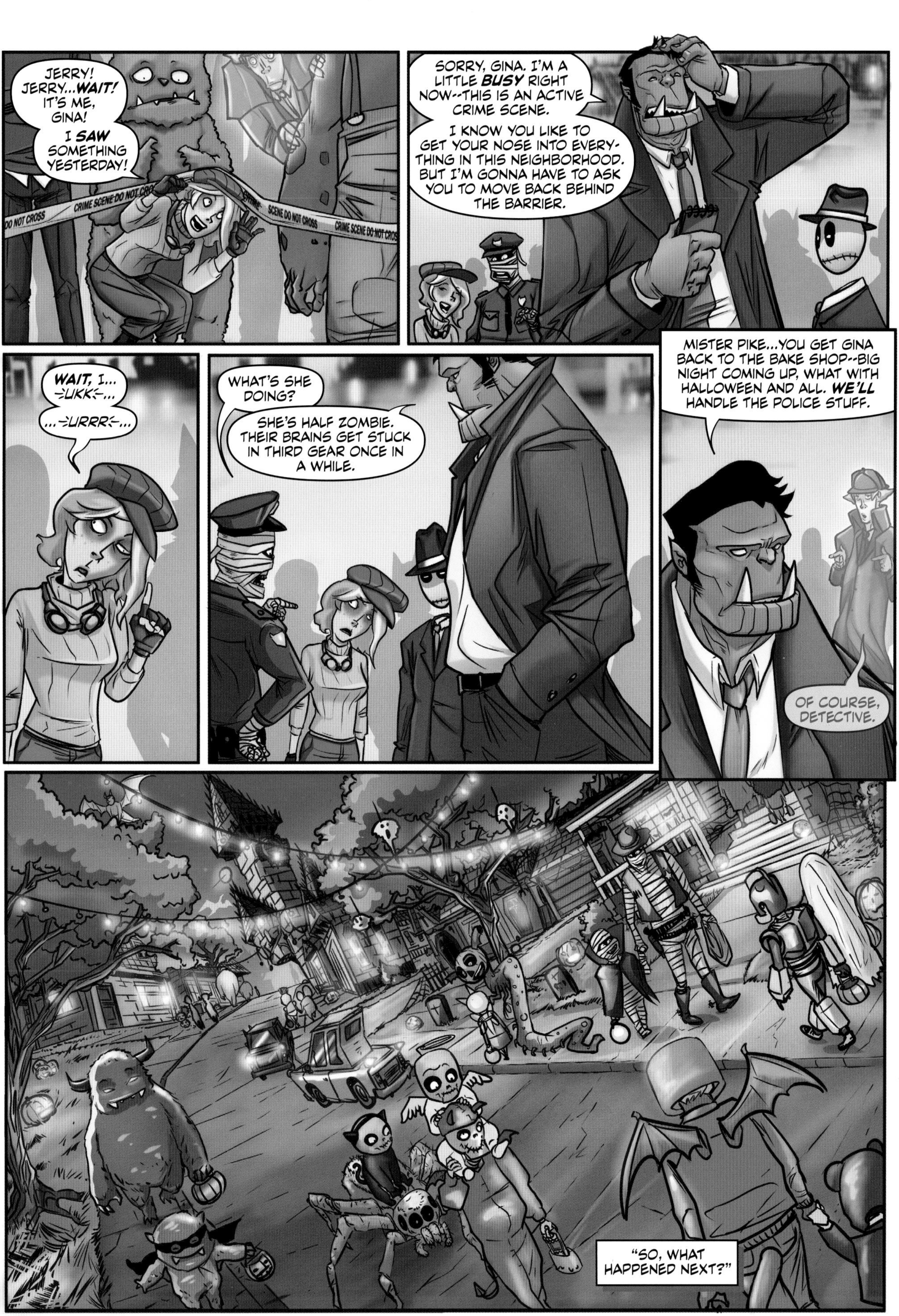
JERRY! JERRY...**WAIT!** IT'S ME, GINA!
I **SAW** SOMETHING YESTERDAY!
CRIME SCENE DO NOT CROSS
SORRY, GINA. I'M A LITTLE **BUSY** RIGHT NOW--THIS IS AN ACTIVE CRIME SCENE.
I KNOW YOU LIKE TO GET YOUR NOSE INTO EVERYTHING IN THIS NEIGHBORHOOD. BUT I'M GONNA HAVE TO ASK YOU TO MOVE BACK BEHIND THE BARRIER.
WAIT, I... =UKK=...
...=URRR=...
WHAT'S SHE DOING?
SHE'S HALF ZOMBIE. THEIR BRAINS GET STUCK IN THIRD GEAR ONCE IN A WHILE.
MISTER PIKE...YOU GET GINA BACK TO THE BAKE SHOP--BIG NIGHT COMING UP, WHAT WITH HALLOWEEN AND ALL. **WE'LL** HANDLE THE POLICE STUFF.
OF COURSE, DETECTIVE.
"SO, WHAT HAPPENED NEXT?"

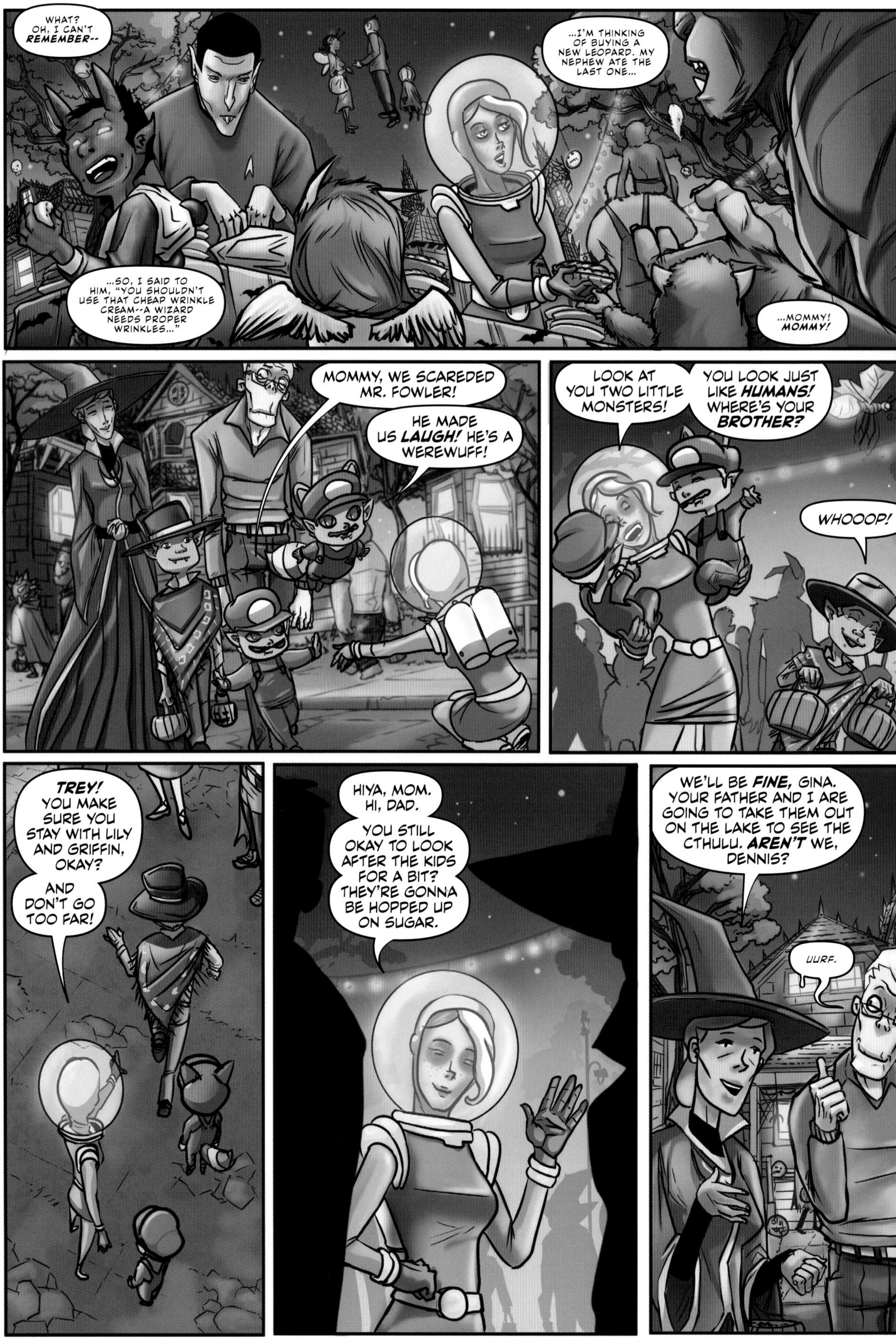
WHAT? OH, I CAN'T REMEMBER--
...I'M THINKING OF BUYING A NEW LEOPARD. MY NEPHEW ATE THE LAST ONE...
...SO, I SAID TO HIM, "YOU SHOULDN'T USE THAT CHEAP WRINKLE CREAM--A WIZARD NEEDS PROPER WRINKLES..."
...MOMMY! MOMMY!
MOMMY, WE SCAREDED MR. FOWLER!
HE MADE US LAUGH! HE'S A WEREWUFF!
LOOK AT YOU TWO LITTLE MONSTERS!
YOU LOOK JUST LIKE HUMANS! WHERE'S YOUR BROTHER?
WHOOOP!
TREY! YOU MAKE SURE YOU STAY WITH LILY AND GRIFFIN, OKAY?
AND DON'T GO TOO FAR!
HIYA, MOM. HI, DAD.
YOU STILL OKAY TO LOOK AFTER THE KIDS FOR A BIT? THEY'RE GONNA BE HOPPED UP ON SUGAR.
WE'LL BE FINE, GINA. YOUR FATHER AND I ARE GOING TO TAKE THEM OUT ON THE LAKE TO SEE THE CTHULU. AREN'T WE, DENNIS?
UURF.

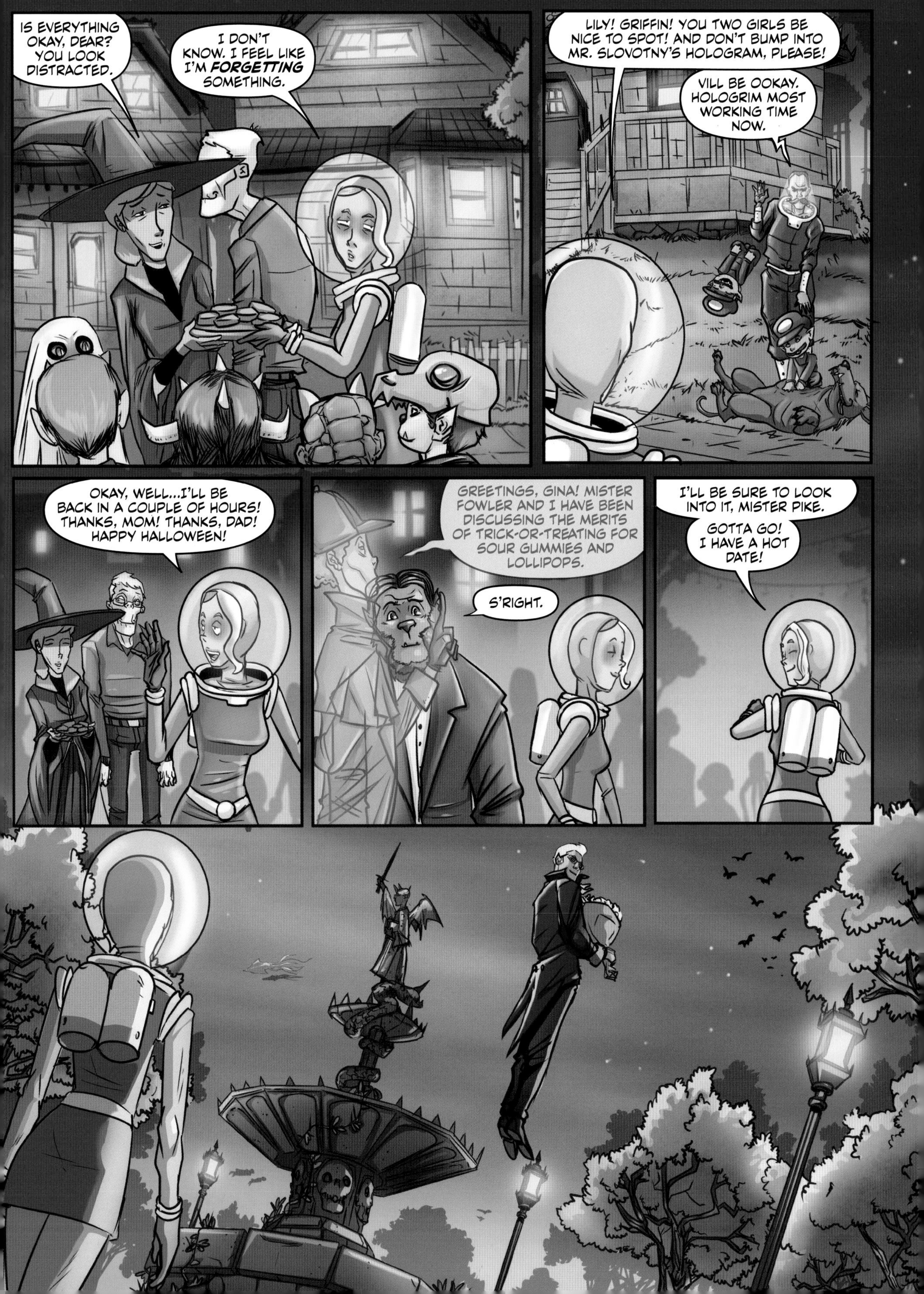
IS EVERYTHING OKAY, DEAR? YOU LOOK DISTRACTED.
I DON'T KNOW. I FEEL LIKE I'M FORGETTING SOMETHING.
LILY! GRIFFIN! YOU TWO GIRLS BE NICE TO SPOT! AND DON'T BUMP INTO MR. SLOVOTNY'S HOLOGRAM, PLEASE!
VILL BE OOKAY. HOLOGRIM MOST WORKING TIME NOW.
OKAY, WELL...I'LL BE BACK IN A COUPLE OF HOURS! THANKS, MOM! THANKS, DAD! HAPPY HALLOWEEN!
GREETINGS, GINA! MISTER FOWLER AND I HAVE BEEN DISCUSSING THE MERITS OF TRICK-OR-TREATING FOR SOUR GUMMIES AND LOLLIPOPS.
S'RIGHT.
I'LL BE SURE TO LOOK INTO IT, MISTER PIKE.
GOTTA GO! I HAVE A HOT DATE!

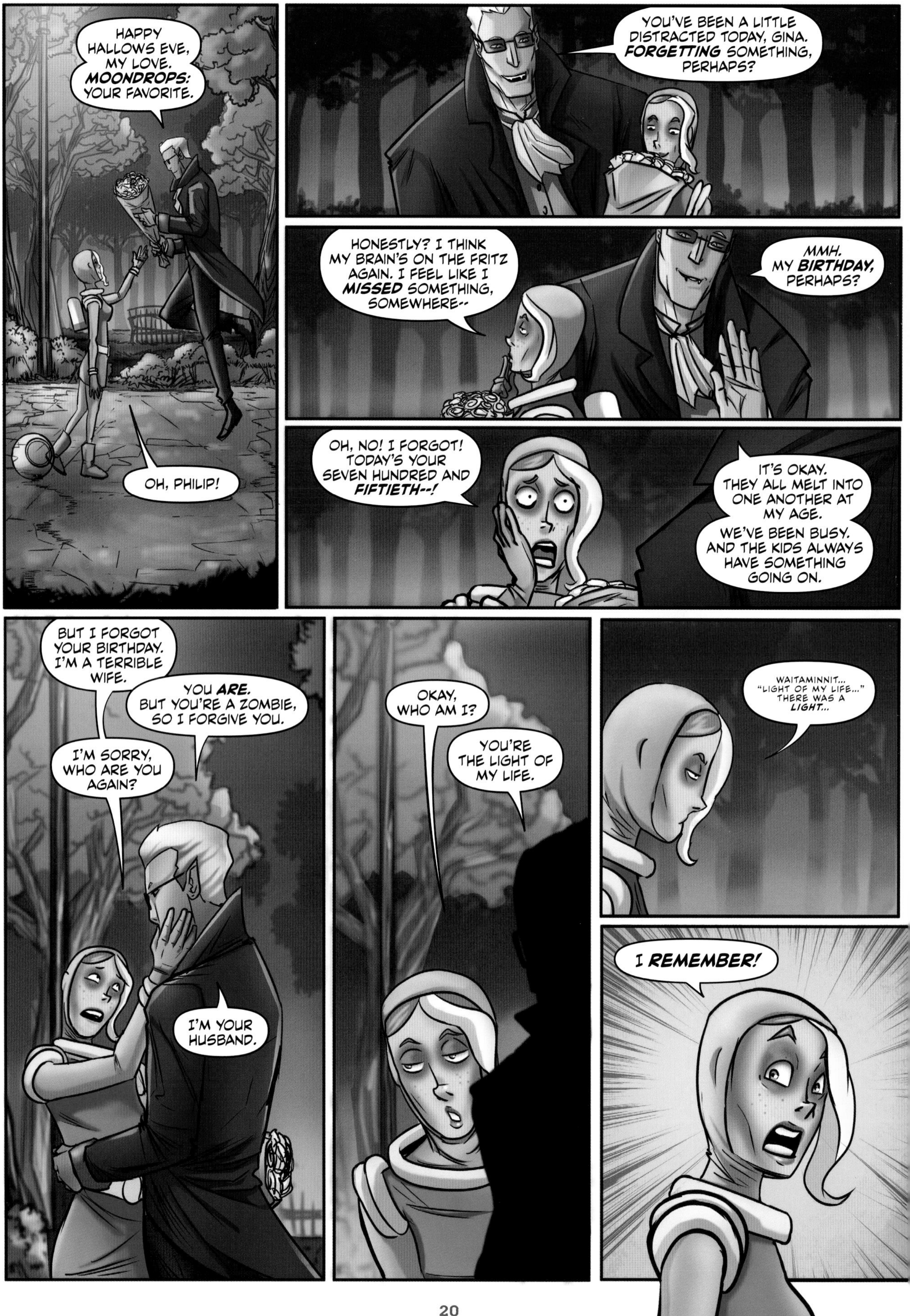
HAPPY HALLOWS EVE, MY LOVE. MOONDROPS: YOUR FAVORITE.
OH, PHILIP!
YOU'VE BEEN A LITTLE DISTRACTED TODAY, GINA. FORGETTING SOMETHING, PERHAPS?
HONESTLY? I THINK MY BRAIN'S ON THE FRITZ AGAIN. I FEEL LIKE I MISSED SOMETHING, SOMEWHERE--
MMH. MY BIRTHDAY, PERHAPS?
OH, NO! I FORGOT! TODAY'S YOUR SEVEN HUNDRED AND FIFTIETH--!
IT'S OKAY. THEY ALL MELT INTO ONE ANOTHER AT MY AGE.
WE'VE BEEN BUSY. AND THE KIDS ALWAYS HAVE SOMETHING GOING ON.
BUT I FORGOT YOUR BIRTHDAY. I'M A TERRIBLE WIFE.
YOU ARE. BUT YOU'RE A ZOMBIE, SO I FORGIVE YOU.
I'M SORRY, WHO ARE YOU AGAIN?
I'M YOUR HUSBAND.
OKAY, WHO AM I?
YOU'RE THE LIGHT OF MY LIFE.
WAITAMINNIT... "LIGHT OF MY LIFE..." THERE WAS A LIGHT...
I REMEMBER!

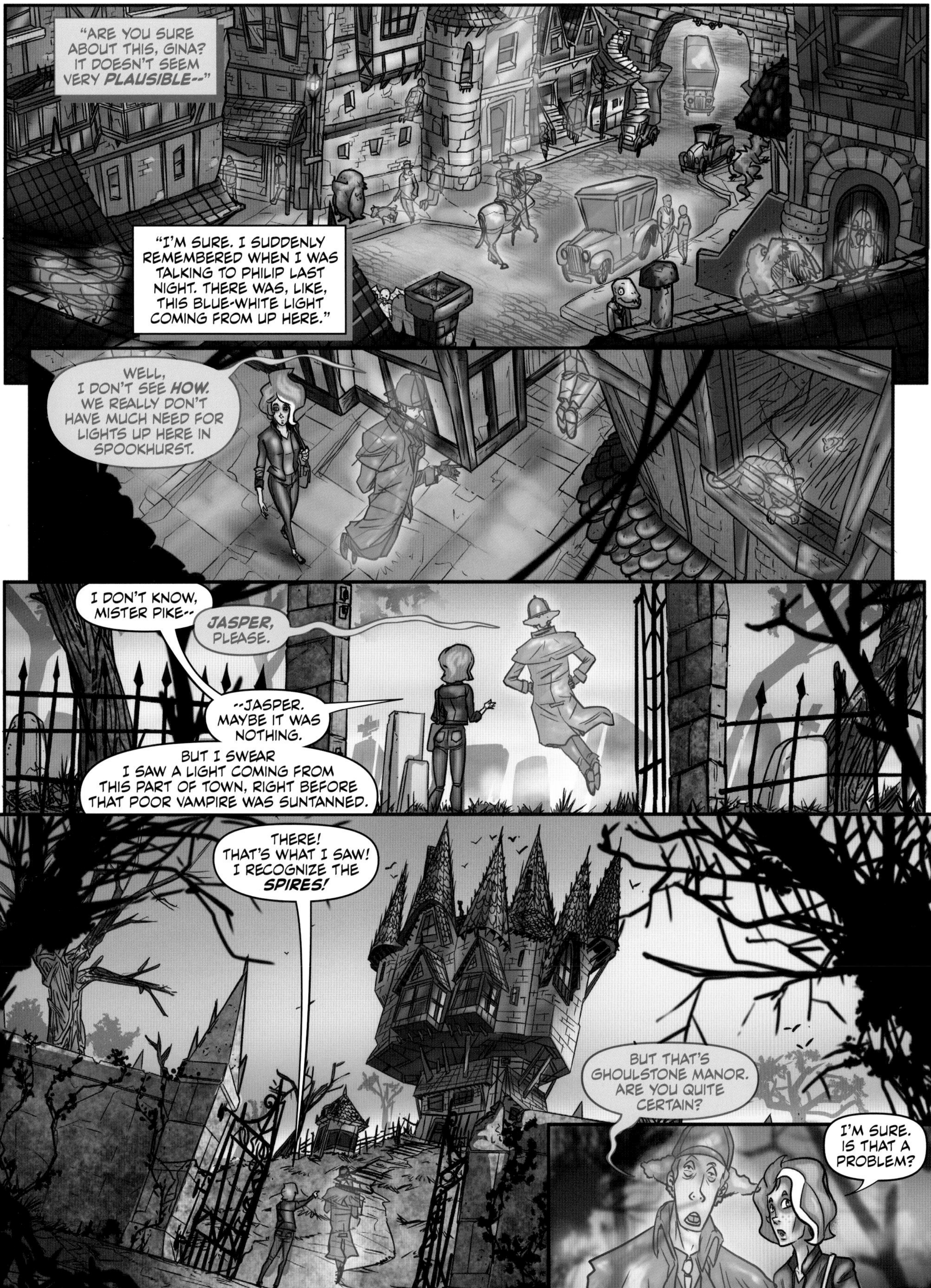
"ARE YOU SURE ABOUT THIS, GINA? IT DOESN'T SEEM VERY *PLAUSIBLE*--"
"I'M SURE. I SUDDENLY REMEMBERED WHEN I WAS TALKING TO PHILIP LAST NIGHT. THERE WAS, LIKE, THIS BLUE-WHITE LIGHT COMING FROM UP HERE."
WELL, I DON'T SEE *HOW*. WE REALLY DON'T HAVE MUCH NEED FOR LIGHTS UP HERE IN SPOOKHURST.
I DON'T KNOW, MISTER PIKE--
JASPER, PLEASE.
--JASPER. MAYBE IT WAS NOTHING.
BUT I SWEAR I SAW A LIGHT COMING FROM THIS PART OF TOWN, RIGHT BEFORE THAT POOR VAMPIRE WAS SUNTANNED.
THERE! THAT'S WHAT I SAW! I RECOGNIZE THE *SPIRES!*
BUT THAT'S GHOULSTONE MANOR. ARE YOU QUITE CERTAIN?
I'M SURE. IS THAT A PROBLEM?

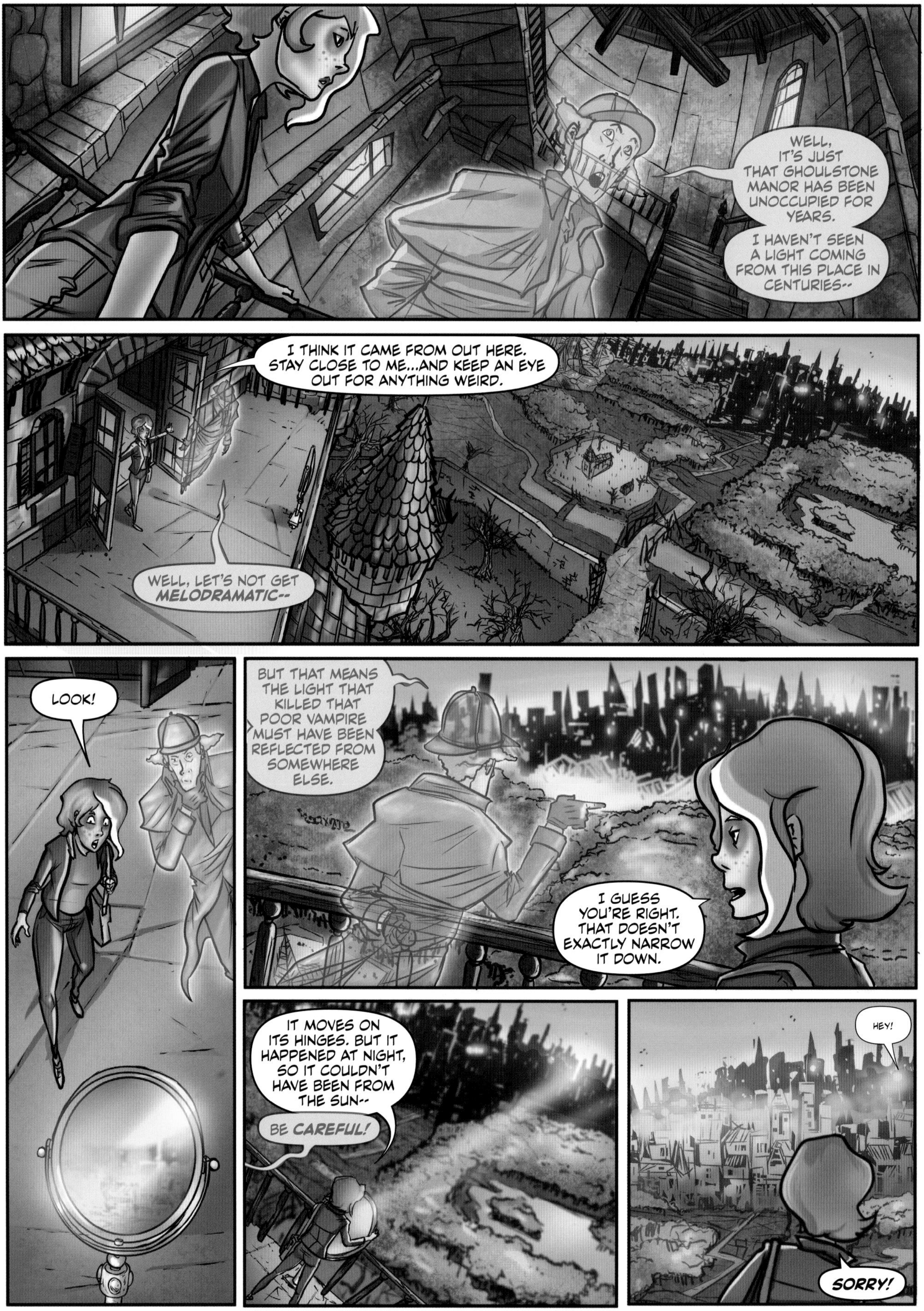
WELL, IT'S JUST THAT GHOULSTONE MANOR HAS BEEN UNOCCUPIED FOR YEARS.
I HAVEN'T SEEN A LIGHT COMING FROM THIS PLACE IN CENTURIES--
I THINK IT CAME FROM OUT HERE. STAY CLOSE TO ME...AND KEEP AN EYE OUT FOR ANYTHING WEIRD.
WELL, LET'S NOT GET *MELODRAMATIC*--
LOOK!
BUT THAT MEANS THE LIGHT THAT KILLED THAT POOR VAMPIRE MUST HAVE BEEN REFLECTED FROM SOMEWHERE ELSE.
I GUESS YOU'RE RIGHT. THAT DOESN'T EXACTLY NARROW IT DOWN.
IT MOVES ON ITS HINGES. BUT IT HAPPENED AT NIGHT, SO IT COULDN'T HAVE BEEN FROM THE SUN--
BE *CAREFUL!*
HEY!
SORRY!

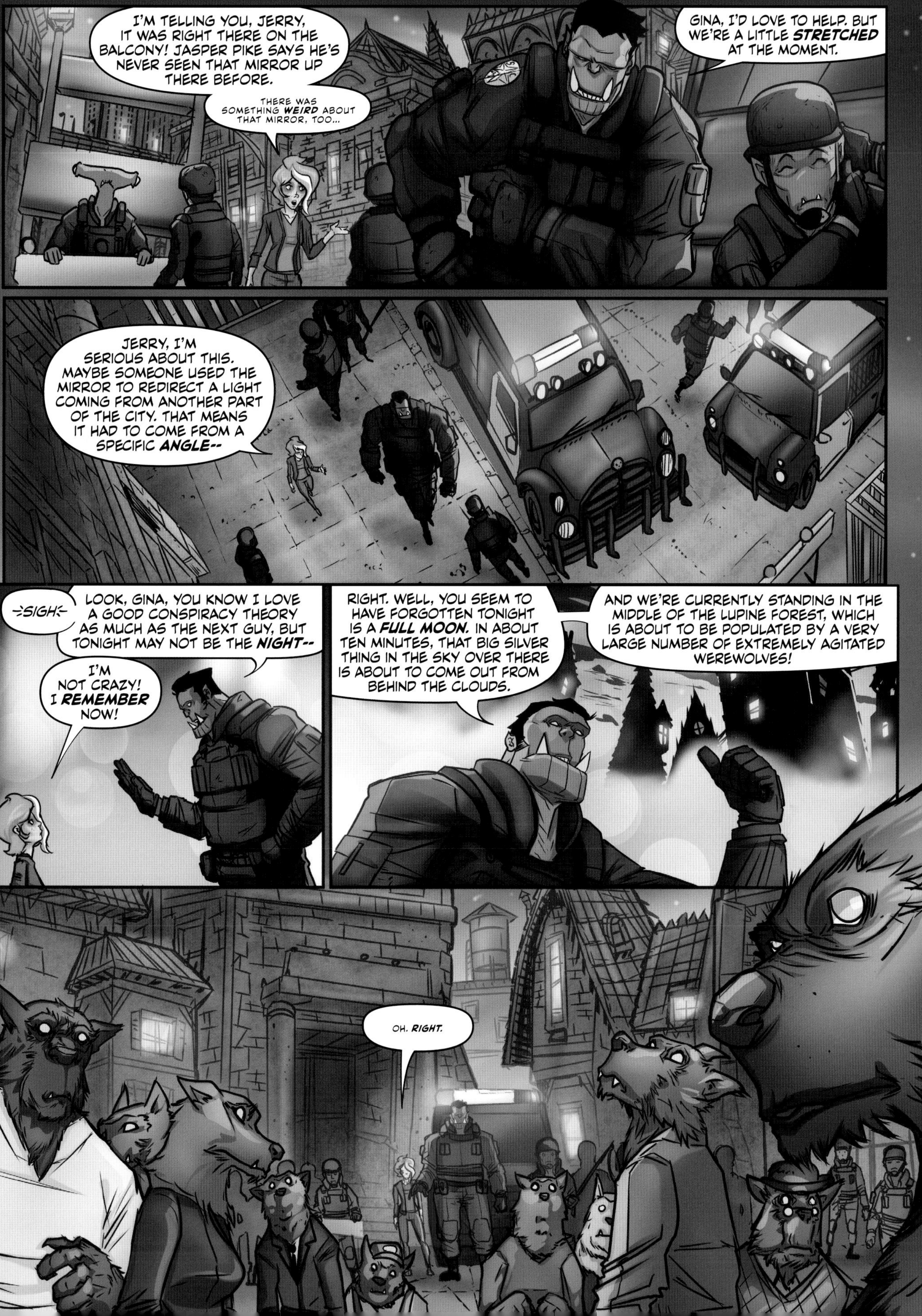
I'M TELLING YOU, JERRY, IT WAS RIGHT THERE ON THE BALCONY! JASPER PIKE SAYS HE'S NEVER SEEN THAT MIRROR UP THERE BEFORE.
THERE WAS SOMETHING WEIRD ABOUT THAT MIRROR, TOO...
GINA, I'D LOVE TO HELP. BUT WE'RE A LITTLE STRETCHED AT THE MOMENT.
JERRY, I'M SERIOUS ABOUT THIS. MAYBE SOMEONE USED THE MIRROR TO REDIRECT A LIGHT COMING FROM ANOTHER PART OF THE CITY. THAT MEANS IT HAD TO COME FROM A SPECIFIC ANGLE--
SIGH
LOOK, GINA, YOU KNOW I LOVE A GOOD CONSPIRACY THEORY AS MUCH AS THE NEXT GUY, BUT TONIGHT MAY NOT BE THE NIGHT--
I'M NOT CRAZY! I REMEMBER NOW!
RIGHT. WELL, YOU SEEM TO HAVE FORGOTTEN TONIGHT IS A FULL MOON. IN ABOUT TEN MINUTES, THAT BIG SILVER THING IN THE SKY OVER THERE IS ABOUT TO COME OUT FROM BEHIND THE CLOUDS.
AND WE'RE CURRENTLY STANDING IN THE MIDDLE OF THE LUPINE FOREST, WHICH IS ABOUT TO BE POPULATED BY A VERY LARGE NUMBER OF EXTREMELY AGITATED WEREWOLVES!
OH. RIGHT.

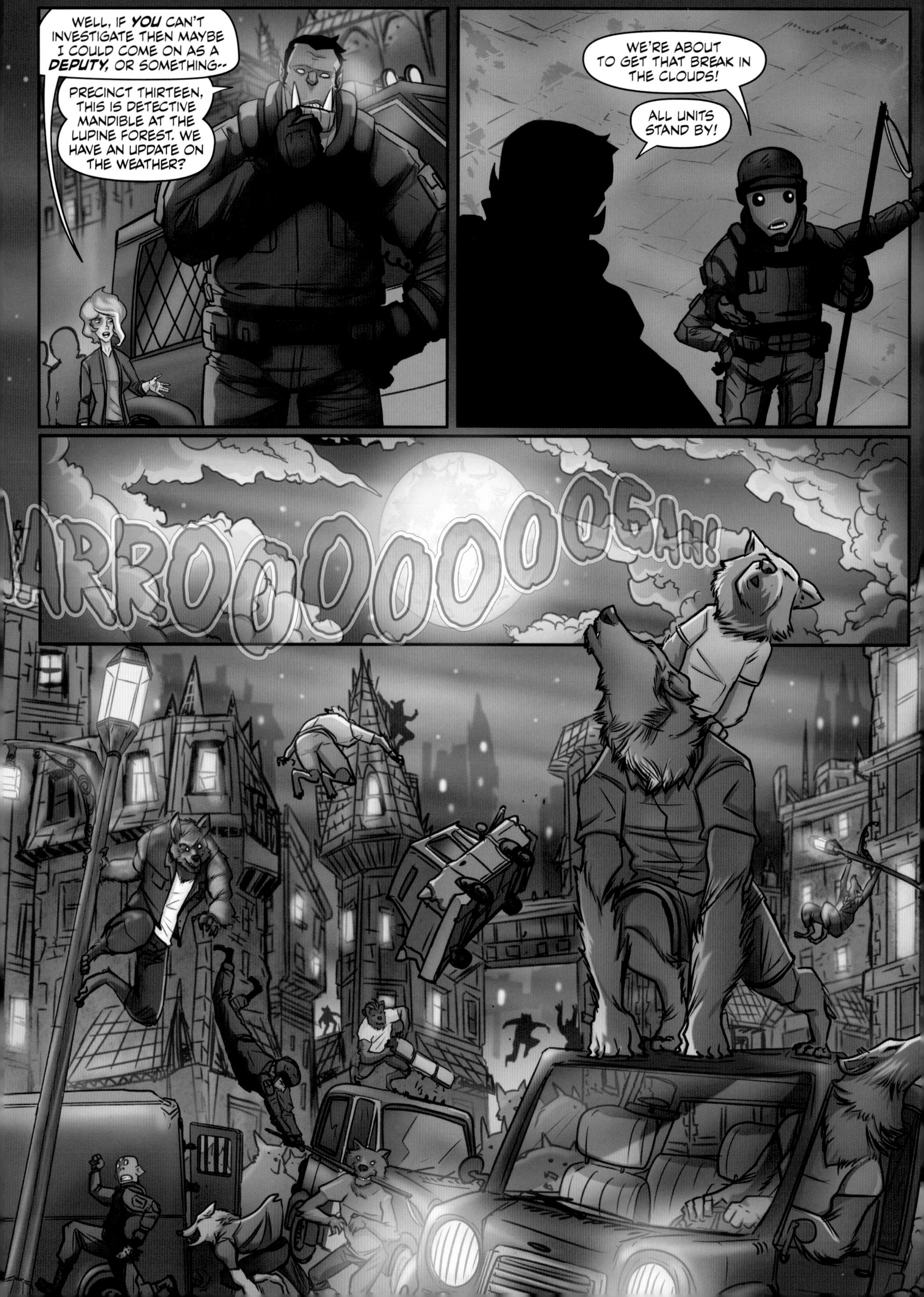

WELL, IF *YOU* CAN'T INVESTIGATE THEN MAYBE I COULD COME ON AS A *DEPUTY*, OR SOMETHING--
PRECINCT THIRTEEN, THIS IS DETECTIVE MANDIBLE AT THE LUPINE FOREST. WE HAVE AN UPDATE ON THE WEATHER?
WE'RE ABOUT TO GET THAT BREAK IN THE CLOUDS!
ALL UNITS STAND BY!
ARROOOOOOOOGHH!

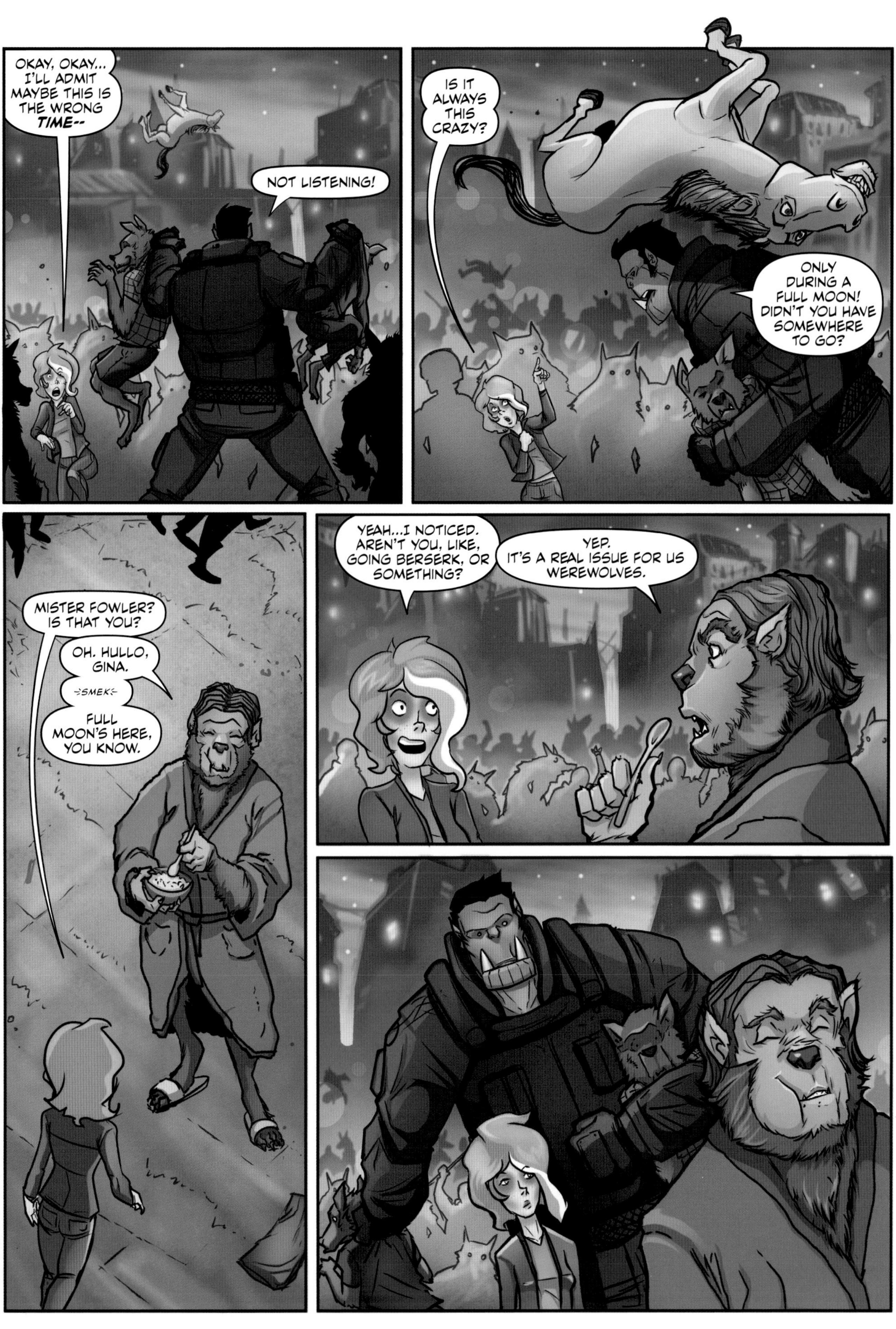

OKAY, OKAY... I'LL ADMIT MAYBE THIS IS THE WRONG *TIME--*
NOT LISTENING!
IS IT ALWAYS THIS CRAZY?
ONLY DURING A FULL MOON! DIDN'T YOU HAVE SOMEWHERE TO GO?
MISTER FOWLER? IS THAT YOU?
OH. HULLO, GINA.
SMEK
FULL MOON'S HERE, YOU KNOW.
YEAH...I NOTICED. AREN'T YOU, LIKE, GOING BERSERK, OR SOMETHING?
YEP. IT'S A REAL ISSUE FOR US WEREWOLVES.

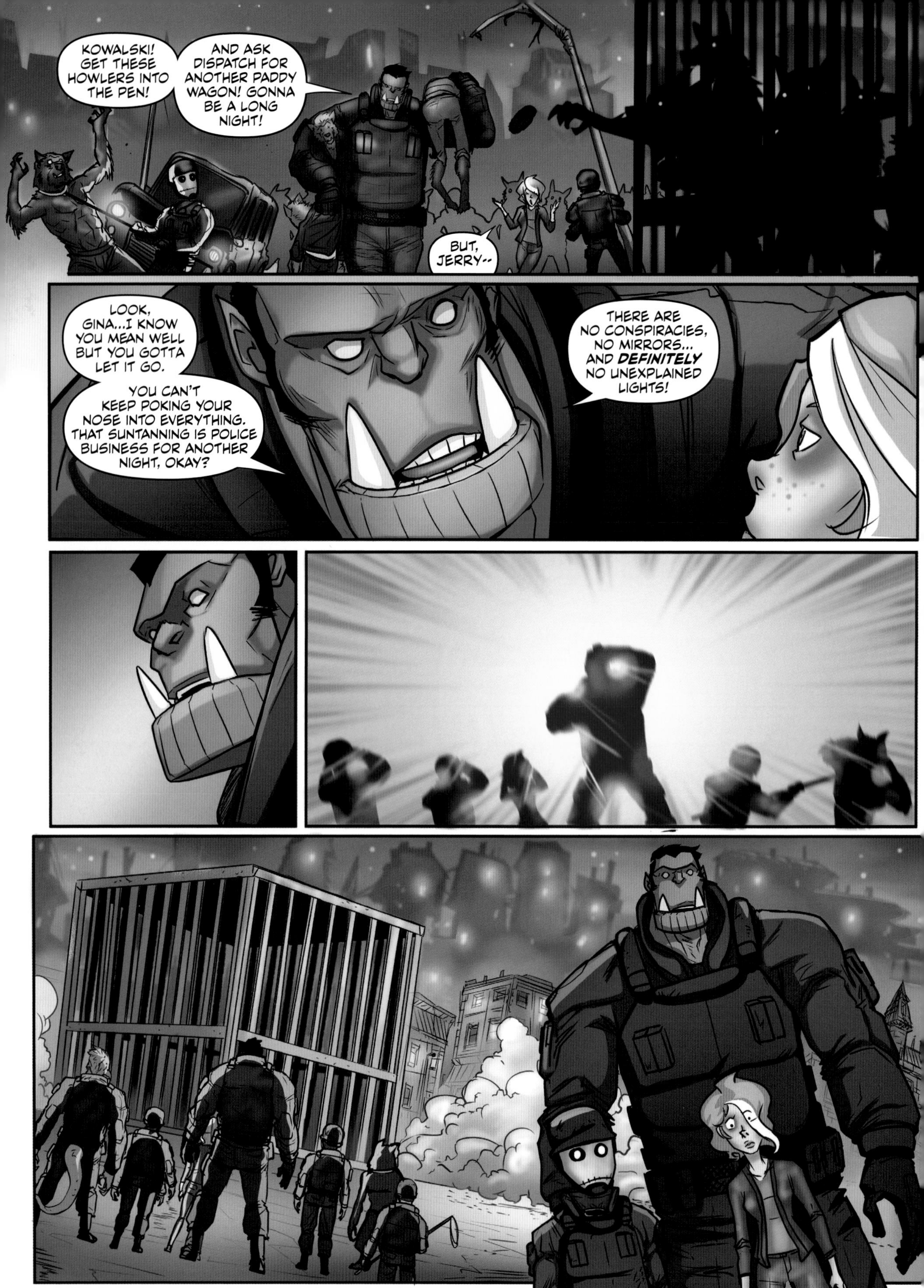
KOWALSKI! GET THESE HOWLERS INTO THE PEN!
AND ASK DISPATCH FOR ANOTHER PADDY WAGON! GONNA BE A LONG NIGHT!
BUT, JERRY--
LOOK, GINA...I KNOW YOU MEAN WELL BUT YOU GOTTA LET IT GO.
YOU CAN'T KEEP POKING YOUR NOSE INTO EVERYTHING. THAT SUNTANNING IS POLICE BUSINESS FOR ANOTHER NIGHT, OKAY?
THERE ARE NO CONSPIRACIES, NO MIRRORS... AND *DEFINITELY* NO UNEXPLAINED LIGHTS!

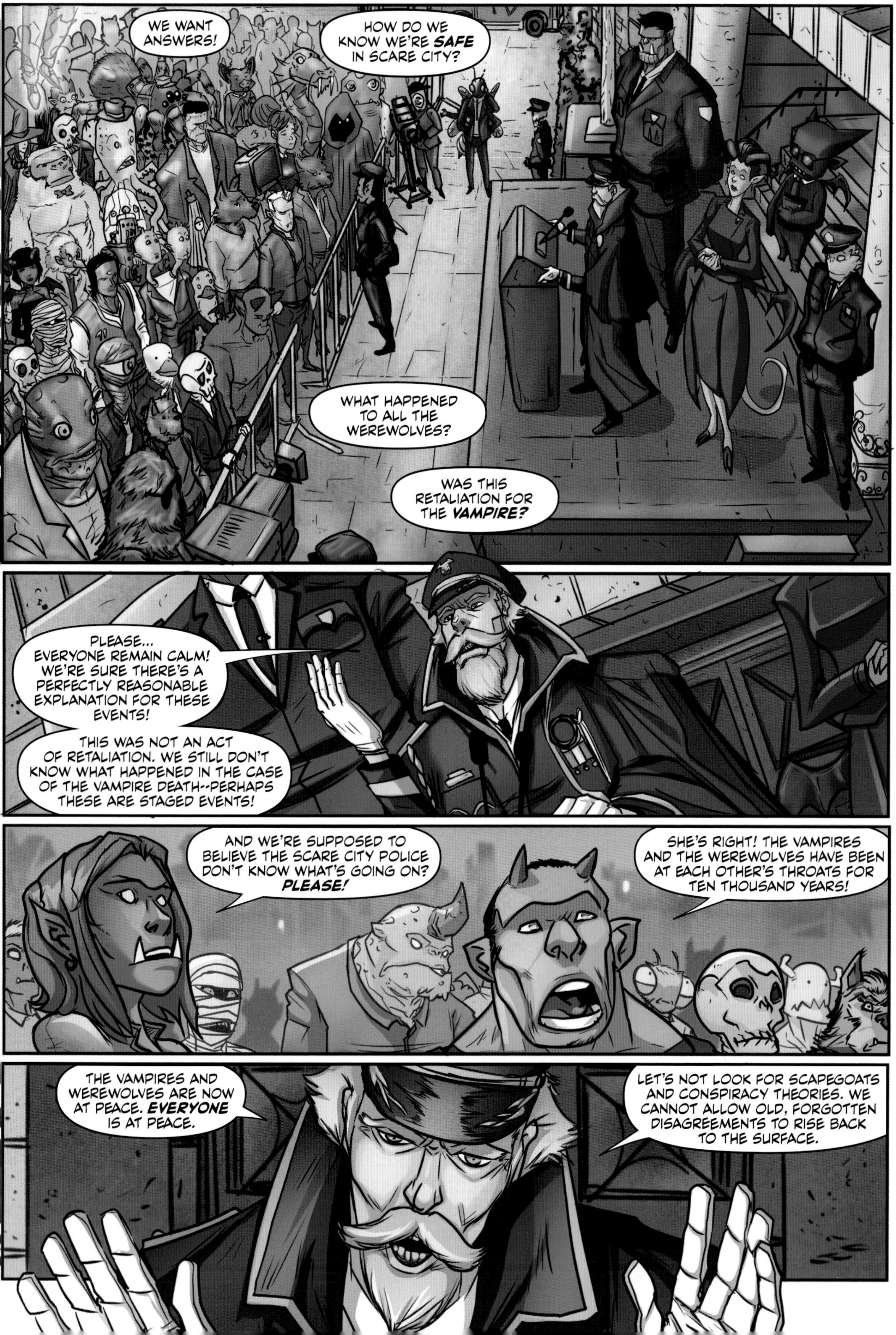
WE WANT ANSWERS!
HOW DO WE KNOW WE'RE **SAFE** IN SCARE CITY?
WHAT HAPPENED TO ALL THE WEREWOLVES?
WAS THIS RETALIATION FOR THE **VAMPIRE?**
PLEASE... EVERYONE REMAIN CALM! WE'RE SURE THERE'S A PERFECTLY REASONABLE EXPLANATION FOR THESE EVENTS!
THIS WAS NOT AN ACT OF RETALIATION. WE STILL DON'T KNOW WHAT HAPPENED IN THE CASE OF THE VAMPIRE DEATH--PERHAPS THESE ARE STAGED EVENTS!
AND WE'RE SUPPOSED TO BELIEVE THE SCARE CITY POLICE DON'T KNOW WHAT'S GOING ON? **PLEASE!**
SHE'S RIGHT! THE VAMPIRES AND THE WEREWOLVES HAVE BEEN AT EACH OTHER'S THROATS FOR TEN THOUSAND YEARS!
THE VAMPIRES AND WEREWOLVES ARE NOW AT PEACE. **EVERYONE** IS AT PEACE.
LET'S NOT LOOK FOR SCAPEGOATS AND CONSPIRACY THEORIES. WE CANNOT ALLOW OLD, FORGOTTEN DISAGREEMENTS TO RISE BACK TO THE SURFACE.

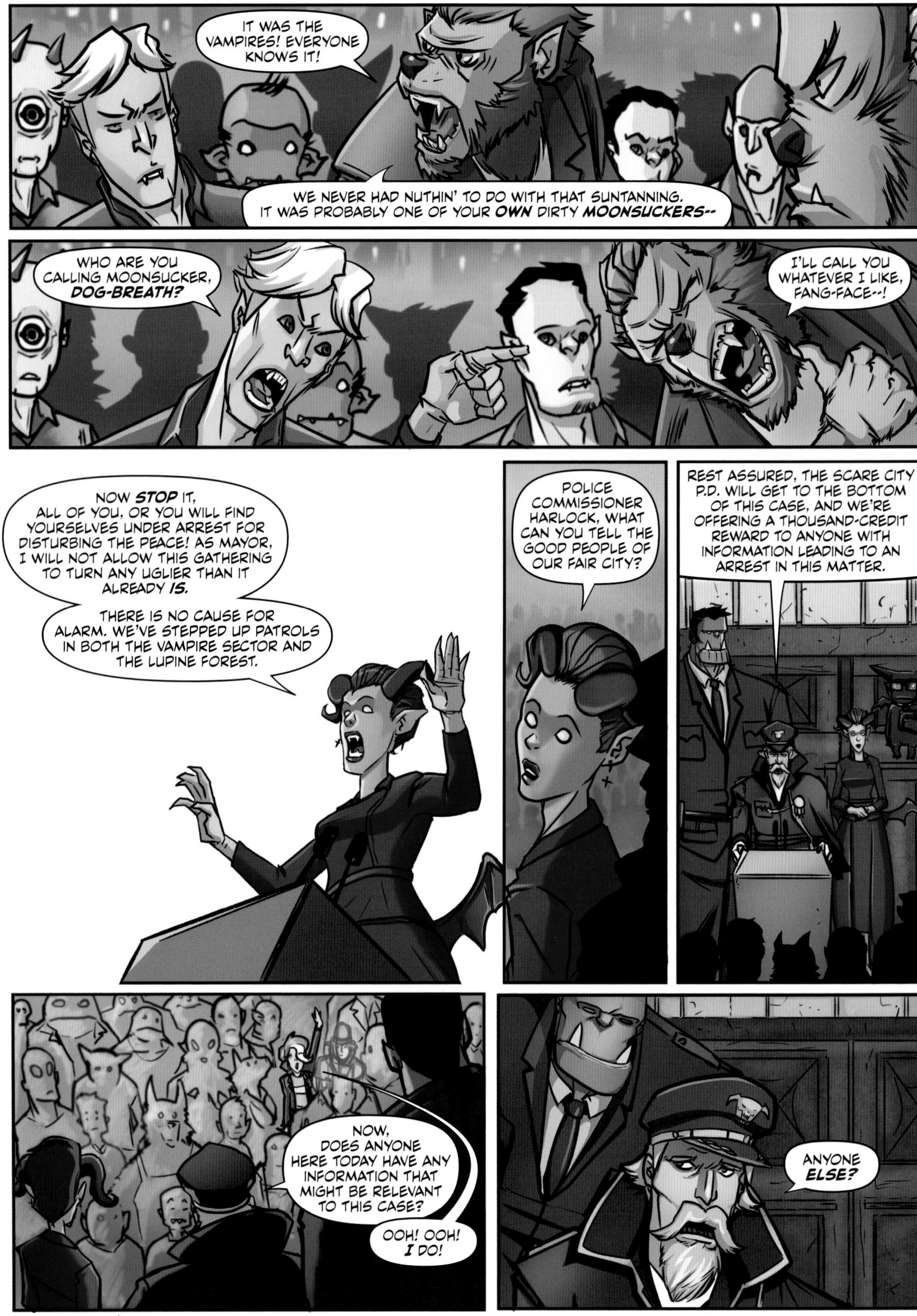

IT WAS THE VAMPIRES! EVERYONE KNOWS IT!
WE NEVER HAD NUTHIN' TO DO WITH THAT SUNTANNING. IT WAS PROBABLY ONE OF YOUR OWN DIRTY MOONSUCKERS--
WHO ARE YOU CALLING MOONSUCKER, DOG-BREATH?
I'LL CALL YOU WHATEVER I LIKE, FANG-FACE--!
NOW STOP IT, ALL OF YOU, OR YOU WILL FIND YOURSELVES UNDER ARREST FOR DISTURBING THE PEACE! AS MAYOR, I WILL NOT ALLOW THIS GATHERING TO TURN ANY UGLIER THAN IT ALREADY IS.
THERE IS NO CAUSE FOR ALARM. WE'VE STEPPED UP PATROLS IN BOTH THE VAMPIRE SECTOR AND THE LUPINE FOREST.
POLICE COMMISSIONER HARLOCK, WHAT CAN YOU TELL THE GOOD PEOPLE OF OUR FAIR CITY?
REST ASSURED, THE SCARE CITY P.D. WILL GET TO THE BOTTOM OF THIS CASE, AND WE'RE OFFERING A THOUSAND-CREDIT REWARD TO ANYONE WITH INFORMATION LEADING TO AN ARREST IN THIS MATTER.
NOW, DOES ANYONE HERE TODAY HAVE ANY INFORMATION THAT MIGHT BE RELEVANT TO THIS CASE?
OOH! OOH! I DO!
ANYONE ELSE?

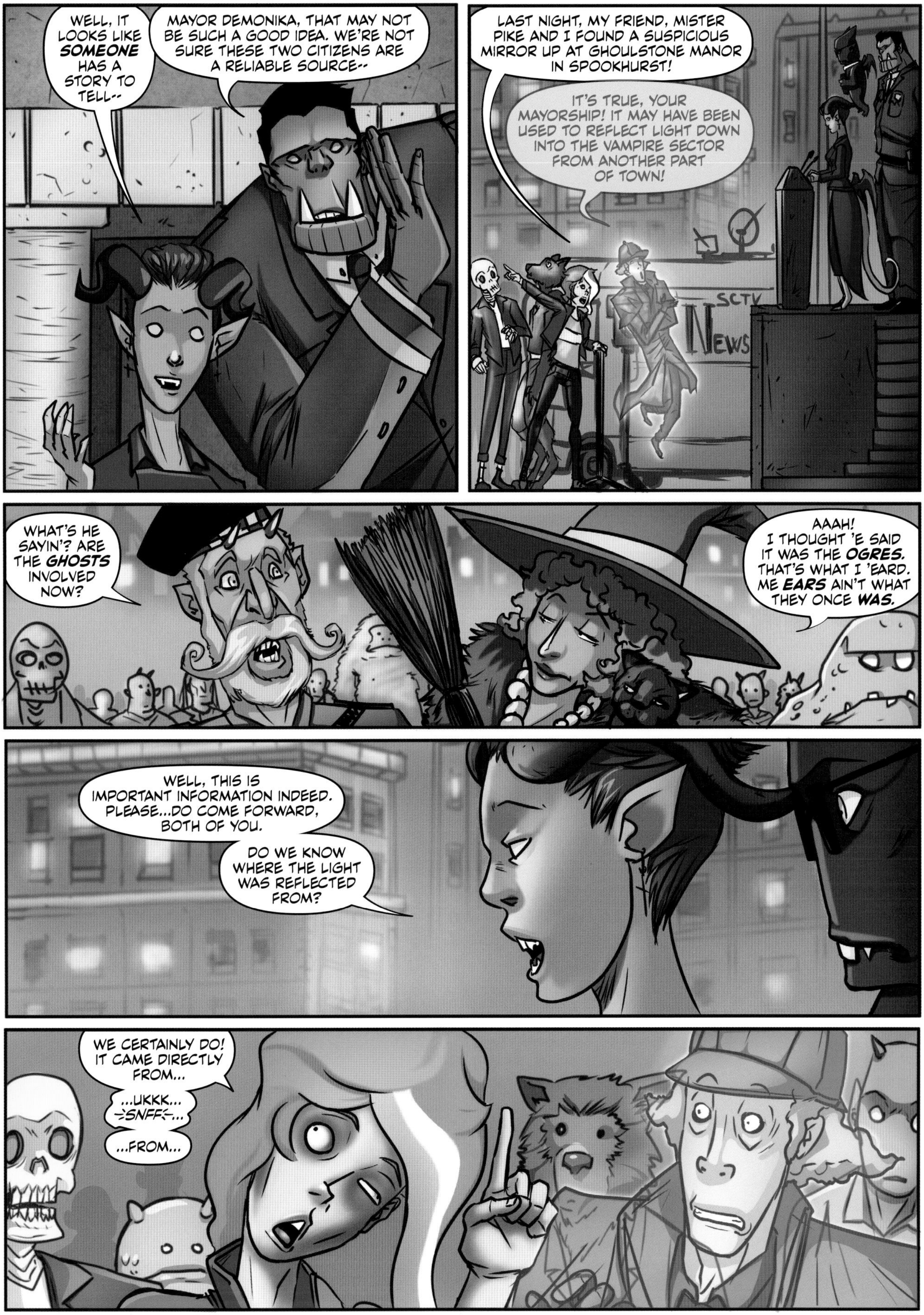
WELL, IT LOOKS LIKE **SOMEONE** HAS A STORY TO TELL--
MAYOR DEMONIKA, THAT MAY NOT BE SUCH A GOOD IDEA. WE'RE NOT SURE THESE TWO CITIZENS ARE A RELIABLE SOURCE--
LAST NIGHT, MY FRIEND, MISTER PIKE AND I FOUND A SUSPICIOUS MIRROR UP AT GHOULSTONE MANOR IN SPOOKHURST!
IT'S TRUE, YOUR MAYORSHIP! IT MAY HAVE BEEN USED TO REFLECT LIGHT DOWN INTO THE VAMPIRE SECTOR FROM ANOTHER PART OF TOWN!
SCTV
NEWS
WHAT'S HE SAYIN'? ARE THE **GHOSTS** INVOLVED NOW?
AAAH! I THOUGHT 'E SAID IT WAS THE **OGRES.** THAT'S WHAT I 'EARD. ME **EARS** AIN'T WHAT THEY ONCE **WAS.**
WELL, THIS IS IMPORTANT INFORMATION INDEED. PLEASE...DO COME FORWARD, BOTH OF YOU.
DO WE KNOW WHERE THE LIGHT WAS REFLECTED FROM?
WE CERTAINLY DO! IT CAME DIRECTLY FROM...
...UKKK...
-SNFF-...
...FROM...

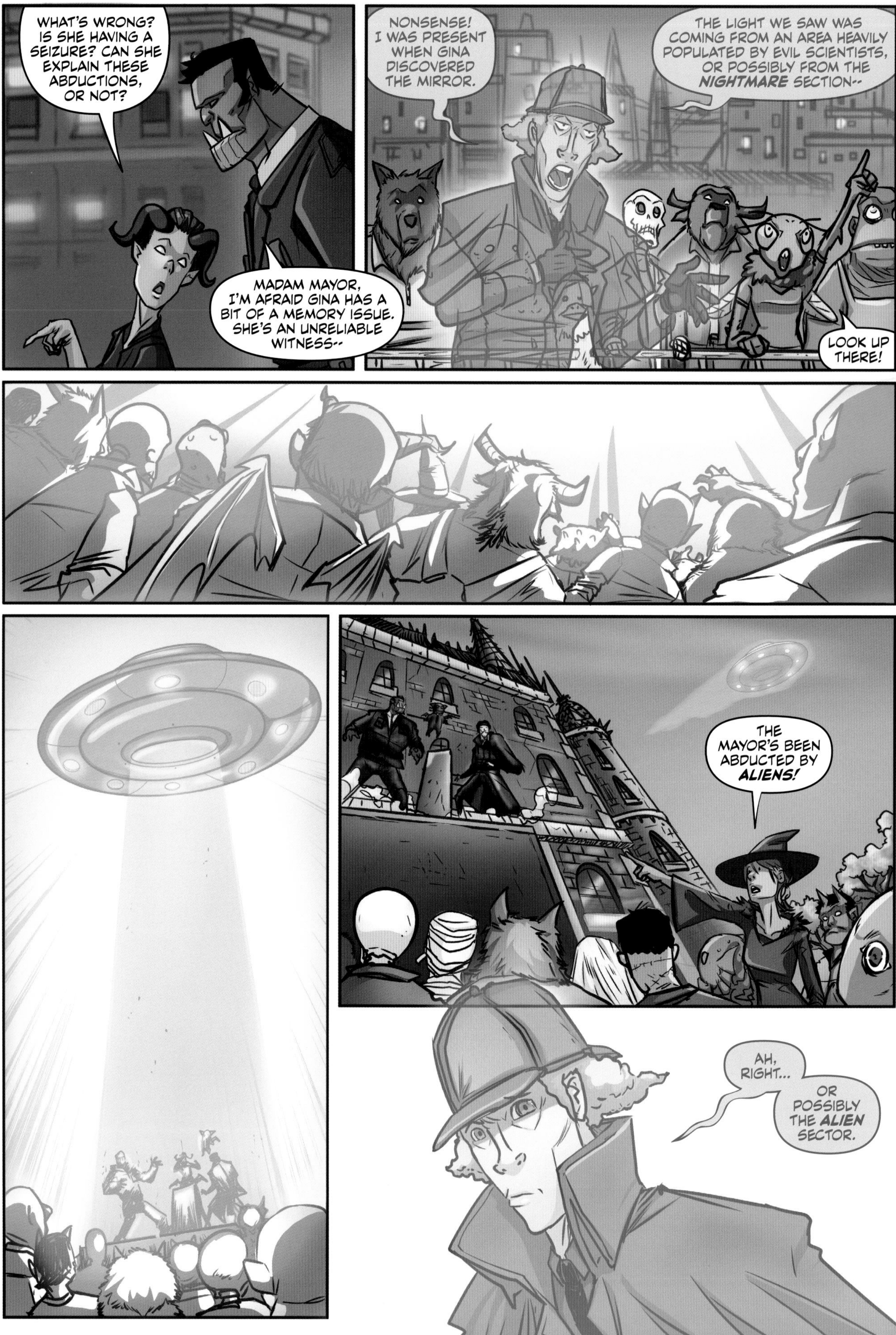
WHAT'S WRONG? IS SHE HAVING A SEIZURE? CAN SHE EXPLAIN THESE ABDUCTIONS, OR NOT?
MADAM MAYOR, I'M AFRAID GINA HAS A BIT OF A MEMORY ISSUE. SHE'S AN UNRELIABLE WITNESS--
NONSENSE! I WAS PRESENT WHEN GINA DISCOVERED THE MIRROR.
THE LIGHT WE SAW WAS COMING FROM AN AREA HEAVILY POPULATED BY EVIL SCIENTISTS, OR POSSIBLY FROM THE NIGHTMARE SECTION--
LOOK UP THERE!
THE MAYOR'S BEEN ABDUCTED BY ALIENS!
AH, RIGHT... OR POSSIBLY THE ALIEN SECTOR.

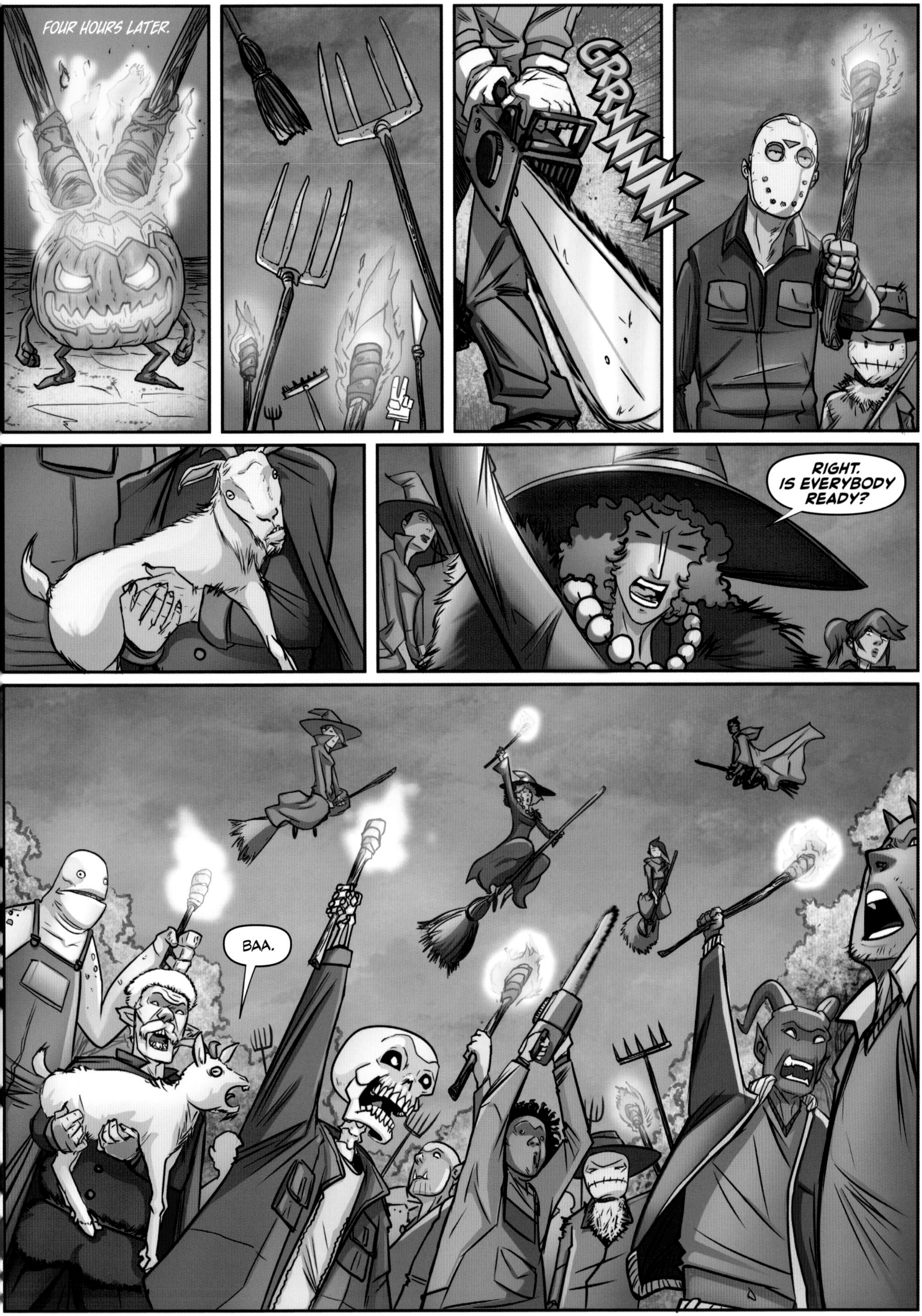
FOUR HOURS LATER.
GRRNNNN
RIGHT. IS EVERYBODY READY?
BAA.

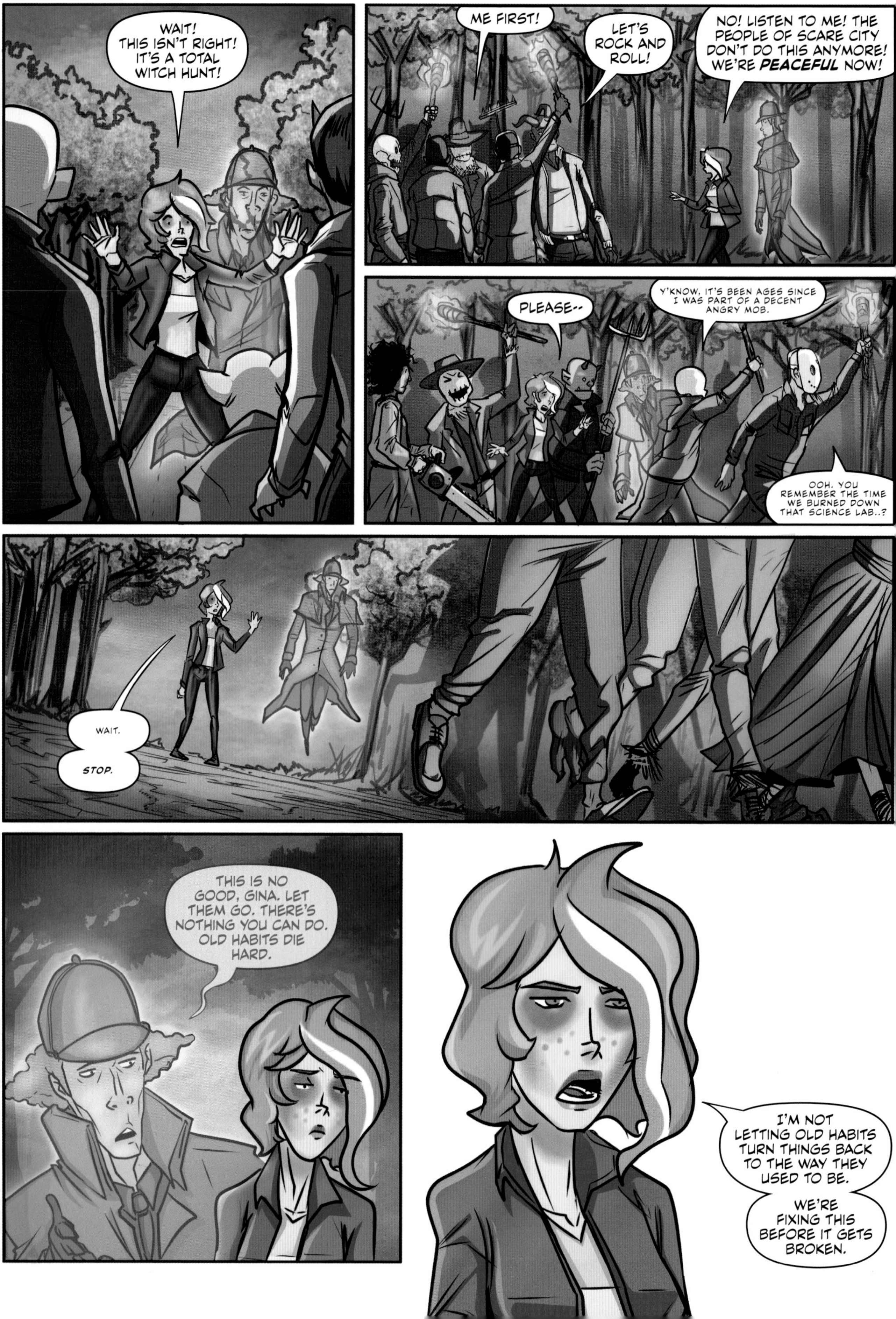
WAIT! THIS ISN'T RIGHT! IT'S A TOTAL WITCH HUNT!
ME FIRST!
LET'S ROCK AND ROLL!
NO! LISTEN TO ME! THE PEOPLE OF SCARE CITY DON'T DO THIS ANYMORE! WE'RE *PEACEFUL* NOW!
PLEASE--
Y'KNOW, IT'S BEEN AGES SINCE I WAS PART OF A DECENT ANGRY MOB.
OOH. YOU REMEMBER THE TIME WE BURNED DOWN THAT SCIENCE LAB..?
WAIT.
STOP.
THIS IS NO GOOD, GINA. LET THEM GO. THERE'S NOTHING YOU CAN DO. OLD HABITS DIE HARD.
I'M NOT LETTING OLD HABITS TURN THINGS BACK TO THE WAY THEY USED TO BE.
WE'RE FIXING THIS BEFORE IT GETS BROKEN.

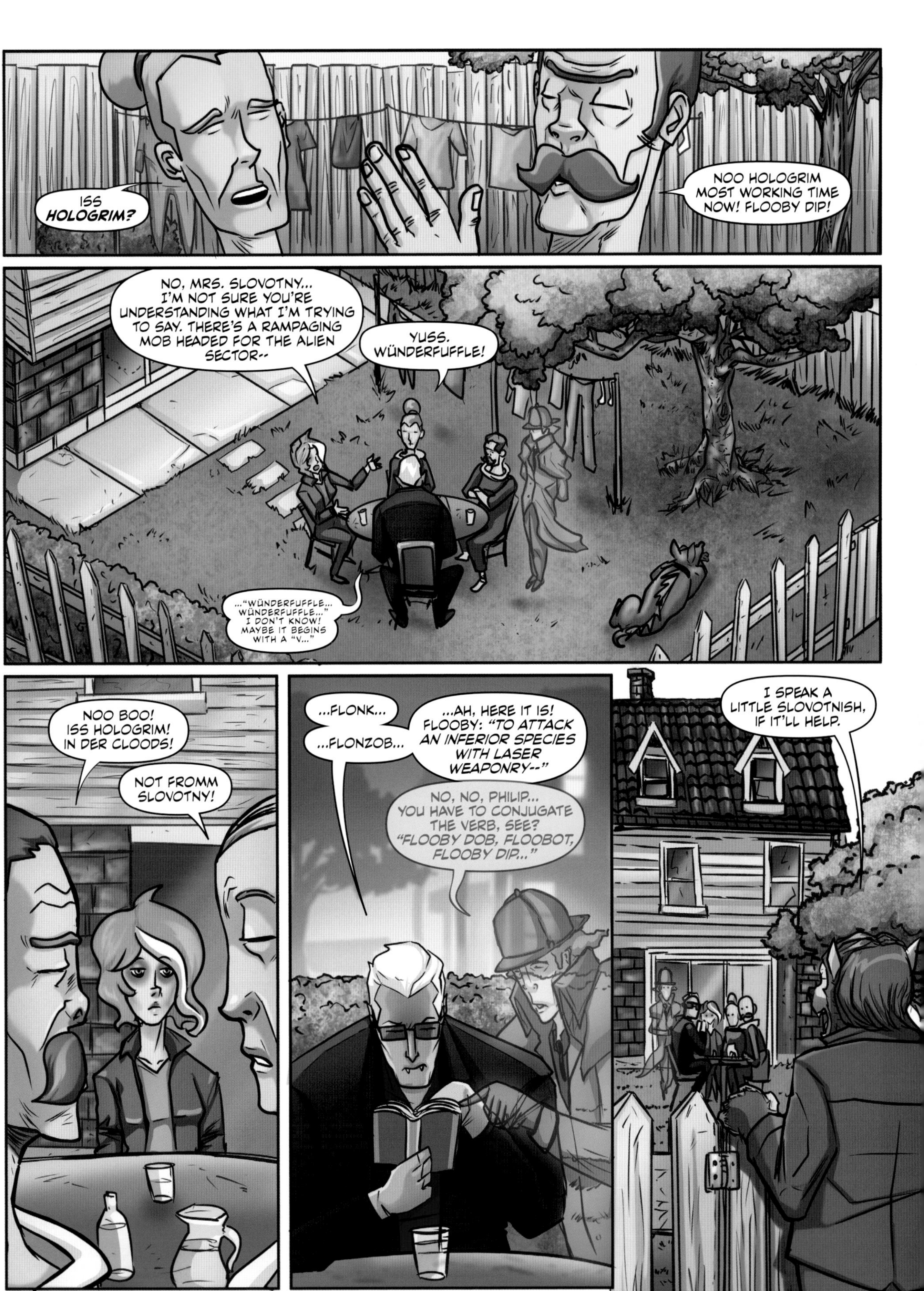
ISS *HOLOGRIM?*
NOO HOLOGRIM MOST WORKING TIME NOW! FLOOBY DIP!
NO, MRS. SLOVOTNY... I'M NOT SURE YOU'RE UNDERSTANDING WHAT I'M TRYING TO SAY. THERE'S A RAMPAGING MOB HEADED FOR THE ALIEN SECTOR--
YUSS. WÜNDERFUFFLE!
..."WÜNDERFUFFLE... WÜNDERFUFFLE..." I DON'T KNOW! MAYBE IT BEGINS WITH A "V..."
NOO BOO! ISS HOLOGRIM! IN DER CLOODS!
NOT FROMM SLOVOTNY!
...FLONK...
...FLONZOB...
...AH, HERE IT IS! FLOOBY: *"TO ATTACK AN INFERIOR SPECIES WITH LASER WEAPONRY--"*
NO, NO, PHILIP... YOU HAVE TO CONJUGATE THE VERB, SEE? *"FLOOBY DOB, FLOOBOT, FLOOBY DIP..."*
I SPEAK A LITTLE SLOVOTNISH, IF IT'LL HELP.

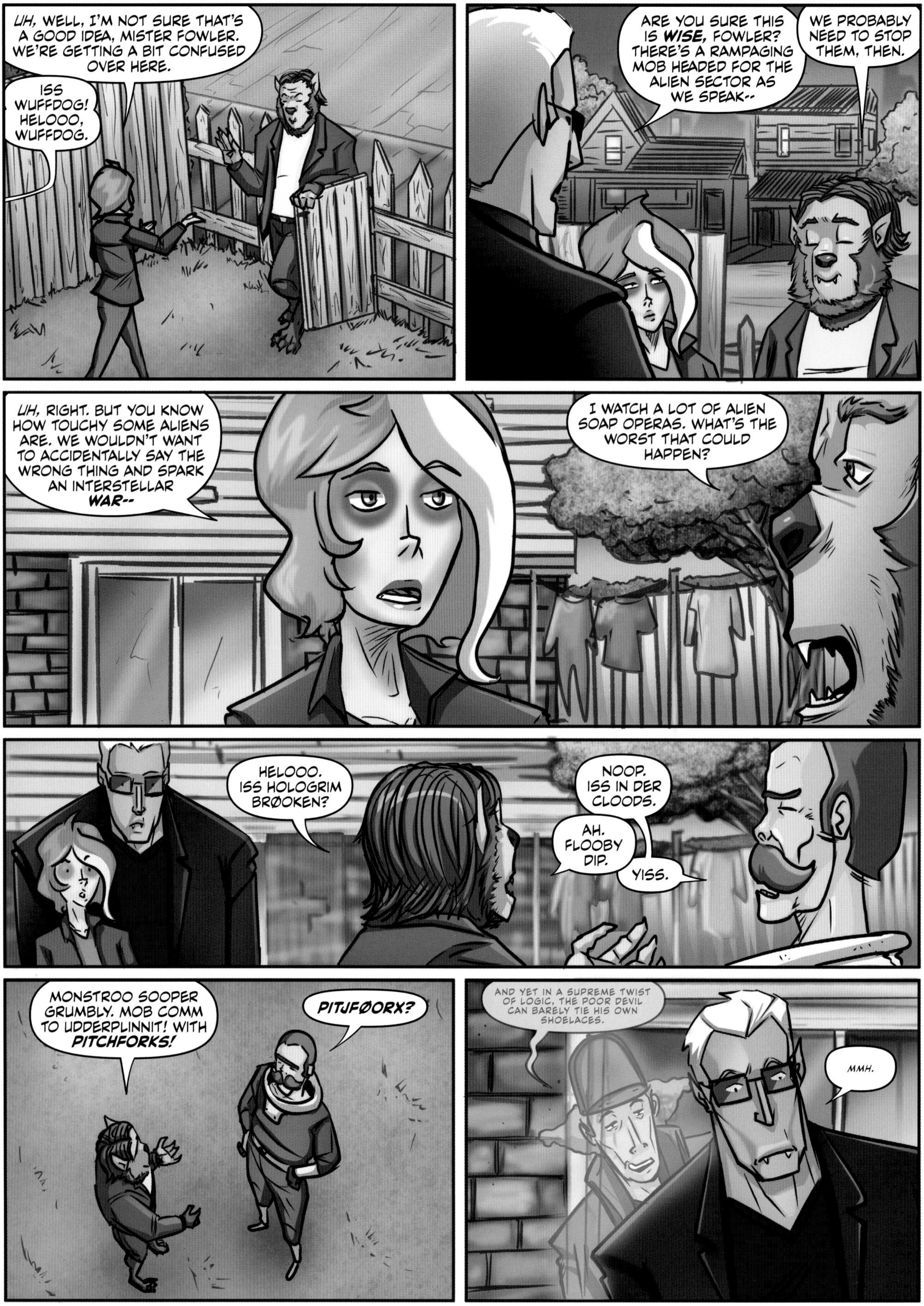
UH, WELL, I'M NOT SURE THAT'S A GOOD IDEA, MISTER FOWLER. WE'RE GETTING A BIT CONFUSED OVER HERE.
ISS WUFFDOG! HELOOO, WUFFDOG.
ARE YOU SURE THIS IS WISE, FOWLER? THERE'S A RAMPAGING MOB HEADED FOR THE ALIEN SECTOR AS WE SPEAK--
WE PROBABLY NEED TO STOP THEM, THEN.
UH, RIGHT. BUT YOU KNOW HOW TOUCHY SOME ALIENS ARE. WE WOULDN'T WANT TO ACCIDENTALLY SAY THE WRONG THING AND SPARK AN INTERSTELLAR WAR--
I WATCH A LOT OF ALIEN SOAP OPERAS. WHAT'S THE WORST THAT COULD HAPPEN?
HELOOO. ISS HOLOGRIM BRØKEN?
NOOP. ISS IN DER CLOODS.
AH. FLOOBY DIP.
YISS.
MONSTROO SOOPER GRUMBLY. MOB COMM TO UDDERPLINNIT! WITH PITCHFORKS!
PITJFØORX?
AND YET IN A SUPREME TWIST OF LOGIC, THE POOR DEVIL CAN BARELY TIE HIS OWN SHOELACES.
MMH.

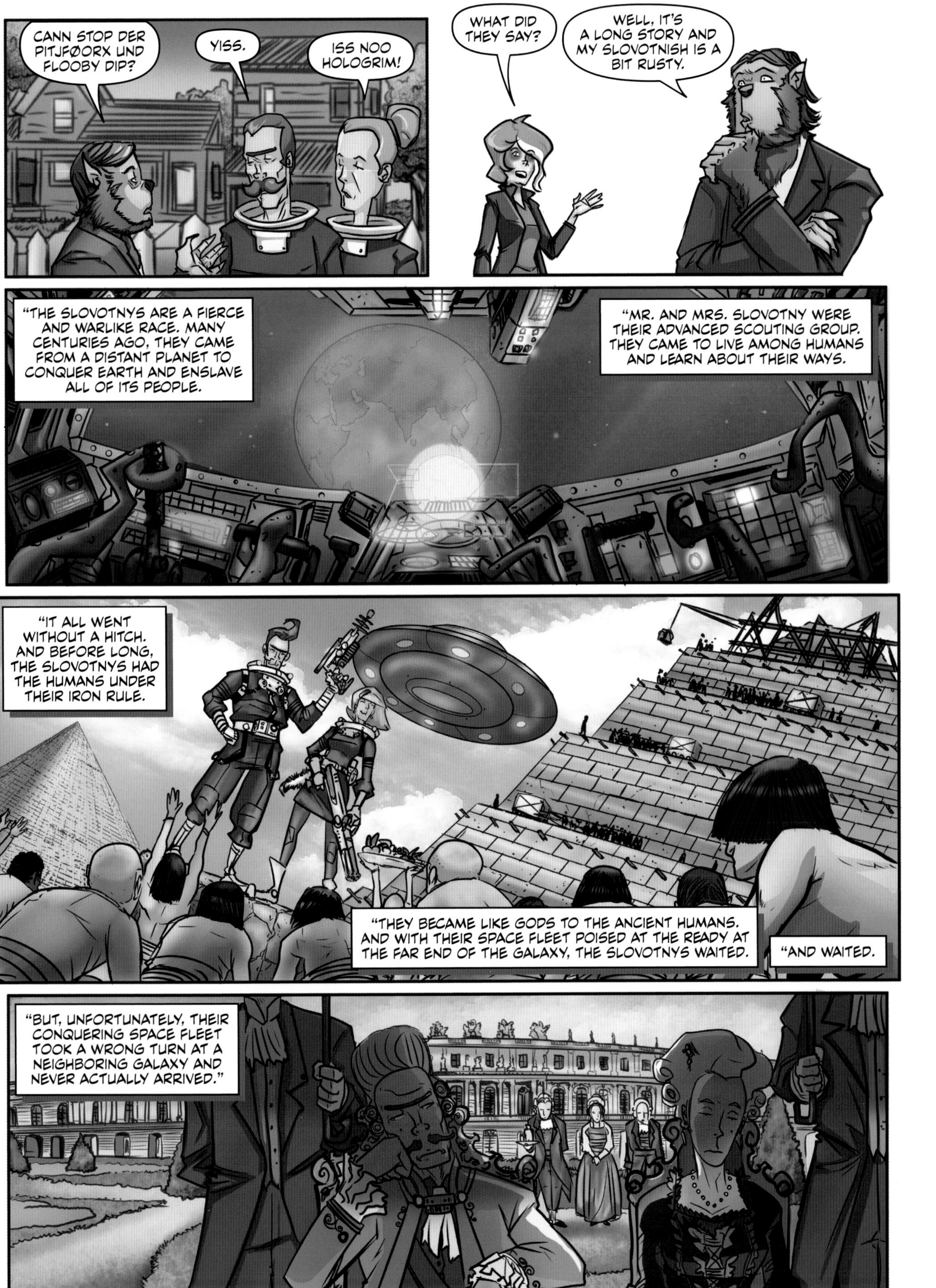
CANN STOP DER PITJFØORX UND FLOOBY DIP?
YISS.
ISS NOO HOLOGRIM!
WHAT DID THEY SAY?
WELL, IT'S A LONG STORY AND MY SLOVOTNISH IS A BIT RUSTY.
"THE SLOVOTNYS ARE A FIERCE AND WARLIKE RACE. MANY CENTURIES AGO, THEY CAME FROM A DISTANT PLANET TO CONQUER EARTH AND ENSLAVE ALL OF ITS PEOPLE.
"MR. AND MRS. SLOVOTNY WERE THEIR ADVANCED SCOUTING GROUP. THEY CAME TO LIVE AMONG HUMANS AND LEARN ABOUT THEIR WAYS.
"IT ALL WENT WITHOUT A HITCH. AND BEFORE LONG, THE SLOVOTNYS HAD THE HUMANS UNDER THEIR IRON RULE.
"THEY BECAME LIKE GODS TO THE ANCIENT HUMANS. AND WITH THEIR SPACE FLEET POISED AT THE READY AT THE FAR END OF THE GALAXY, THE SLOVOTNYS WAITED.
"AND WAITED.
"BUT, UNFORTUNATELY, THEIR CONQUERING SPACE FLEET TOOK A WRONG TURN AT A NEIGHBORING GALAXY AND NEVER ACTUALLY ARRIVED."

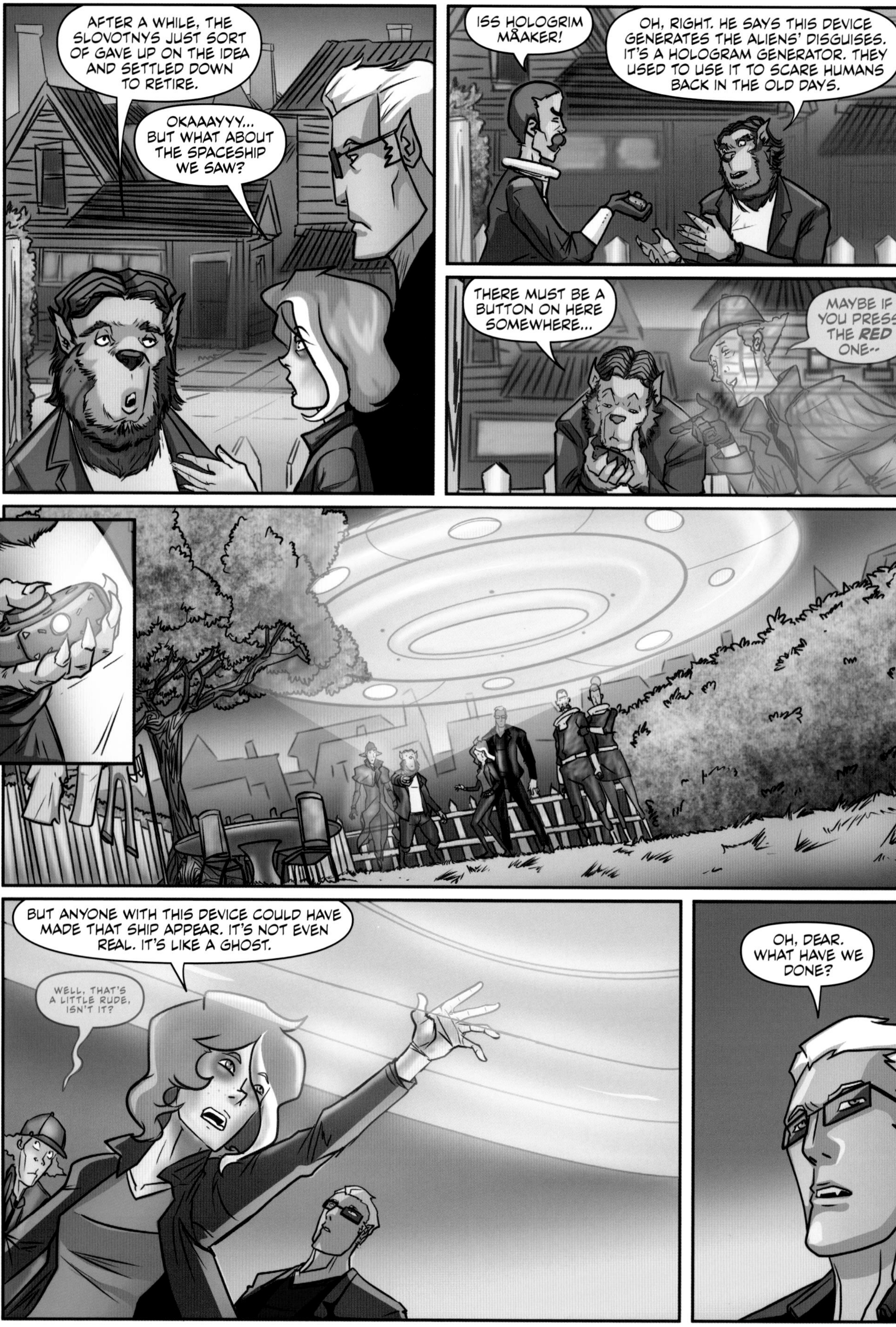

AFTER A WHILE, THE SLOVOTNYS JUST SORT OF GAVE UP ON THE IDEA AND SETTLED DOWN TO RETIRE.
OKAAAYYY... BUT WHAT ABOUT THE SPACESHIP WE SAW?
ISS HOLOGRIM MÅAKER!
OH, RIGHT. HE SAYS THIS DEVICE GENERATES THE ALIENS' DISGUISES. IT'S A HOLOGRAM GENERATOR. THEY USED TO USE IT TO SCARE HUMANS BACK IN THE OLD DAYS.
THERE MUST BE A BUTTON ON HERE SOMEWHERE...
MAYBE IF YOU PRESS THE *RED* ONE--
BUT ANYONE WITH THIS DEVICE COULD HAVE MADE THAT SHIP APPEAR. IT'S NOT EVEN REAL. IT'S LIKE A GHOST.
WELL, THAT'S A LITTLE RUDE, ISN'T IT?
OH, DEAR. WHAT HAVE WE DONE?

I CAN'T DO THIS RIGHT NOW.

"I CAN'T DO THIS RIGHT NOW?" IS THAT YOUR STANDARD REPLY TO **EVERYTHING**, JERRY?

THE MAYOR DISAPPEARED RIGHT IN FRONT OF OUR EYES! BUT IT WASN'T THE ALIENS!

DETECTIVE, I REALLY THINK YOU SHOULD LISTEN TO GINA. THE ALIEN SHIP WAS APPARENTLY SOMETHING THEY CALL A "HOLOGRAM."

QUITE A REMARKABLE DEVICE, TOO--ONE MIGHT THINK OF IT AS A GHOST PROJECTOR--

NOT IN THE MOOD.

--HEY!

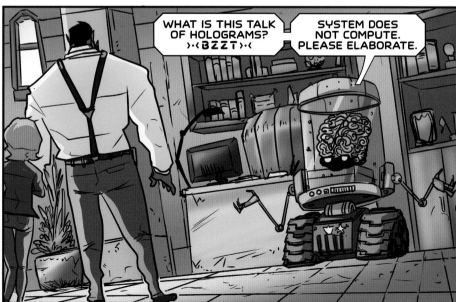

WHAT IS THIS TALK OF HOLOGRAMS? >·‹ BZZT ›·‹

SYSTEM DOES NOT COMPUTE. PLEASE ELABORATE.

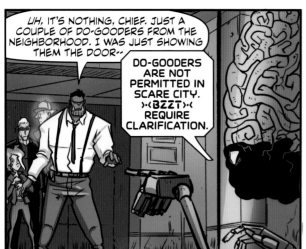

UH, IT'S NOTHING, CHIEF. JUST A COUPLE OF DO-GOODERS FROM THE NEIGHBORHOOD. I WAS JUST SHOWING THEM THE DOOR--
DO-GOODERS ARE NOT PERMITTED IN SCARE CITY. ›‹BZZT›‹ REQUIRE CLARIFICATION.
WHAT TYPE OF MONSTER IS THE POLICE CHIEF?
EVIL RAMPAGING ROBOT, I BELIEVE. THEY'RE A SUB-GENRE. A THROWBACK TO A SIMPLER TIME.
OH.
POLICE CHIEF MIND-MELD, I NEED YOU TO LISTEN TO ME. WE HAVE EVIDENCE PROVING THE VAMPIRE WHO WAS SUNTANNED IN THE MOONWALK DISTRICT MAY HAVE BEEN MURDERED FROM A DISTANCE.
IF DETECTIVE MANDIBLE HERE ISN'T WILLING TO LISTEN THEN PERHAPS YOU WILL--
AFFIRMATIVE. PROCEED WITH YOUR EXPLANATION.
SPOOKHURST
X MY HOME
X ALIENS AREA
LOOK! HERE'S THE EXACT SPOT IN SPOOKHURST WHERE THE LIGHT CAME FROM. IT'S THE SAME LIGHT WE'VE BEEN SEEING ALL OVER TOWN.
BUT THE ALIEN SECTOR IS ACROSS TOWN, AND IT'S NOT IN THE LINE OF SIGHT. THE SOURCE COULDN'T POSSIBLY HAVE COME FROM THERE!

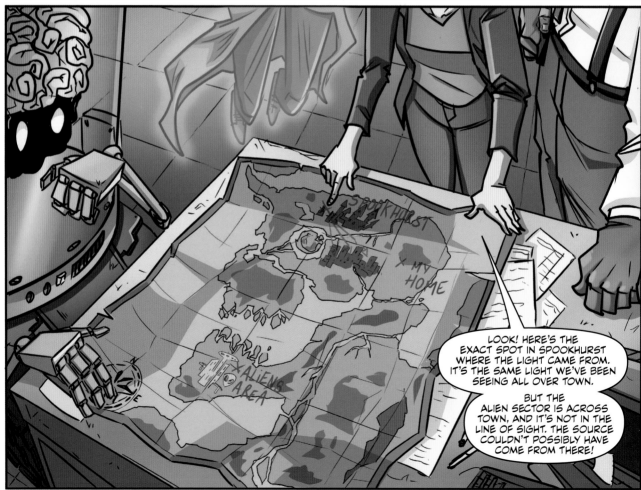

CHIEF! LOOKS LIKE THE MOB IS DYING DOWN OUT THERE!

I HAVEN'T HAD THAT MUCH FUN IN AGES.

OH, YEAH! WE REALLY SHOULD DO THIS MORE OFTEN--

IF THE ALIEN SECTOR IS NOT RESPONSIBLE FOR ABDUCTIONS WITHIN THE CITY, YOU MUST PROVIDE PROOF OF YOUR HYPOTHESIS, AND AN EXPLANATION.

YES! THANK YOU!

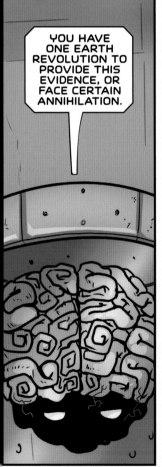

YOU HAVE ONE EARTH REVOLUTION TO PROVIDE THIS EVIDENCE, OR FACE CERTAIN ANNIHILATION.

DON'T WORRY ABOUT THE CHIEF. HE ALWAYS SAYS STUFF LIKE THAT.

BUT YOU NEED TO BE *CAREFUL*, OKAY? WAY I HEAR IT, YOU GOT SOME PRETTY SCARY PEOPLE LOOKIN' IN YOUR DIRECTION. AN' TRUST ME, THESE ARE PEOPLE YOU'D RATHER HAVE LOOKIN' THE OTHER WAY.

DON'T PUSH TOO MANY BUTTONS ON THIS ONE, GINA.

NO ONE WANTS TO LOSE THEIR HEAD OVER SOMETHIN' LIKE THIS--ESPECIALLY NOT A *ZOMBIE*, IF YOU CATCH MY DRIFT?

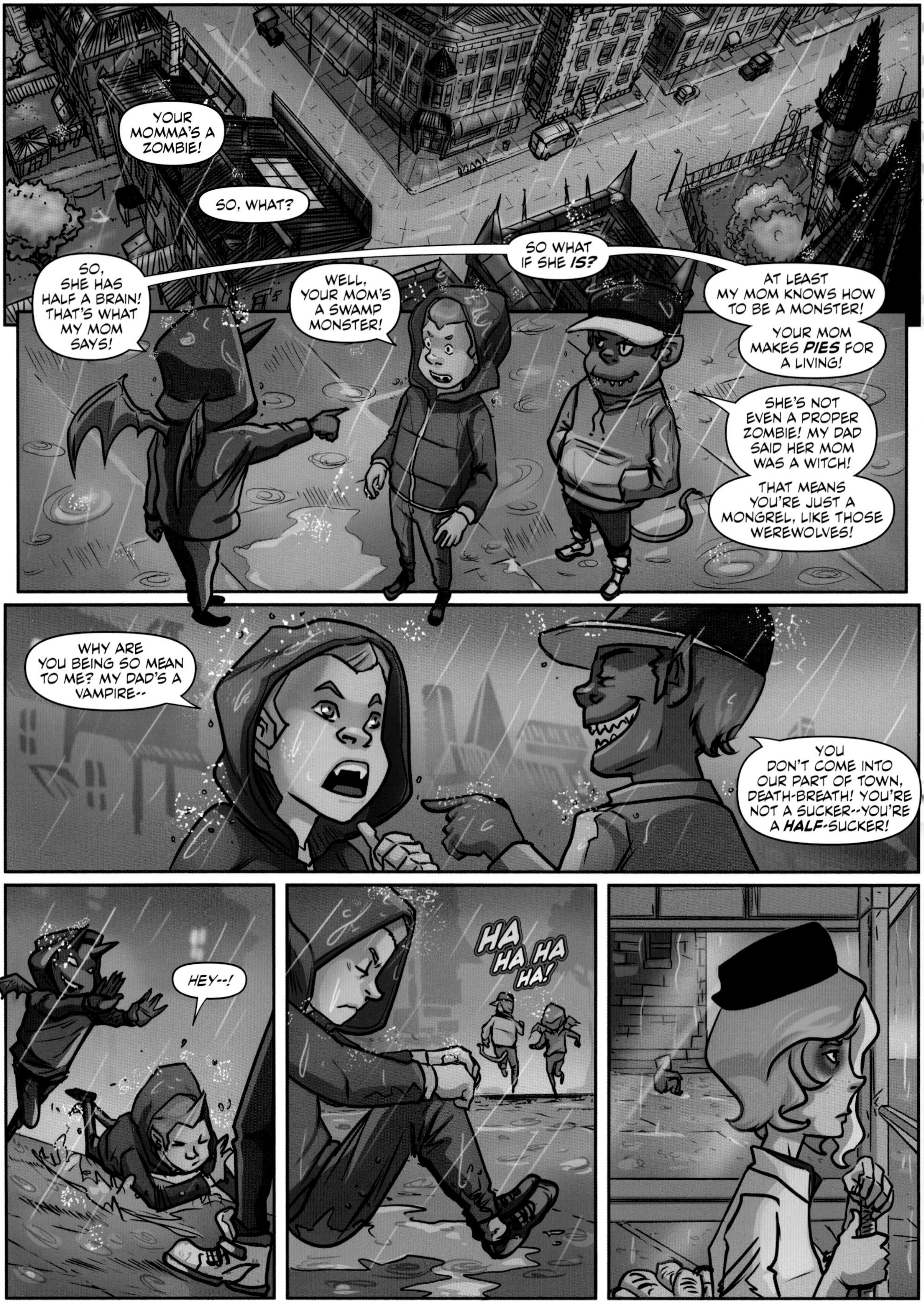
YOUR MOMMA'S A ZOMBIE!
SO, WHAT?
SO, SHE HAS HALF A BRAIN! THAT'S WHAT MY MOM SAYS!
SO WHAT IF SHE *IS?*
WELL, YOUR MOM'S A SWAMP MONSTER!
AT LEAST MY MOM KNOWS HOW TO BE A MONSTER!
YOUR MOM MAKES *PIES* FOR A LIVING!
SHE'S NOT EVEN A PROPER ZOMBIE! MY DAD SAID HER MOM WAS A WITCH!
THAT MEANS YOU'RE JUST A MONGREL, LIKE THOSE WEREWOLVES!
WHY ARE YOU BEING SO MEAN TO ME? MY DAD'S A VAMPIRE--
YOU DON'T COME INTO OUR PART OF TOWN, DEATH-BREATH! YOU'RE NOT A SUCKER--YOU'RE A *HALF*-SUCKER!
HEY--!
HA HA HA HA!

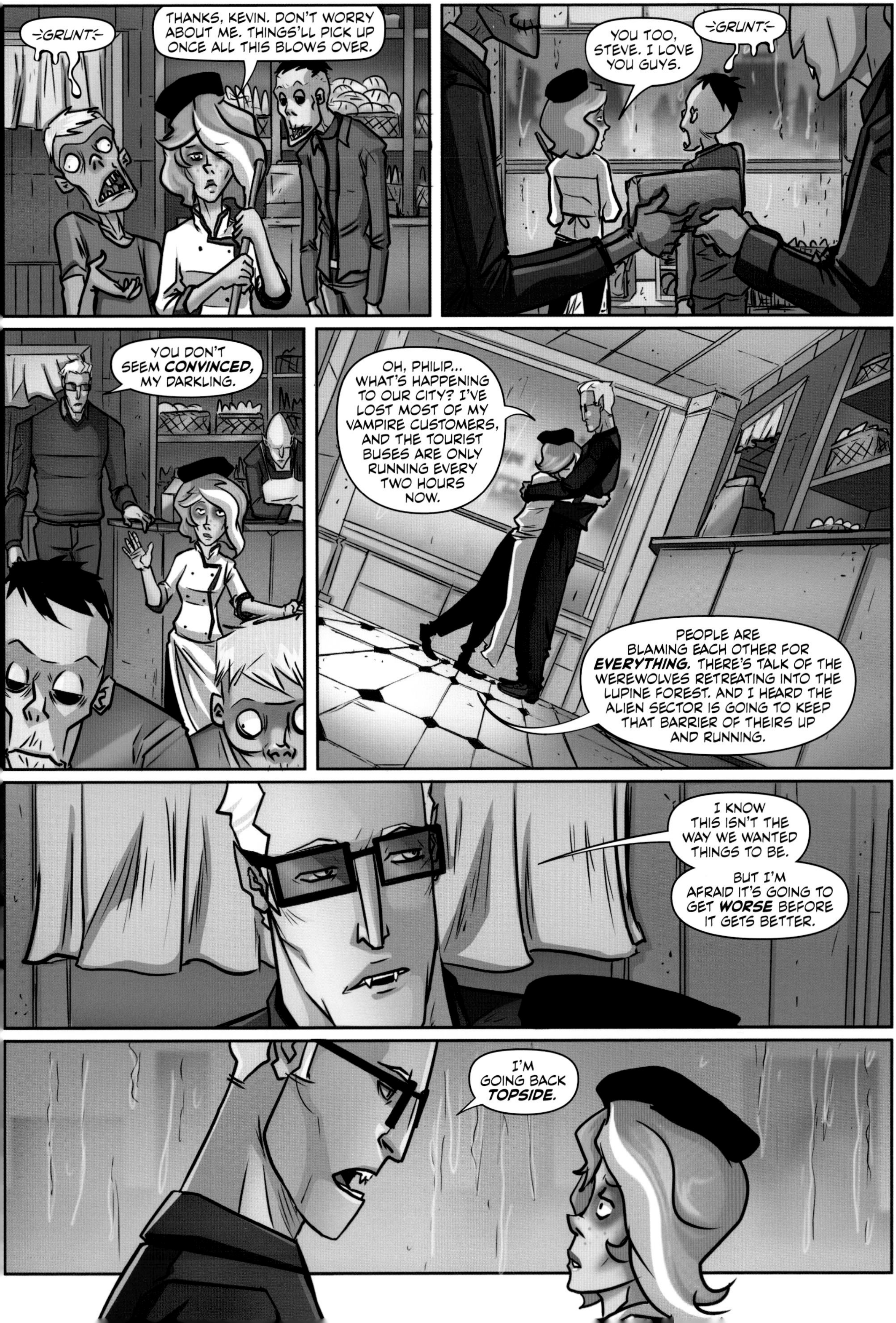

GRUNT
THANKS, KEVIN. DON'T WORRY ABOUT ME. THINGS'LL PICK UP ONCE ALL THIS BLOWS OVER.
YOU TOO, STEVE. I LOVE YOU GUYS.
GRUNT
YOU DON'T SEEM CONVINCED, MY DARLING.
OH, PHILIP... WHAT'S HAPPENING TO OUR CITY? I'VE LOST MOST OF MY VAMPIRE CUSTOMERS, AND THE TOURIST BUSES ARE ONLY RUNNING EVERY TWO HOURS NOW.
PEOPLE ARE BLAMING EACH OTHER FOR EVERYTHING. THERE'S TALK OF THE WEREWOLVES RETREATING INTO THE LUPINE FOREST. AND I HEARD THE ALIEN SECTOR IS GOING TO KEEP THAT BARRIER OF THEIRS UP AND RUNNING.
I KNOW THIS ISN'T THE WAY WE WANTED THINGS TO BE.
BUT I'M AFRAID IT'S GOING TO GET WORSE BEFORE IT GETS BETTER.
I'M GOING BACK TOPSIDE.

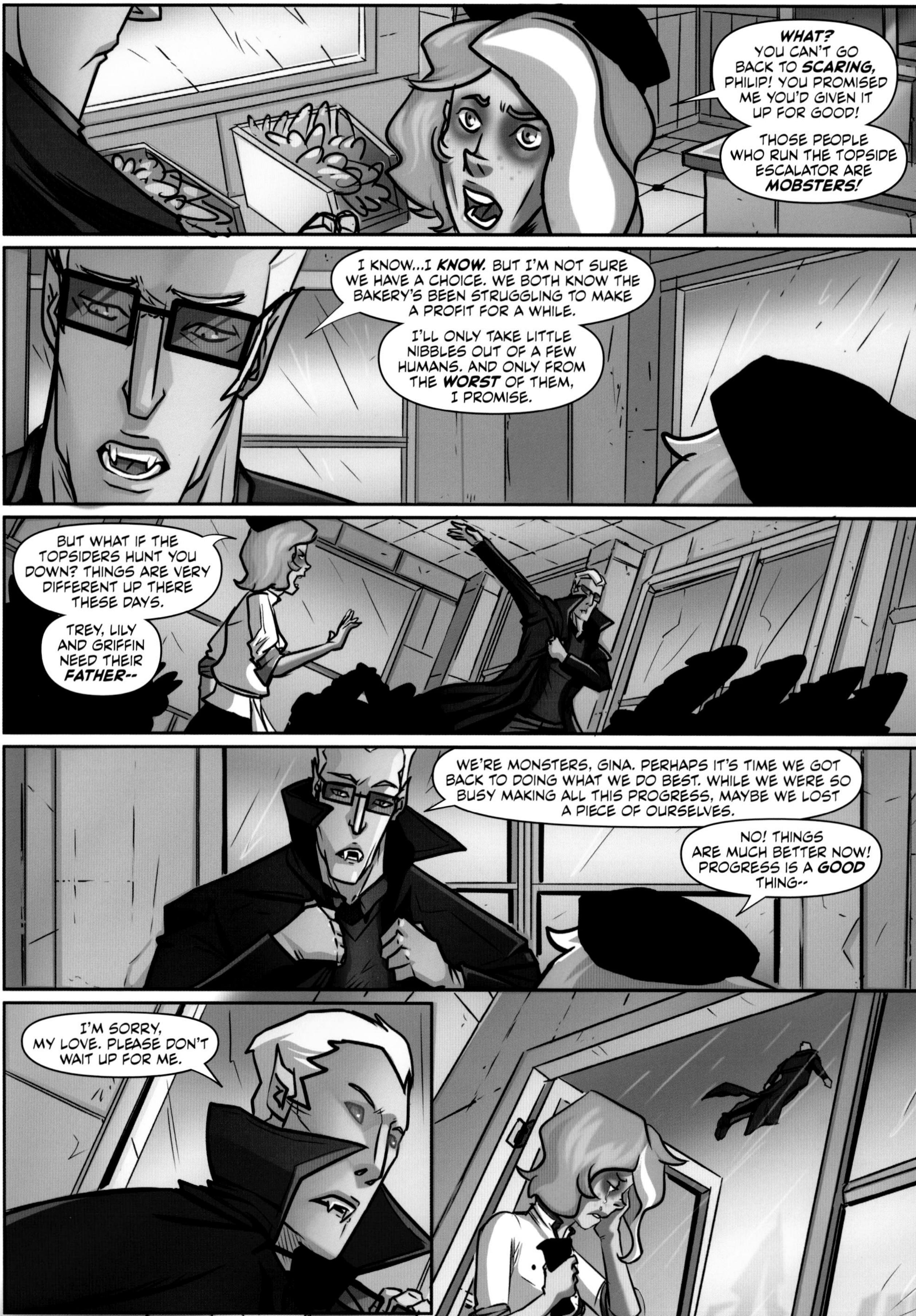
WHAT? YOU CAN'T GO BACK TO SCARING, PHILIP! YOU PROMISED ME YOU'D GIVEN IT UP FOR GOOD!
THOSE PEOPLE WHO RUN THE TOPSIDE ESCALATOR ARE MOBSTERS!
I KNOW...I KNOW. BUT I'M NOT SURE WE HAVE A CHOICE. WE BOTH KNOW THE BAKERY'S BEEN STRUGGLING TO MAKE A PROFIT FOR A WHILE.
I'LL ONLY TAKE LITTLE NIBBLES OUT OF A FEW HUMANS. AND ONLY FROM THE WORST OF THEM, I PROMISE.
BUT WHAT IF THE TOPSIDERS HUNT YOU DOWN? THINGS ARE VERY DIFFERENT UP THERE THESE DAYS.
TREY, LILY AND GRIFFIN NEED THEIR FATHER--
WE'RE MONSTERS, GINA. PERHAPS IT'S TIME WE GOT BACK TO DOING WHAT WE DO BEST. WHILE WE WERE SO BUSY MAKING ALL THIS PROGRESS, MAYBE WE LOST A PIECE OF OURSELVES.
NO! THINGS ARE MUCH BETTER NOW! PROGRESS IS A GOOD THING--
I'M SORRY, MY LOVE. PLEASE DON'T WAIT UP FOR ME.

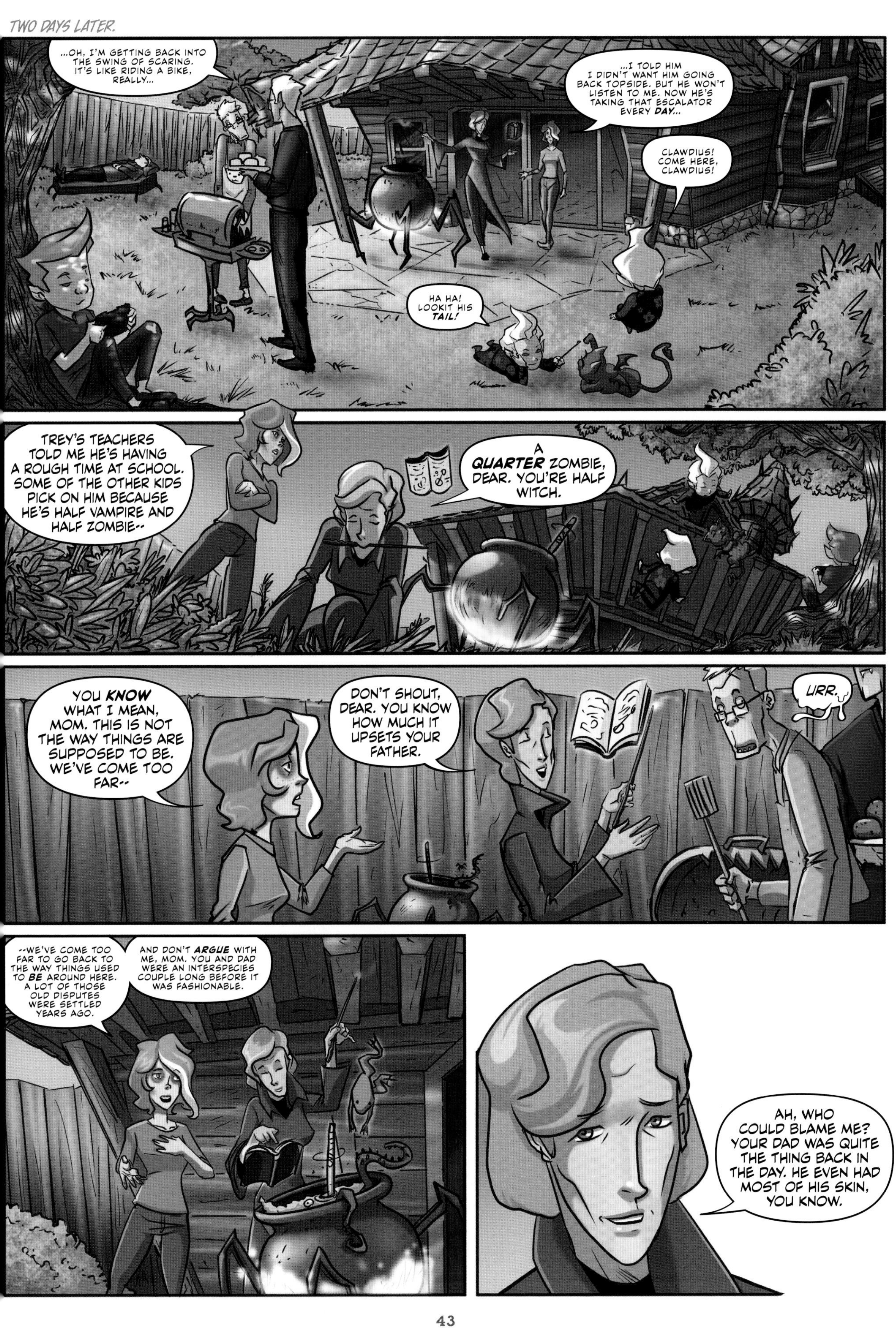
TWO DAYS LATER.
...OH, I'M GETTING BACK INTO THE SWING OF SCARING. IT'S LIKE RIDING A BIKE, REALLY...
...I TOLD HIM I DIDN'T WANT HIM GOING BACK TOPSIDE. BUT HE WON'T LISTEN TO ME. NOW HE'S TAKING THAT ESCALATOR EVERY DAY...
CLAWDIUS! COME HERE, CLAWDIUS!
HA HA! LOOKIT HIS TAIL!
TREY'S TEACHERS TOLD ME HE'S HAVING A ROUGH TIME AT SCHOOL. SOME OF THE OTHER KIDS PICK ON HIM BECAUSE HE'S HALF VAMPIRE AND HALF ZOMBIE--
A QUARTER ZOMBIE, DEAR. YOU'RE HALF WITCH.
YOU KNOW WHAT I MEAN, MOM. THIS IS NOT THE WAY THINGS ARE SUPPOSED TO BE. WE'VE COME TOO FAR--
DON'T SHOUT, DEAR. YOU KNOW HOW MUCH IT UPSETS YOUR FATHER.
URR.
--WE'VE COME TOO FAR TO GO BACK TO THE WAY THINGS USED TO BE AROUND HERE. A LOT OF THOSE OLD DISPUTES WERE SETTLED YEARS AGO.
AND DON'T ARGUE WITH ME, MOM. YOU AND DAD WERE AN INTERSPECIES COUPLE LONG BEFORE IT WAS FASHIONABLE.
AH, WHO COULD BLAME ME? YOUR DAD WAS QUITE THE THING BACK IN THE DAY. HE EVEN HAD MOST OF HIS SKIN, YOU KNOW.

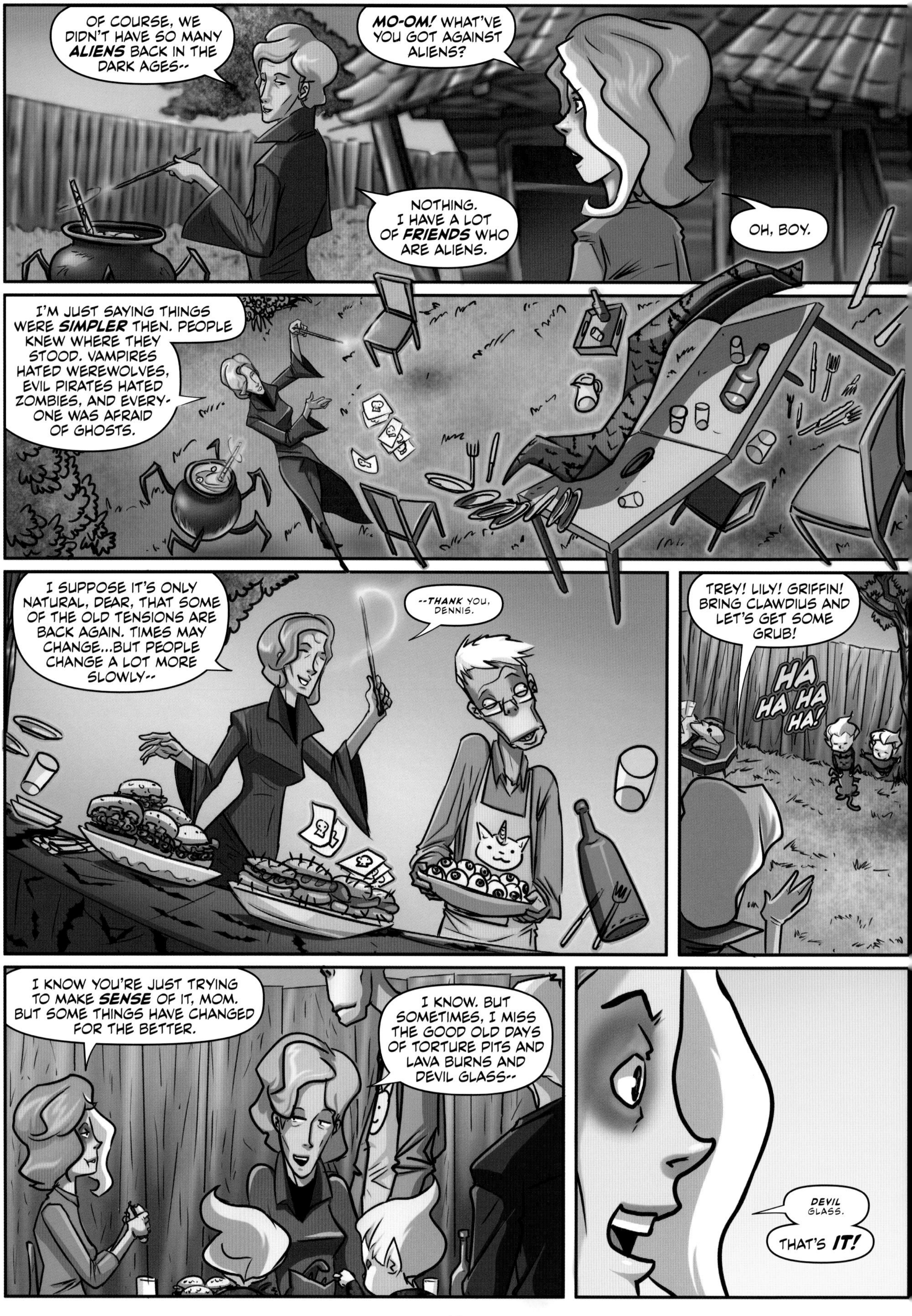
OF COURSE, WE DIDN'T HAVE SO MANY ALIENS BACK IN THE DARK AGES--
MO-OM! WHAT'VE YOU GOT AGAINST ALIENS?
NOTHING. I HAVE A LOT OF FRIENDS WHO ARE ALIENS.
OH, BOY.
I'M JUST SAYING THINGS WERE SIMPLER THEN. PEOPLE KNEW WHERE THEY STOOD. VAMPIRES HATED WEREWOLVES, EVIL PIRATES HATED ZOMBIES, AND EVERY-ONE WAS AFRAID OF GHOSTS.
I SUPPOSE IT'S ONLY NATURAL, DEAR, THAT SOME OF THE OLD TENSIONS ARE BACK AGAIN. TIMES MAY CHANGE...BUT PEOPLE CHANGE A LOT MORE SLOWLY--
--THANK YOU, DENNIS.
TREY! LILY! GRIFFIN! BRING CLAWDIUS AND LET'S GET SOME GRUB!
HA HA HA HA!
I KNOW YOU'RE JUST TRYING TO MAKE SENSE OF IT, MOM. BUT SOME THINGS HAVE CHANGED FOR THE BETTER.
I KNOW. BUT SOMETIMES, I MISS THE GOOD OLD DAYS OF TORTURE PITS AND LAVA BURNS AND DEVIL GLASS--
DEVIL GLASS.
THAT'S IT!

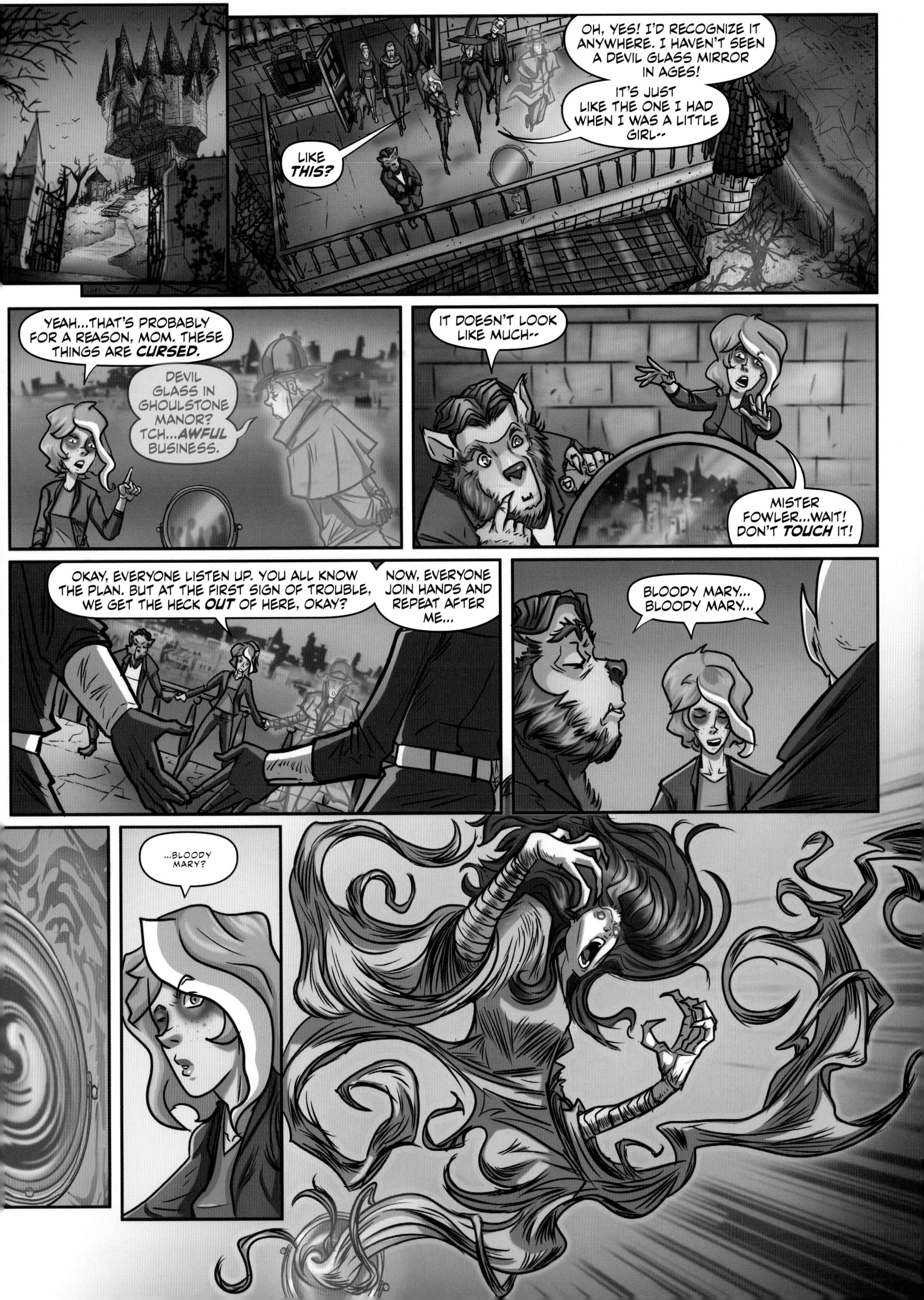
OH, YES! I'D RECOGNIZE IT ANYWHERE. I HAVEN'T SEEN A DEVIL GLASS MIRROR IN AGES!
IT'S JUST LIKE THE ONE I HAD WHEN I WAS A LITTLE GIRL--
LIKE THIS?
YEAH...THAT'S PROBABLY FOR A REASON, MOM. THESE THINGS ARE CURSED.
DEVIL GLASS IN GHOULSTONE MANOR? TCH...AWFUL BUSINESS.
IT DOESN'T LOOK LIKE MUCH--
MISTER FOWLER...WAIT! DON'T TOUCH IT!
OKAY, EVERYONE LISTEN UP. YOU ALL KNOW THE PLAN. BUT AT THE FIRST SIGN OF TROUBLE, WE GET THE HECK OUT OF HERE, OKAY?
NOW, EVERYONE JOIN HANDS AND REPEAT AFTER ME...
BLOODY MARY... BLOODY MARY...
...BLOODY MARY?

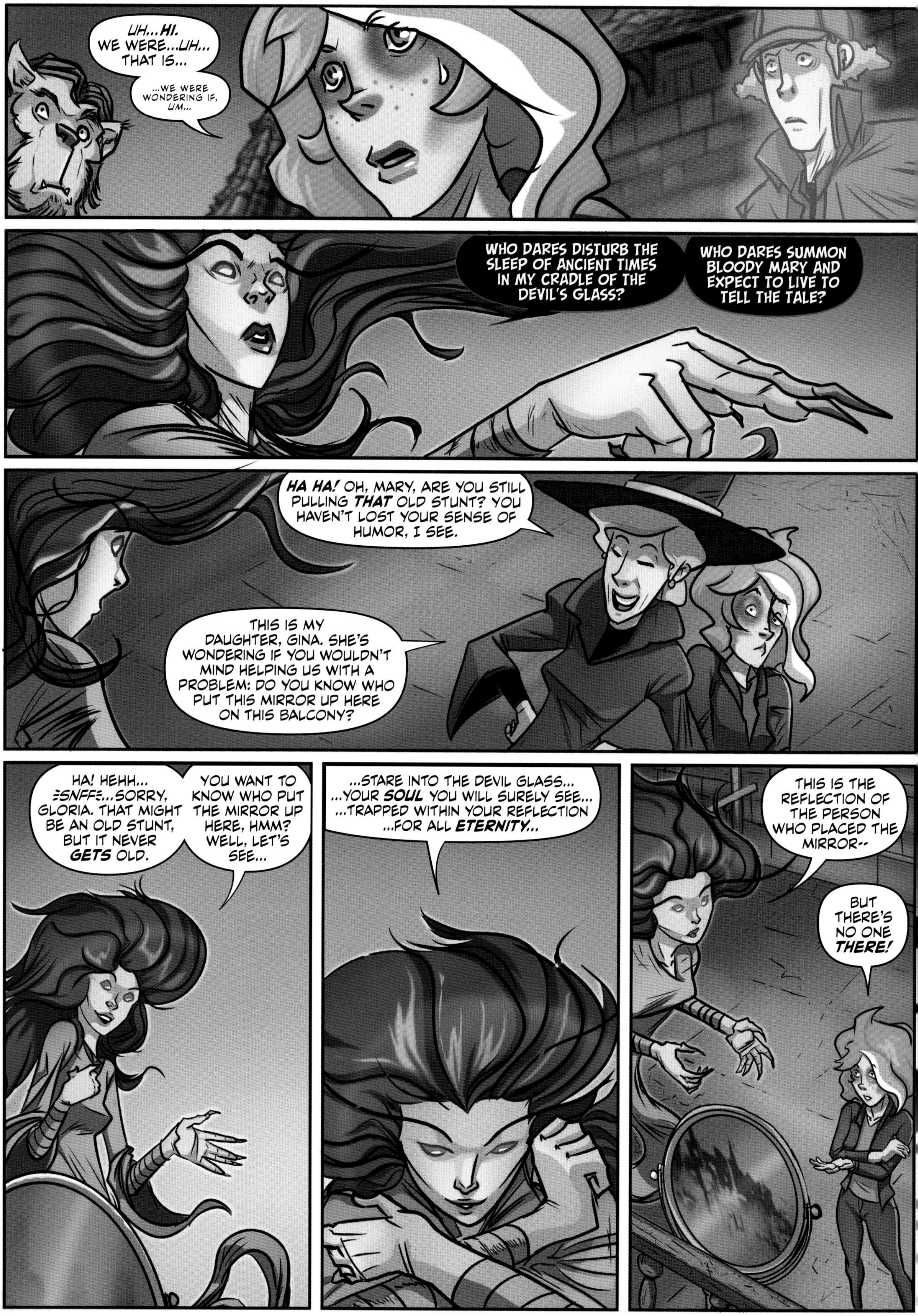

UH...HI. WE WERE...UH... THAT IS...
...WE WERE WONDERING IF, UM...
WHO DARES DISTURB THE SLEEP OF ANCIENT TIMES IN MY CRADLE OF THE DEVIL'S GLASS?
WHO DARES SUMMON BLOODY MARY AND EXPECT TO LIVE TO TELL THE TALE?
HA HA! OH, MARY, ARE YOU STILL PULLING THAT OLD STUNT? YOU HAVEN'T LOST YOUR SENSE OF HUMOR, I SEE.
THIS IS MY DAUGHTER, GINA. SHE'S WONDERING IF YOU WOULDN'T MIND HELPING US WITH A PROBLEM: DO YOU KNOW WHO PUT THIS MIRROR UP HERE ON THIS BALCONY?
HA! HEHH... SNFF... SORRY, GLORIA. THAT MIGHT BE AN OLD STUNT, BUT IT NEVER GETS OLD.
YOU WANT TO KNOW WHO PUT THE MIRROR UP HERE, HMM? WELL, LET'S SEE...
...STARE INTO THE DEVIL GLASS... ...YOUR SOUL YOU WILL SURELY SEE... ...TRAPPED WITHIN YOUR REFLECTION ...FOR ALL ETERNITY...
THIS IS THE REFLECTION OF THE PERSON WHO PLACED THE MIRROR--
BUT THERE'S NO ONE THERE!

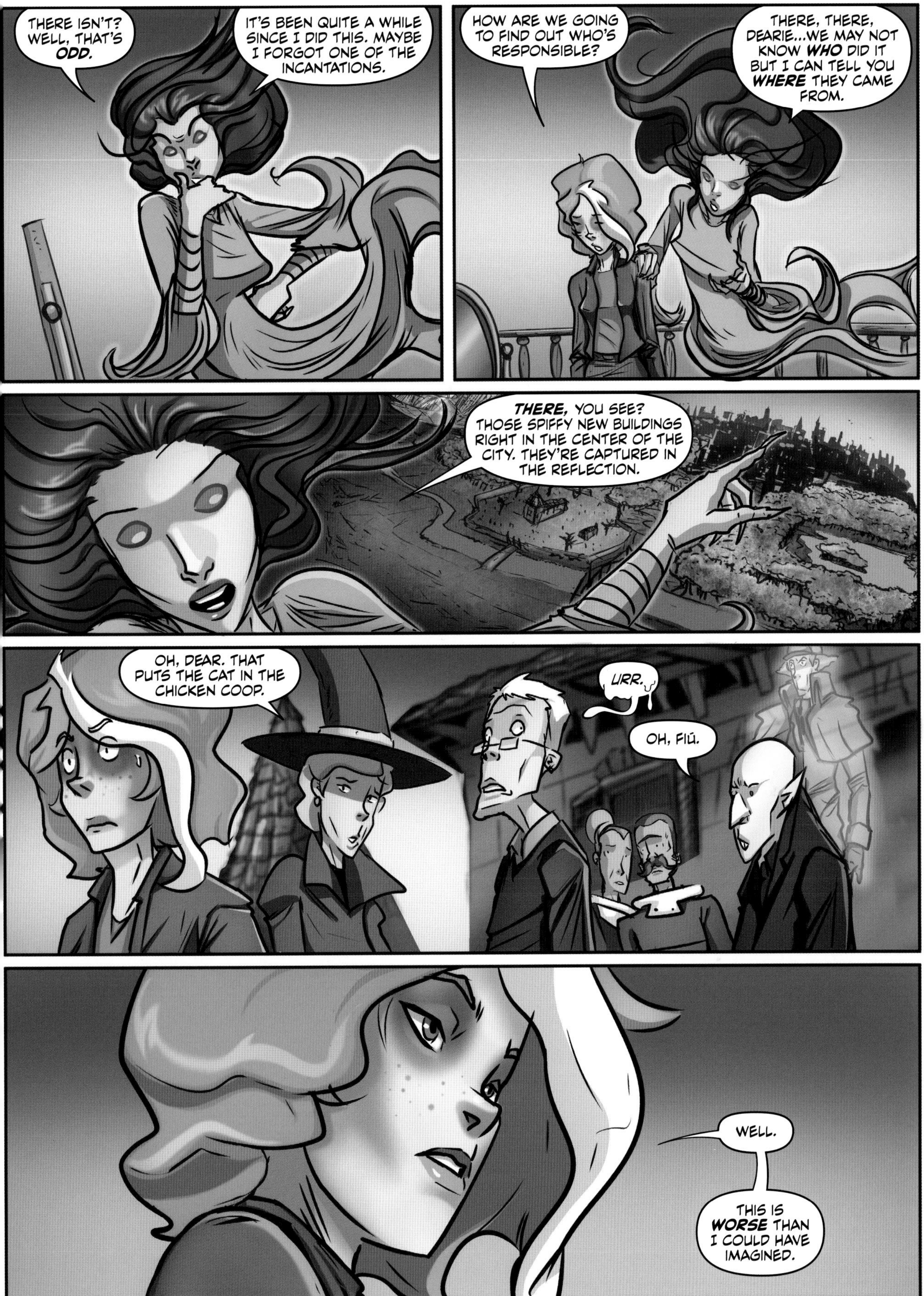
THERE ISN'T? WELL, THAT'S ***ODD.***
IT'S BEEN QUITE A WHILE SINCE I DID THIS. MAYBE I FORGOT ONE OF THE INCANTATIONS.
HOW ARE WE GOING TO FIND OUT WHO'S RESPONSIBLE?
THERE, THERE, DEARIE...WE MAY NOT KNOW ***WHO*** DID IT BUT I CAN TELL YOU ***WHERE*** THEY CAME FROM.
THERE, YOU SEE? THOSE SPIFFY NEW BUILDINGS RIGHT IN THE CENTER OF THE CITY. THEY'RE CAPTURED IN THE REFLECTION.
OH, DEAR. THAT PUTS THE CAT IN THE CHICKEN COOP.
URR.
OH, FIÚ.
WELL.
THIS IS ***WORSE*** THAN I COULD HAVE IMAGINED.

LATER.

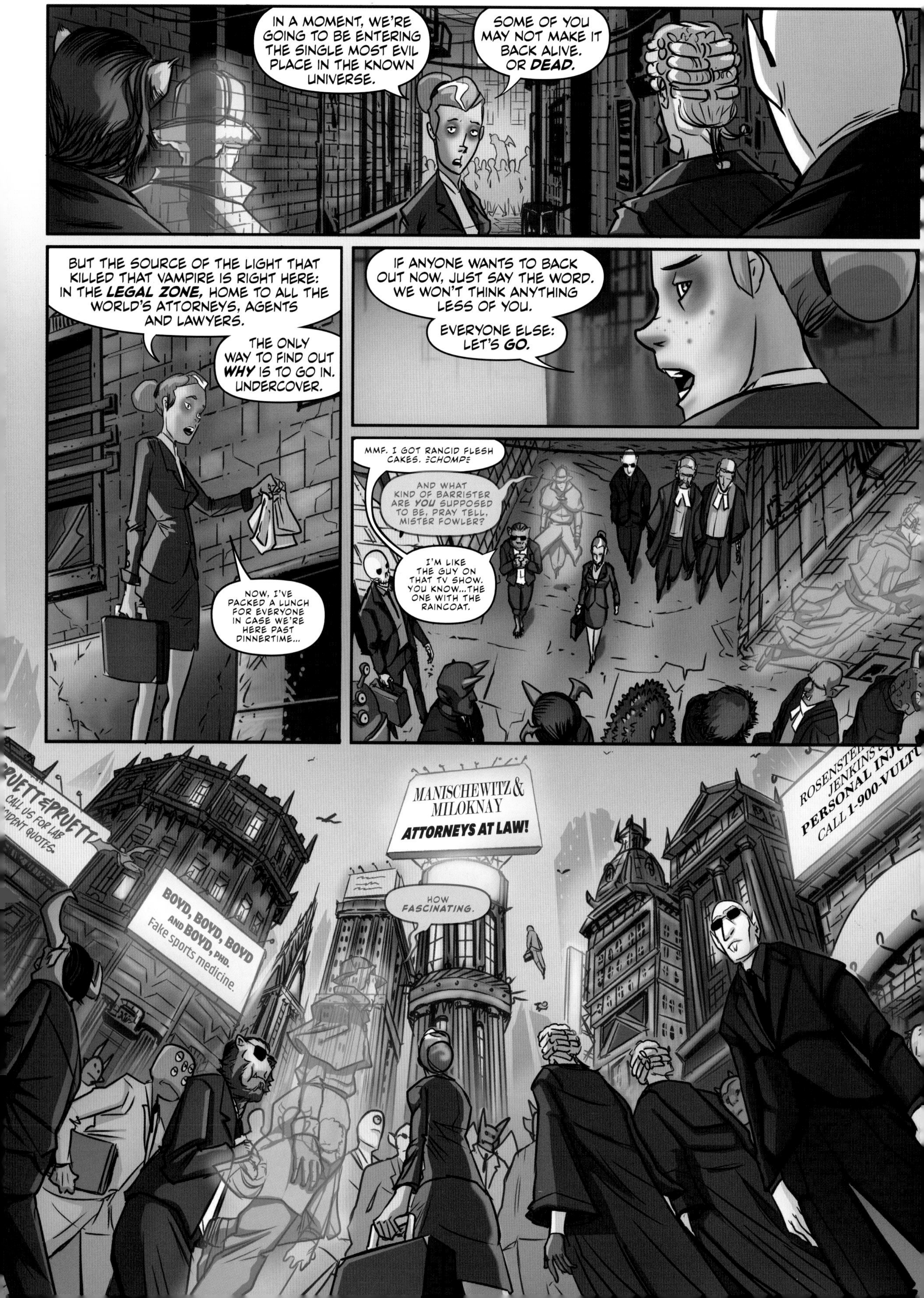
IN A MOMENT, WE'RE GOING TO BE ENTERING THE SINGLE MOST EVIL PLACE IN THE KNOWN UNIVERSE.
SOME OF YOU MAY NOT MAKE IT BACK ALIVE. OR DEAD.
BUT THE SOURCE OF THE LIGHT THAT KILLED THAT VAMPIRE IS RIGHT HERE: IN THE LEGAL ZONE, HOME TO ALL THE WORLD'S ATTORNEYS, AGENTS AND LAWYERS.
THE ONLY WAY TO FIND OUT WHY IS TO GO IN. UNDERCOVER.
NOW, I'VE PACKED A LUNCH FOR EVERYONE IN CASE WE'RE HERE PAST DINNERTIME...
IF ANYONE WANTS TO BACK OUT NOW, JUST SAY THE WORD. WE WON'T THINK ANYTHING LESS OF YOU.
EVERYONE ELSE: LET'S GO.
MMF. I GOT RANCID FLESH CAKES. =CHOMP=
AND WHAT KIND OF BARRISTER ARE YOU SUPPOSED TO BE, PRAY TELL, MISTER FOWLER?
I'M LIKE THE GUY ON THAT TV SHOW. YOU KNOW...THE ONE WITH THE RAINCOAT.
PRUETT&PRUETT
CALL US FOR LAB
MANISCHEWITZ & MILOKNAY
ATTORNEYS AT LAW!
JENKINS
CALL 1-900-VULTU
BOYD, BOYD, BOYD AND BOYD, PHD.
Fake sports medicine.
HOW FASCINATING.

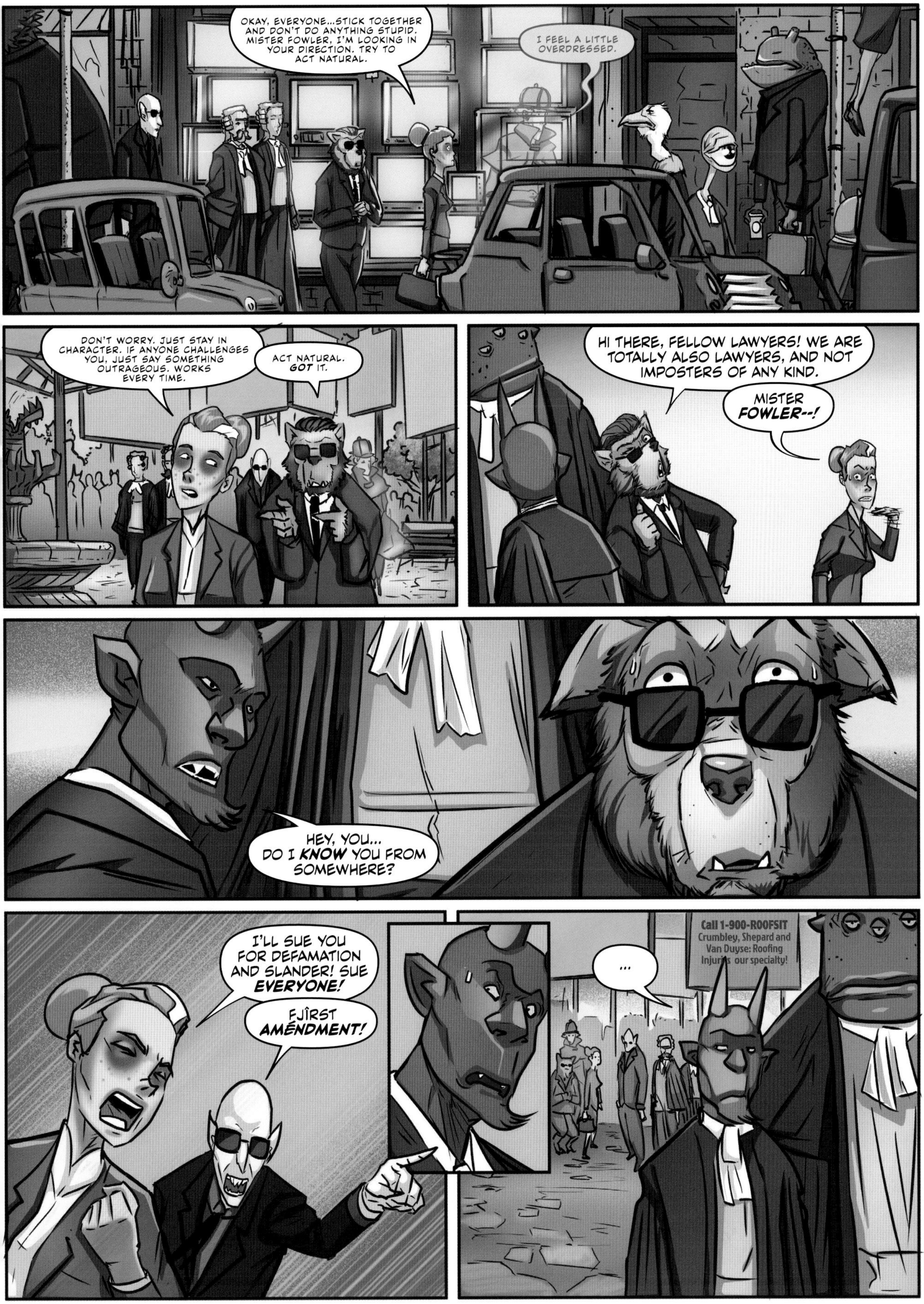
OKAY, EVERYONE...STICK TOGETHER AND DON'T DO ANYTHING STUPID. MISTER FOWLER, I'M LOOKING IN YOUR DIRECTION. TRY TO ACT NATURAL.
I FEEL A LITTLE OVERDRESSED.
DON'T WORRY. JUST STAY IN CHARACTER. IF ANYONE CHALLENGES YOU, JUST SAY SOMETHING OUTRAGEOUS. WORKS EVERY TIME.
ACT NATURAL. **GOT** IT.
HI THERE, FELLOW LAWYERS! WE ARE TOTALLY ALSO LAWYERS, AND NOT IMPOSTERS OF ANY KIND.
MISTER **FOWLER--!**
HEY, YOU... DO I **KNOW** YOU FROM SOMEWHERE?
I'LL SUE YOU FOR DEFAMATION AND SLANDER! SUE **EVERYONE!**
FJÎRST **AMÉNDMENT!**
...
Call 1-900-ROOFSIT
Crumbley, Shepard and Van Duyse: Roofing
our specialty!

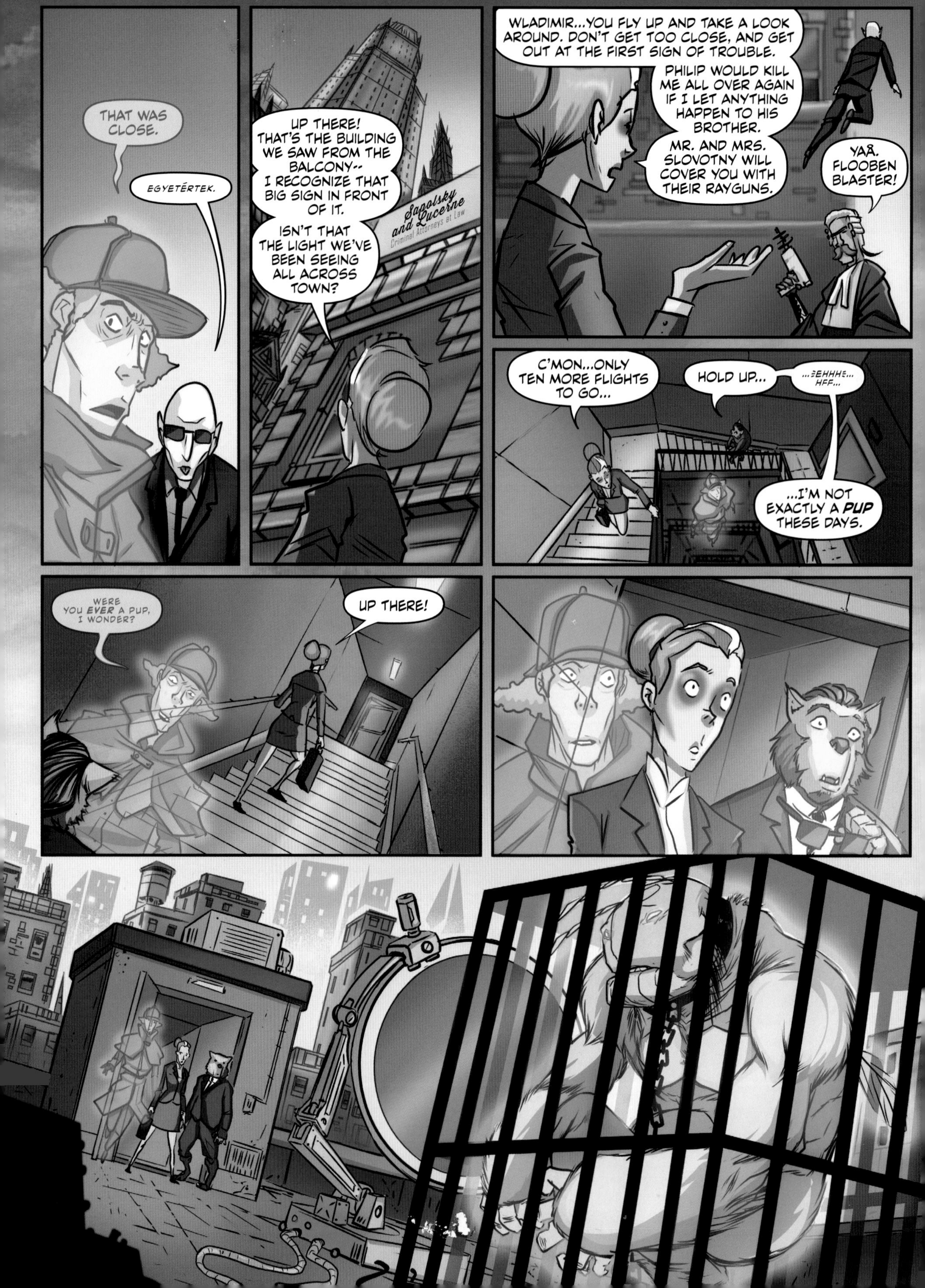
THAT WAS CLOSE.
EGYETÉRTEK.
UP THERE! THAT'S THE BUILDING WE SAW FROM THE BALCONY-- I RECOGNIZE THAT BIG SIGN IN FRONT OF IT.
Sapolsky and Lucerne
Criminal Attorneys at Law
ISN'T THAT THE LIGHT WE'VE BEEN SEEING ALL ACROSS TOWN?
WLADIMIR...YOU FLY UP AND TAKE A LOOK AROUND. DON'T GET TOO CLOSE, AND GET OUT AT THE FIRST SIGN OF TROUBLE.
PHILIP WOULD KILL ME ALL OVER AGAIN IF I LET ANYTHING HAPPEN TO HIS BROTHER.
MR. AND MRS. SLOVOTNY WILL COVER YOU WITH THEIR RAYGUNS.
YAÅ. FLOOBEN BLASTER!
C'MON...ONLY TEN MORE FLIGHTS TO GO...
HOLD UP...
...ƎEHHHƎ... HFF...
...I'M NOT EXACTLY A PUP THESE DAYS.
WERE YOU EVER A PUP, I WONDER?
UP THERE!

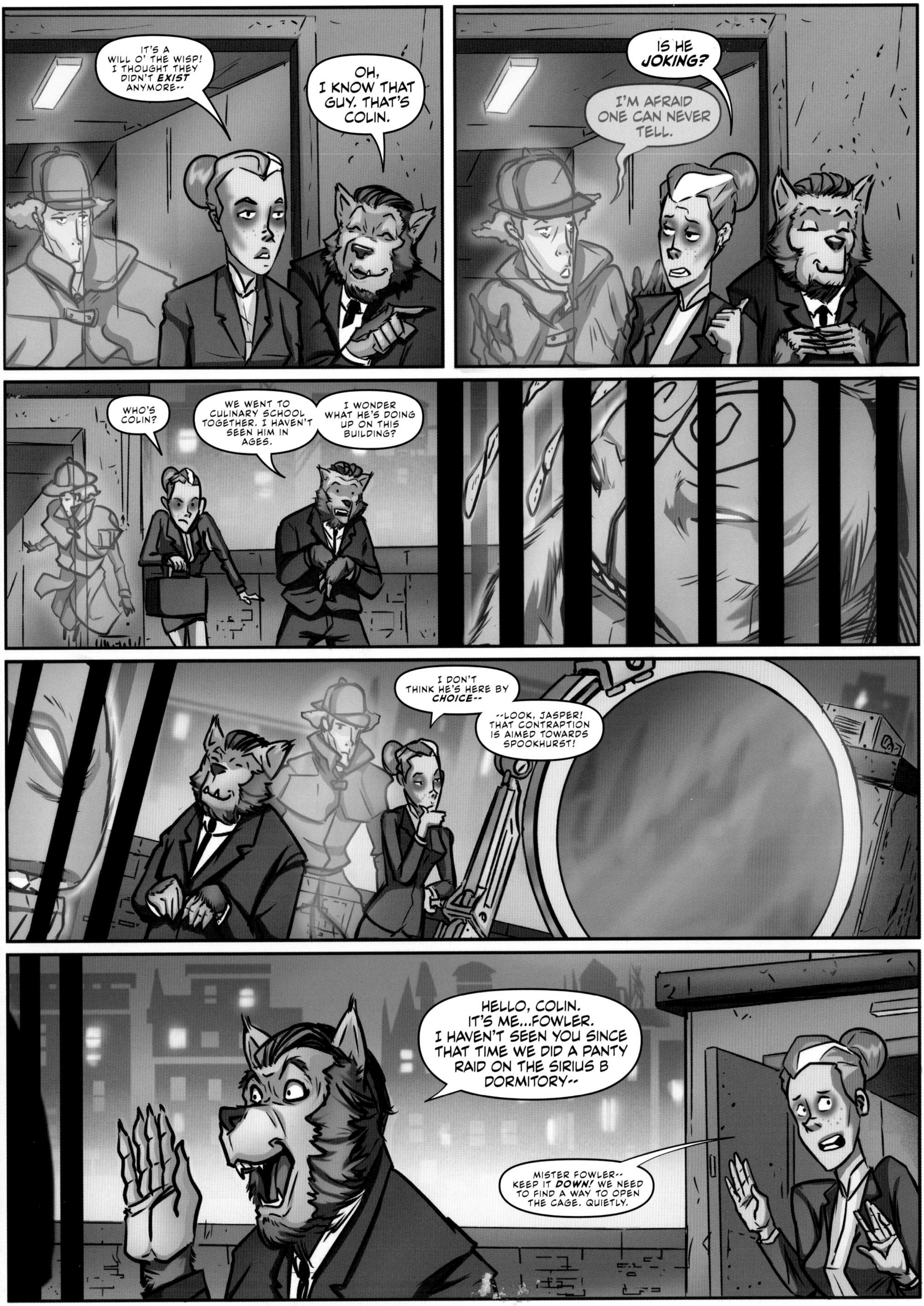
IT'S A WILL O' THE WISP! I THOUGHT THEY DIDN'T *EXIST* ANYMORE--
OH, I KNOW THAT GUY. THAT'S COLIN.
IS HE *JOKING?*
I'M AFRAID ONE CAN NEVER TELL.
WHO'S COLIN?
WE WENT TO CULINARY SCHOOL TOGETHER. I HAVEN'T SEEN HIM IN AGES.
I WONDER WHAT HE'S DOING UP ON THIS BUILDING?
I DON'T THINK HE'S HERE BY *CHOICE*--
--LOOK, JASPER! THAT CONTRAPTION IS AIMED TOWARDS SPOOKHURST!
HELLO, COLIN. IT'S ME...FOWLER. I HAVEN'T SEEN YOU SINCE THAT TIME WE DID A PANTY RAID ON THE SIRIUS B DORMITORY--
MISTER FOWLER-- KEEP IT *DOWN!* WE NEED TO FIND A WAY TO OPEN THE CAGE. QUIETLY.

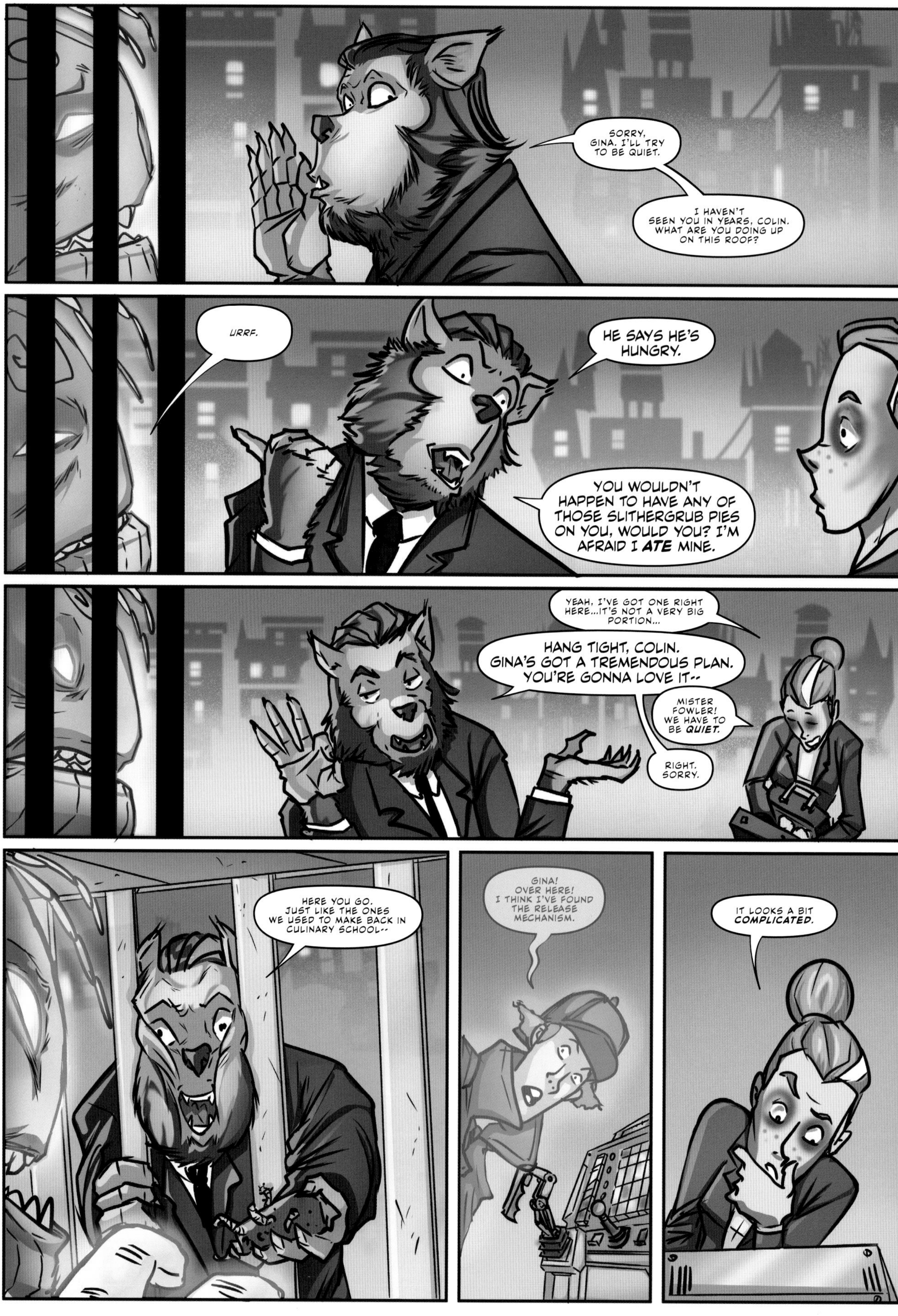
SORRY, GINA. I'LL TRY TO BE QUIET.
I HAVEN'T SEEN YOU IN YEARS, COLIN. WHAT ARE YOU DOING UP ON THIS ROOF?
URRF.
HE SAYS HE'S HUNGRY.
YOU WOULDN'T HAPPEN TO HAVE ANY OF THOSE SLITHERGRUB PIES ON YOU, WOULD YOU? I'M AFRAID I ATE MINE.
YEAH, I'VE GOT ONE RIGHT HERE...IT'S NOT A VERY BIG PORTION...
HANG TIGHT, COLIN. GINA'S GOT A TREMENDOUS PLAN. YOU'RE GONNA LOVE IT--
MISTER FOWLER! WE HAVE TO BE QUIET.
RIGHT. SORRY.
HERE YOU GO. JUST LIKE THE ONES WE USED TO MAKE BACK IN CULINARY SCHOOL--
GINA! OVER HERE! I THINK I'VE FOUND THE RELEASE MECHANISM.
IT LOOKS A BIT COMPLICATED.

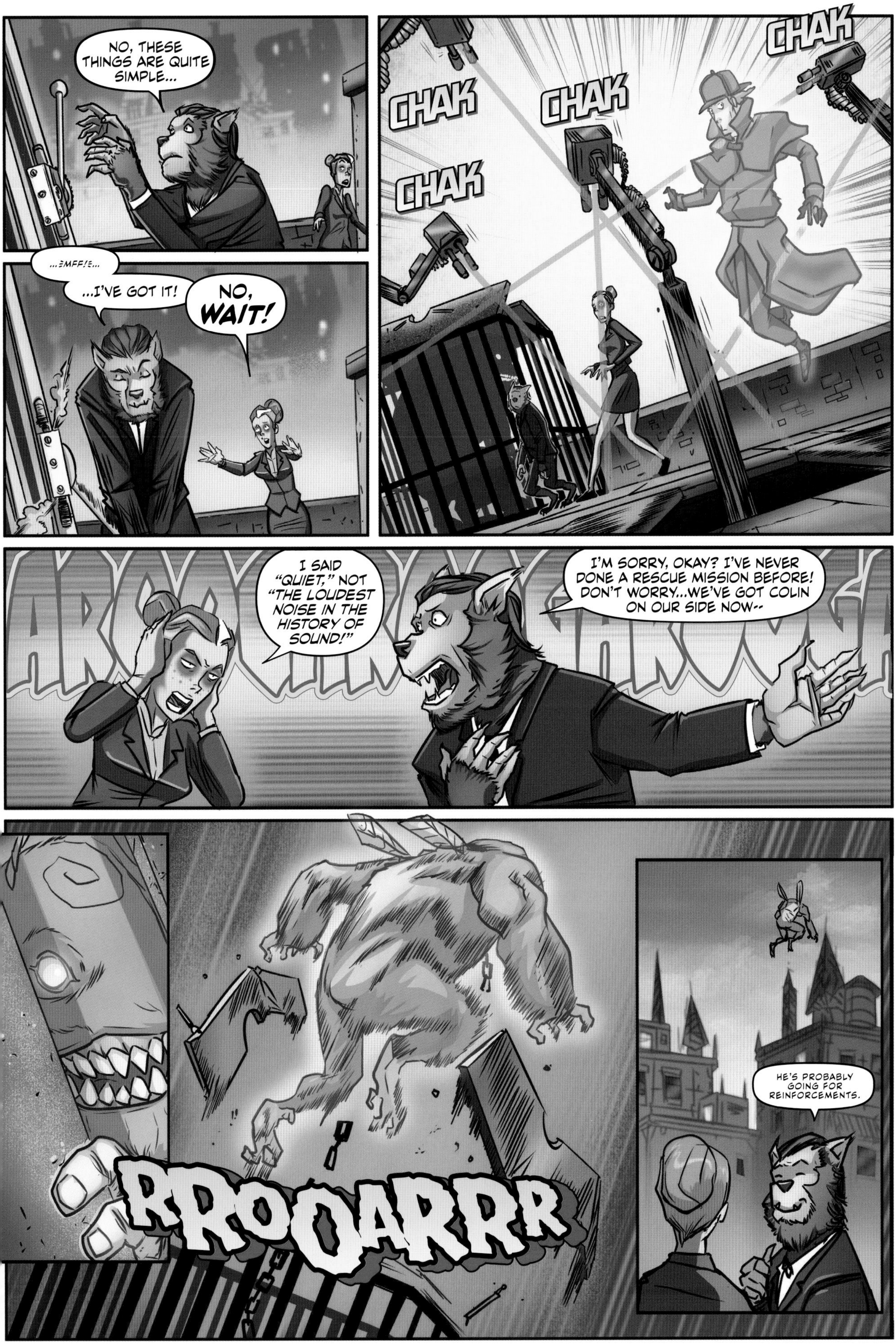

NO, THESE THINGS ARE QUITE SIMPLE...
...SMFF!S...
...I'VE GOT IT!
NO, WAIT!
CHAK
CHAK
CHAK
CHAK
I SAID "QUIET," NOT "THE LOUDEST NOISE IN THE HISTORY OF SOUND!"
I'M SORRY, OKAY? I'VE NEVER DONE A RESCUE MISSION BEFORE! DON'T WORRY...WE'VE GOT COLIN ON OUR SIDE NOW--
RROOARRR
HE'S PROBABLY GOING FOR REINFORCEMENTS.

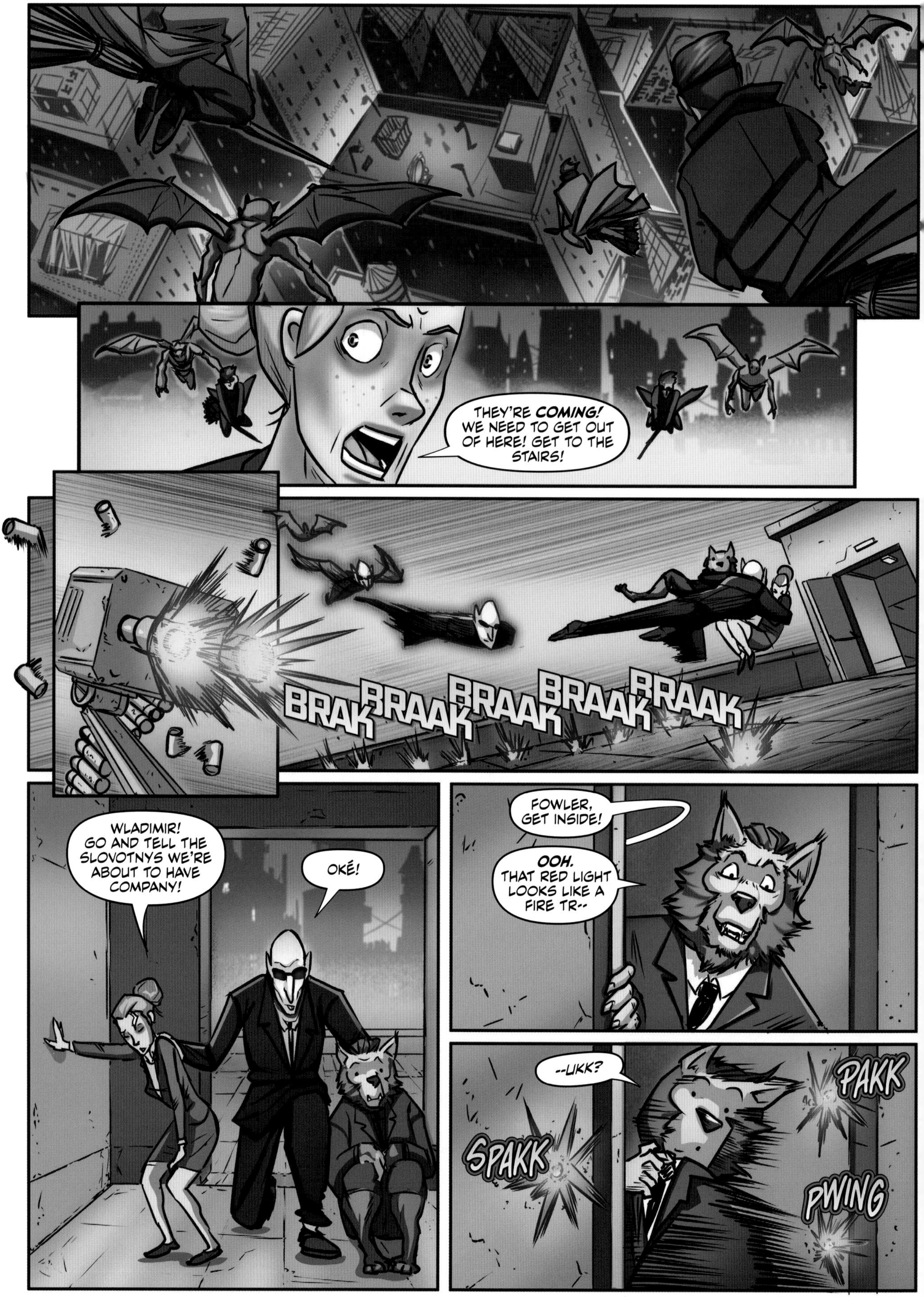
THEY'RE COMING! WE NEED TO GET OUT OF HERE! GET TO THE STAIRS!
BRAK BRAAK BRAAK BRAAK BRAAK
WLADIMIR! GO AND TELL THE SLOVOTNYS WE'RE ABOUT TO HAVE COMPANY!
OKÉ!
FOWLER, GET INSIDE!
OOH. THAT RED LIGHT LOOKS LIKE A FIRE TR--
--UKK?
PAKK
SPAKK
PWING

OMIGOD...OMIGOD...OMIGOD...

...OKAY, GINA...JUST *THINK*...

THER FLÜDEN IN DER STROOTEN! WAS ISS?

THEY WANT TO KNOW WHAT JUST *HAPPENED.*

I DON'T *KNOW!*

OKAY, LOOK... WLAD, YOU GET BACK TO MONSTRAVIA AND MAKE SURE THE DOORS TO THE BAKERY ARE UNLOCKED.

JASPER CAN PASS THROUGH WALLS SO HE CAN SCOUT AHEAD. WE'LL FOLLOW ON WHEN THE COAST IS CLEAR.

CHARMED, I'M SURE.

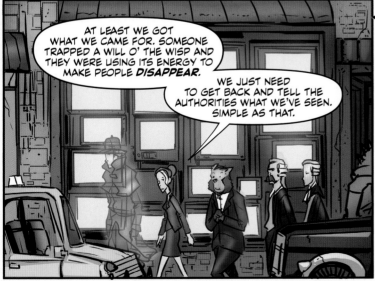

AT LEAST WE GOT WHAT WE CAME FOR. SOMEONE TRAPPED A WILL O' THE WISP AND THEY WERE USING ITS ENERGY TO MAKE PEOPLE *DISAPPEAR.*

WE JUST NEED TO GET BACK AND TELL THE AUTHORITIES WHAT WE'VE SEEN. SIMPLE AS THAT.

SYIMPLE?

IT'S A FIGURE OF *SPEECH.*

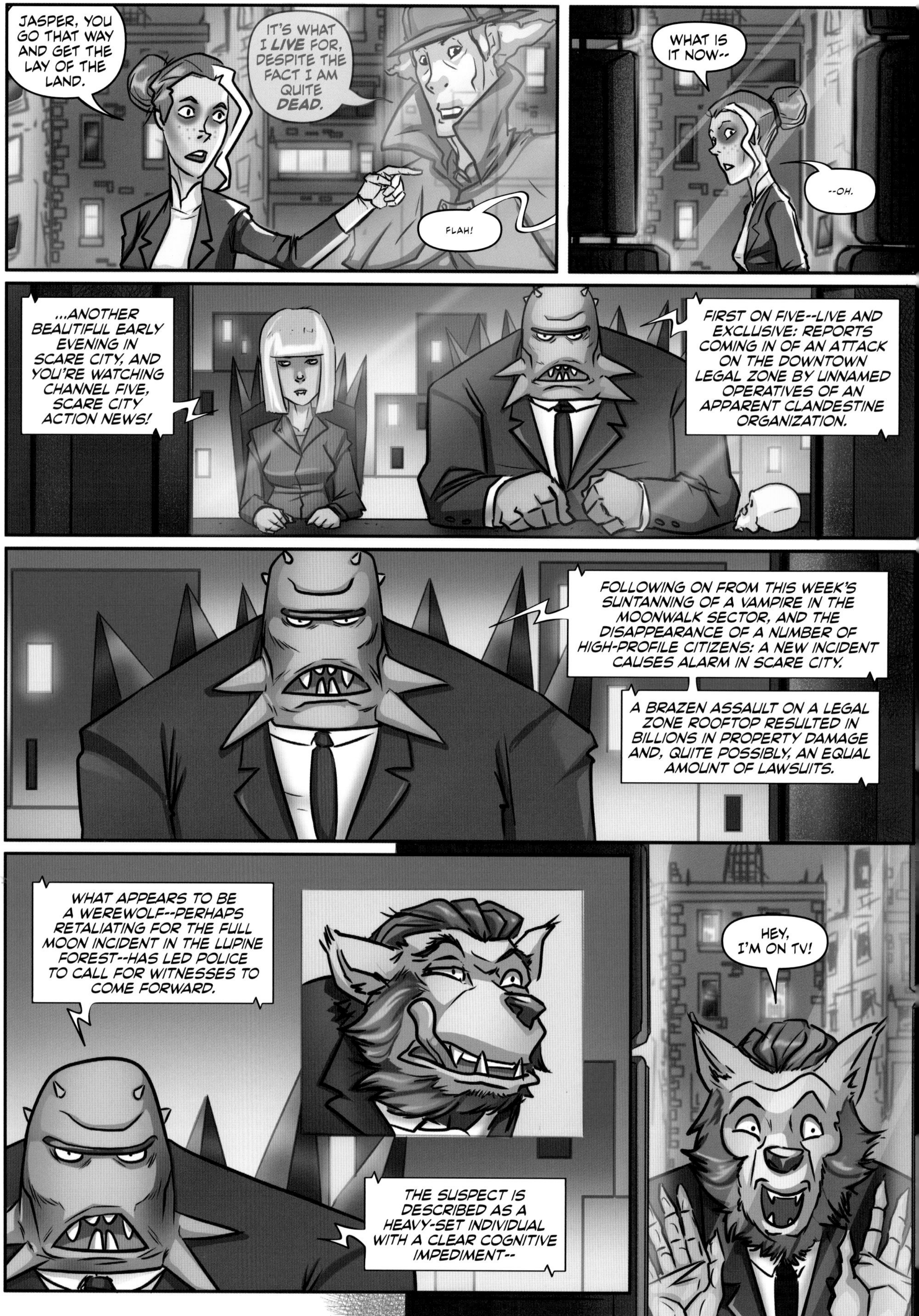
JASPER, YOU GO THAT WAY AND GET THE LAY OF THE LAND.
IT'S WHAT I LIVE FOR, DESPITE THE FACT I AM QUITE DEAD.
FLAH!
WHAT IS IT NOW--
--OH.
...ANOTHER BEAUTIFUL EARLY EVENING IN SCARE CITY, AND YOU'RE WATCHING CHANNEL FIVE, SCARE CITY ACTION NEWS!
FIRST ON FIVE--LIVE AND EXCLUSIVE: REPORTS COMING IN OF AN ATTACK ON THE DOWNTOWN LEGAL ZONE BY UNNAMED OPERATIVES OF AN APPARENT CLANDESTINE ORGANIZATION.
FOLLOWING ON FROM THIS WEEK'S SUNTANNING OF A VAMPIRE IN THE MOONWALK SECTOR, AND THE DISAPPEARANCE OF A NUMBER OF HIGH-PROFILE CITIZENS: A NEW INCIDENT CAUSES ALARM IN SCARE CITY.
A BRAZEN ASSAULT ON A LEGAL ZONE ROOFTOP RESULTED IN BILLIONS IN PROPERTY DAMAGE AND, QUITE POSSIBLY, AN EQUAL AMOUNT OF LAWSUITS.
WHAT APPEARS TO BE A WEREWOLF--PERHAPS RETALIATING FOR THE FULL MOON INCIDENT IN THE LUPINE FOREST--HAS LED POLICE TO CALL FOR WITNESSES TO COME FORWARD.
HEY, I'M ON TV!
THE SUSPECT IS DESCRIBED AS A HEAVY-SET INDIVIDUAL WITH A CLEAR COGNITIVE IMPEDIMENT--

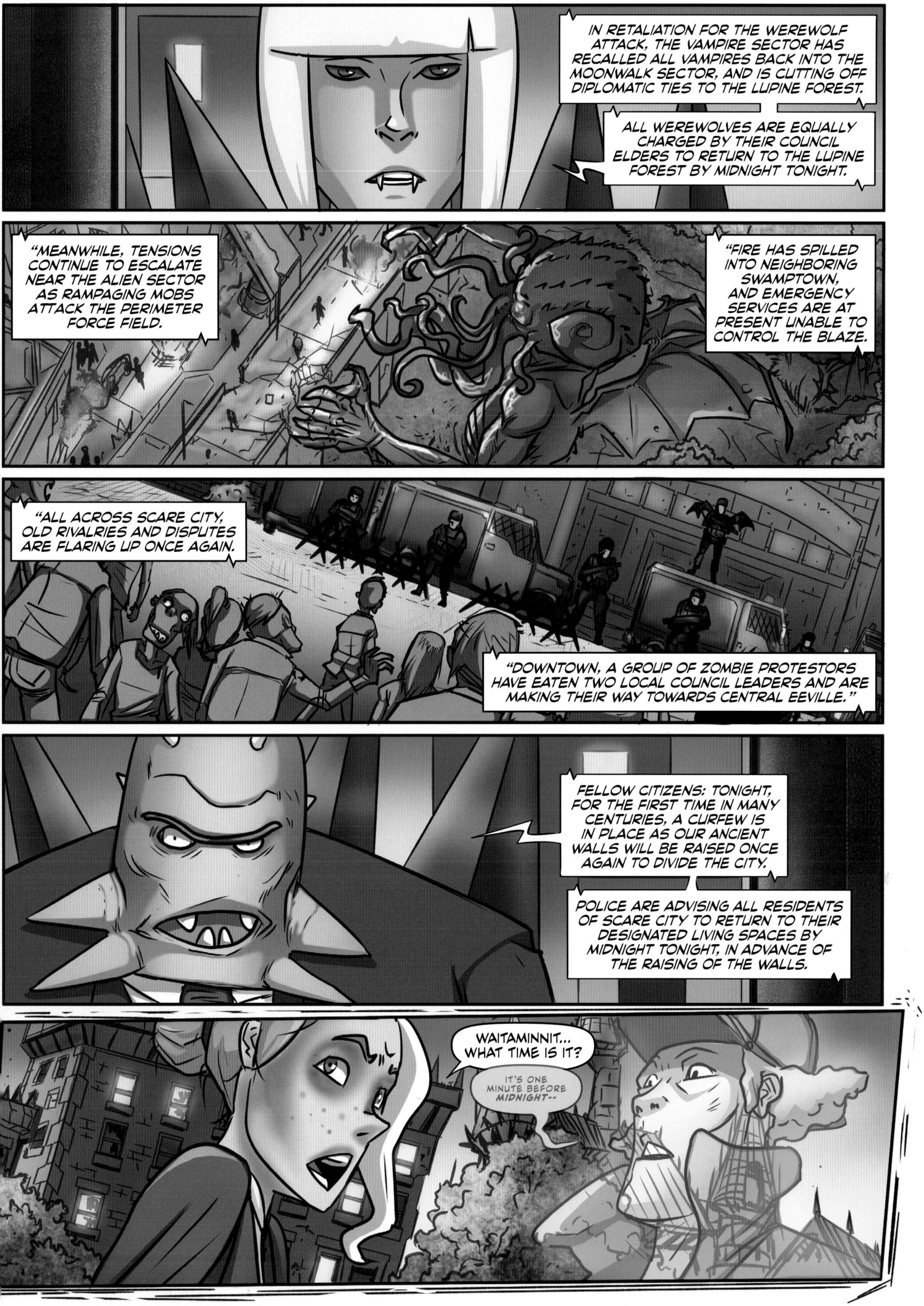
IN RETALIATION FOR THE WEREWOLF ATTACK, THE VAMPIRE SECTOR HAS RECALLED ALL VAMPIRES BACK INTO THE MOONWALK SECTOR, AND IS CUTTING OFF DIPLOMATIC TIES TO THE LUPINE FOREST.
ALL WEREWOLVES ARE EQUALLY CHARGED BY THEIR COUNCIL ELDERS TO RETURN TO THE LUPINE FOREST BY MIDNIGHT TONIGHT.
"MEANWHILE, TENSIONS CONTINUE TO ESCALATE NEAR THE ALIEN SECTOR AS RAMPAGING MOBS ATTACK THE PERIMETER FORCE FIELD.
"FIRE HAS SPILLED INTO NEIGHBORING SWAMPTOWN, AND EMERGENCY SERVICES ARE AT PRESENT UNABLE TO CONTROL THE BLAZE.
"ALL ACROSS SCARE CITY, OLD RIVALRIES AND DISPUTES ARE FLARING UP ONCE AGAIN.
"DOWNTOWN, A GROUP OF ZOMBIE PROTESTORS HAVE EATEN TWO LOCAL COUNCIL LEADERS AND ARE MAKING THEIR WAY TOWARDS CENTRAL EEVILLE."
FELLOW CITIZENS: TONIGHT, FOR THE FIRST TIME IN MANY CENTURIES, A CURFEW IS IN PLACE AS OUR ANCIENT WALLS WILL BE RAISED ONCE AGAIN TO DIVIDE THE CITY.
POLICE ARE ADVISING ALL RESIDENTS OF SCARE CITY TO RETURN TO THEIR DESIGNATED LIVING SPACES BY MIDNIGHT TONIGHT, IN ADVANCE OF THE RAISING OF THE WALLS.
WAITAMINNIT... WHAT TIME IS IT?
IT'S ONE MINUTE BEFORE MIDNIGHT--

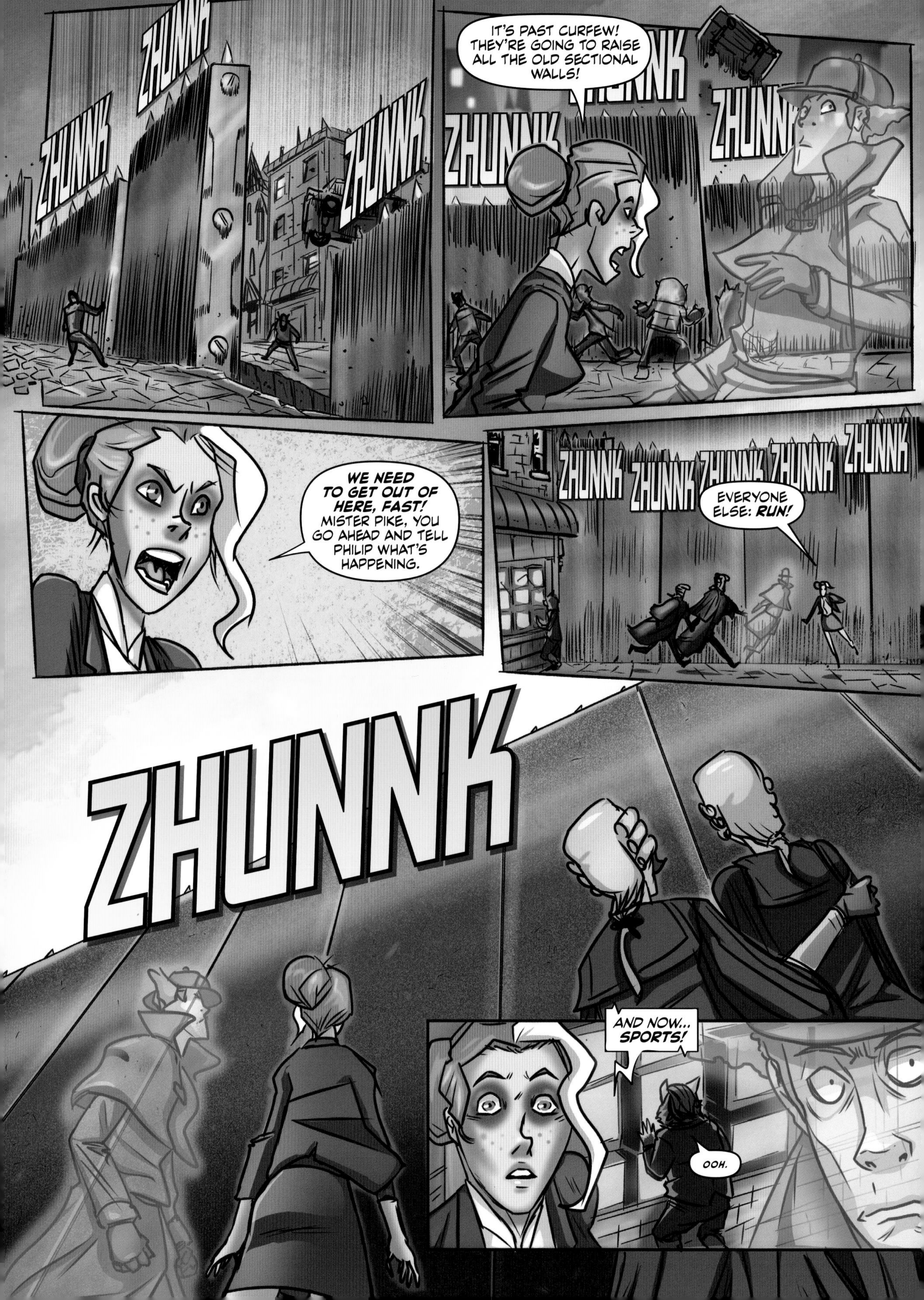
ZHUNNK
ZHUNNK
ZHUNNK
IT'S PAST CURFEW! THEY'RE GOING TO RAISE ALL THE OLD SECTIONAL WALLS!
ZHUNNK
ZHUNNK
ZHUNNK
WE NEED TO GET OUT OF HERE, FAST! MISTER PIKE, YOU GO AHEAD AND TELL PHILIP WHAT'S HAPPENING.
ZHUNNK ZHUNNK ZHUNNK ZHUNNK ZHUNNK
EVERYONE ELSE: RUN!
ZHUNNK
AND NOW... SPORTS!
OOH.

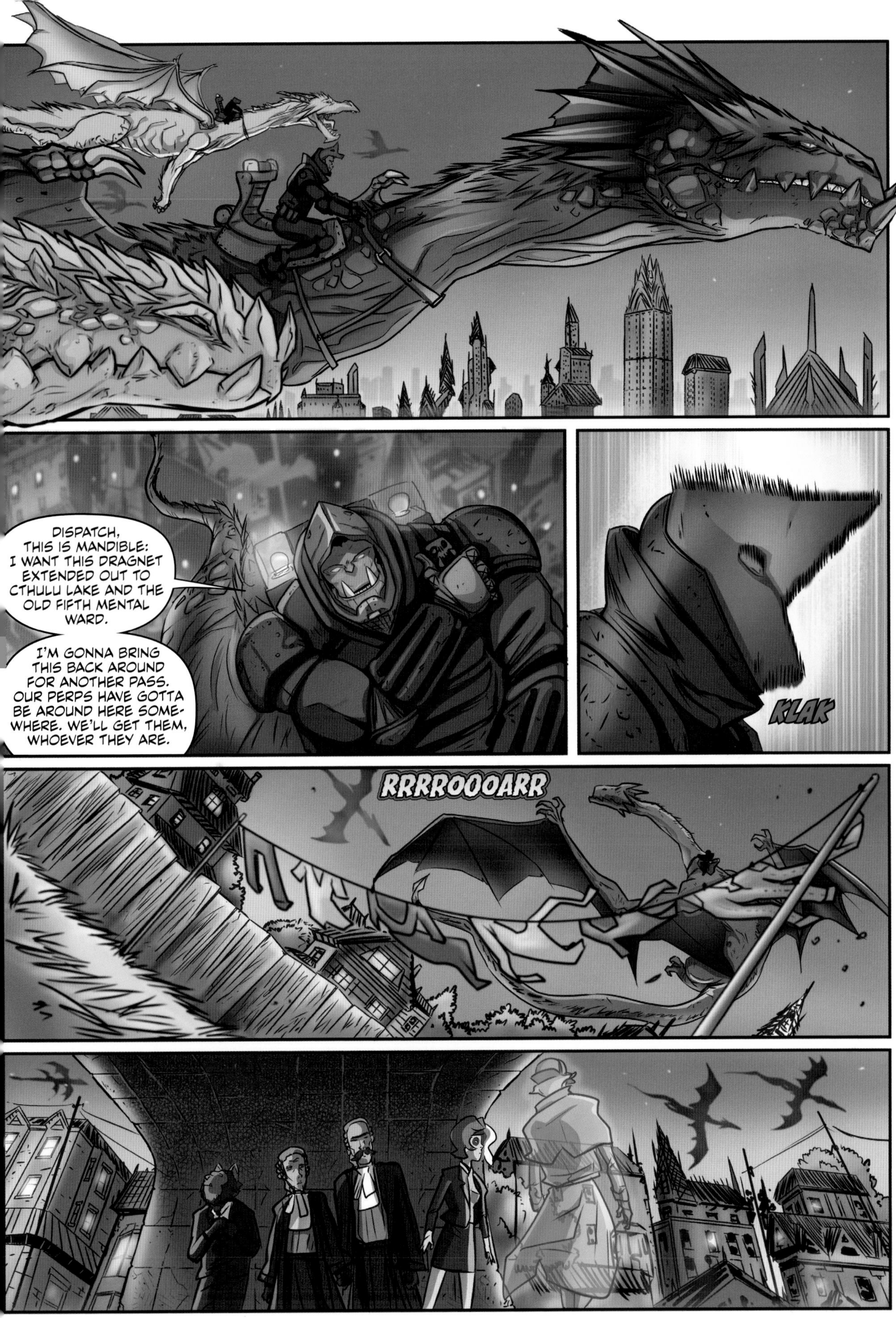
DISPATCH, THIS IS MANDIBLE: I WANT THIS DRAGNET EXTENDED OUT TO CTHULU LAKE AND THE OLD FIFTH MENTAL WARD.
I'M GONNA BRING THIS BACK AROUND FOR ANOTHER PASS. OUR PERPS HAVE GOTTA BE AROUND HERE SOME-WHERE. WE'LL GET THEM, WHOEVER THEY ARE.
KLAK
RRRROOOARR

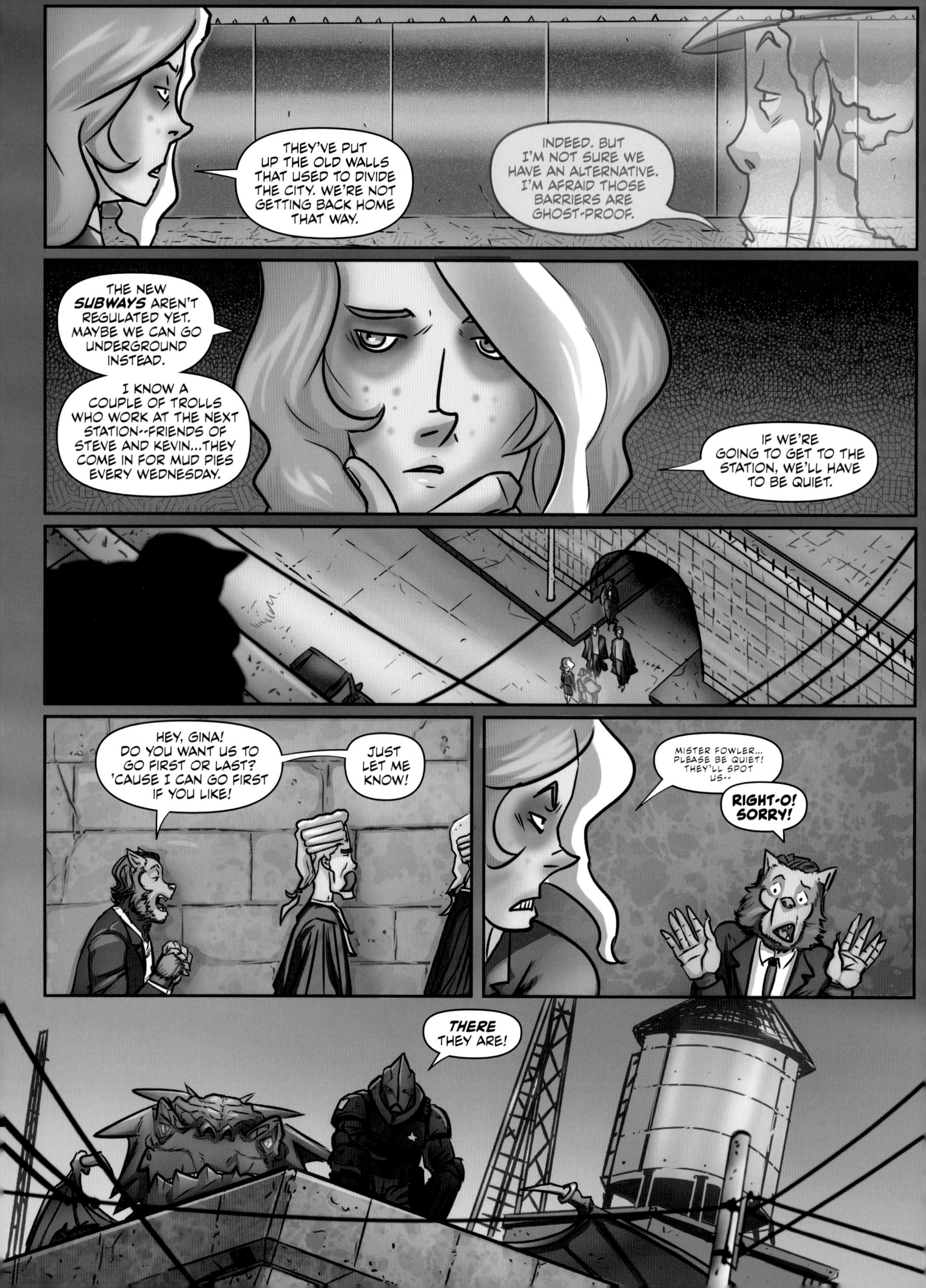
THEY'VE PUT UP THE OLD WALLS THAT USED TO DIVIDE THE CITY. WE'RE NOT GETTING BACK HOME THAT WAY.
INDEED. BUT I'M NOT SURE WE HAVE AN ALTERNATIVE. I'M AFRAID THOSE BARRIERS ARE GHOST-PROOF.
THE NEW *SUBWAYS* AREN'T REGULATED YET. MAYBE WE CAN GO UNDERGROUND INSTEAD.
I KNOW A COUPLE OF TROLLS WHO WORK AT THE NEXT STATION--FRIENDS OF STEVE AND KEVIN...THEY COME IN FOR MUD PIES EVERY WEDNESDAY.
IF WE'RE GOING TO GET TO THE STATION, WE'LL HAVE TO BE QUIET.
HEY, GINA! DO YOU WANT US TO GO FIRST OR LAST? 'CAUSE I CAN GO FIRST IF YOU LIKE!
JUST LET ME KNOW!
MISTER FOWLER... PLEASE BE QUIET! THEY'LL SPOT US--
RIGHT-O! SORRY!
THERE THEY ARE!

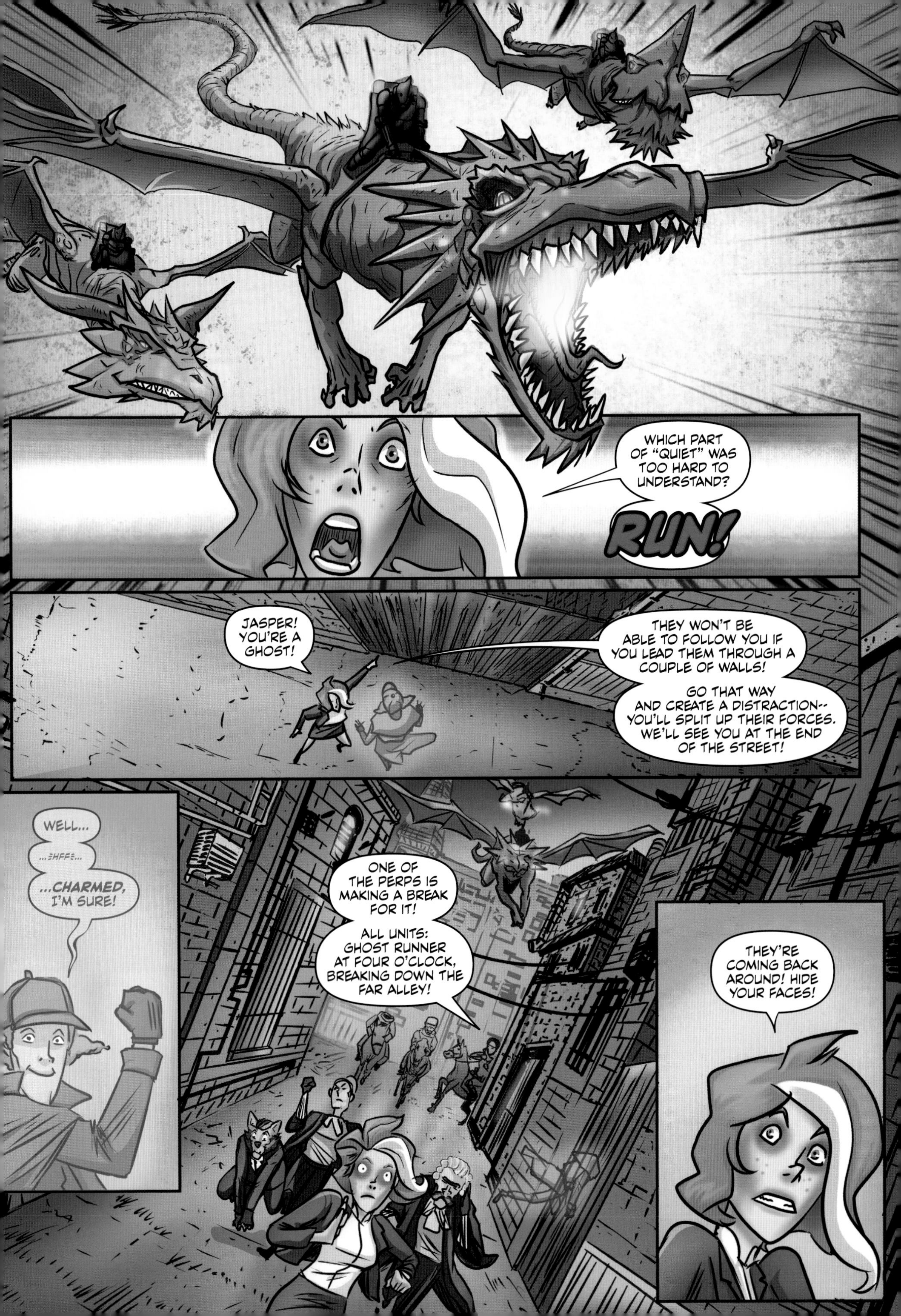
WHICH PART OF "QUIET" WAS TOO HARD TO UNDERSTAND?
RUN!
JASPER! YOU'RE A GHOST!
THEY WON'T BE ABLE TO FOLLOW YOU IF YOU LEAD THEM THROUGH A COUPLE OF WALLS!
GO THAT WAY AND CREATE A DISTRACTION-- YOU'LL SPLIT UP THEIR FORCES. WE'LL SEE YOU AT THE END OF THE STREET!
WELL...
...HFF...
...CHARMED, I'M SURE!
ONE OF THE PERPS IS MAKING A BREAK FOR IT!
ALL UNITS: GHOST RUNNER AT FOUR O'CLOCK, BREAKING DOWN THE FAR ALLEY!
THEY'RE COMING BACK AROUND! HIDE YOUR FACES!

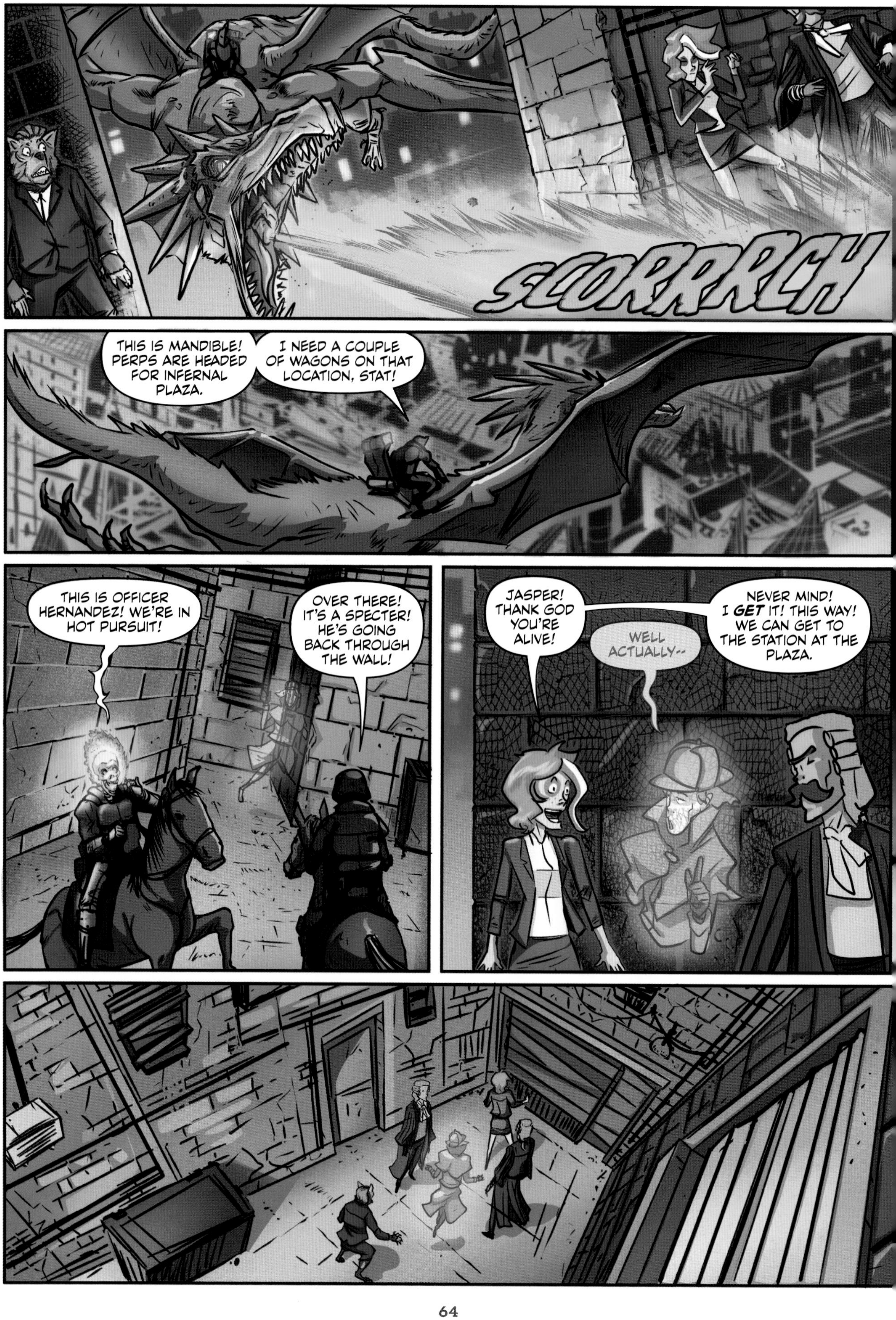
SCORRRCH
THIS IS MANDIBLE! PERPS ARE HEADED FOR INFERNAL PLAZA.
I NEED A COUPLE OF WAGONS ON THAT LOCATION, STAT!
THIS IS OFFICER HERNANDEZ! WE'RE IN HOT PURSUIT!
OVER THERE! IT'S A SPECTER! HE'S GOING BACK THROUGH THE WALL!
JASPER! THANK GOD YOU'RE ALIVE!
WELL ACTUALLY--
NEVER MIND! I **GET** IT! THIS WAY! WE CAN GET TO THE STATION AT THE PLAZA.

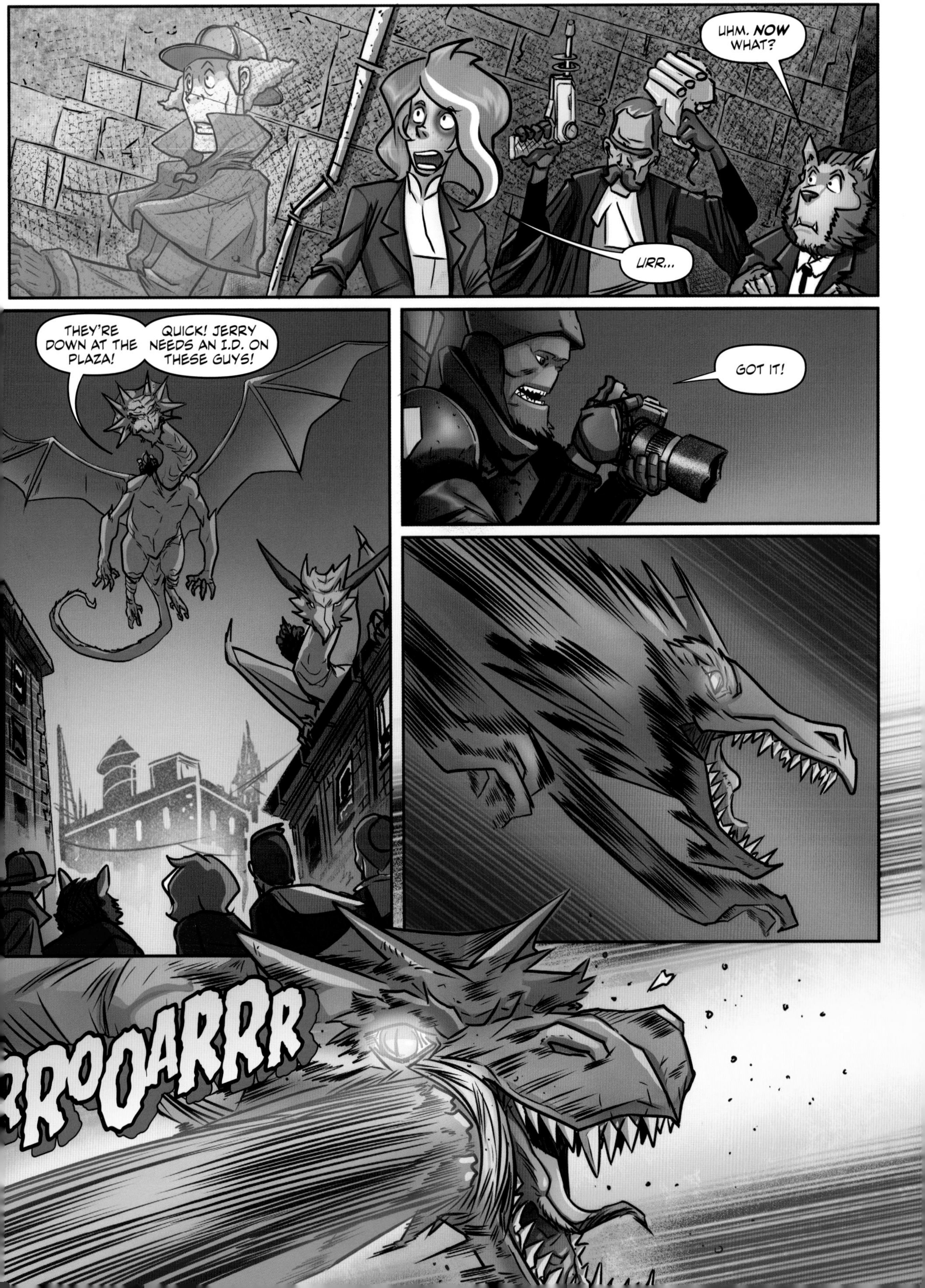
UHM. NOW WHAT?
URR...
THEY'RE DOWN AT THE PLAZA!
QUICK! JERRY NEEDS AN I.D. ON THESE GUYS!
GOT IT!
RROOARRR

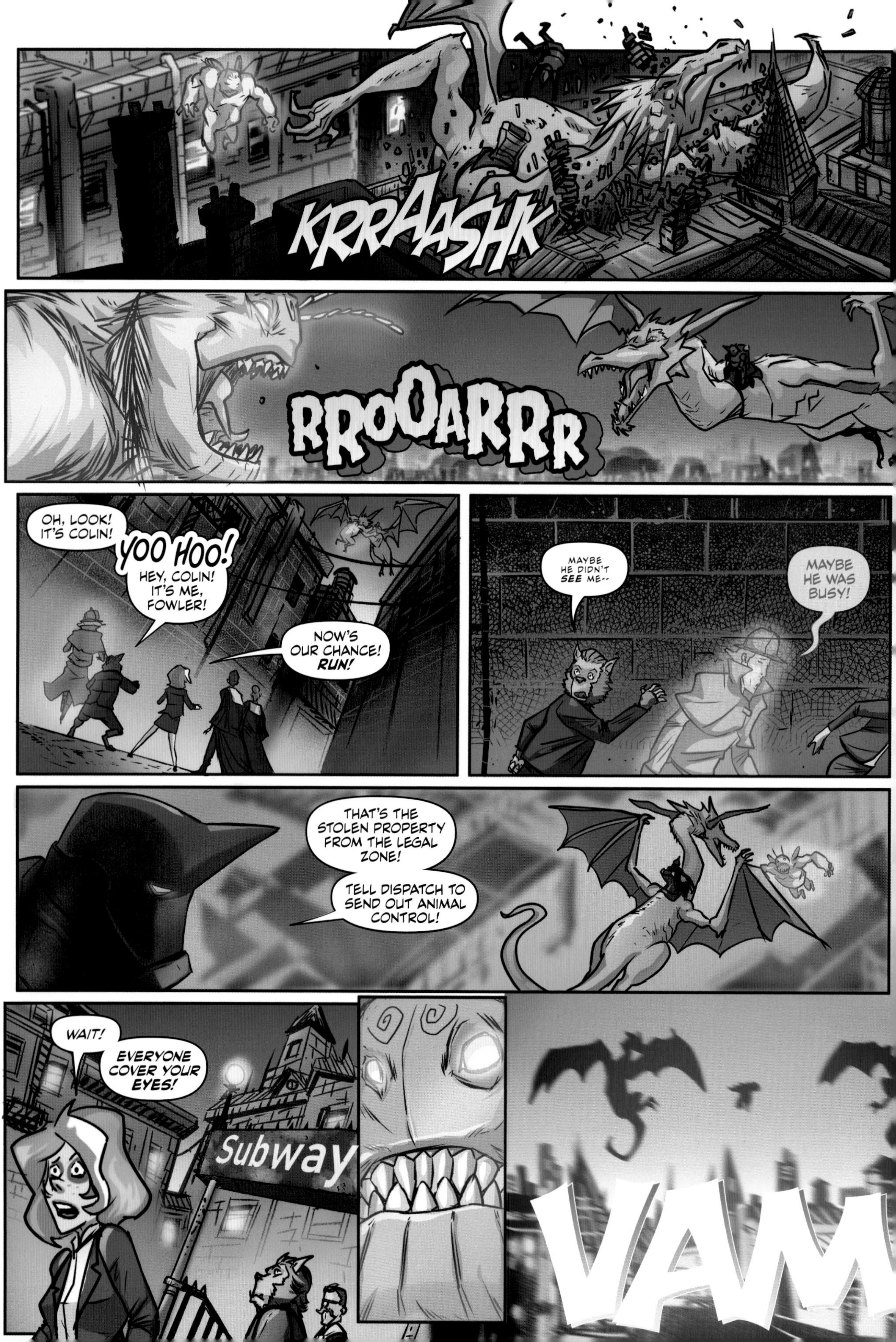

KRRAASHK
RROOARRRR
OH, LOOK! IT'S COLIN!
YOO HOO!
HEY, COLIN! IT'S ME, FOWLER!
NOW'S OUR CHANCE! RUN!
MAYBE HE DIDN'T SEE ME--
MAYBE HE WAS BUSY!
THAT'S THE STOLEN PROPERTY FROM THE LEGAL ZONE!
TELL DISPATCH TO SEND OUT ANIMAL CONTROL!
WAIT!
EVERYONE COVER YOUR EYES!
Subway
VAM

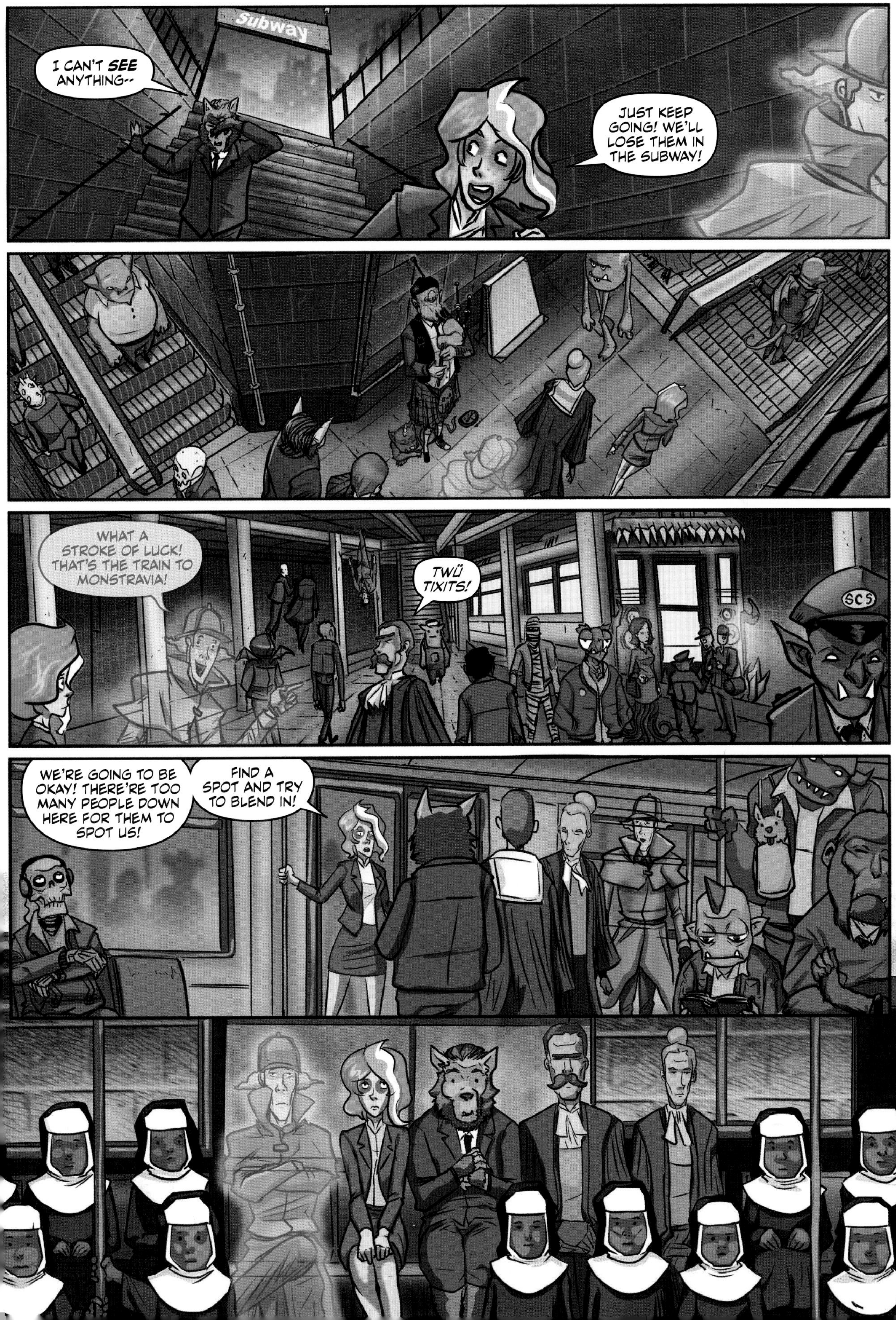
Subway
I CAN'T SEE ANYTHING--
JUST KEEP GOING! WE'LL LOSE THEM IN THE SUBWAY!
WHAT A STROKE OF LUCK! THAT'S THE TRAIN TO MONSTRAVIA!
TWÜ TIXITS!
SCS
WE'RE GOING TO BE OKAY! THERE'RE TOO MANY PEOPLE DOWN HERE FOR THEM TO SPOT US!
FIND A SPOT AND TRY TO BLEND IN!

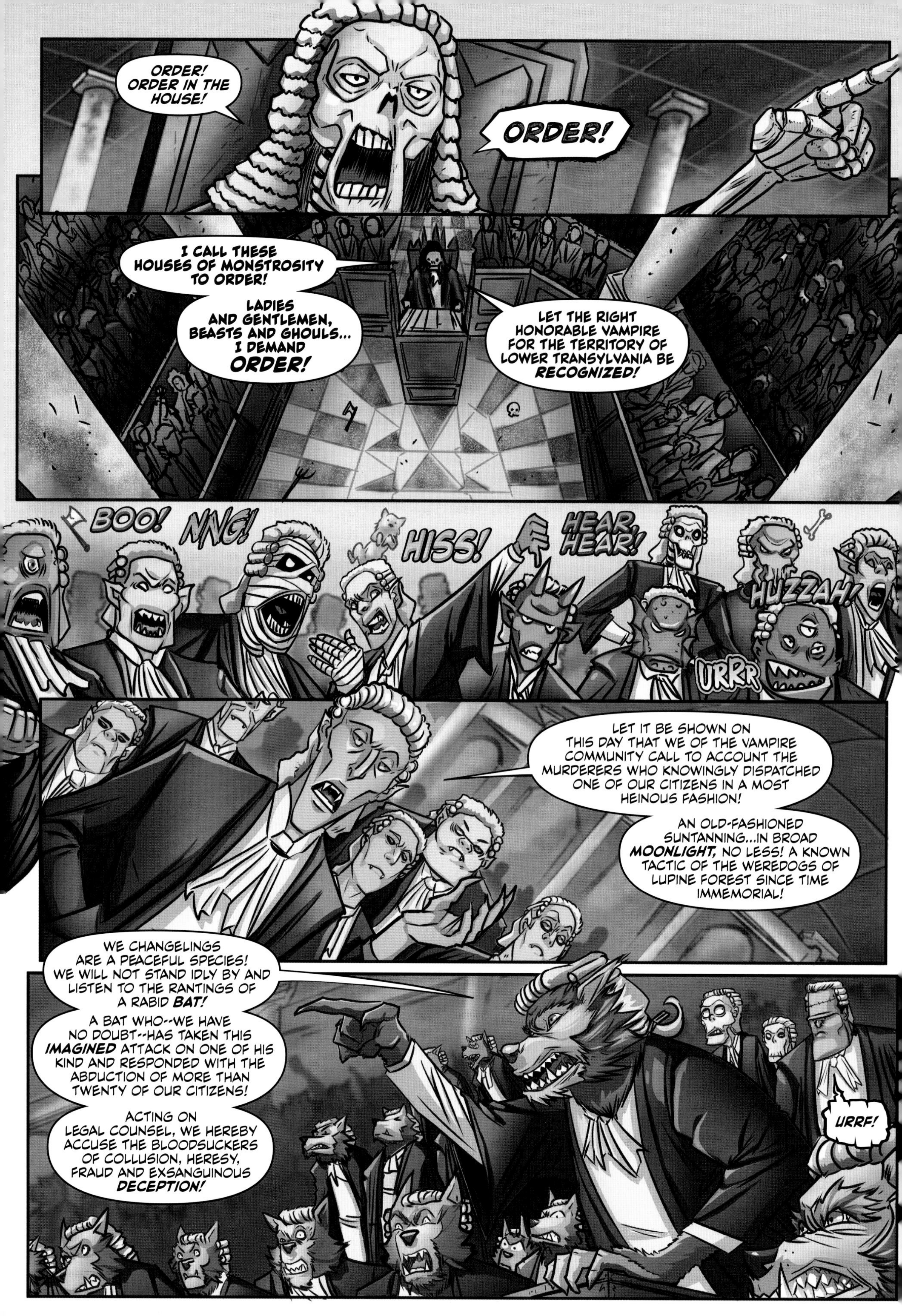
ORDER! ORDER IN THE HOUSE!
ORDER!
I CALL THESE HOUSES OF MONSTROSITY TO ORDER!
LADIES AND GENTLEMEN, BEASTS AND GHOULS... I DEMAND ORDER!
LET THE RIGHT HONORABLE VAMPIRE FOR THE TERRITORY OF LOWER TRANSYLVANIA BE RECOGNIZED!
BOO!
NNG!
HISS!
HEAR, HEAR!
HUZZAH!
URRR
LET IT BE SHOWN ON THIS DAY THAT WE OF THE VAMPIRE COMMUNITY CALL TO ACCOUNT THE MURDERERS WHO KNOWINGLY DISPATCHED ONE OF OUR CITIZENS IN A MOST HEINOUS FASHION!
AN OLD-FASHIONED SUNTANNING...IN BROAD MOONLIGHT, NO LESS! A KNOWN TACTIC OF THE WEREDOGS OF LUPINE FOREST SINCE TIME IMMEMORIAL!
WE CHANGELINGS ARE A PEACEFUL SPECIES! WE WILL NOT STAND IDLY BY AND LISTEN TO THE RANTINGS OF A RABID BAT!
A BAT WHO--WE HAVE NO DOUBT--HAS TAKEN THIS IMAGINED ATTACK ON ONE OF HIS KIND AND RESPONDED WITH THE ABDUCTION OF MORE THAN TWENTY OF OUR CITIZENS!
ACTING ON LEGAL COUNSEL, WE HEREBY ACCUSE THE BLOODSUCKERS OF COLLUSION, HERESY, FRAUD AND EXSANGUINOUS DECEPTION!
URRF!

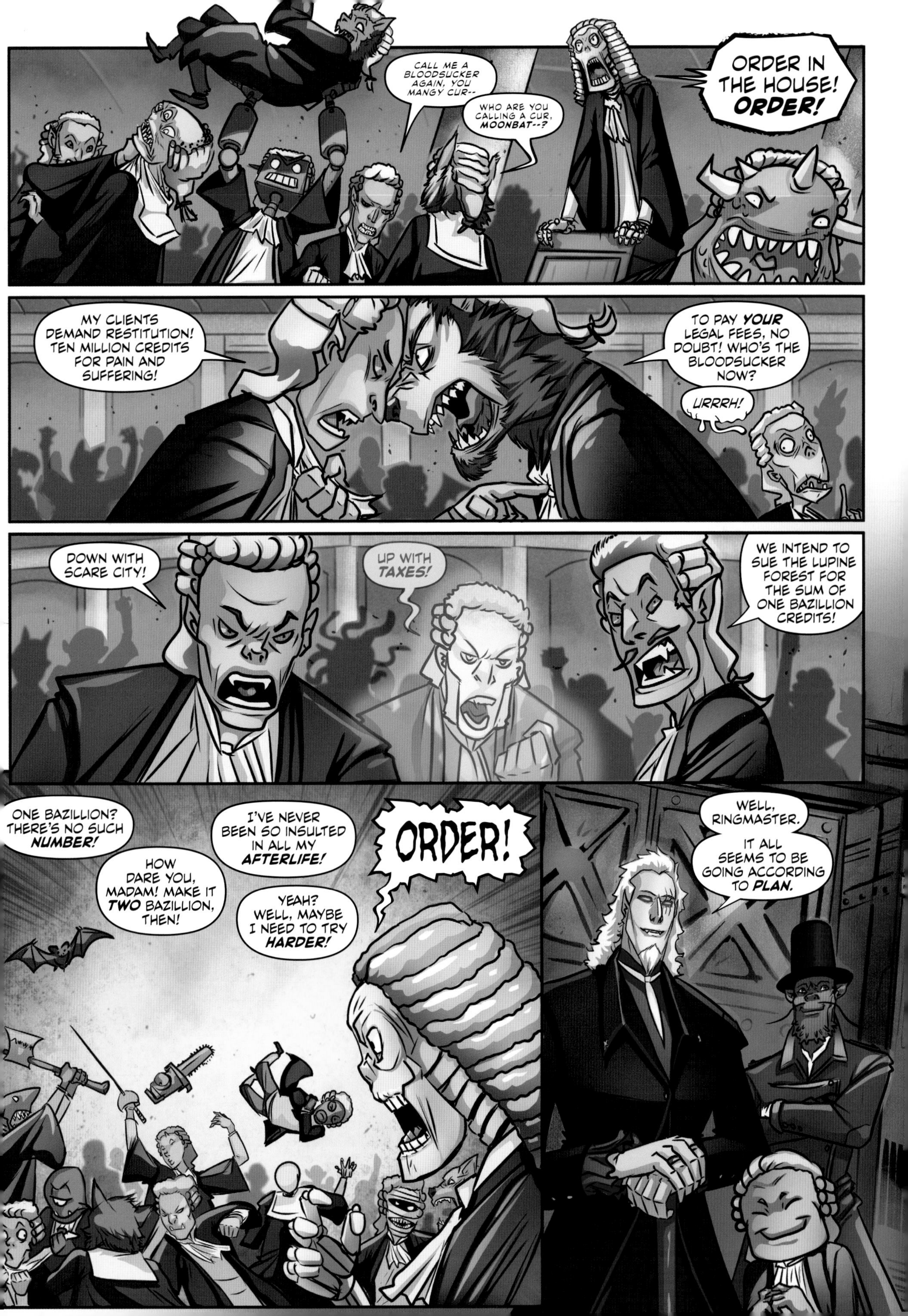
CALL ME A BLOODSUCKER AGAIN, YOU MANGY CUR--
WHO ARE YOU CALLING A CUR, MOONBAT--?
ORDER IN THE HOUSE! ORDER!
MY CLIENTS DEMAND RESTITUTION! TEN MILLION CREDITS FOR PAIN AND SUFFERING!
TO PAY YOUR LEGAL FEES, NO DOUBT! WHO'S THE BLOODSUCKER NOW?
URRRH!
DOWN WITH SCARE CITY!
UP WITH TAXES!
WE INTEND TO SUE THE LUPINE FOREST FOR THE SUM OF ONE BAZILLION CREDITS!
ONE BAZILLION? THERE'S NO SUCH NUMBER!
HOW DARE YOU, MADAM! MAKE IT TWO BAZILLION, THEN!
I'VE NEVER BEEN SO INSULTED IN ALL MY AFTERLIFE!
YEAH? WELL, MAYBE I NEED TO TRY HARDER!
ORDER!
WELL, RINGMASTER.
IT ALL SEEMS TO BE GOING ACCORDING TO PLAN.

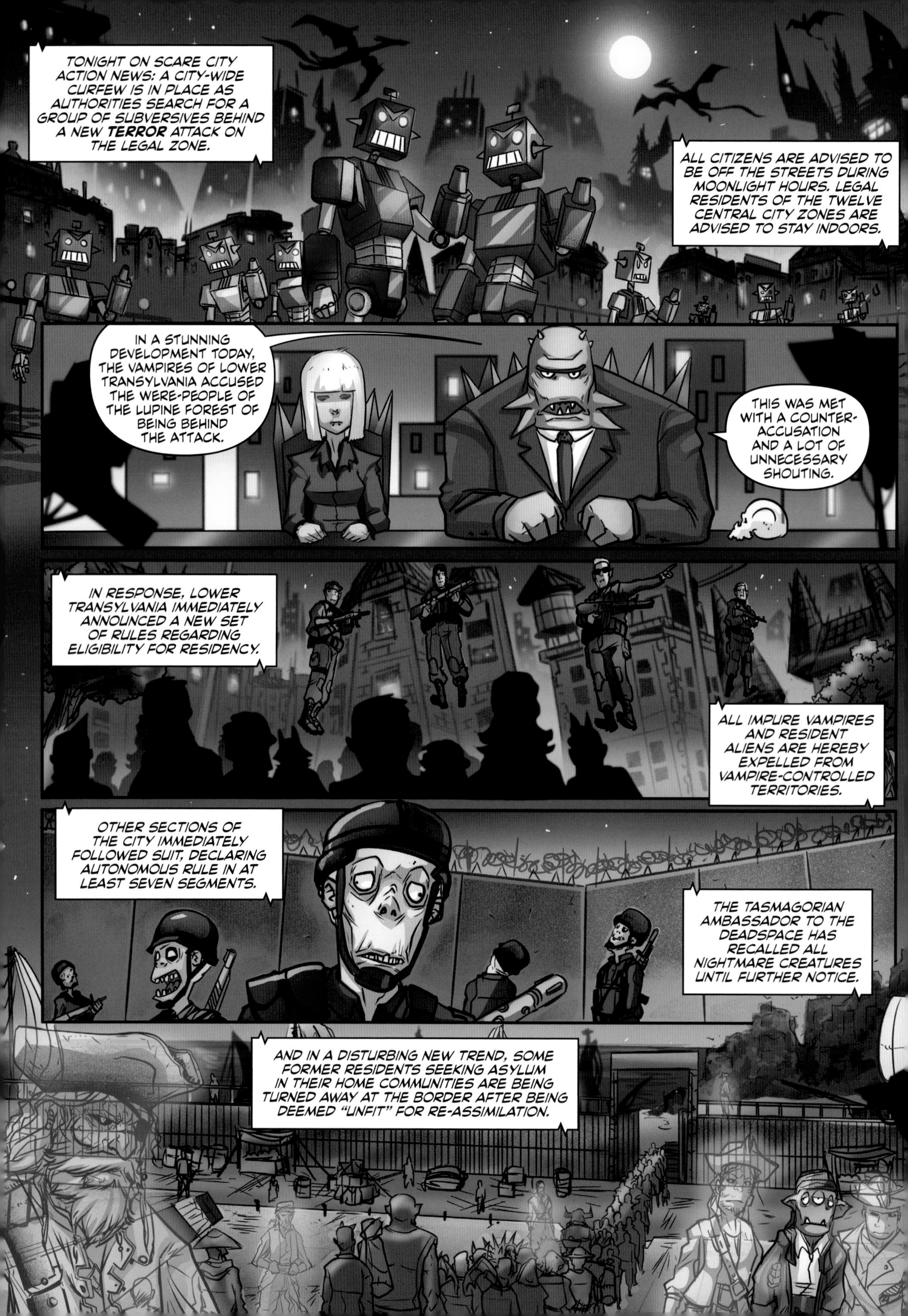
TONIGHT ON SCARE CITY ACTION NEWS: A CITY-WIDE CURFEW IS IN PLACE AS AUTHORITIES SEARCH FOR A GROUP OF SUBVERSIVES BEHIND A NEW TERROR ATTACK ON THE LEGAL ZONE.
ALL CITIZENS ARE ADVISED TO BE OFF THE STREETS DURING MOONLIGHT HOURS. LEGAL RESIDENTS OF THE TWELVE CENTRAL CITY ZONES ARE ADVISED TO STAY INDOORS.
IN A STUNNING DEVELOPMENT TODAY, THE VAMPIRES OF LOWER TRANSYLVANIA ACCUSED THE WERE-PEOPLE OF THE LUPINE FOREST OF BEING BEHIND THE ATTACK.
THIS WAS MET WITH A COUNTER-ACCUSATION AND A LOT OF UNNECESSARY SHOUTING.
IN RESPONSE, LOWER TRANSYLVANIA IMMEDIATELY ANNOUNCED A NEW SET OF RULES REGARDING ELIGIBILITY FOR RESIDENCY.
ALL IMPURE VAMPIRES AND RESIDENT ALIENS ARE HEREBY EXPELLED FROM VAMPIRE-CONTROLLED TERRITORIES.
OTHER SECTIONS OF THE CITY IMMEDIATELY FOLLOWED SUIT, DECLARING AUTONOMOUS RULE IN AT LEAST SEVEN SEGMENTS.
THE TASMAGORIAN AMBASSADOR TO THE DEADSPACE HAS RECALLED ALL NIGHTMARE CREATURES UNTIL FURTHER NOTICE.
AND IN A DISTURBING NEW TREND, SOME FORMER RESIDENTS SEEKING ASYLUM IN THEIR HOME COMMUNITIES ARE BEING TURNED AWAY AT THE BORDER AFTER BEING DEEMED "UNFIT" FOR RE-ASSIMILATION.

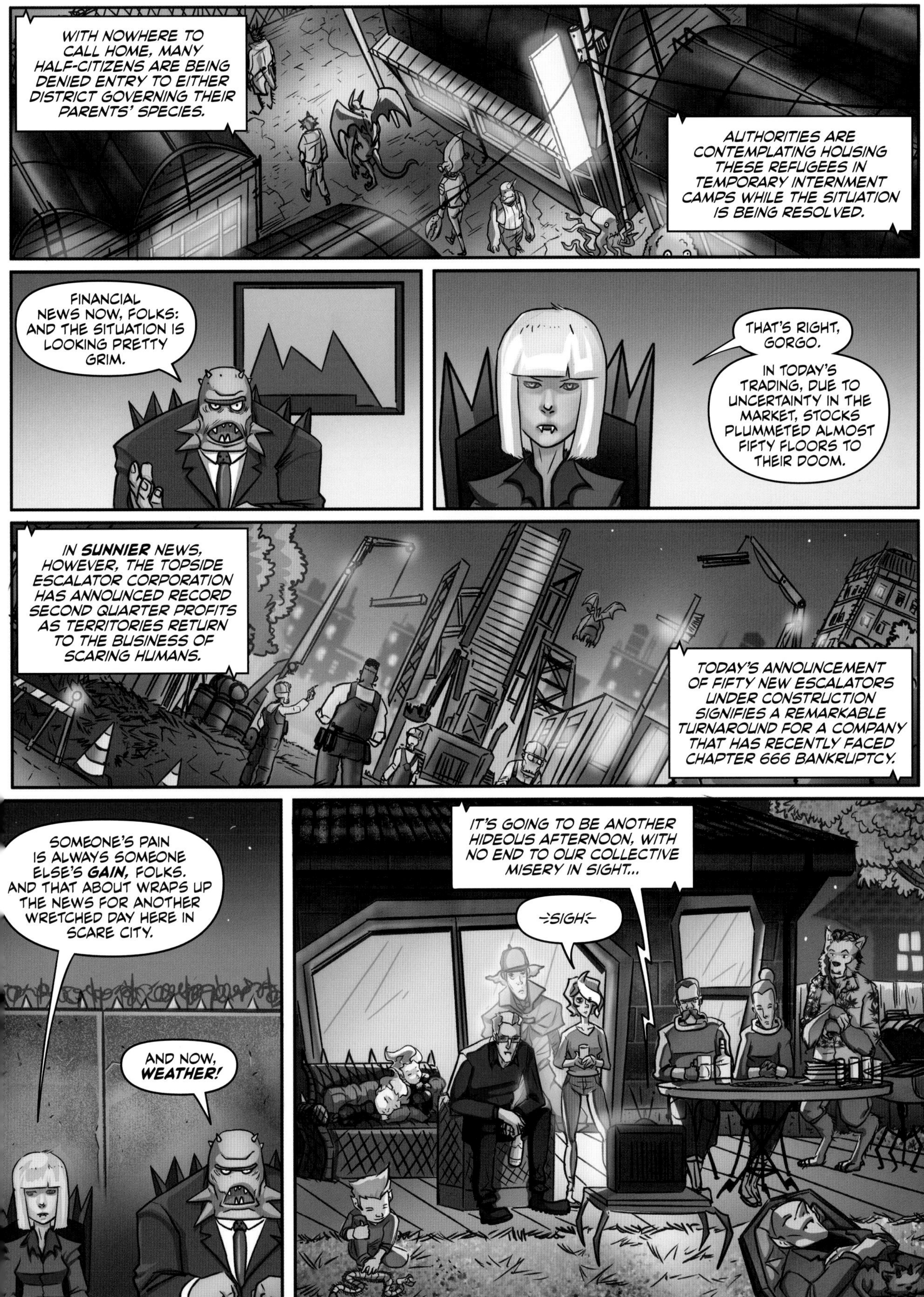

WITH NOWHERE TO CALL HOME, MANY HALF-CITIZENS ARE BEING DENIED ENTRY TO EITHER DISTRICT GOVERNING THEIR PARENTS' SPECIES.
AUTHORITIES ARE CONTEMPLATING HOUSING THESE REFUGEES IN TEMPORARY INTERNMENT CAMPS WHILE THE SITUATION IS BEING RESOLVED.
FINANCIAL NEWS NOW, FOLKS: AND THE SITUATION IS LOOKING PRETTY GRIM.
THAT'S RIGHT, GORGO.
IN TODAY'S TRADING, DUE TO UNCERTAINTY IN THE MARKET, STOCKS PLUMMETED ALMOST FIFTY FLOORS TO THEIR DOOM.
IN **SUNNIER** NEWS, HOWEVER, THE TOPSIDE ESCALATOR CORPORATION HAS ANNOUNCED RECORD SECOND QUARTER PROFITS AS TERRITORIES RETURN TO THE BUSINESS OF SCARING HUMANS.
TODAY'S ANNOUNCEMENT OF FIFTY NEW ESCALATORS UNDER CONSTRUCTION SIGNIFIES A REMARKABLE TURNAROUND FOR A COMPANY THAT HAS RECENTLY FACED CHAPTER 666 BANKRUPTCY.
SOMEONE'S PAIN IS ALWAYS SOMEONE ELSE'S **GAIN,** FOLKS. AND THAT ABOUT WRAPS UP THE NEWS FOR ANOTHER WRETCHED DAY HERE IN SCARE CITY.
AND NOW, ***WEATHER!***
IT'S GOING TO BE ANOTHER HIDEOUS AFTERNOON, WITH NO END TO OUR COLLECTIVE MISERY IN SIGHT...
-SIGH-

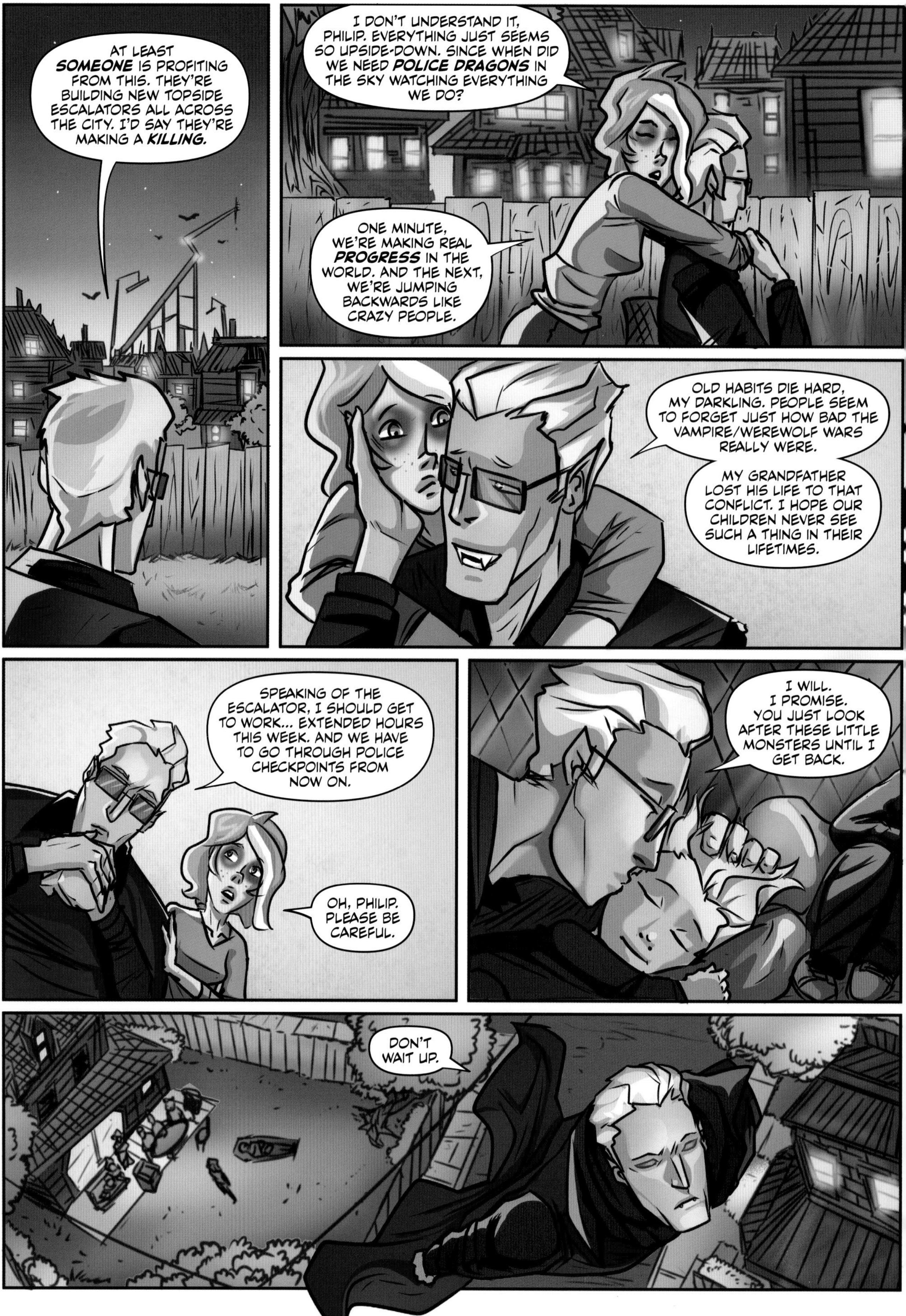
AT LEAST SOMEONE IS PROFITING FROM THIS. THEY'RE BUILDING NEW TOPSIDE ESCALATORS ALL ACROSS THE CITY. I'D SAY THEY'RE MAKING A KILLING.
I DON'T UNDERSTAND IT, PHILIP. EVERYTHING JUST SEEMS SO UPSIDE-DOWN. SINCE WHEN DID WE NEED POLICE DRAGONS IN THE SKY WATCHING EVERYTHING WE DO?
ONE MINUTE, WE'RE MAKING REAL PROGRESS IN THE WORLD. AND THE NEXT, WE'RE JUMPING BACKWARDS LIKE CRAZY PEOPLE.
OLD HABITS DIE HARD, MY DARKLING. PEOPLE SEEM TO FORGET JUST HOW BAD THE VAMPIRE/WEREWOLF WARS REALLY WERE.
MY GRANDFATHER LOST HIS LIFE TO THAT CONFLICT. I HOPE OUR CHILDREN NEVER SEE SUCH A THING IN THEIR LIFETIMES.
SPEAKING OF THE ESCALATOR, I SHOULD GET TO WORK... EXTENDED HOURS THIS WEEK. AND WE HAVE TO GO THROUGH POLICE CHECKPOINTS FROM NOW ON.
OH, PHILIP. PLEASE BE CAREFUL.
I WILL. I PROMISE. YOU JUST LOOK AFTER THESE LITTLE MONSTERS UNTIL I GET BACK.
DON'T WAIT UP.

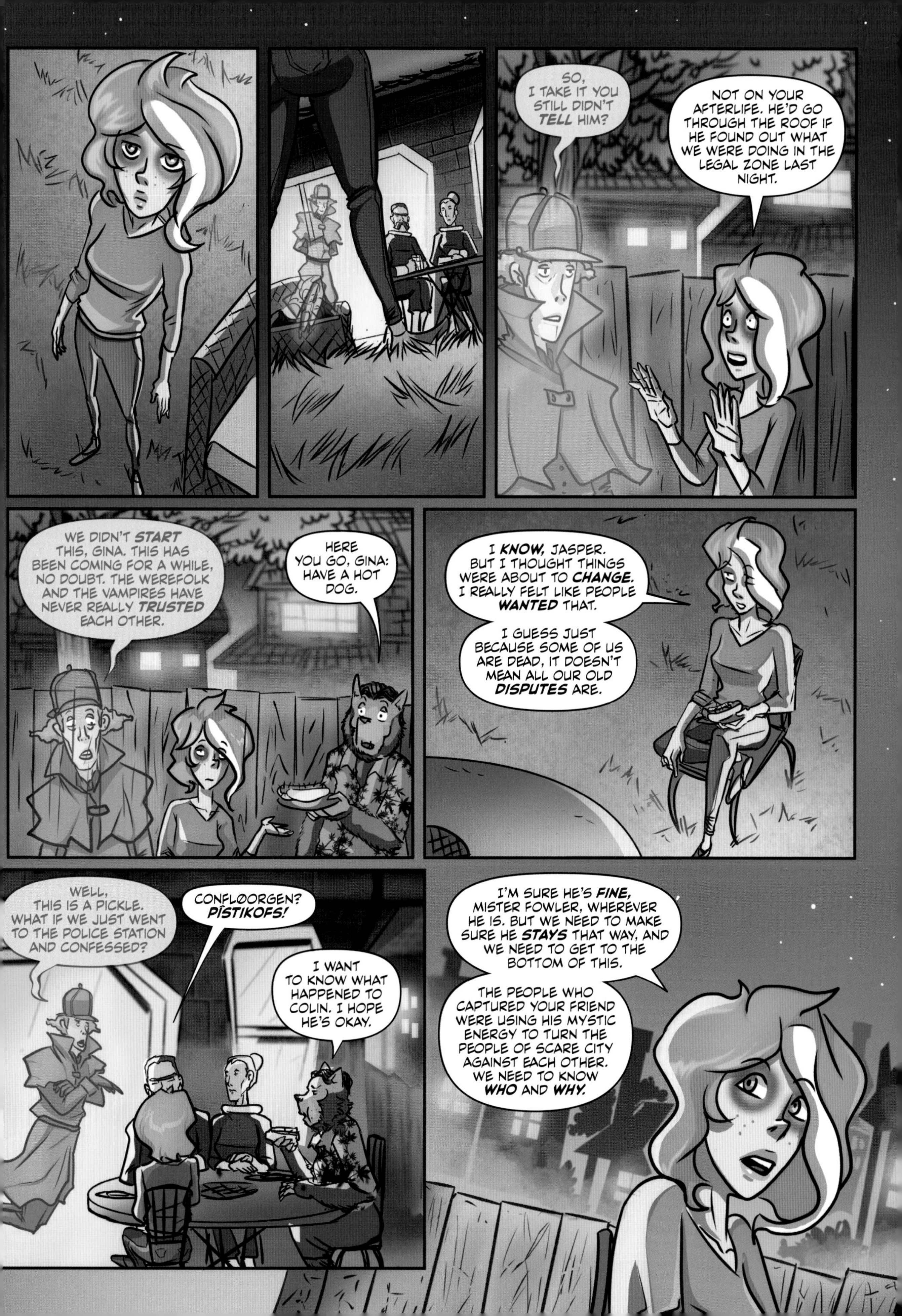

SO, I TAKE IT YOU STILL DIDN'T TELL HIM?
NOT ON YOUR AFTERLIFE. HE'D GO THROUGH THE ROOF IF HE FOUND OUT WHAT WE WERE DOING IN THE LEGAL ZONE LAST NIGHT.
WE DIDN'T START THIS, GINA. THIS HAS BEEN COMING FOR A WHILE, NO DOUBT. THE WEREFOLK AND THE VAMPIRES HAVE NEVER REALLY TRUSTED EACH OTHER.
HERE YOU GO, GINA: HAVE A HOT DOG.
I KNOW, JASPER. BUT I THOUGHT THINGS WERE ABOUT TO CHANGE. I REALLY FELT LIKE PEOPLE WANTED THAT.
I GUESS JUST BECAUSE SOME OF US ARE DEAD, IT DOESN'T MEAN ALL OUR OLD DISPUTES ARE.
WELL, THIS IS A PICKLE. WHAT IF WE JUST WENT TO THE POLICE STATION AND CONFESSED?
CONFLØORGEN? PÍSTIKOFS!
I WANT TO KNOW WHAT HAPPENED TO COLIN. I HOPE HE'S OKAY.
I'M SURE HE'S FINE, MISTER FOWLER, WHEREVER HE IS. BUT WE NEED TO MAKE SURE HE STAYS THAT WAY, AND WE NEED TO GET TO THE BOTTOM OF THIS.
THE PEOPLE WHO CAPTURED YOUR FRIEND WERE USING HIS MYSTIC ENERGY TO TURN THE PEOPLE OF SCARE CITY AGAINST EACH OTHER. WE NEED TO KNOW WHO AND WHY.

=MFF=...

...Y'KNOW, MY UNCLE HAROLD ALWAYS USED TO SAY WHEN EVERYONE'S ACTING ALL WEIRD AND ANGRY, THERE'S ALWAYS SOMEONE **BEHIND** IT AND AN UNLUCKY PERSON RIGHT IN **FRONT** OF IT.

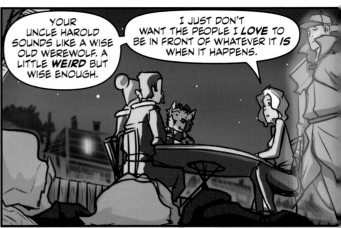

YOUR UNCLE HAROLD SOUNDS LIKE A WISE OLD WEREWOLF. A LITTLE **WEIRD** BUT WISE ENOUGH.

I JUST DON'T WANT THE PEOPLE I **LOVE** TO BE IN FRONT OF WHATEVER IT **IS** WHEN IT HAPPENS.

WELL, THERE'S NO USE SITTING AROUND MOPING. IT'S UP TO US TO **DO** SOMETHING ABOUT IT. WHAT DO WE KNOW SO FAR?

WELL, SOMEONE'S EITHER KILLING INNOCENT PEOPLE OR STEALING THEM AWAY. WE DON'T KNOW **WHO** AND WE DON'T KNOW WHY.

THE WEREWOLVES AND VAMPIRES ARE FIGHTING AGAIN, WE'VE LOST **COLIN,** AND WE JUST CREATED A MAJOR INCIDENT IN THE LEGAL ZONE. DID I **MISS** ANYTHING?

BUT WE DO HAVE ONE **ADVANTAGE:** WE **KNOW** THERE ARE DARK FORCES AT PLAY...

AND WE ARE ON THEIR TRAIL.

DØRK **FJÜRCES!**

WELL, WITH MAYOR DEMONIKA MISSING, THE BAD NEWS IS, WE'RE GOING TO HAVE TO FIGURE OUT A WAY TO SOLVE ALL OF THIS WITHOUT THE CITY'S HELP.

THE GOOD NEWS IS, AT LEAST NO ONE KNOWS WE'RE **INVOLVED--**

ATTENTION, OCCUPANTS! THIS IS DETECTIVE JERRY MANDIBLE OF THE THIRTEENTH PRECINCT!

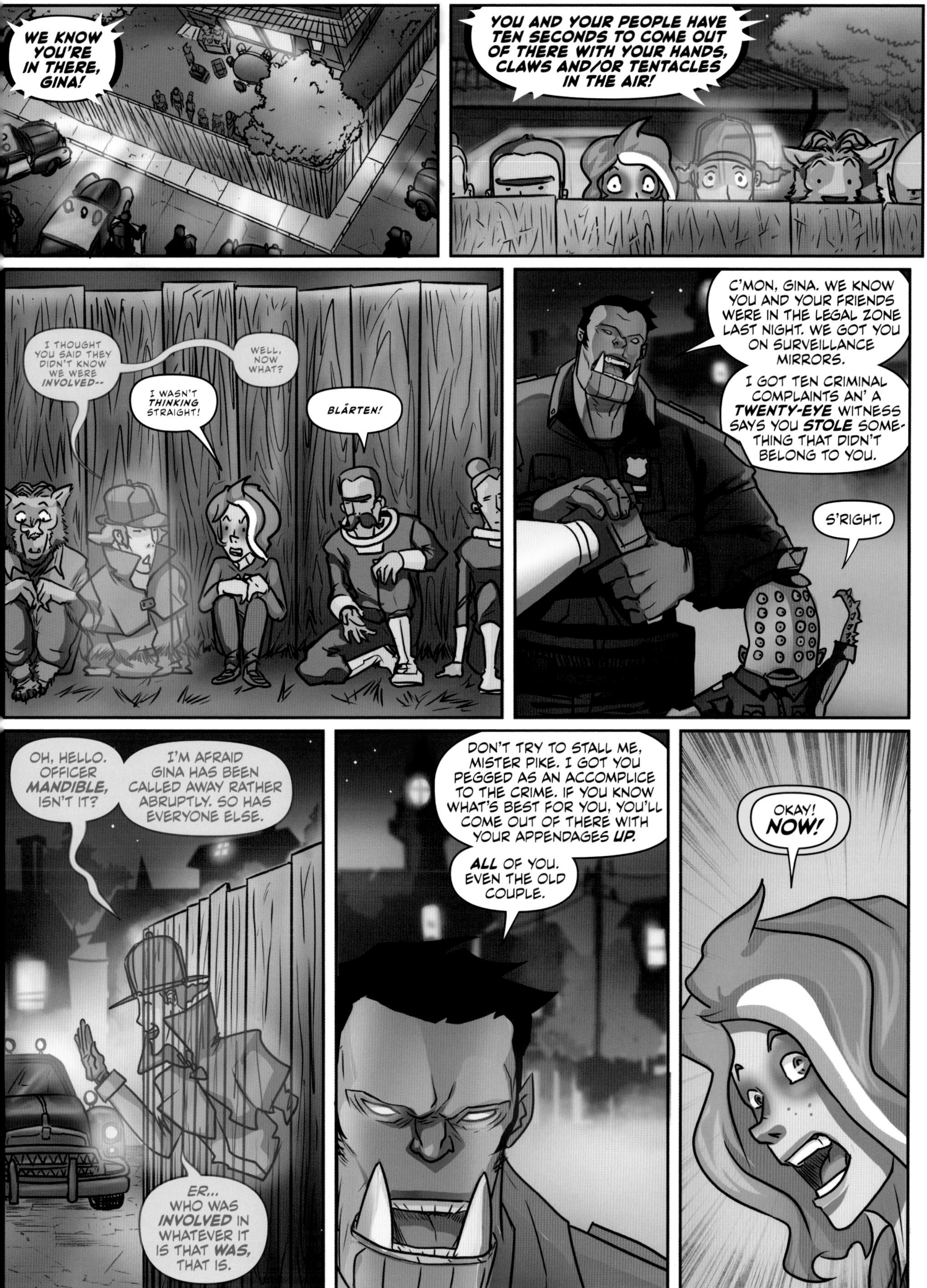
WE KNOW YOU'RE IN THERE, GINA!
YOU AND YOUR PEOPLE HAVE TEN SECONDS TO COME OUT OF THERE WITH YOUR HANDS, CLAWS AND/OR TENTACLES IN THE AIR!
I THOUGHT YOU SAID THEY DIDN'T KNOW WE WERE INVOLVED--
WELL, NOW WHAT?
I WASN'T THINKING STRAIGHT!
BLÄRTEN!
C'MON, GINA. WE KNOW YOU AND YOUR FRIENDS WERE IN THE LEGAL ZONE LAST NIGHT. WE GOT YOU ON SURVEILLANCE MIRRORS.
I GOT TEN CRIMINAL COMPLAINTS AN' A TWENTY-EYE WITNESS SAYS YOU STOLE SOMETHING THAT DIDN'T BELONG TO YOU.
S'RIGHT.
OH, HELLO. OFFICER MANDIBLE, ISN'T IT?
I'M AFRAID GINA HAS BEEN CALLED AWAY RATHER ABRUPTLY. SO HAS EVERYONE ELSE.
ER... WHO WAS INVOLVED IN WHATEVER IT IS THAT WAS, THAT IS.
DON'T TRY TO STALL ME, MISTER PIKE. I GOT YOU PEGGED AS AN ACCOMPLICE TO THE CRIME. IF YOU KNOW WHAT'S BEST FOR YOU, YOU'LL COME OUT OF THERE WITH YOUR APPENDAGES UP.
ALL OF YOU. EVEN THE OLD COUPLE.
OKAY! NOW!

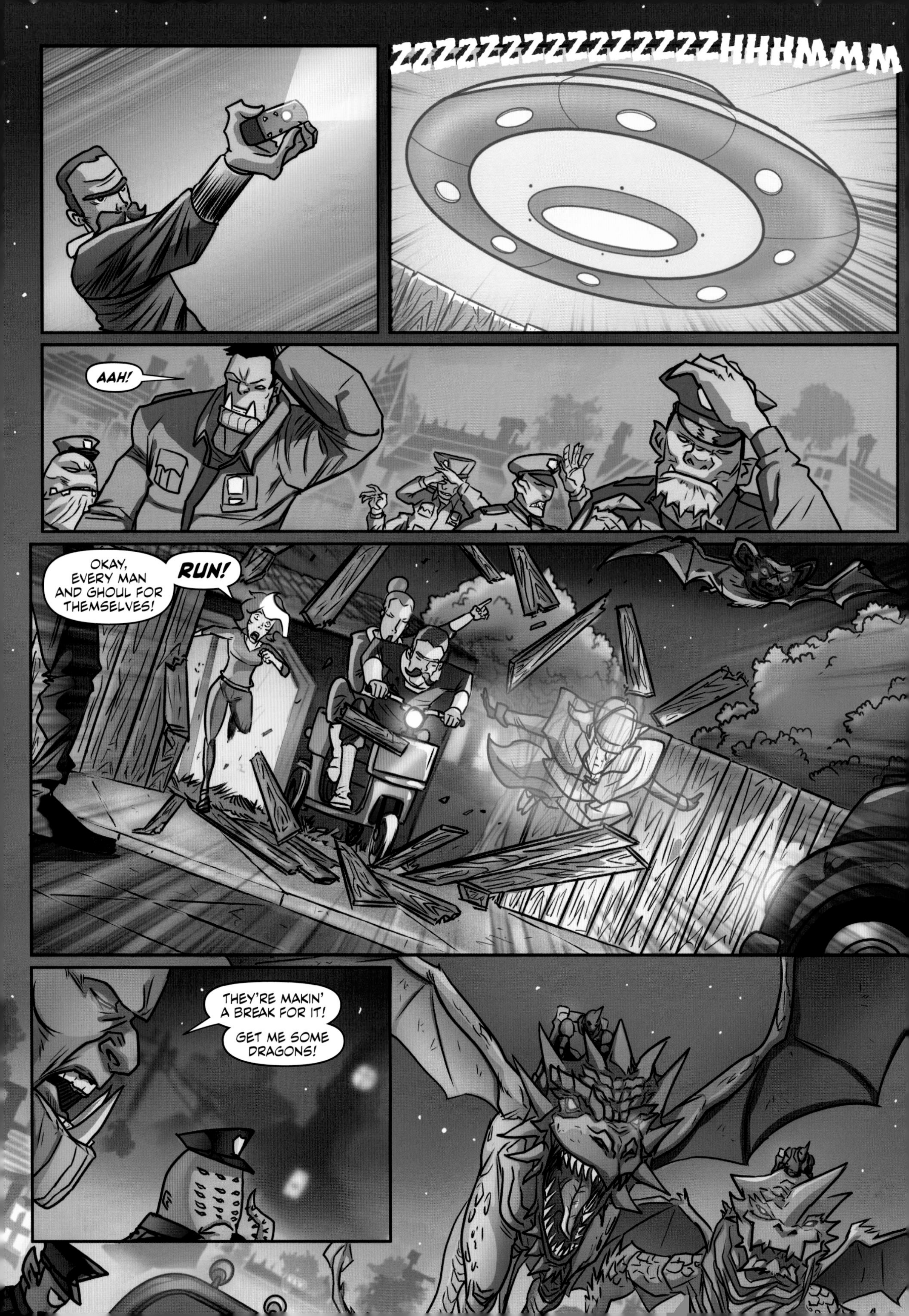

ZZZZZZZZZZZZZZZZHHHMMM
AAH!
OKAY, EVERY MAN AND GHOUL FOR THEMSELVES!
RUN!
THEY'RE MAKIN' A BREAK FOR IT!
GET ME SOME DRAGONS!

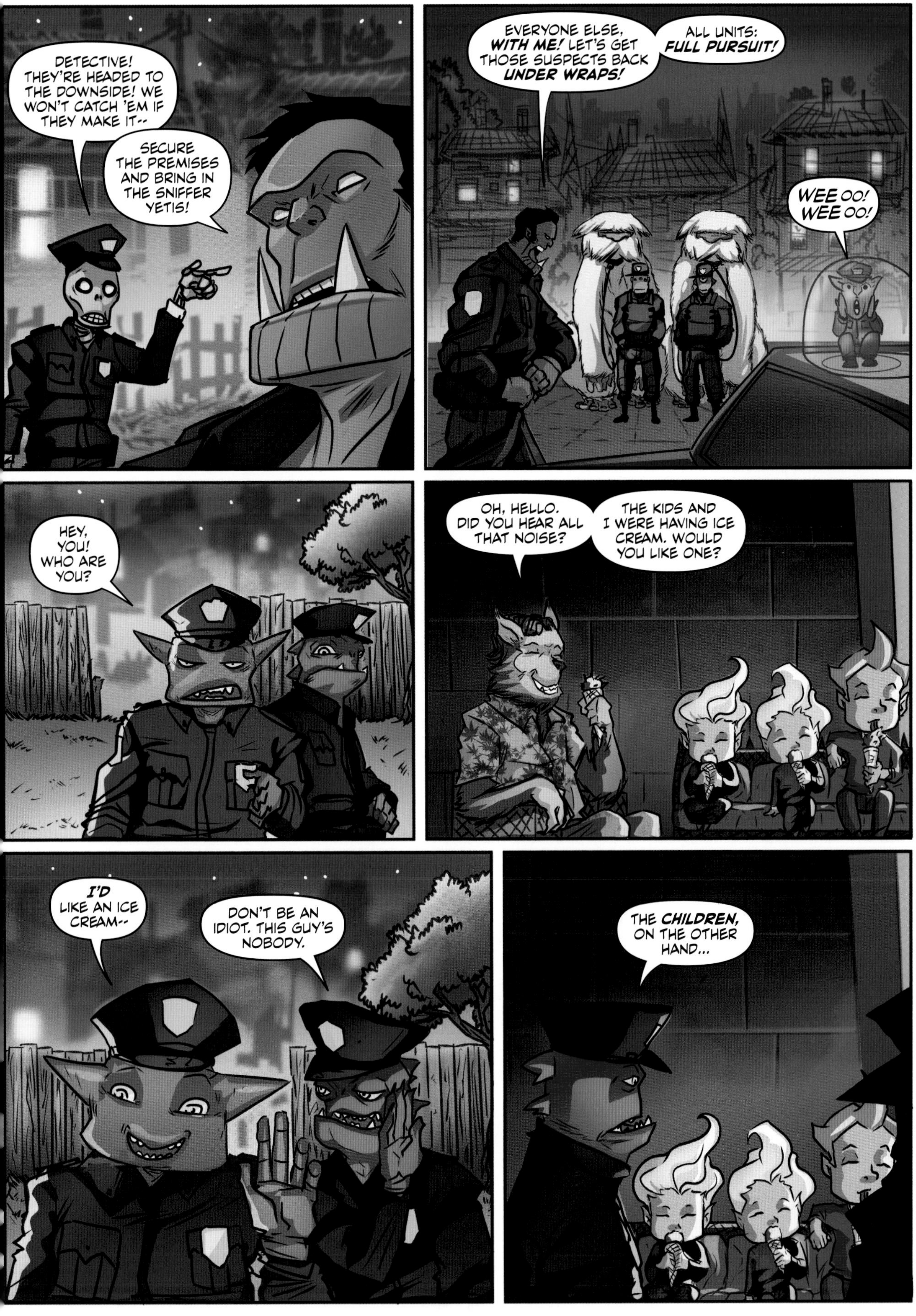
DETECTIVE! THEY'RE HEADED TO THE DOWNSIDE! WE WON'T CATCH 'EM IF THEY MAKE IT--
SECURE THE PREMISES AND BRING IN THE SNIFFER YETIS!
EVERYONE ELSE, WITH ME! LET'S GET THOSE SUSPECTS BACK UNDER WRAPS!
ALL UNITS: FULL PURSUIT!
WEE OO! WEE OO!
HEY, YOU! WHO ARE YOU?
OH, HELLO. DID YOU HEAR ALL THAT NOISE?
THE KIDS AND I WERE HAVING ICE CREAM. WOULD YOU LIKE ONE?
I'D LIKE AN ICE CREAM--
DON'T BE AN IDIOT. THIS GUY'S NOBODY.
THE CHILDREN, ON THE OTHER HAND...

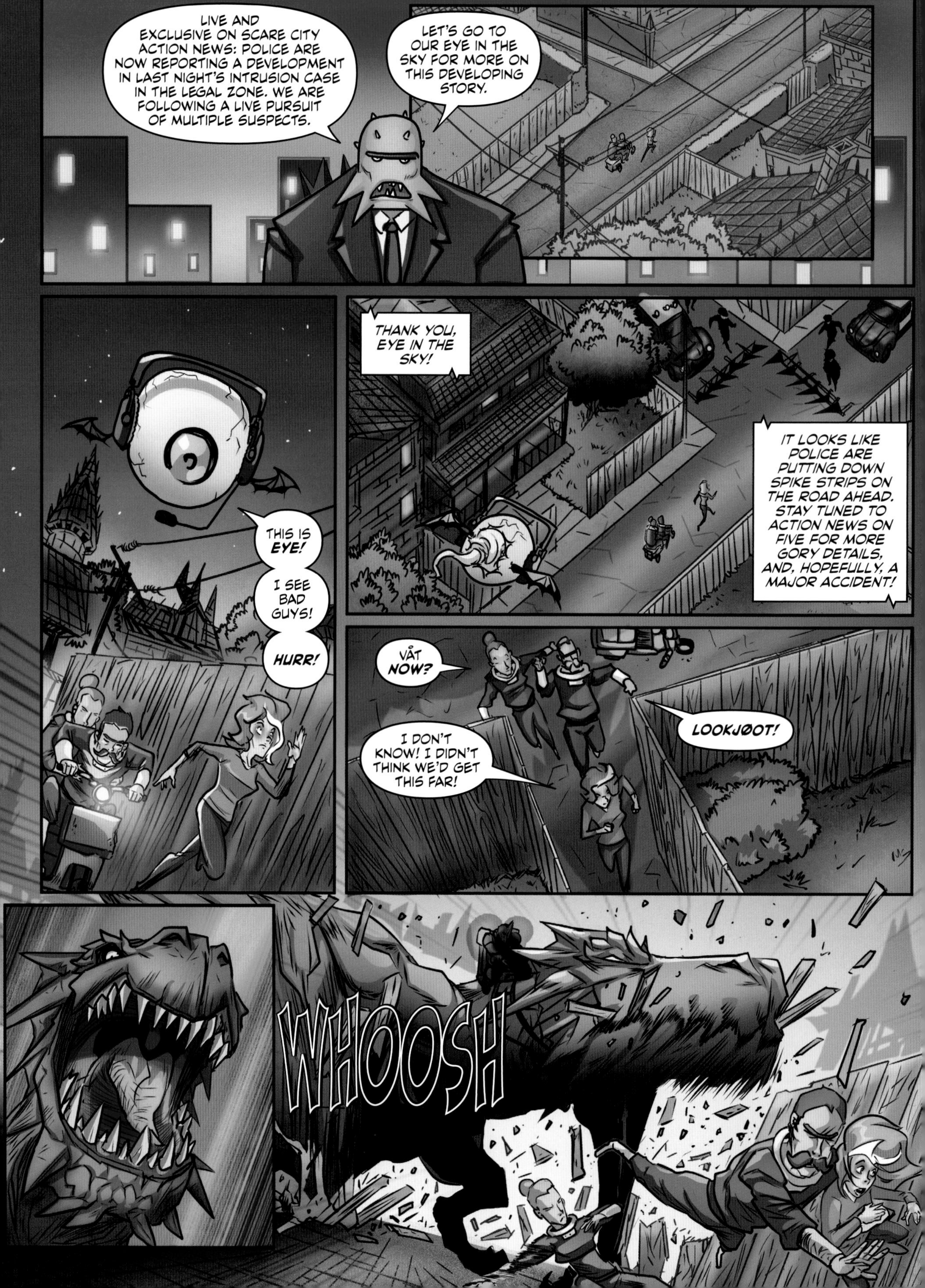
LIVE AND EXCLUSIVE ON SCARE CITY ACTION NEWS: POLICE ARE NOW REPORTING A DEVELOPMENT IN LAST NIGHT'S INTRUSION CASE IN THE LEGAL ZONE. WE ARE FOLLOWING A LIVE PURSUIT OF MULTIPLE SUSPECTS.
LET'S GO TO OUR EYE IN THE SKY FOR MORE ON THIS DEVELOPING STORY.
THIS IS *EYE!*
I SEE BAD GUYS!
HURR!
THANK YOU, EYE IN THE SKY!
IT LOOKS LIKE POLICE ARE PUTTING DOWN SPIKE STRIPS ON THE ROAD AHEAD. STAY TUNED TO ACTION NEWS ON FIVE FOR MORE GORY DETAILS, AND, HOPEFULLY, A MAJOR ACCIDENT!
VÅT ***NOW?***
I DON'T KNOW! I DIDN'T THINK WE'D GET THIS FAR!
LOOKJØOT!
WHOOSH

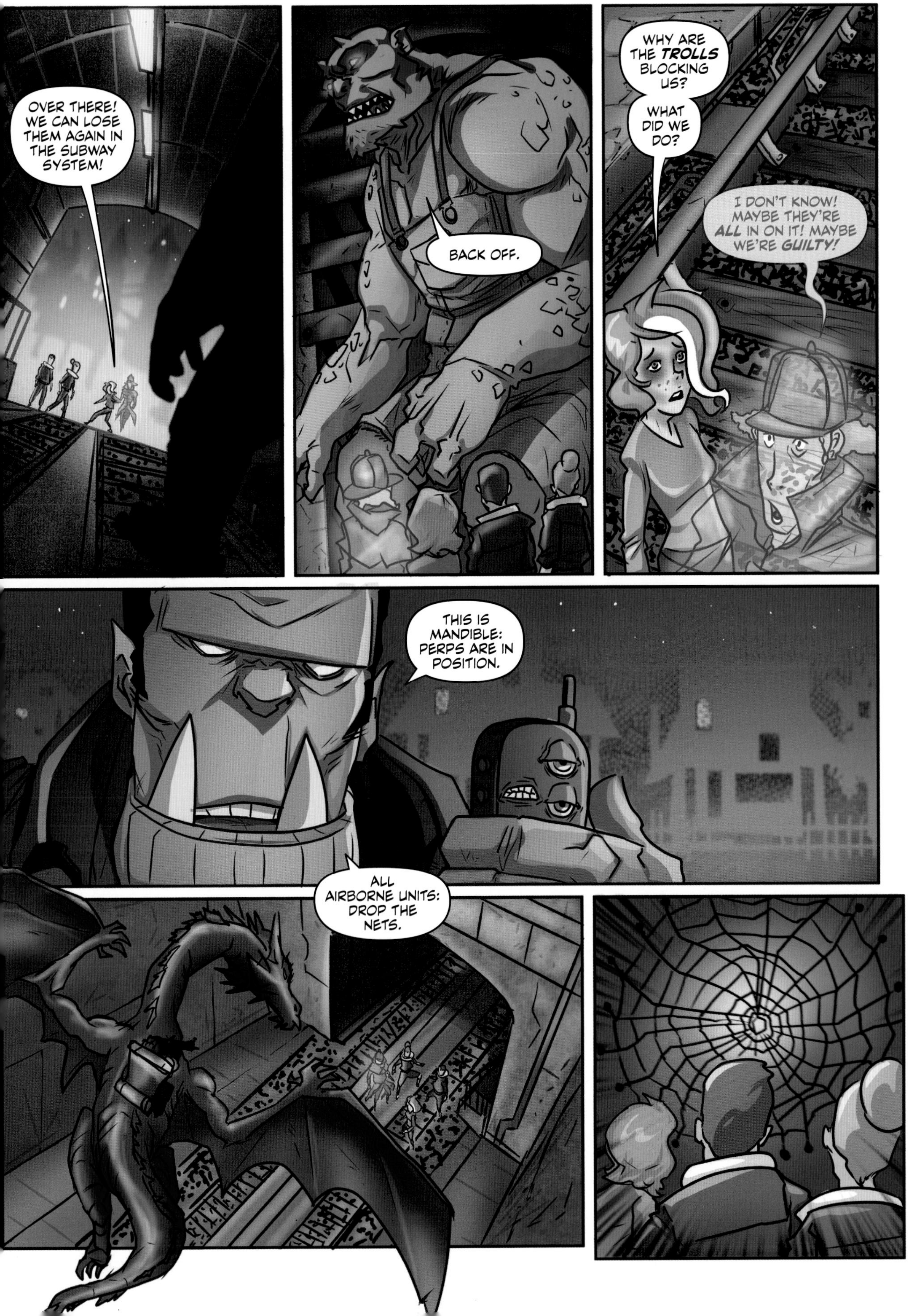
OVER THERE! WE CAN LOSE THEM AGAIN IN THE SUBWAY SYSTEM!
BACK OFF.
WHY ARE THE **TROLLS** BLOCKING US?
WHAT DID WE DO?
I DON'T KNOW! MAYBE THEY'RE **ALL** IN ON IT! MAYBE WE'RE **GUILTY!**
THIS IS MANDIBLE: PERPS ARE IN POSITION.
ALL AIRBORNE UNITS: DROP THE NETS.

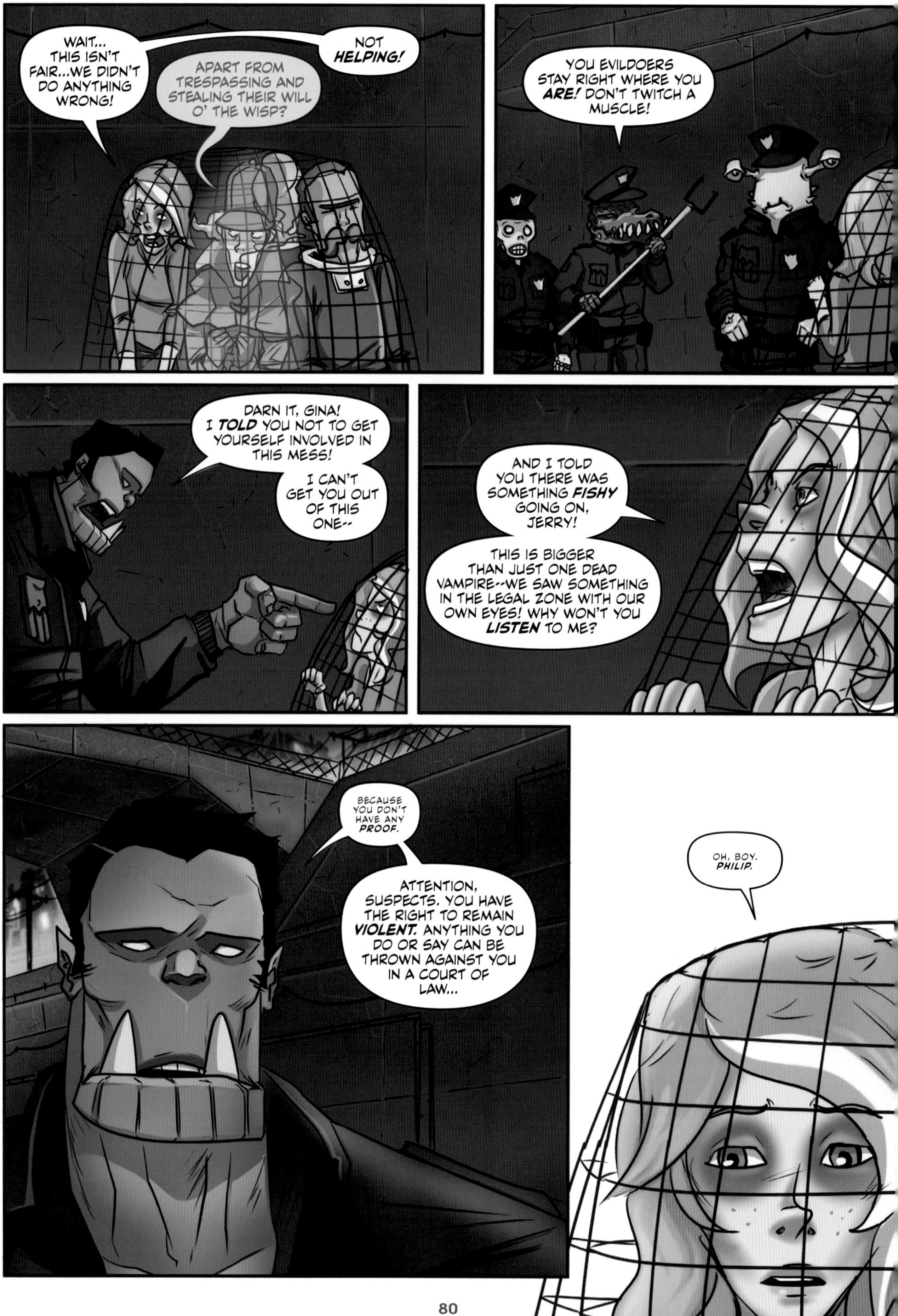
WAIT... THIS ISN'T FAIR...WE DIDN'T DO ANYTHING WRONG!
APART FROM TRESPASSING AND STEALING THEIR WILL O' THE WISP?
NOT HELPING!
YOU EVILDOERS STAY RIGHT WHERE YOU ARE! DON'T TWITCH A MUSCLE!
DARN IT, GINA! I TOLD YOU NOT TO GET YOURSELF INVOLVED IN THIS MESS!
I CAN'T GET YOU OUT OF THIS ONE--
AND I TOLD YOU THERE WAS SOMETHING FISHY GOING ON, JERRY!
THIS IS BIGGER THAN JUST ONE DEAD VAMPIRE--WE SAW SOMETHING IN THE LEGAL ZONE WITH OUR OWN EYES! WHY WON'T YOU LISTEN TO ME?
BECAUSE YOU DON'T HAVE ANY PROOF.
ATTENTION, SUSPECTS. YOU HAVE THE RIGHT TO REMAIN VIOLENT. ANYTHING YOU DO OR SAY CAN BE THROWN AGAINST YOU IN A COURT OF LAW...
OH, BOY. PHILIP.

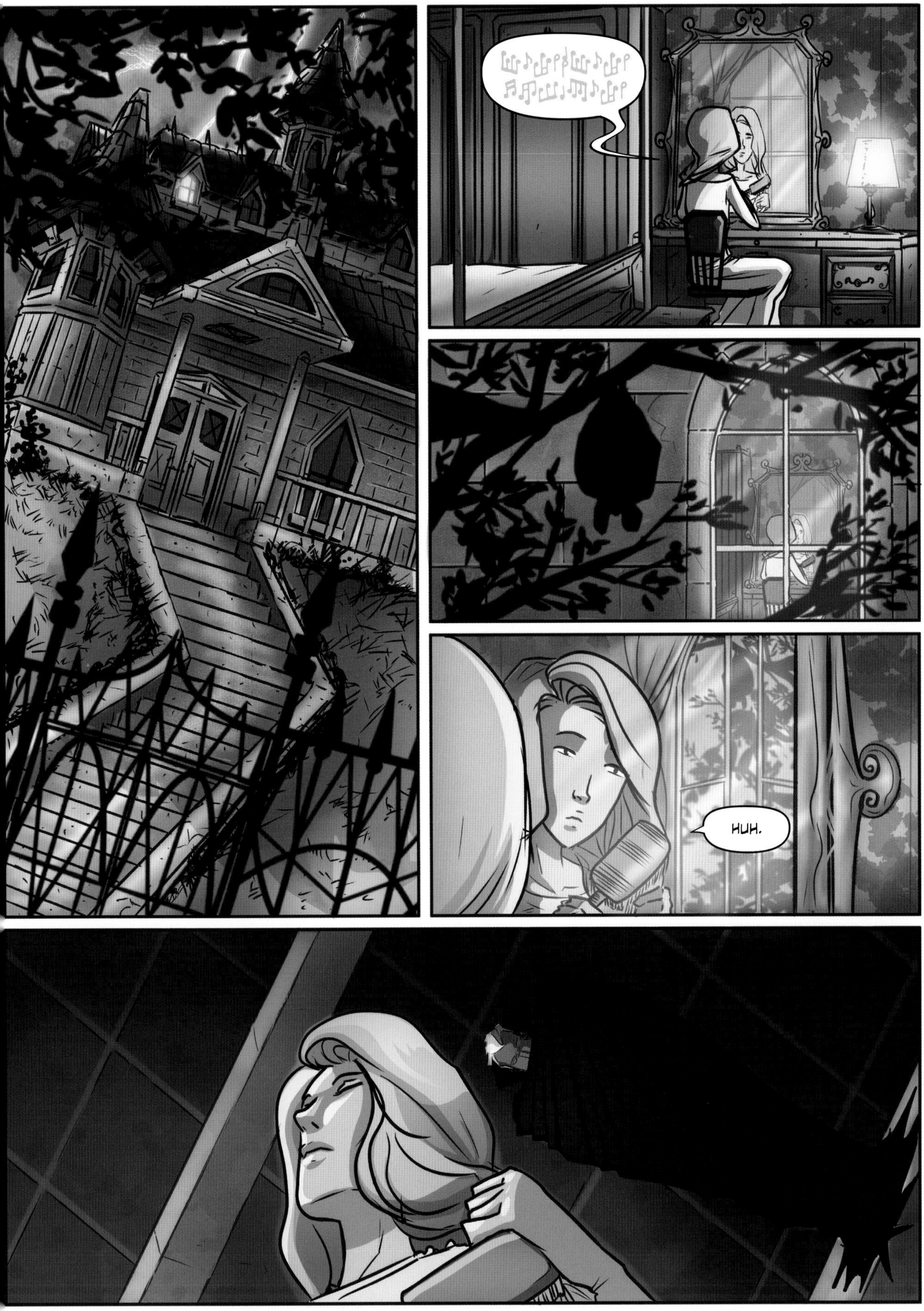
HUH.

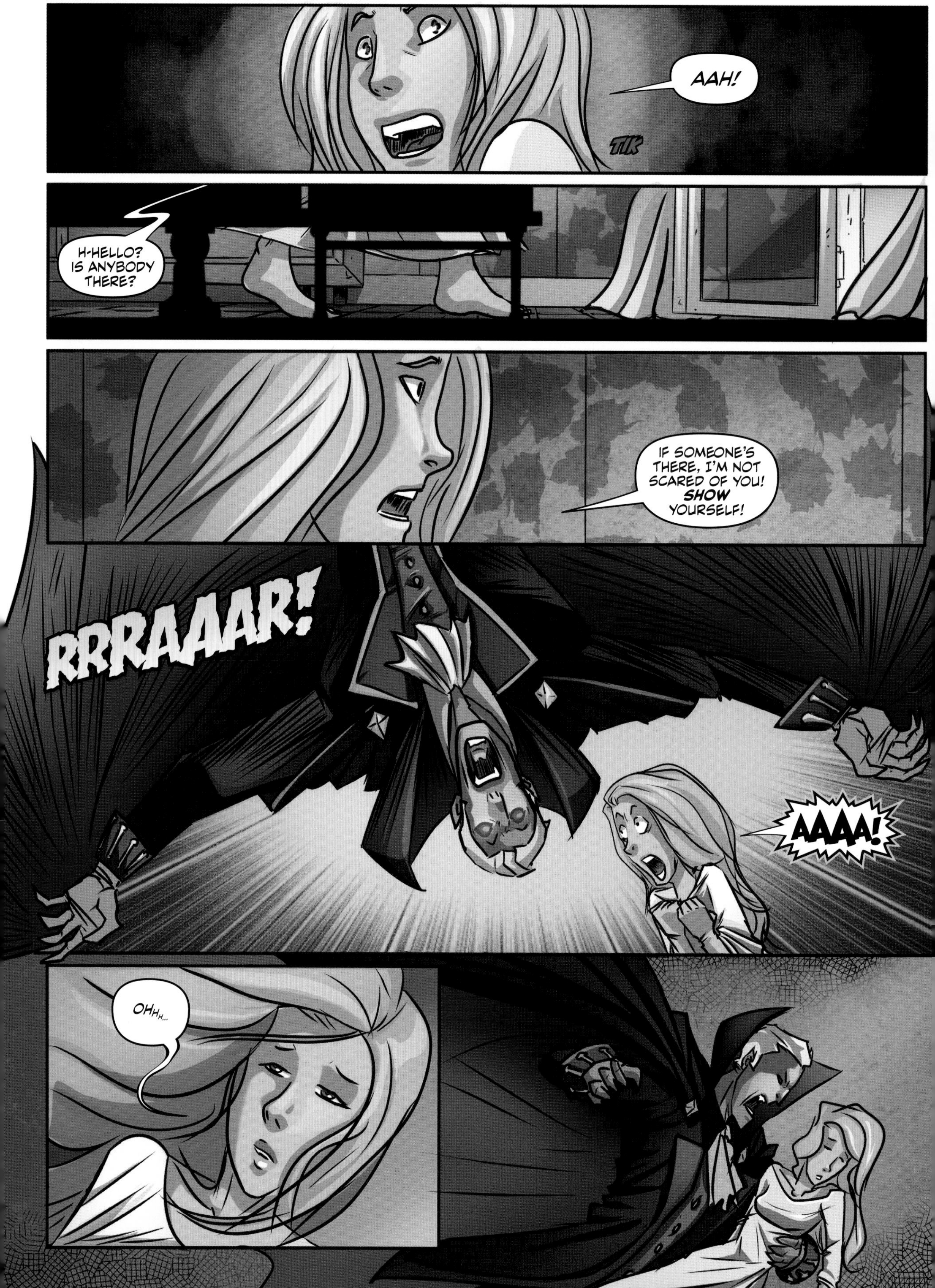
AAH!
TIK
H-HELLO? IS ANYBODY THERE?
IF SOMEONE'S THERE, I'M NOT SCARED OF YOU! SHOW YOURSELF!
RRRAAAR!
AAAA!
OHHH...

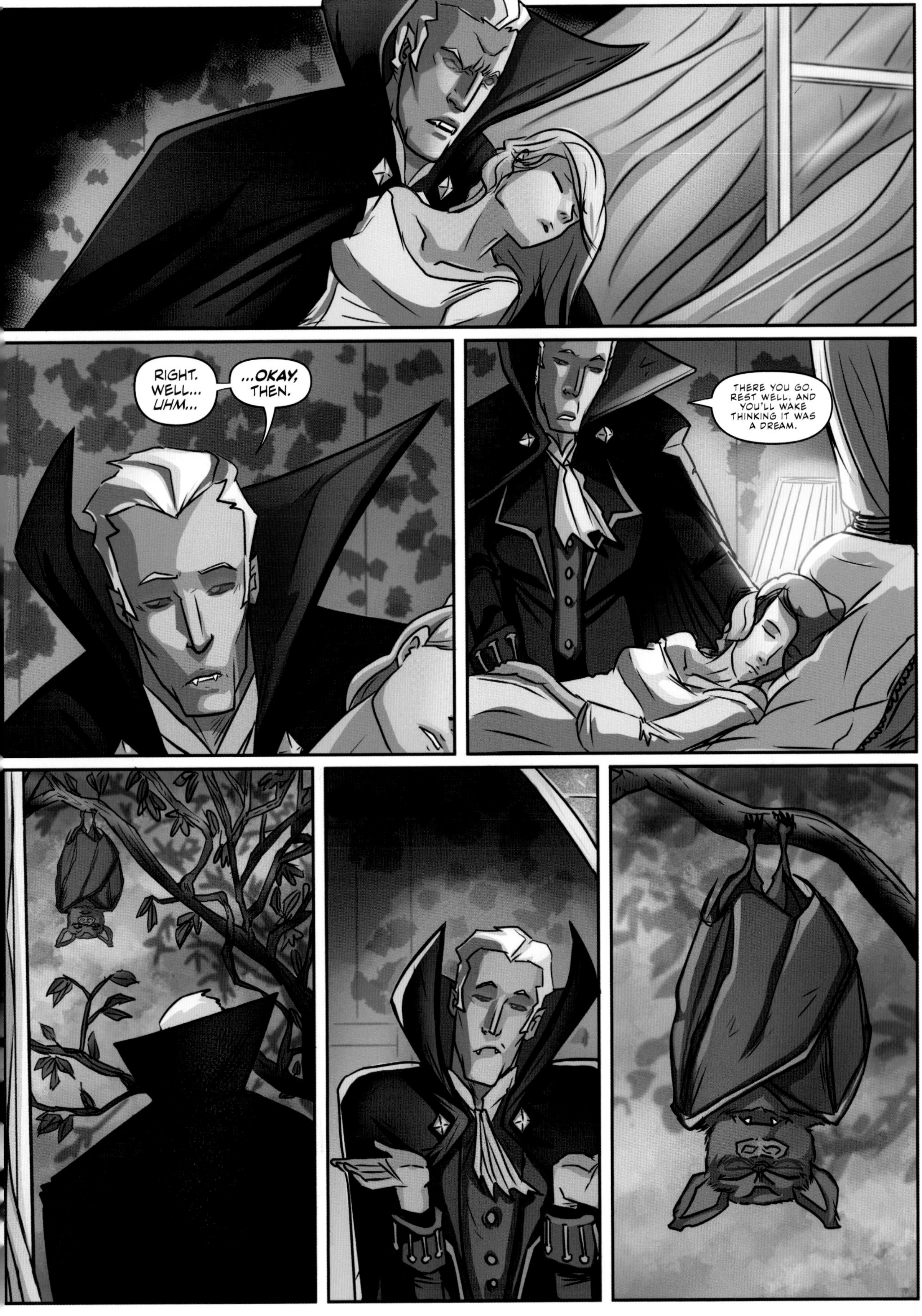
RIGHT. WELL... UHM...
...OKAY, THEN.
THERE YOU GO. REST WELL, AND YOU'LL WAKE THINKING IT WAS A DREAM.

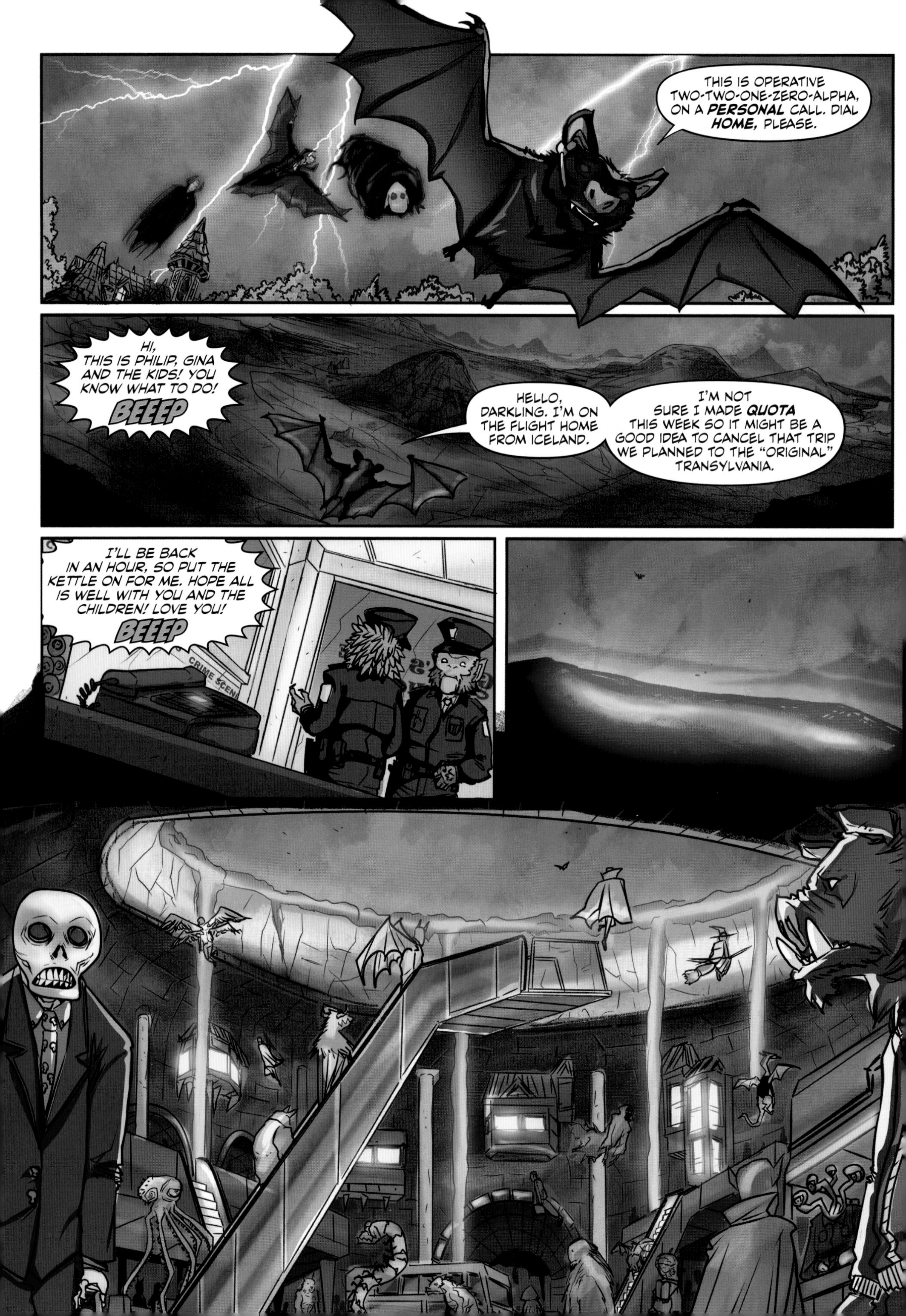
THIS IS OPERATIVE TWO-TWO-ONE-ZERO-ALPHA, ON A PERSONAL CALL. DIAL HOME, PLEASE.
HI, THIS IS PHILIP, GINA AND THE KIDS! YOU KNOW WHAT TO DO!
BEEEP
HELLO, DARKLING. I'M ON THE FLIGHT HOME FROM ICELAND.
I'M NOT SURE I MADE QUOTA THIS WEEK SO IT MIGHT BE A GOOD IDEA TO CANCEL THAT TRIP WE PLANNED TO THE "ORIGINAL" TRANSYLVANIA.
I'LL BE BACK IN AN HOUR, SO PUT THE KETTLE ON FOR ME. HOPE ALL IS WELL WITH YOU AND THE CHILDREN! LOVE YOU!
BEEEP
CRIME SCENE

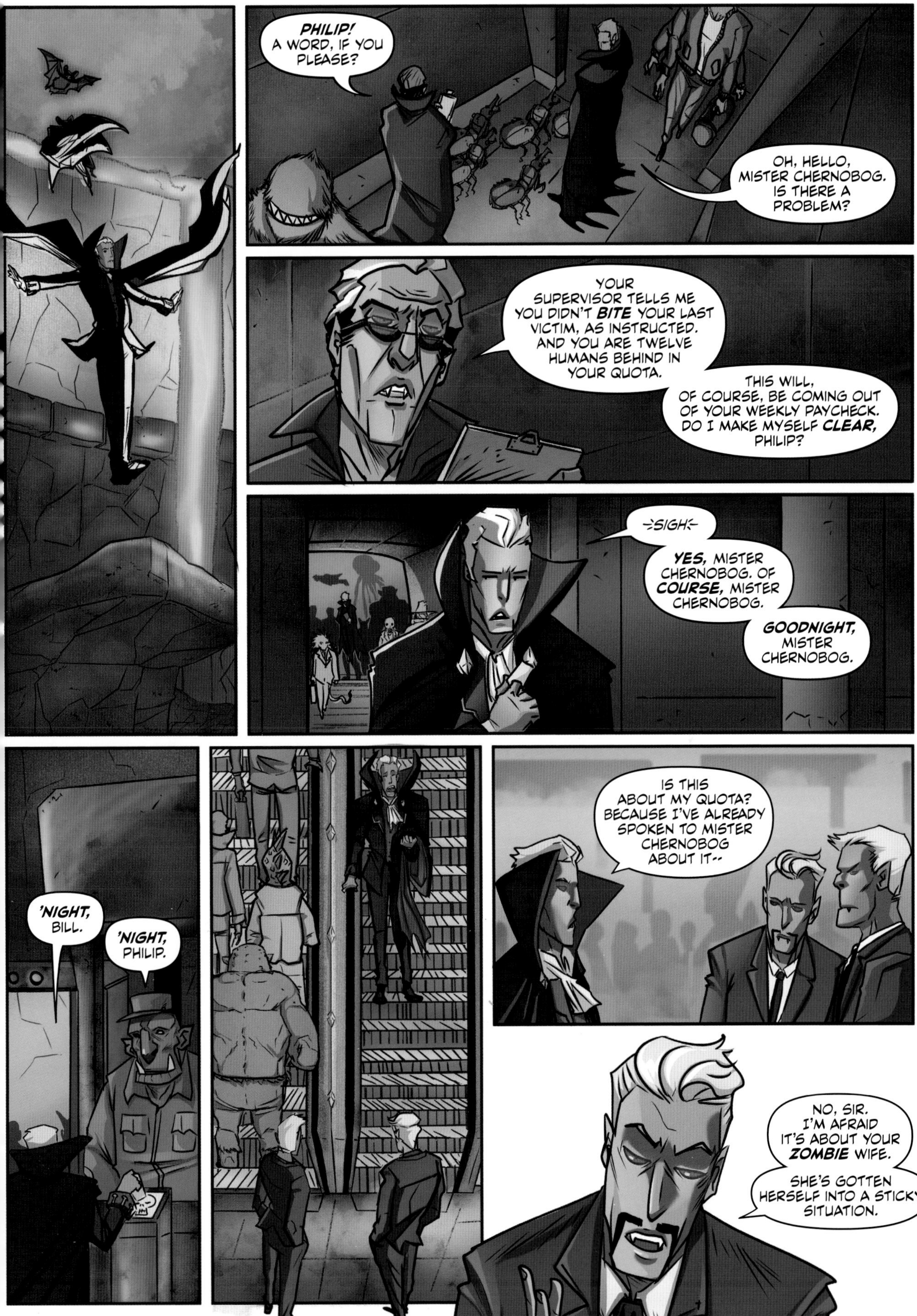
PHILIP! A WORD, IF YOU PLEASE?
OH, HELLO, MISTER CHERNOBOG. IS THERE A PROBLEM?
YOUR SUPERVISOR TELLS ME YOU DIDN'T BITE YOUR LAST VICTIM, AS INSTRUCTED. AND YOU ARE TWELVE HUMANS BEHIND IN YOUR QUOTA.
THIS WILL, OF COURSE, BE COMING OUT OF YOUR WEEKLY PAYCHECK. DO I MAKE MYSELF CLEAR, PHILIP?
SIGH
YES, MISTER CHERNOBOG. OF COURSE, MISTER CHERNOBOG.
GOODNIGHT, MISTER CHERNOBOG.
'NIGHT, BILL.
'NIGHT, PHILIP.
IS THIS ABOUT MY QUOTA? BECAUSE I'VE ALREADY SPOKEN TO MISTER CHERNOBOG ABOUT IT--
NO, SIR. I'M AFRAID IT'S ABOUT YOUR ZOMBIE WIFE.
SHE'S GOTTEN HERSELF INTO A STICKY SITUATION.

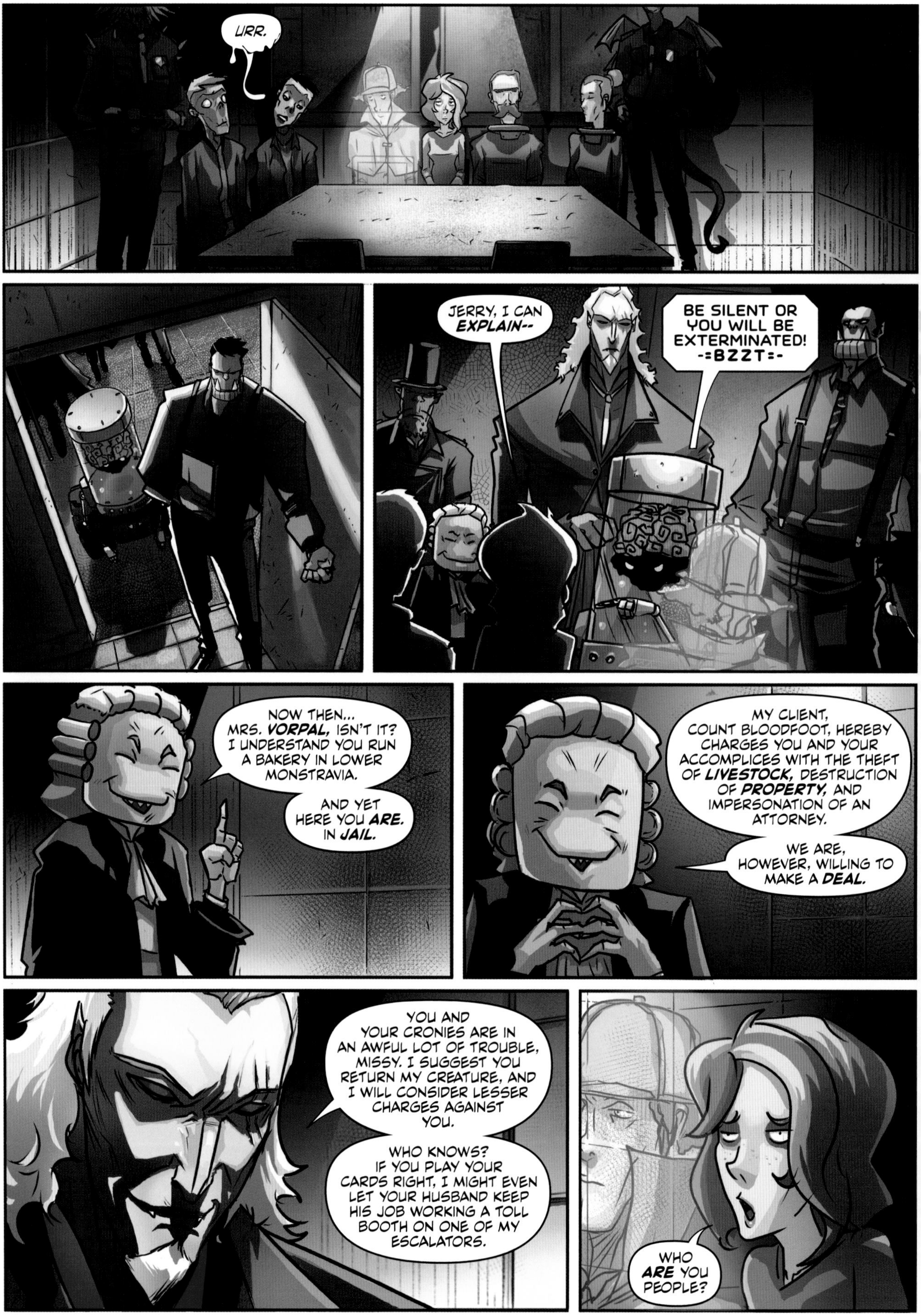
URR.
JERRY, I CAN *EXPLAIN*--
BE SILENT OR YOU WILL BE EXTERMINATED! -=BZZT=-
NOW THEN... MRS. *VORPAL,* ISN'T IT? I UNDERSTAND YOU RUN A BAKERY IN LOWER MONSTRAVIA.
AND YET HERE YOU *ARE.* IN *JAIL.*
MY CLIENT, COUNT BLOODFOOT, HEREBY CHARGES YOU AND YOUR ACCOMPLICES WITH THE THEFT OF *LIVESTOCK,* DESTRUCTION OF *PROPERTY,* AND IMPERSONATION OF AN ATTORNEY.
WE ARE, HOWEVER, WILLING TO MAKE A *DEAL.*
YOU AND YOUR CRONIES ARE IN AN AWFUL LOT OF TROUBLE, MISSY. I SUGGEST YOU RETURN MY CREATURE, AND I WILL CONSIDER LESSER CHARGES AGAINST YOU.
WHO KNOWS? IF YOU PLAY YOUR CARDS RIGHT, I MIGHT EVEN LET YOUR HUSBAND KEEP HIS JOB WORKING A TOLL BOOTH ON ONE OF MY ESCALATORS.
WHO *ARE* YOU PEOPLE?

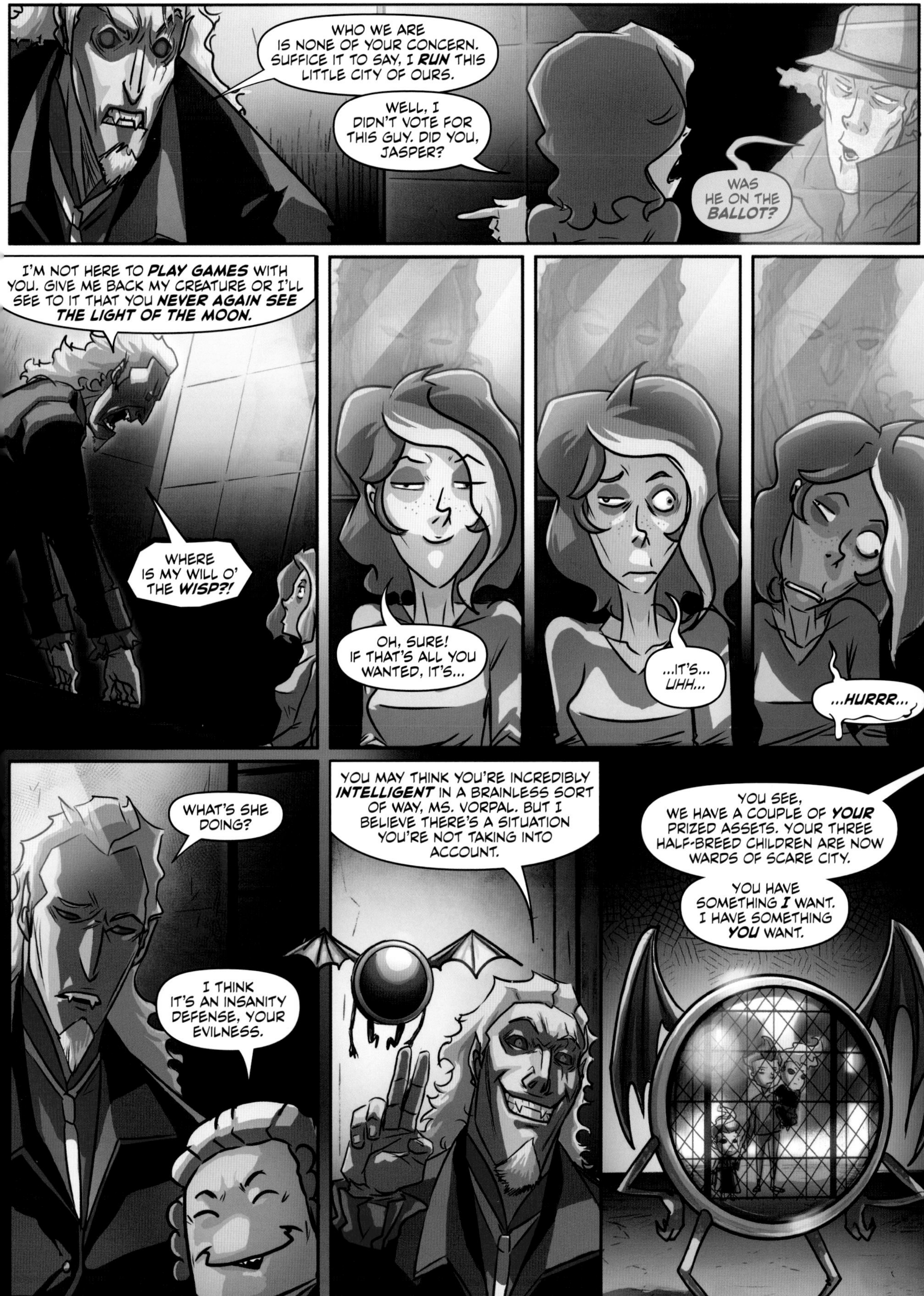
WHO WE ARE IS NONE OF YOUR CONCERN. SUFFICE IT TO SAY, I RUN THIS LITTLE CITY OF OURS.
WELL, I DIDN'T VOTE FOR THIS GUY. DID YOU, JASPER?
WAS HE ON THE BALLOT?
I'M NOT HERE TO PLAY GAMES WITH YOU. GIVE ME BACK MY CREATURE OR I'LL SEE TO IT THAT YOU NEVER AGAIN SEE THE LIGHT OF THE MOON.
WHERE IS MY WILL O' THE WISP?!
OH, SURE! IF THAT'S ALL YOU WANTED, IT'S...
...IT'S... UHH...
...HURRR...
WHAT'S SHE DOING?
I THINK IT'S AN INSANITY DEFENSE, YOUR EVILNESS.
YOU MAY THINK YOU'RE INCREDIBLY INTELLIGENT IN A BRAINLESS SORT OF WAY, MS. VORPAL. BUT I BELIEVE THERE'S A SITUATION YOU'RE NOT TAKING INTO ACCOUNT.
YOU SEE, WE HAVE A COUPLE OF YOUR PRIZED ASSETS. YOUR THREE HALF-BREED CHILDREN ARE NOW WARDS OF SCARE CITY.
YOU HAVE SOMETHING I WANT. I HAVE SOMETHING YOU WANT.

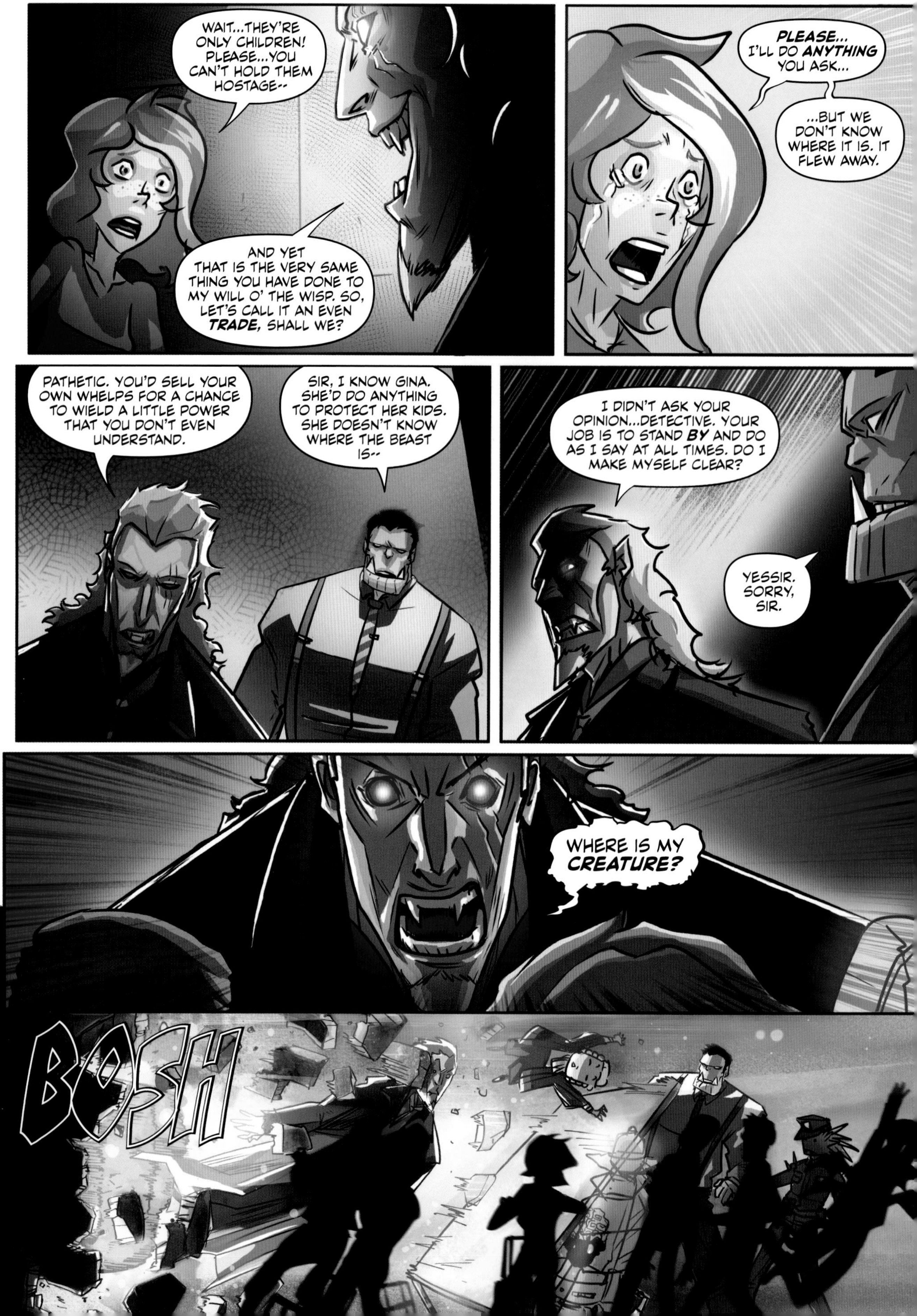
WAIT...THEY'RE ONLY CHILDREN! PLEASE...YOU CAN'T HOLD THEM HOSTAGE--
AND YET THAT IS THE VERY SAME THING YOU HAVE DONE TO MY WILL O' THE WISP. SO, LET'S CALL IT AN EVEN TRADE, SHALL WE?
PLEASE... I'LL DO ANYTHING YOU ASK...
...BUT WE DON'T KNOW WHERE IT IS. IT FLEW AWAY.
PATHETIC. YOU'D SELL YOUR OWN WHELPS FOR A CHANCE TO WIELD A LITTLE POWER THAT YOU DON'T EVEN UNDERSTAND.
SIR, I KNOW GINA. SHE'D DO ANYTHING TO PROTECT HER KIDS. SHE DOESN'T KNOW WHERE THE BEAST IS--
I DIDN'T ASK YOUR OPINION...DETECTIVE. YOUR JOB IS TO STAND BY AND DO AS I SAY AT ALL TIMES. DO I MAKE MYSELF CLEAR?
YESSIR. SORRY, SIR.
WHERE IS MY CREATURE?
BOSH

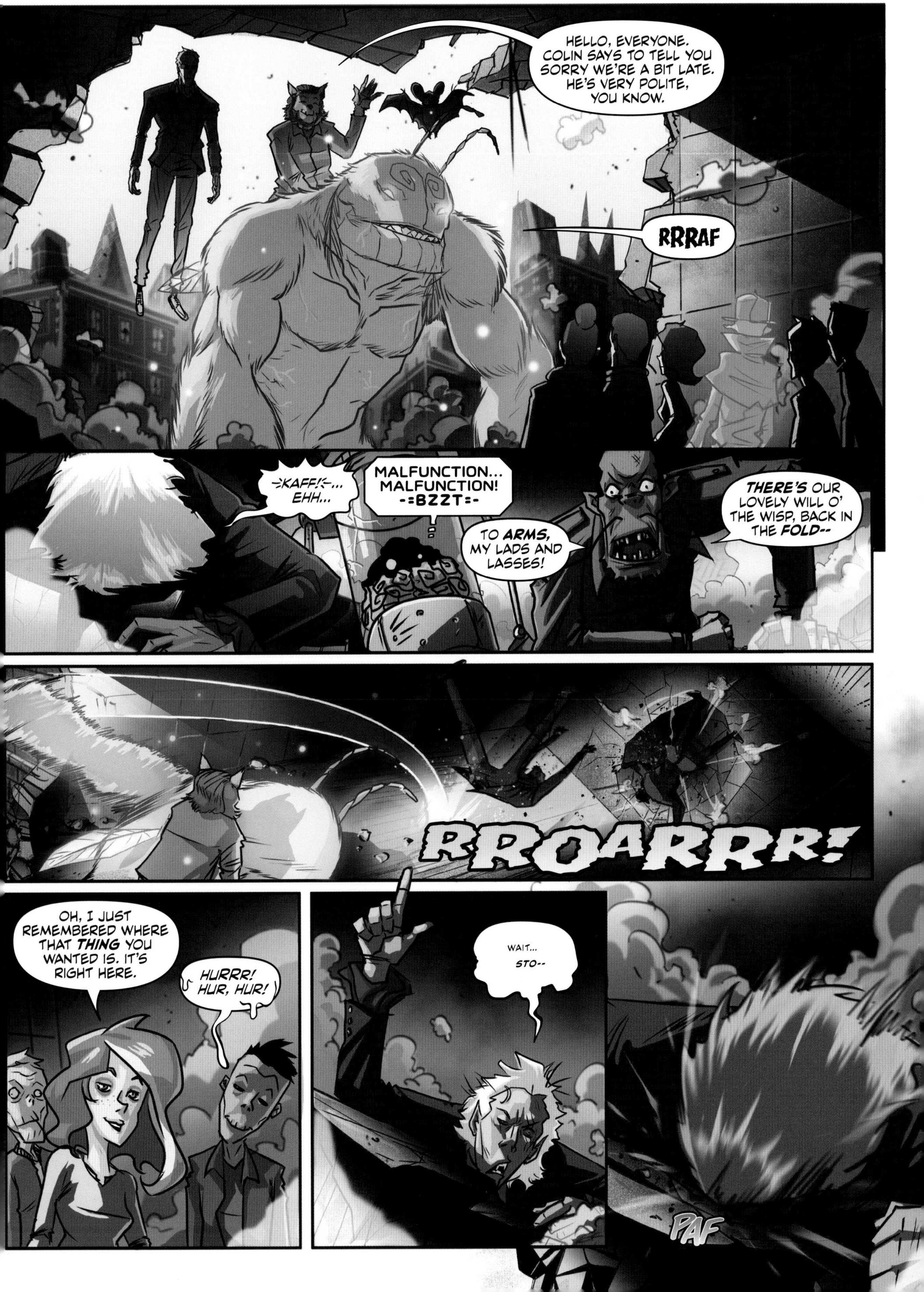
HELLO, EVERYONE. COLIN SAYS TO TELL YOU SORRY WE'RE A BIT LATE. HE'S VERY POLITE, YOU KNOW.
RRRAF
-KAFF!-... EHH...
MALFUNCTION... MALFUNCTION! -=BZZT=-
TO ARMS, MY LADS AND LASSES!
THERE'S OUR LOVELY WILL O' THE WISP, BACK IN THE FOLD--
RROARRR!
OH, I JUST REMEMBERED WHERE THAT THING YOU WANTED IS. IT'S RIGHT HERE.
HURRR! HUR, HUR!
WAIT... STO--
PAF

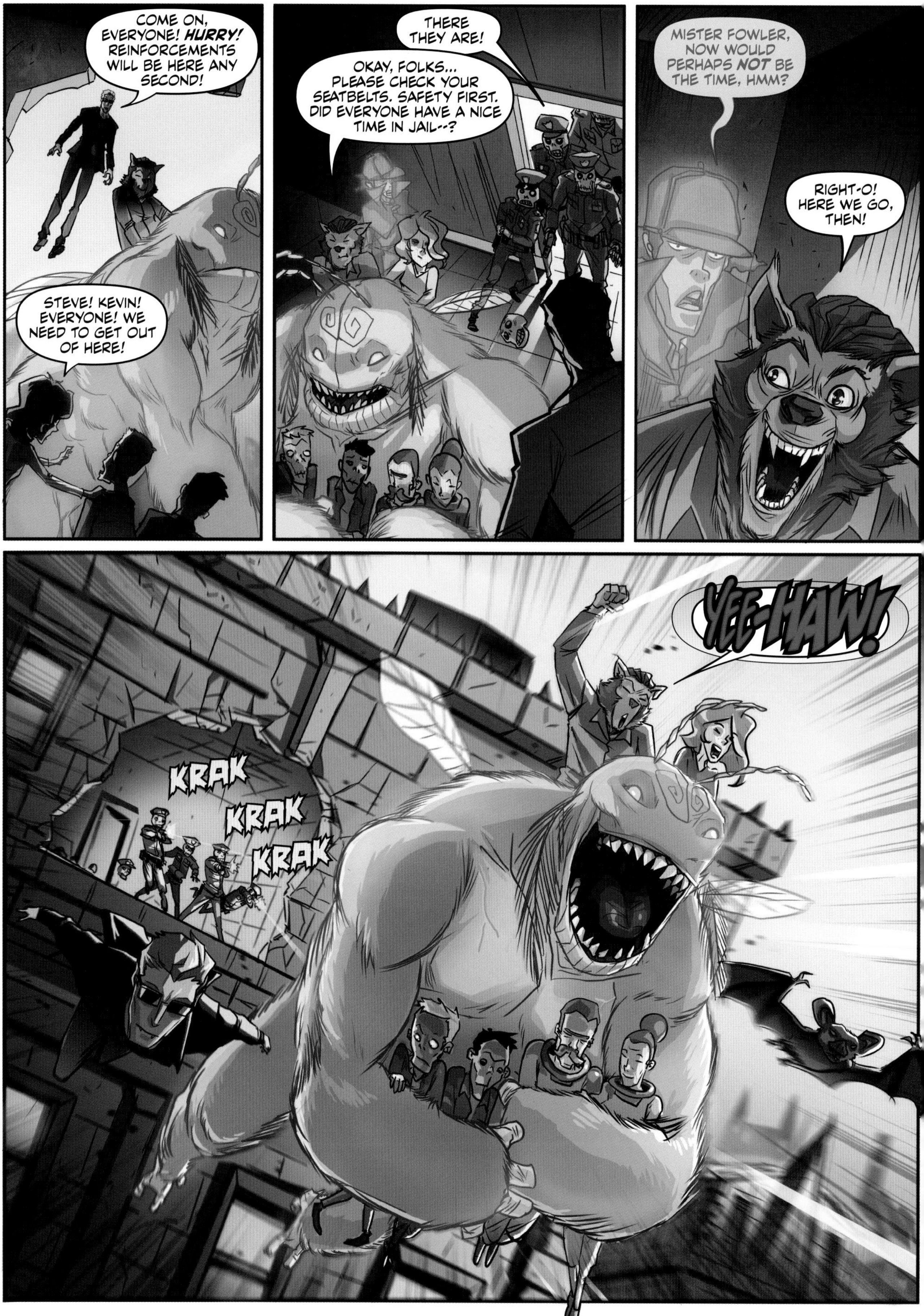
COME ON, EVERYONE! HURRY! REINFORCEMENTS WILL BE HERE ANY SECOND!
STEVE! KEVIN! EVERYONE! WE NEED TO GET OUT OF HERE!
THERE THEY ARE!
OKAY, FOLKS... PLEASE CHECK YOUR SEATBELTS. SAFETY FIRST. DID EVERYONE HAVE A NICE TIME IN JAIL--?
MISTER FOWLER, NOW WOULD PERHAPS NOT BE THE TIME, HMM?
RIGHT-O! HERE WE GO, THEN!
YEE-HAW!
KRAK
KRAK
KRAK

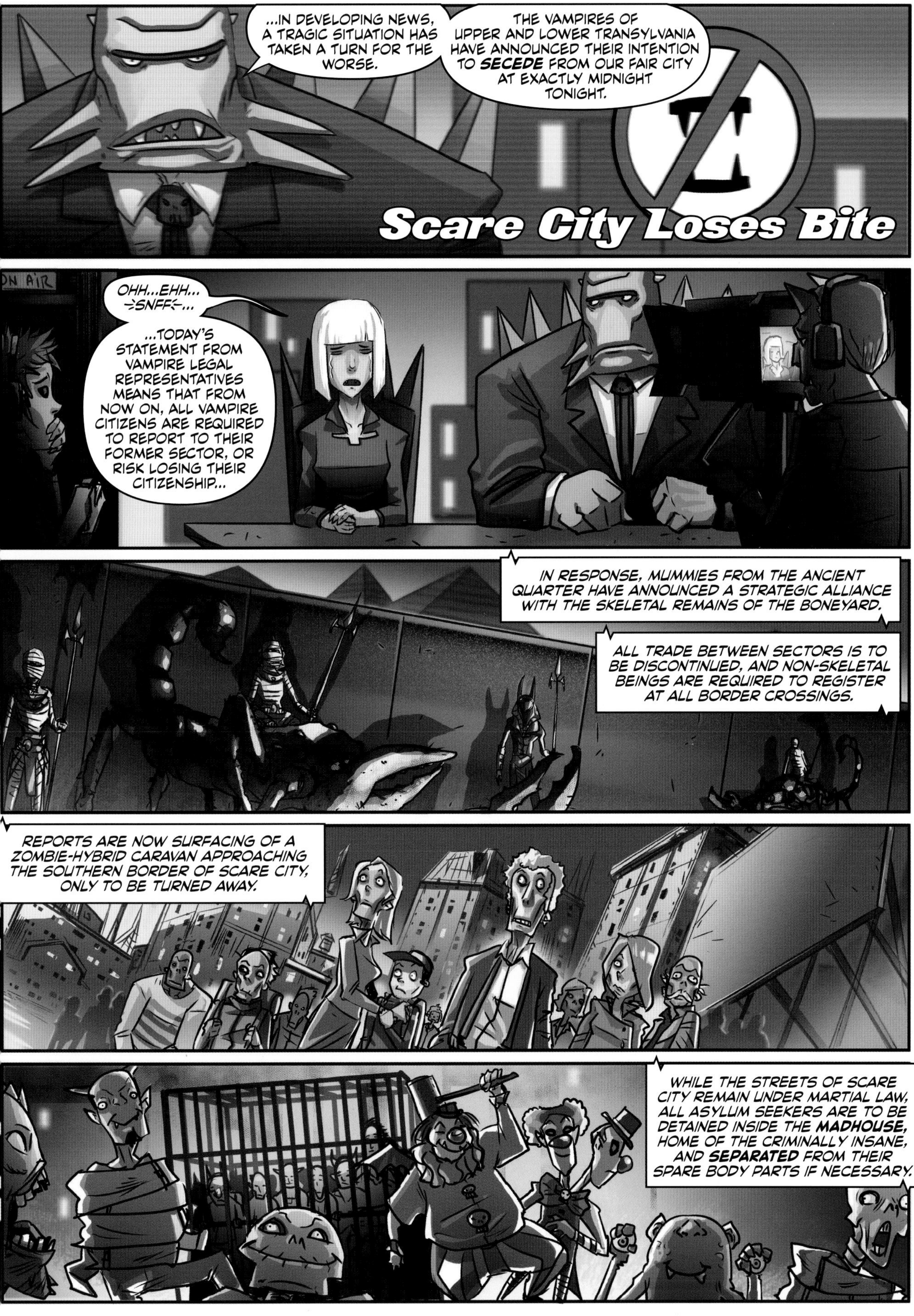
...IN DEVELOPING NEWS, A TRAGIC SITUATION HAS TAKEN A TURN FOR THE WORSE.
THE VAMPIRES OF UPPER AND LOWER TRANSYLVANIA HAVE ANNOUNCED THEIR INTENTION TO **SECEDE** FROM OUR FAIR CITY AT EXACTLY MIDNIGHT TONIGHT.
Scare City Loses Bite
ON AIR
OHH...EHH... >SNFF<...
...TODAY'S STATEMENT FROM VAMPIRE LEGAL REPRESENTATIVES MEANS THAT FROM NOW ON, ALL VAMPIRE CITIZENS ARE REQUIRED TO REPORT TO THEIR FORMER SECTOR, OR RISK LOSING THEIR CITIZENSHIP...
IN RESPONSE, MUMMIES FROM THE ANCIENT QUARTER HAVE ANNOUNCED A STRATEGIC ALLIANCE WITH THE SKELETAL REMAINS OF THE BONEYARD.
ALL TRADE BETWEEN SECTORS IS TO BE DISCONTINUED, AND NON-SKELETAL BEINGS ARE REQUIRED TO REGISTER AT ALL BORDER CROSSINGS.
REPORTS ARE NOW SURFACING OF A ZOMBIE-HYBRID CARAVAN APPROACHING THE SOUTHERN BORDER OF SCARE CITY, ONLY TO BE TURNED AWAY.
WHILE THE STREETS OF SCARE CITY REMAIN UNDER MARTIAL LAW, ALL ASYLUM SEEKERS ARE TO BE DETAINED INSIDE THE **MADHOUSE**, HOME OF THE CRIMINALLY INSANE, AND **SEPARATED** FROM THEIR SPARE BODY PARTS IF NECESSARY.

MEANWHILE, BOTH VAMPIRE SECTORS AND THE LUPINE FOREST ARE NOW OFFICIALLY IN A STATE OF WAR. ROVING BANDS OF BLOODTHIRSTY VAMPIRES AND WEREWOLVES HAVE BEEN SPOTTED MASSING AT THE BORDER.

CITIZENS ARE ADVISED TO STAY IN THEIR HOMES AND AWAIT FURTHER INSTRUCTION IN ANTICIPATION OF WEREWOLF/VAMPIRE HOSTILITIES.

AUTHORITIES ARE EXPECTING A **BLOODBATH.**

HMF. I SUPPOSE WE MUST **HATE** EACH OTHER NOW, FOWLER?

THAT'S WHAT IT SAYS ON THE **NEWS,** PHILIP.

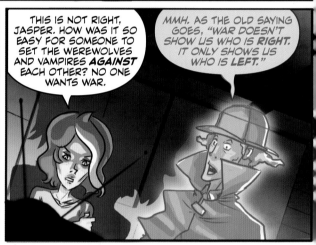

THIS IS NOT RIGHT, JASPER. HOW WAS IT SO EASY FOR SOMEONE TO SET THE WEREWOLVES AND VAMPIRES **AGAINST** EACH OTHER? NO ONE WANTS WAR.

MMH. AS THE OLD SAYING GOES, "WAR DOESN'T SHOW US WHO IS **RIGHT.** IT ONLY SHOWS US WHO IS **LEFT.**"

WE MUST **DO** SOMETHING, GINA. WHATEVER WE **CAN,** AS SOON AS POSSIBLE.

BECAUSE IF WE **FAIL,** THE WARMONGERS **WIN.**

WE CAN'T JUST STAY IN HIDING FOREVER.

OH, I DON'T KNOW, MISTER PIKE... I'VE BEEN DOWN HERE FOR MILLENNIA.

YOU GET QUITE **USED** TO IT AFTER A WHILE.

92

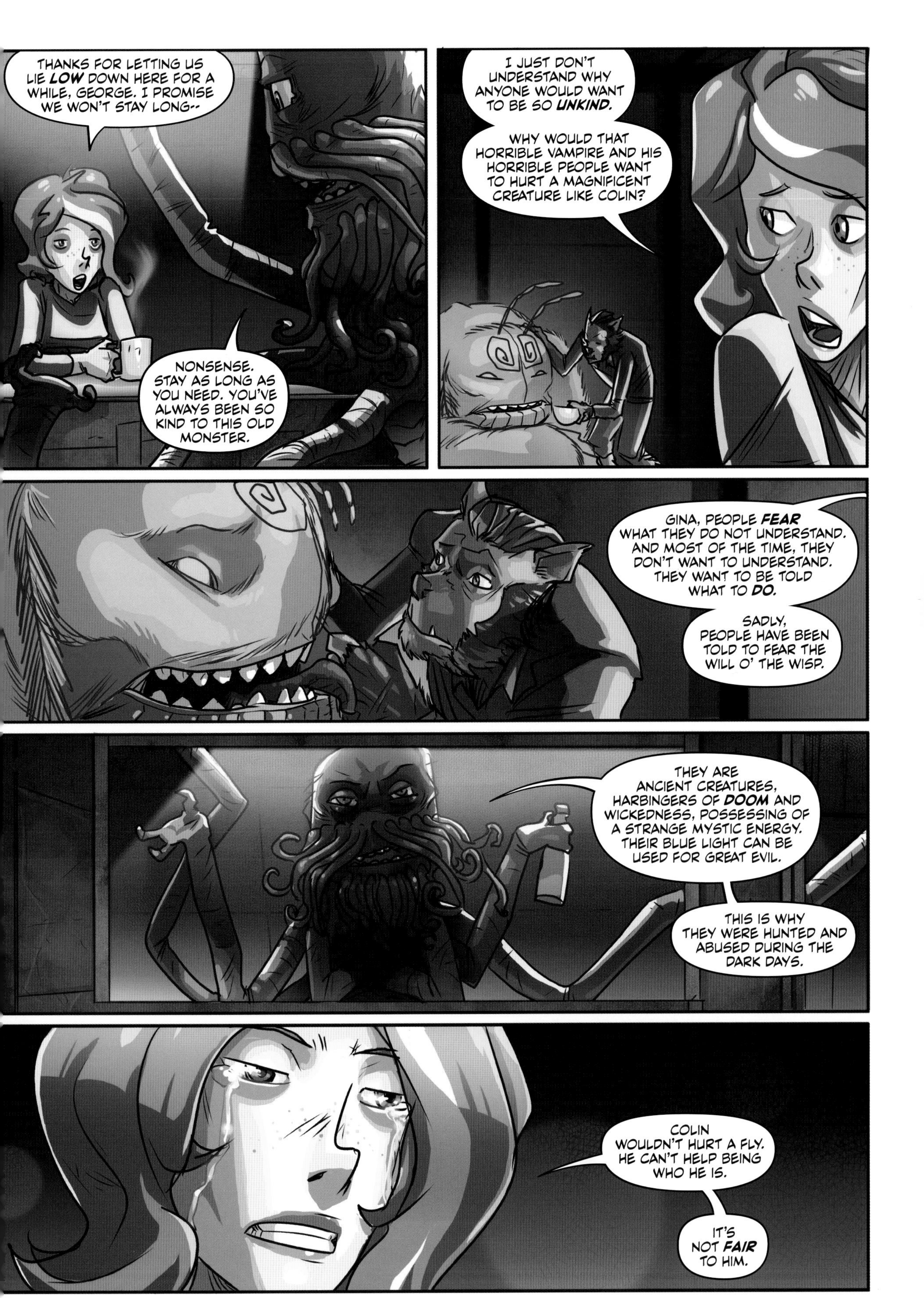
THANKS FOR LETTING US LIE LOW DOWN HERE FOR A WHILE, GEORGE. I PROMISE WE WON'T STAY LONG--
NONSENSE. STAY AS LONG AS YOU NEED. YOU'VE ALWAYS BEEN SO KIND TO THIS OLD MONSTER.
I JUST DON'T UNDERSTAND WHY ANYONE WOULD WANT TO BE SO UNKIND.
WHY WOULD THAT HORRIBLE VAMPIRE AND HIS HORRIBLE PEOPLE WANT TO HURT A MAGNIFICENT CREATURE LIKE COLIN?
GINA, PEOPLE FEAR WHAT THEY DO NOT UNDERSTAND. AND MOST OF THE TIME, THEY DON'T WANT TO UNDERSTAND. THEY WANT TO BE TOLD WHAT TO DO.
SADLY, PEOPLE HAVE BEEN TOLD TO FEAR THE WILL O' THE WISP.
THEY ARE ANCIENT CREATURES, HARBINGERS OF DOOM AND WICKEDNESS, POSSESSING OF A STRANGE MYSTIC ENERGY. THEIR BLUE LIGHT CAN BE USED FOR GREAT EVIL.
THIS IS WHY THEY WERE HUNTED AND ABUSED DURING THE DARK DAYS.
COLIN WOULDN'T HURT A FLY. HE CAN'T HELP BEING WHO HE IS.
IT'S NOT FAIR TO HIM.

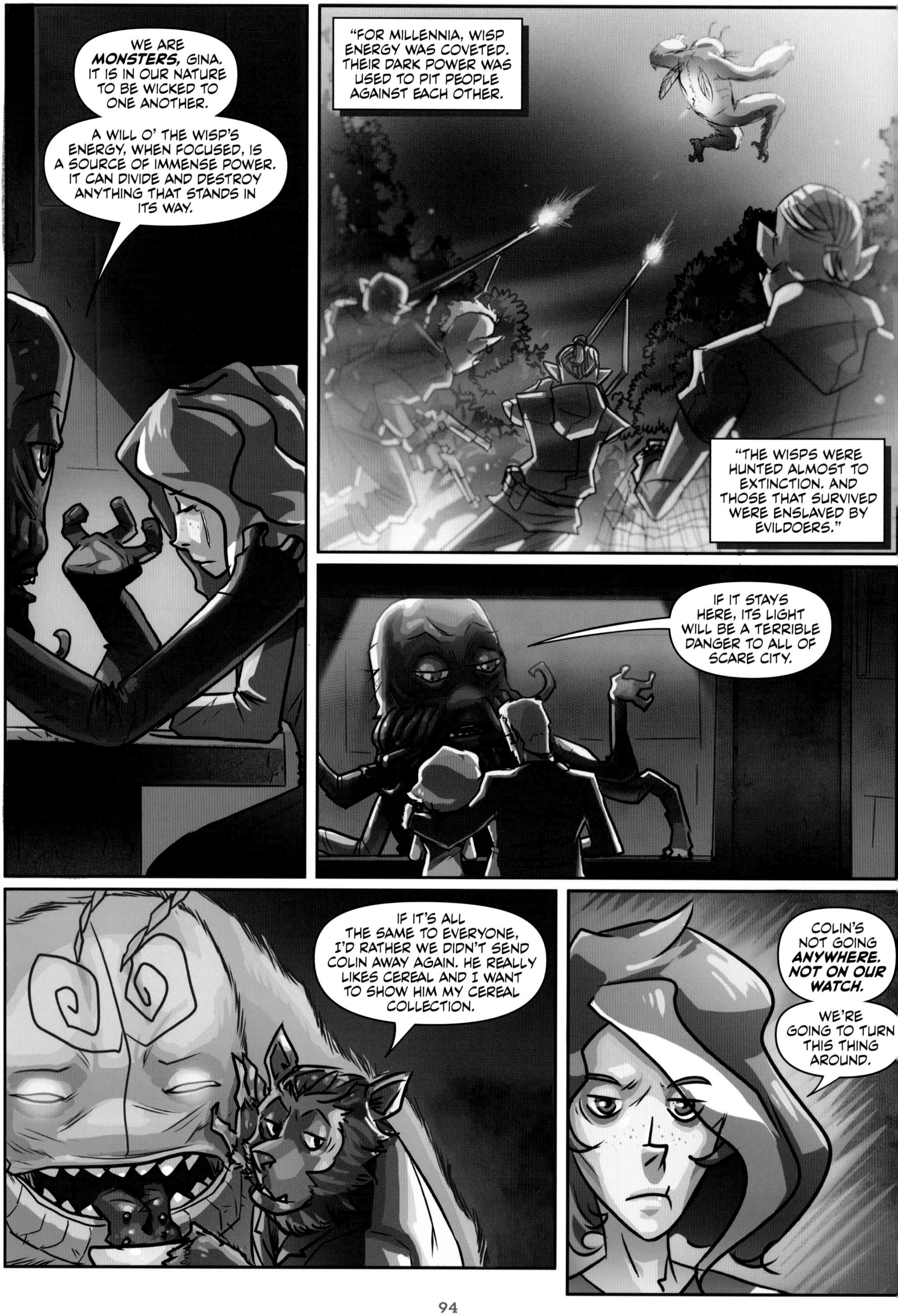
WE ARE **MONSTERS,** GINA. IT IS IN OUR NATURE TO BE WICKED TO ONE ANOTHER.
A WILL O' THE WISP'S ENERGY, WHEN FOCUSED, IS A SOURCE OF IMMENSE POWER. IT CAN DIVIDE AND DESTROY ANYTHING THAT STANDS IN ITS WAY.
"FOR MILLENNIA, WISP ENERGY WAS COVETED. THEIR DARK POWER WAS USED TO PIT PEOPLE AGAINST EACH OTHER.
"THE WISPS WERE HUNTED ALMOST TO EXTINCTION. AND THOSE THAT SURVIVED WERE ENSLAVED BY EVILDOERS."
IF IT STAYS HERE, ITS LIGHT WILL BE A TERRIBLE DANGER TO ALL OF SCARE CITY.
IF IT'S ALL THE SAME TO EVERYONE, I'D RATHER WE DIDN'T SEND COLIN AWAY AGAIN. HE REALLY LIKES CEREAL AND I WANT TO SHOW HIM MY CEREAL COLLECTION.
COLIN'S NOT GOING ***ANYWHERE. NOT ON OUR WATCH.***
WE'RE GOING TO TURN THIS THING AROUND.

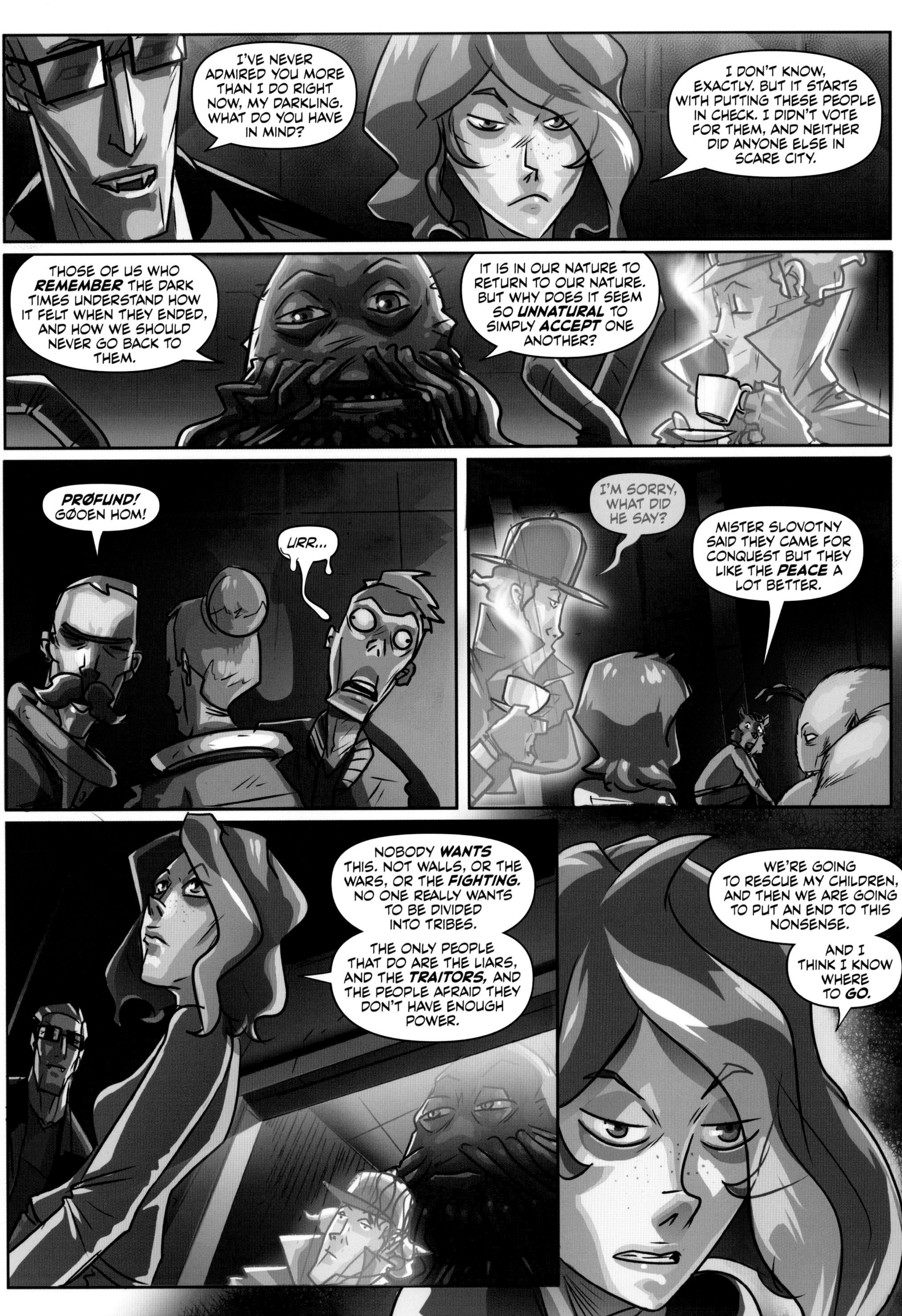

I'VE NEVER ADMIRED YOU MORE THAN I DO RIGHT NOW, MY DARKLING. WHAT DO YOU HAVE IN MIND?
I DON'T KNOW, EXACTLY. BUT IT STARTS WITH PUTTING THESE PEOPLE IN CHECK. I DIDN'T VOTE FOR THEM, AND NEITHER DID ANYONE ELSE IN SCARE CITY.
THOSE OF US WHO ***REMEMBER*** THE DARK TIMES UNDERSTAND HOW IT FELT WHEN THEY ENDED, AND HOW WE SHOULD NEVER GO BACK TO THEM.
IT IS IN OUR NATURE TO RETURN TO OUR NATURE. BUT WHY DOES IT SEEM SO ***UNNATURAL*** TO SIMPLY ***ACCEPT*** ONE ANOTHER?
PRØFUND! GØOEN HOM!
URR...
I'M SORRY, WHAT DID HE SAY?
MISTER SLOVOTNY SAID THEY CAME FOR CONQUEST BUT THEY LIKE THE ***PEACE*** A LOT BETTER.
NOBODY ***WANTS*** THIS. NOT WALLS, OR THE WARS, OR THE ***FIGHTING.*** NO ONE REALLY WANTS TO BE DIVIDED INTO TRIBES.
THE ONLY PEOPLE THAT DO ARE THE LIARS, AND THE ***TRAITORS,*** AND THE PEOPLE AFRAID THEY DON'T HAVE ENOUGH POWER.
WE'RE GOING TO RESCUE MY CHILDREN, AND THEN WE ARE GOING TO PUT AN END TO THIS NONSENSE.
AND I THINK I KNOW WHERE TO ***GO.***

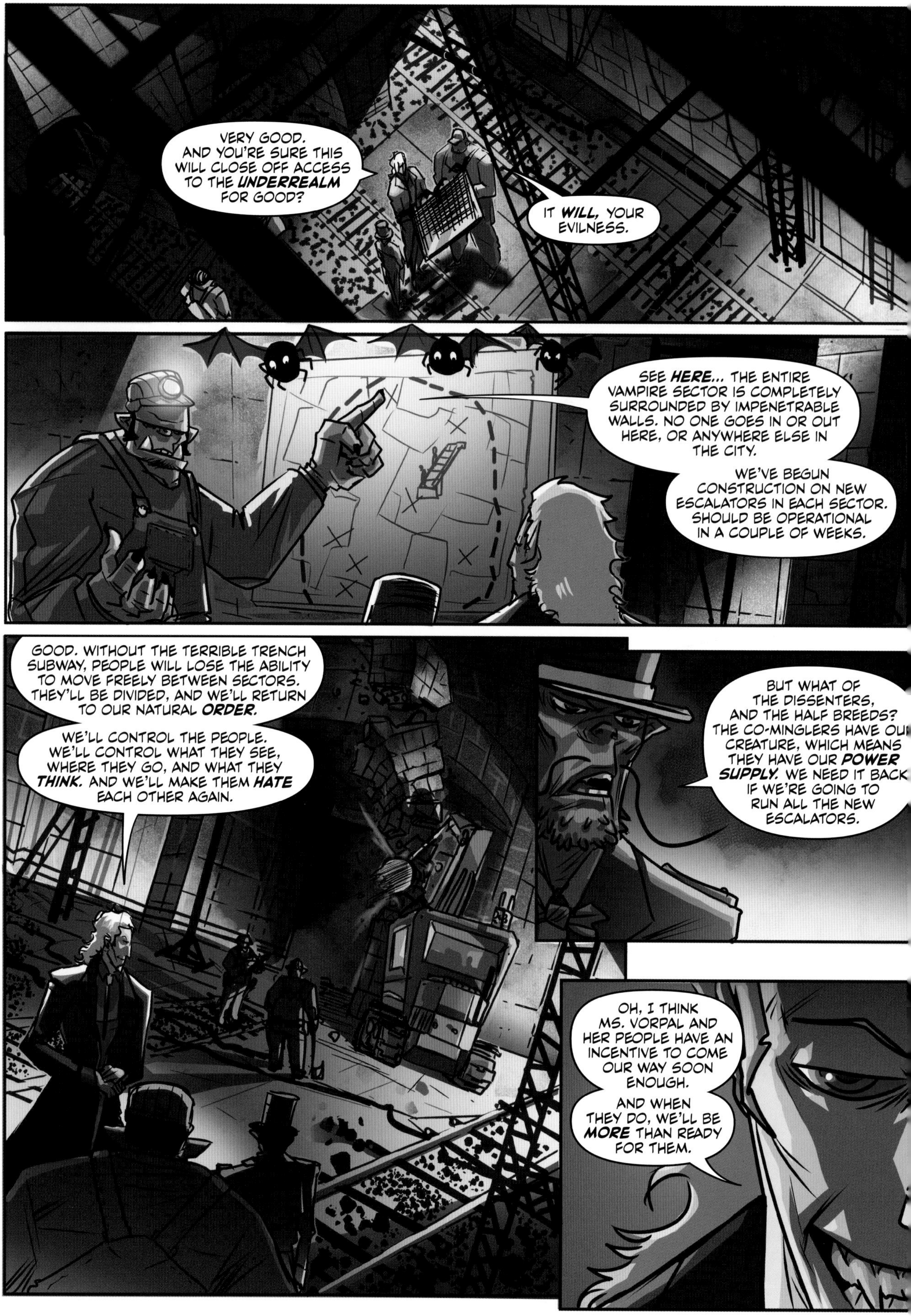
VERY GOOD. AND YOU'RE SURE THIS WILL CLOSE OFF ACCESS TO THE *UNDERREALM* FOR GOOD?
IT *WILL,* YOUR EVILNESS.
SEE *HERE...* THE ENTIRE VAMPIRE SECTOR IS COMPLETELY SURROUNDED BY IMPENETRABLE WALLS. NO ONE GOES IN OR OUT HERE, OR ANYWHERE ELSE IN THE CITY.
WE'VE BEGUN CONSTRUCTION ON NEW ESCALATORS IN EACH SECTOR. SHOULD BE OPERATIONAL IN A COUPLE OF WEEKS.
GOOD. WITHOUT THE TERRIBLE TRENCH SUBWAY, PEOPLE WILL LOSE THE ABILITY TO MOVE FREELY BETWEEN SECTORS. THEY'LL BE DIVIDED, AND WE'LL RETURN TO OUR NATURAL *ORDER.*
WE'LL CONTROL THE PEOPLE. WE'LL CONTROL WHAT THEY SEE, WHERE THEY GO, AND WHAT THEY *THINK.* AND WE'LL MAKE THEM *HATE* EACH OTHER AGAIN.
BUT WHAT OF THE DISSENTERS, AND THE HALF BREEDS? THE CO-MINGLERS HAVE OU CREATURE, WHICH MEANS THEY HAVE OUR *POWER SUPPLY.* WE NEED IT BACK IF WE'RE GOING TO RUN ALL THE NEW ESCALATORS.
OH, I THINK MS. VORPAL AND HER PEOPLE HAVE AN INCENTIVE TO COME OUR WAY SOON ENOUGH.
AND WHEN THEY DO, WE'LL BE *MORE* THAN READY FOR THEM.

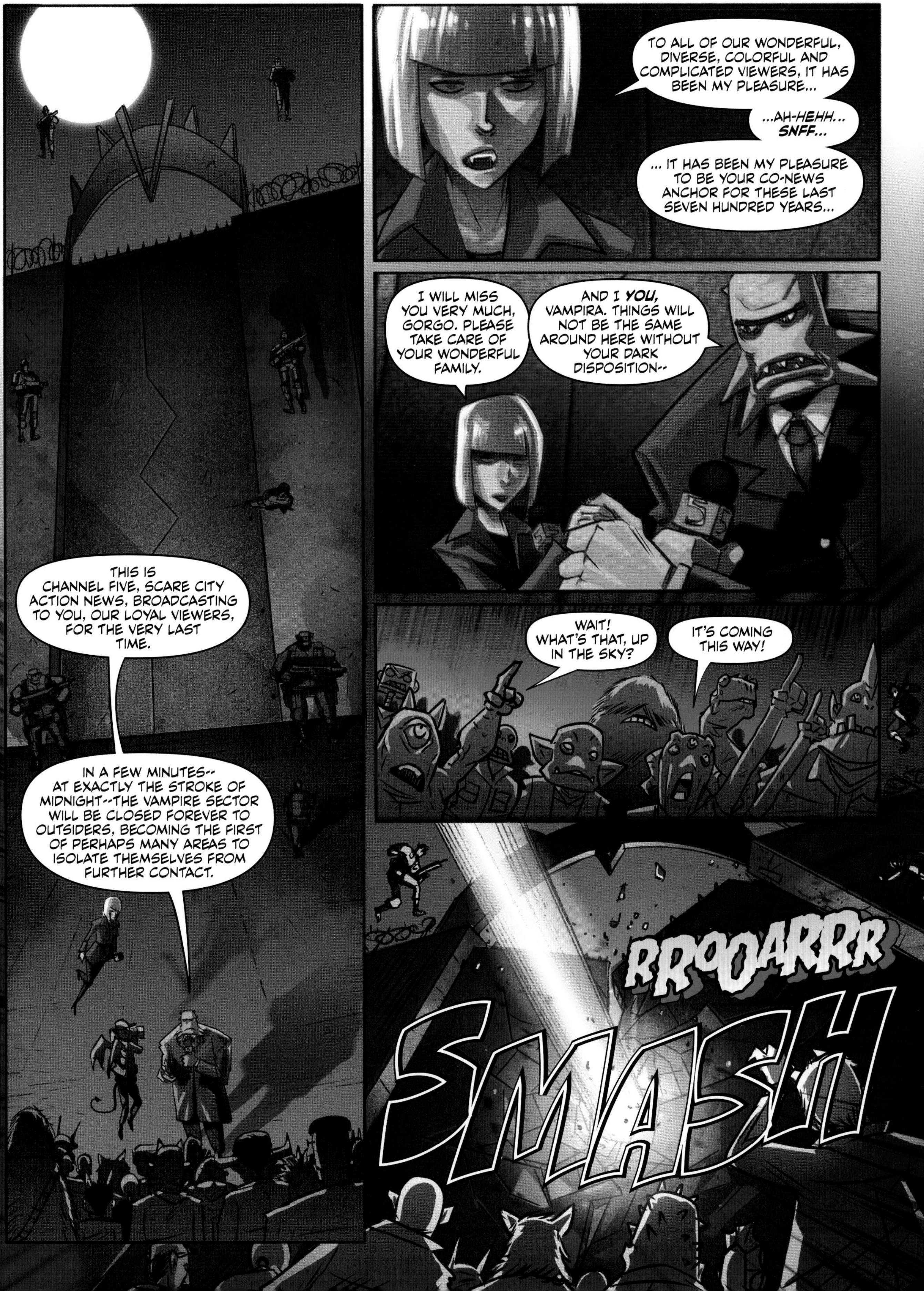
THIS IS CHANNEL FIVE, SCARE CITY ACTION NEWS, BROADCASTING TO YOU, OUR LOYAL VIEWERS, FOR THE VERY LAST TIME.
IN A FEW MINUTES-- AT EXACTLY THE STROKE OF MIDNIGHT--THE VAMPIRE SECTOR WILL BE CLOSED FOREVER TO OUTSIDERS, BECOMING THE FIRST OF PERHAPS MANY AREAS TO ISOLATE THEMSELVES FROM FURTHER CONTACT.
TO ALL OF OUR WONDERFUL, DIVERSE, COLORFUL AND COMPLICATED VIEWERS, IT HAS BEEN MY PLEASURE...
...AH-HEHH... SNFF...
... IT HAS BEEN MY PLEASURE TO BE YOUR CO-NEWS ANCHOR FOR THESE LAST SEVEN HUNDRED YEARS...
I WILL MISS YOU VERY MUCH, GORGO. PLEASE TAKE CARE OF YOUR WONDERFUL FAMILY.
AND I YOU, VAMPIRA. THINGS WILL NOT BE THE SAME AROUND HERE WITHOUT YOUR DARK DISPOSITION--
WAIT! WHAT'S THAT, UP IN THE SKY?
IT'S COMING THIS WAY!
RROOARRR
SMASH

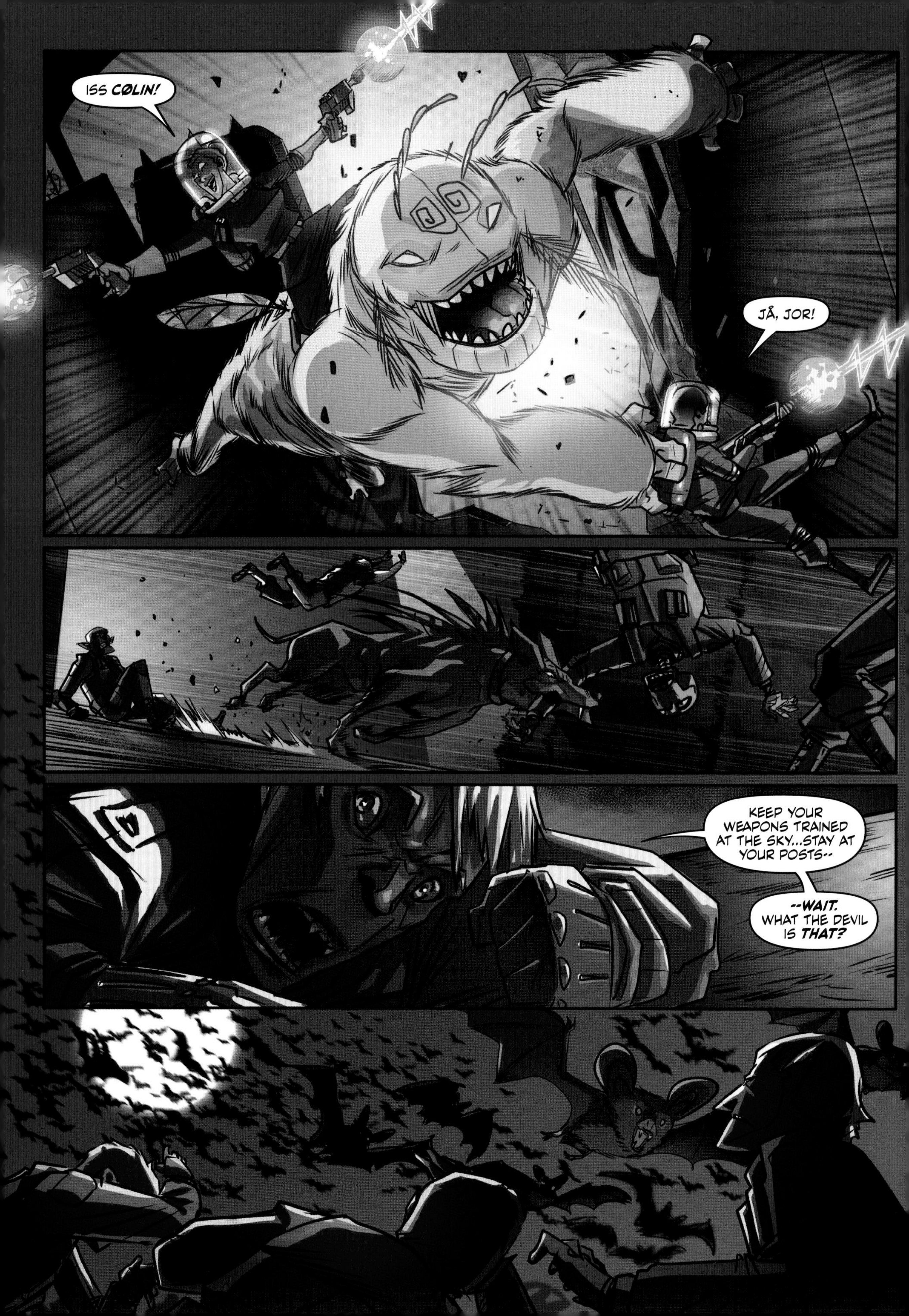
ISS COLIN!
JÅ, JOR!
KEEP YOUR WEAPONS TRAINED AT THE SKY...STAY AT YOUR POSTS--
--WAIT. WHAT THE DEVIL IS THAT?

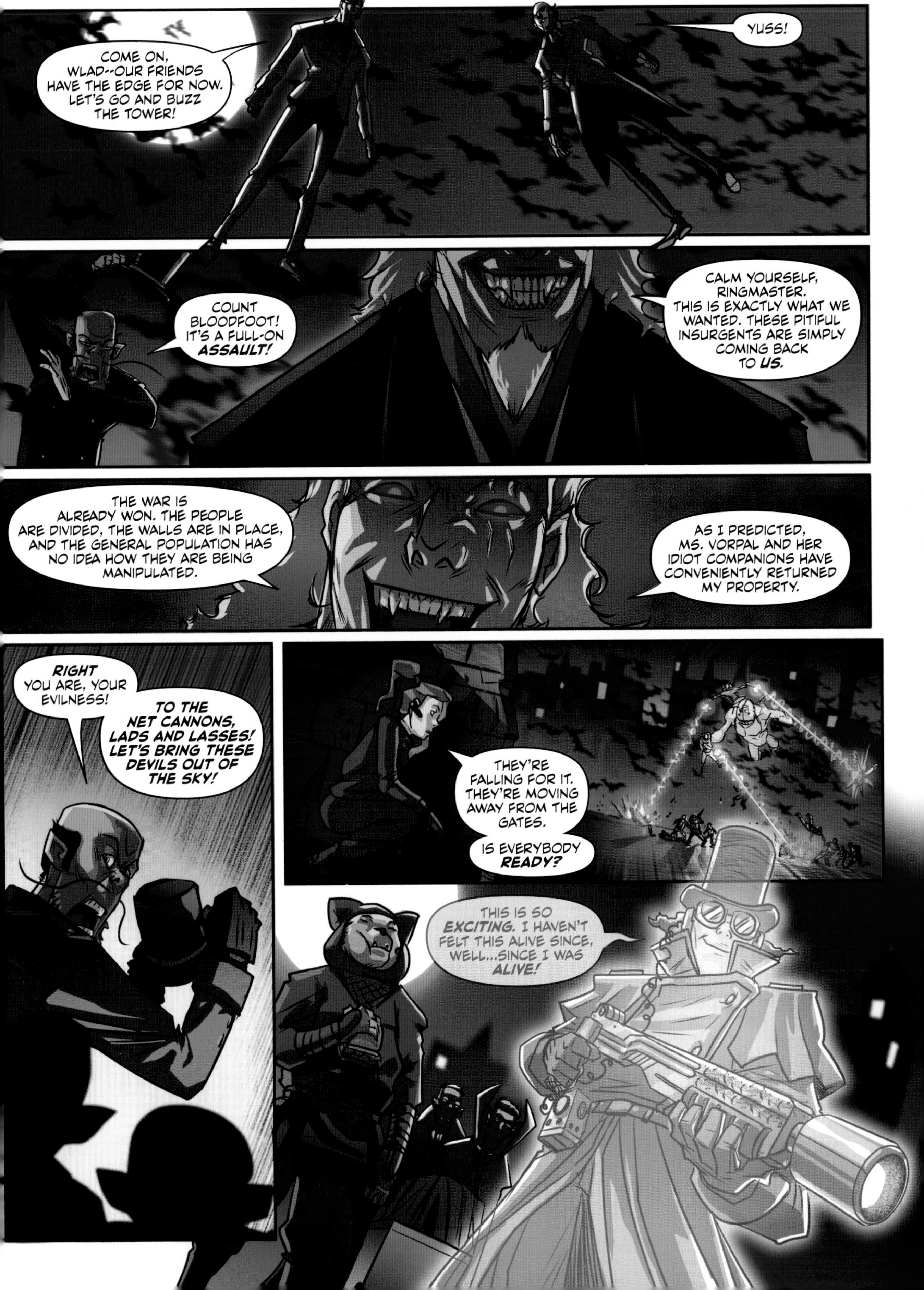

COME ON, WLAD--OUR FRIENDS HAVE THE EDGE FOR NOW. LET'S GO AND BUZZ THE TOWER!
YUSS!
COUNT BLOODFOOT! IT'S A FULL-ON ***ASSAULT!***
CALM YOURSELF, RINGMASTER. THIS IS EXACTLY WHAT WE WANTED. THESE PITIFUL INSURGENTS ARE SIMPLY COMING BACK TO ***US.***
THE WAR IS ALREADY WON. THE PEOPLE ARE DIVIDED, THE WALLS ARE IN PLACE, AND THE GENERAL POPULATION HAS NO IDEA HOW THEY ARE BEING MANIPULATED.
AS I PREDICTED, MS. VORPAL AND HER IDIOT COMPANIONS HAVE CONVENIENTLY RETURNED MY PROPERTY.
RIGHT YOU ARE, YOUR EVILNESS!
TO THE NET CANNONS, LADS AND LASSES! LET'S BRING THESE DEVILS OUT OF THE SKY!
THEY'RE FALLING FOR IT. THEY'RE MOVING AWAY FROM THE GATES.
IS EVERYBODY ***READY?***
THIS IS SO ***EXCITING.*** I HAVEN'T FELT THIS ALIVE SINCE, WELL...SINCE I WAS ***ALIVE!***

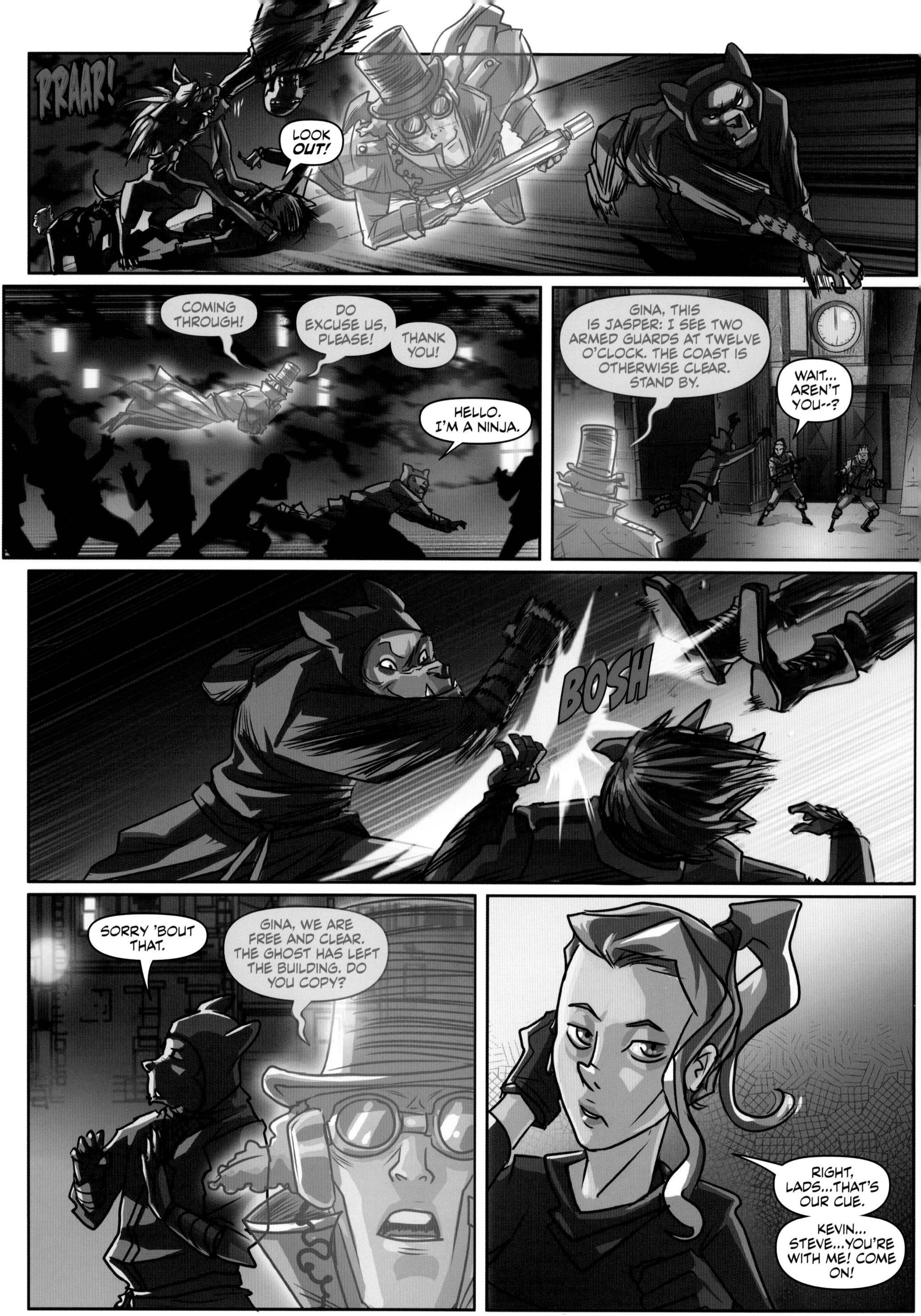
RRAAR!
LOOK OUT!
COMING THROUGH!
DO EXCUSE US, PLEASE!
THANK YOU!
HELLO. I'M A NINJA.
GINA, THIS IS JASPER: I SEE TWO ARMED GUARDS AT TWELVE O'CLOCK. THE COAST IS OTHERWISE CLEAR. STAND BY.
WAIT... AREN'T YOU--?
BOSH
SORRY 'BOUT THAT.
GINA, WE ARE FREE AND CLEAR. THE GHOST HAS LEFT THE BUILDING. DO YOU COPY?
RIGHT, LADS...THAT'S OUR CUE.
KEVIN... STEVE...YOU'RE WITH ME! COME ON!

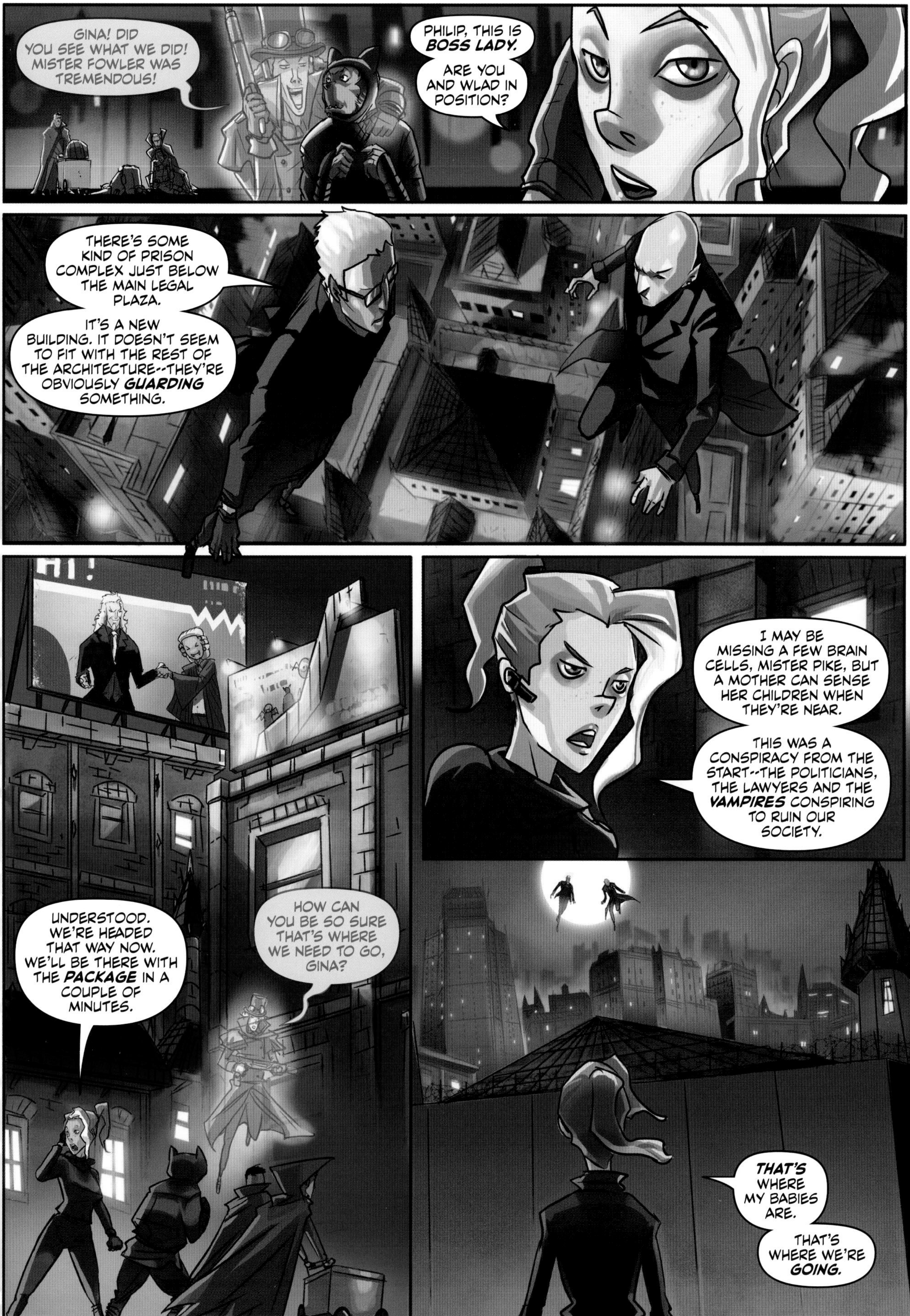

GINA! DID YOU SEE WHAT WE DID! MISTER FOWLER WAS TREMENDOUS!
PHILIP, THIS IS **BOSS LADY.**
ARE YOU AND WLAD IN POSITION?
THERE'S SOME KIND OF PRISON COMPLEX JUST BELOW THE MAIN LEGAL PLAZA.
IT'S A NEW BUILDING. IT DOESN'T SEEM TO FIT WITH THE REST OF THE ARCHITECTURE--THEY'RE OBVIOUSLY **GUARDING** SOMETHING.
UNDERSTOOD. WE'RE HEADED THAT WAY NOW. WE'LL BE THERE WITH THE **PACKAGE** IN A COUPLE OF MINUTES.
HOW CAN YOU BE SO SURE THAT'S WHERE WE NEED TO GO, GINA?
I MAY BE MISSING A FEW BRAIN CELLS, MISTER PIKE, BUT A MOTHER CAN SENSE HER CHILDREN WHEN THEY'RE NEAR.
THIS WAS A CONSPIRACY FROM THE START--THE POLITICIANS, THE LAWYERS AND THE ***VAMPIRES*** CONSPIRING TO RUIN OUR SOCIETY.
THAT'S WHERE MY BABIES ARE.
THAT'S WHERE WE'RE ***GOING.***

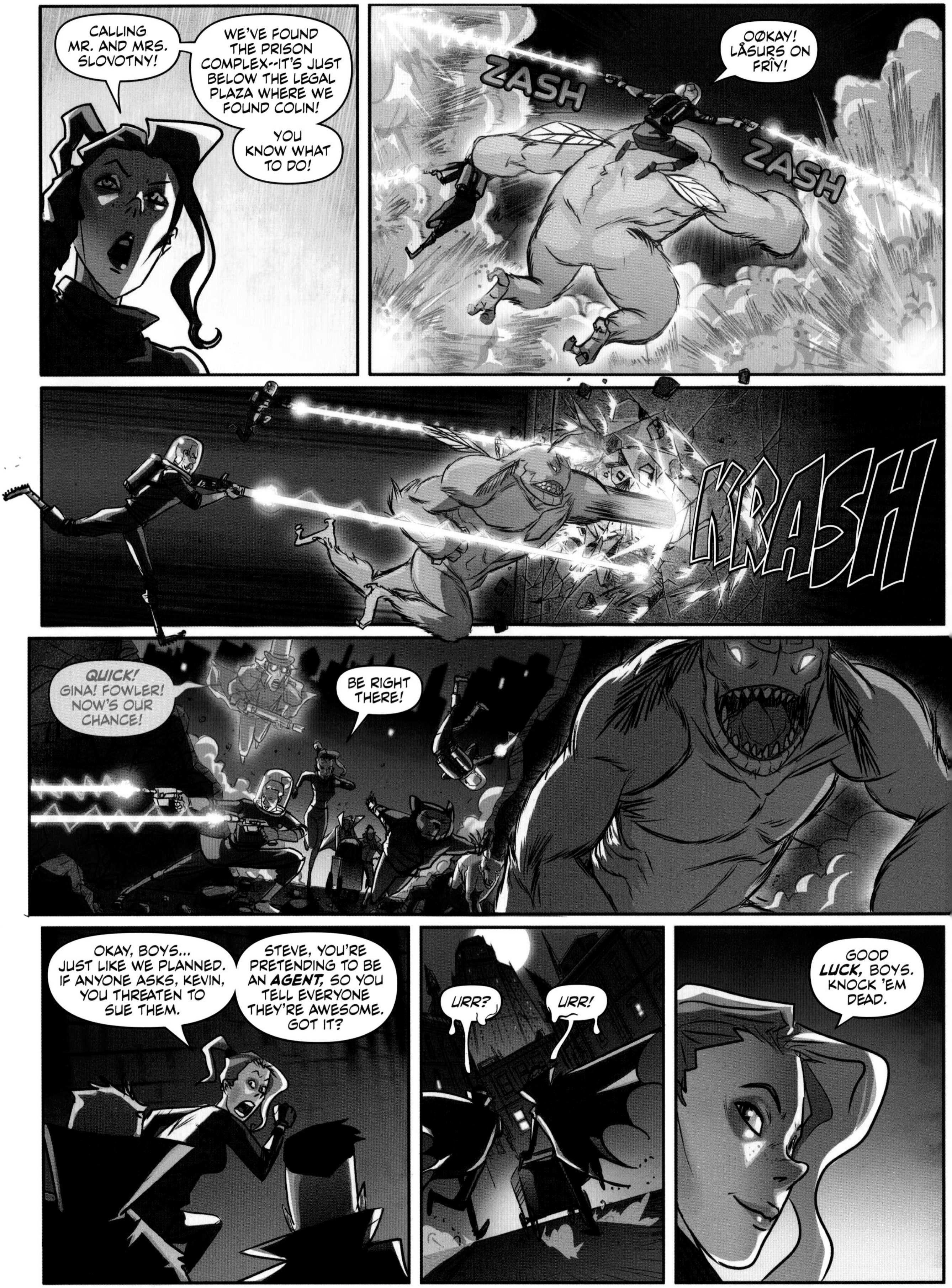
CALLING MR. AND MRS. SLOVOTNY!
WE'VE FOUND THE PRISON COMPLEX--IT'S JUST BELOW THE LEGAL PLAZA WHERE WE FOUND COLIN!
YOU KNOW WHAT TO DO!
ZASH
OØKAY! LÅSURS ON FRÎY!
ZASH
KRASH
QUICK! GINA! FOWLER! NOW'S OUR CHANCE!
BE RIGHT THERE!
OKAY, BOYS... JUST LIKE WE PLANNED. IF ANYONE ASKS, KEVIN, YOU THREATEN TO SUE THEM.
STEVE, YOU'RE PRETENDING TO BE AN AGENT, SO YOU TELL EVERYONE THEY'RE AWESOME. GOT IT?
URR?
URR!
GOOD LUCK, BOYS. KNOCK 'EM DEAD.

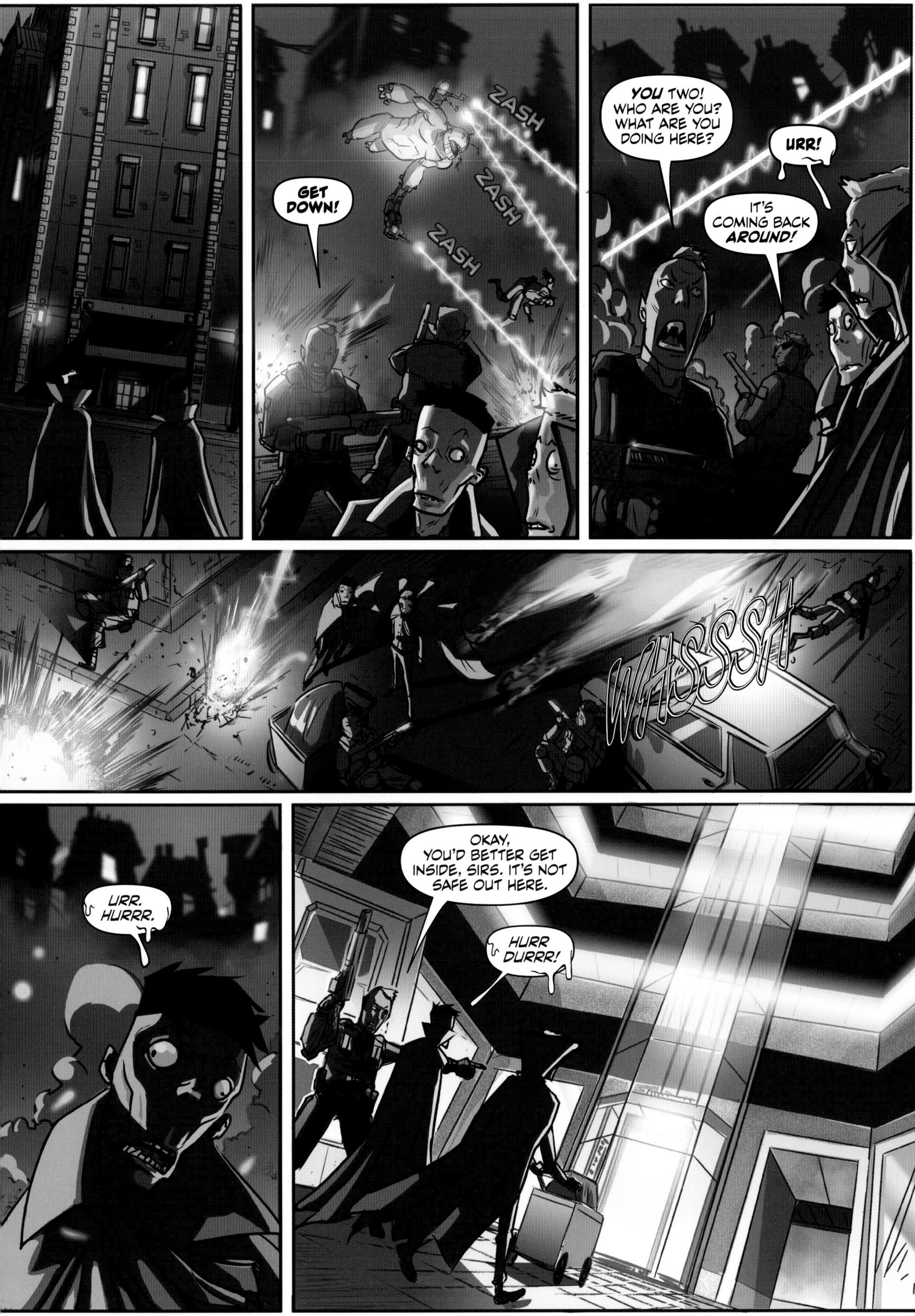
ZASH
ZASH
ZASH
GET DOWN!
YOU TWO! WHO ARE YOU? WHAT ARE YOU DOING HERE?
URR!
IT'S COMING BACK AROUND!
WHSSSH
URR. HURRR.
OKAY, YOU'D BETTER GET INSIDE, SIRS. IT'S NOT SAFE OUT HERE.
HURR DURRR!

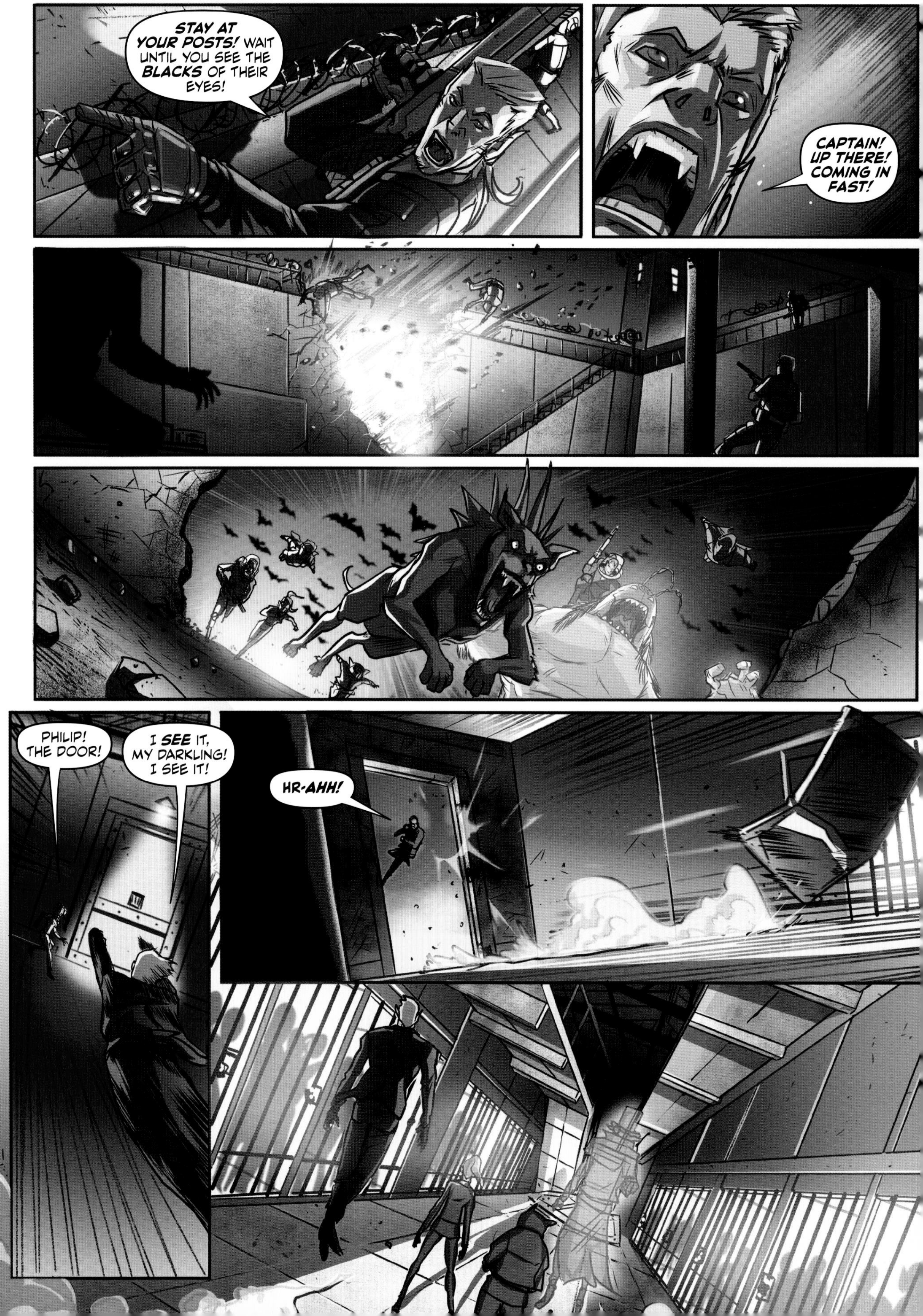
STAY AT YOUR POSTS! WAIT UNTIL YOU SEE THE BLACKS OF THEIR EYES!
CAPTAIN! UP THERE! COMING IN FAST!
PHILIP! THE DOOR!
I SEE IT, MY DARKLING! I SEE IT!
HR-AHH!

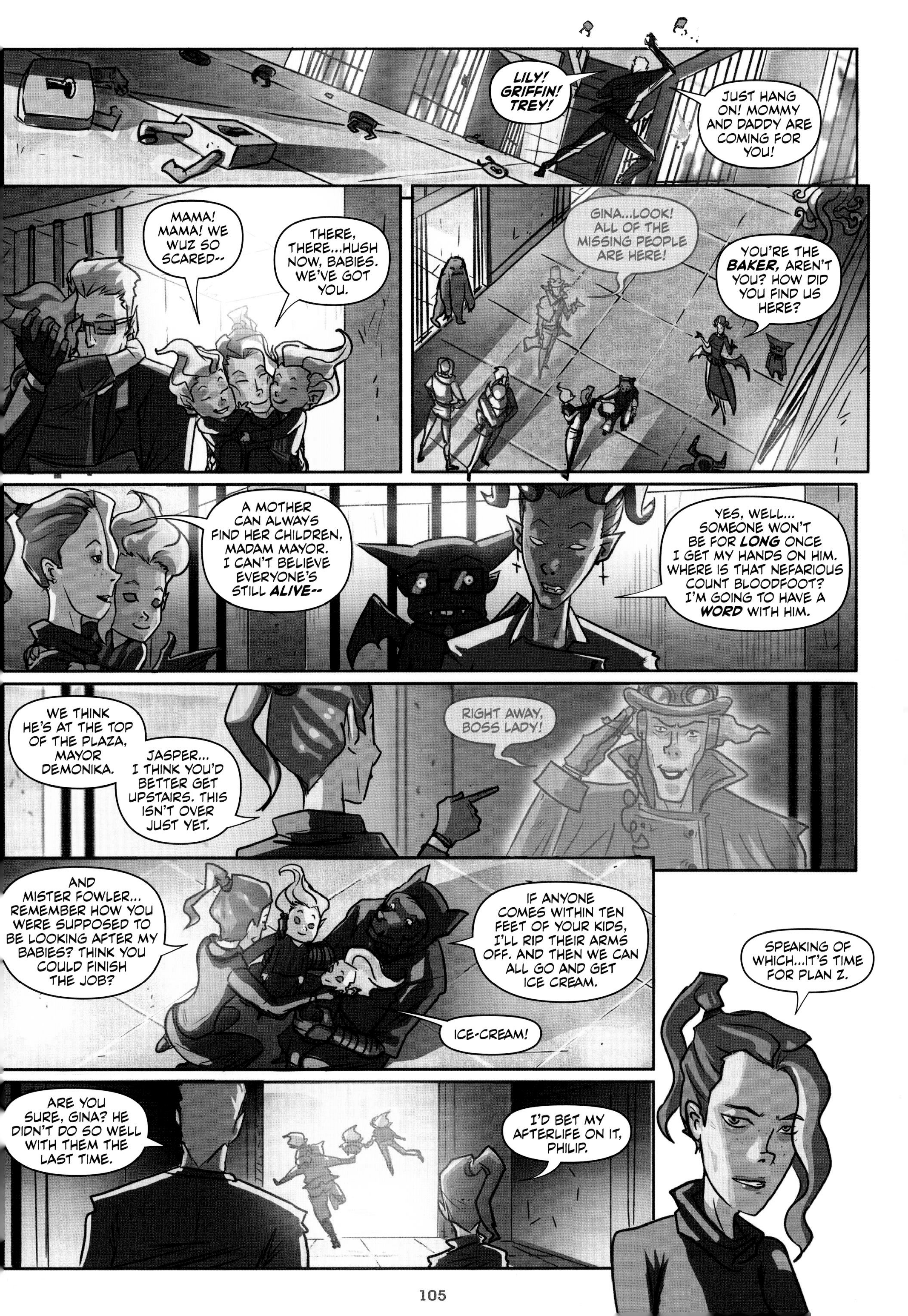
LILY! GRIFFIN! TREY!
JUST HANG ON! MOMMY AND DADDY ARE COMING FOR YOU!
MAMA! MAMA! WE WUZ SO SCARED--
THERE, THERE...HUSH NOW, BABIES. WE'VE GOT YOU.
GINA...LOOK! ALL OF THE MISSING PEOPLE ARE HERE!
YOU'RE THE BAKER, AREN'T YOU? HOW DID YOU FIND US HERE?
A MOTHER CAN ALWAYS FIND HER CHILDREN, MADAM MAYOR. I CAN'T BELIEVE EVERYONE'S STILL ALIVE--
YES, WELL... SOMEONE WON'T BE FOR LONG ONCE I GET MY HANDS ON HIM. WHERE IS THAT NEFARIOUS COUNT BLOODFOOT? I'M GOING TO HAVE A WORD WITH HIM.
WE THINK HE'S AT THE TOP OF THE PLAZA, MAYOR DEMONIKA.
JASPER... I THINK YOU'D BETTER GET UPSTAIRS. THIS ISN'T OVER JUST YET.
RIGHT AWAY, BOSS LADY!
AND MISTER FOWLER... REMEMBER HOW YOU WERE SUPPOSED TO BE LOOKING AFTER MY BABIES? THINK YOU COULD FINISH THE JOB?
IF ANYONE COMES WITHIN TEN FEET OF YOUR KIDS, I'LL RIP THEIR ARMS OFF. AND THEN WE CAN ALL GO AND GET ICE CREAM.
ICE-CREAM!
SPEAKING OF WHICH...IT'S TIME FOR PLAN Z.
ARE YOU SURE, GINA? HE DIDN'T DO SO WELL WITH THEM THE LAST TIME.
I'D BET MY AFTERLIFE ON IT, PHILIP.

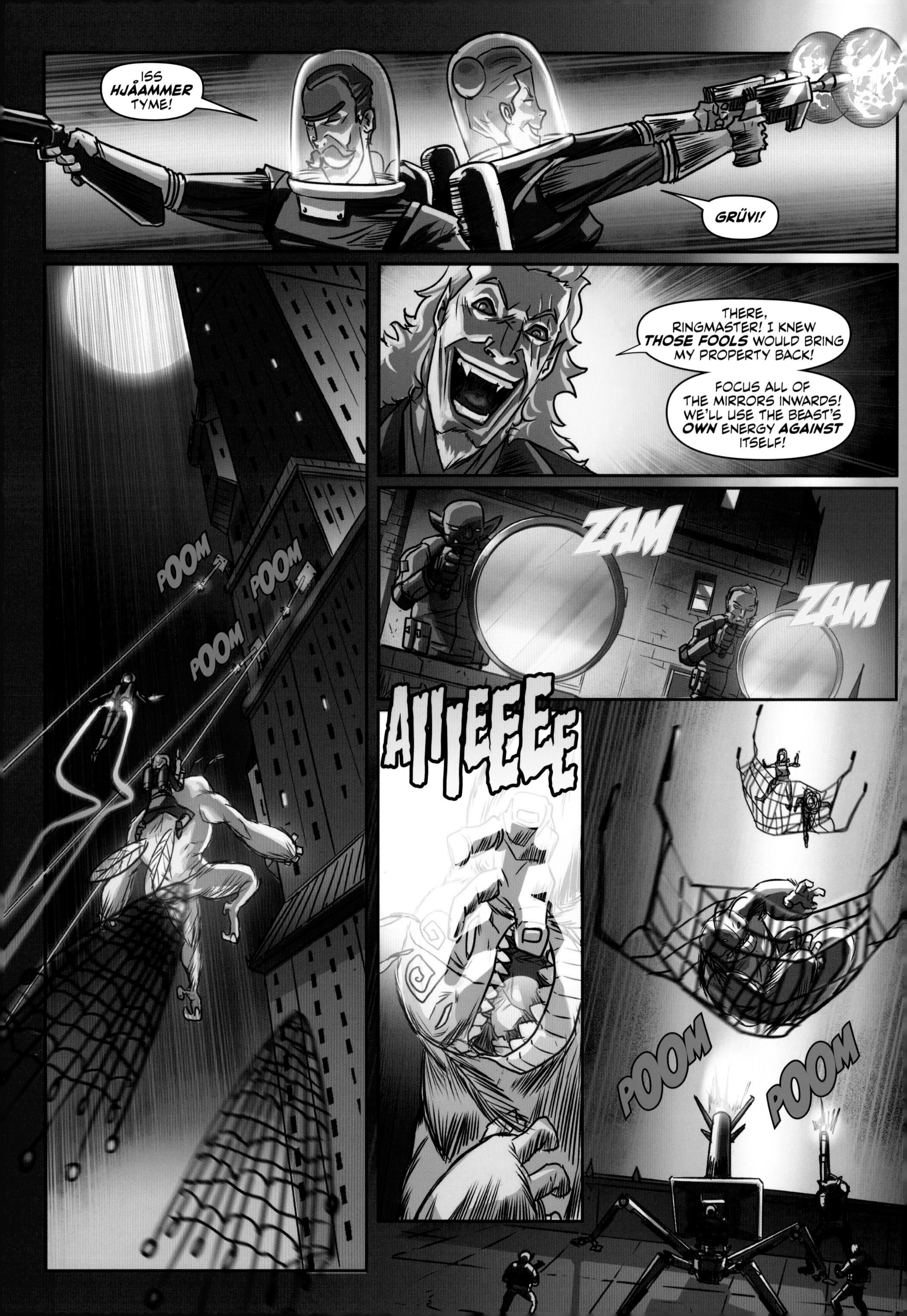
ISS HJÅAMMER TYME!
GRÜVI!
THERE, RINGMASTER! I KNEW THOSE FOOLS WOULD BRING MY PROPERTY BACK!
FOCUS ALL OF THE MIRRORS INWARDS! WE'LL USE THE BEAST'S OWN ENERGY AGAINST ITSELF!
POOM
POOM
POOM
ZAM
ZAM
AIIIEEEE
POOM
POOM

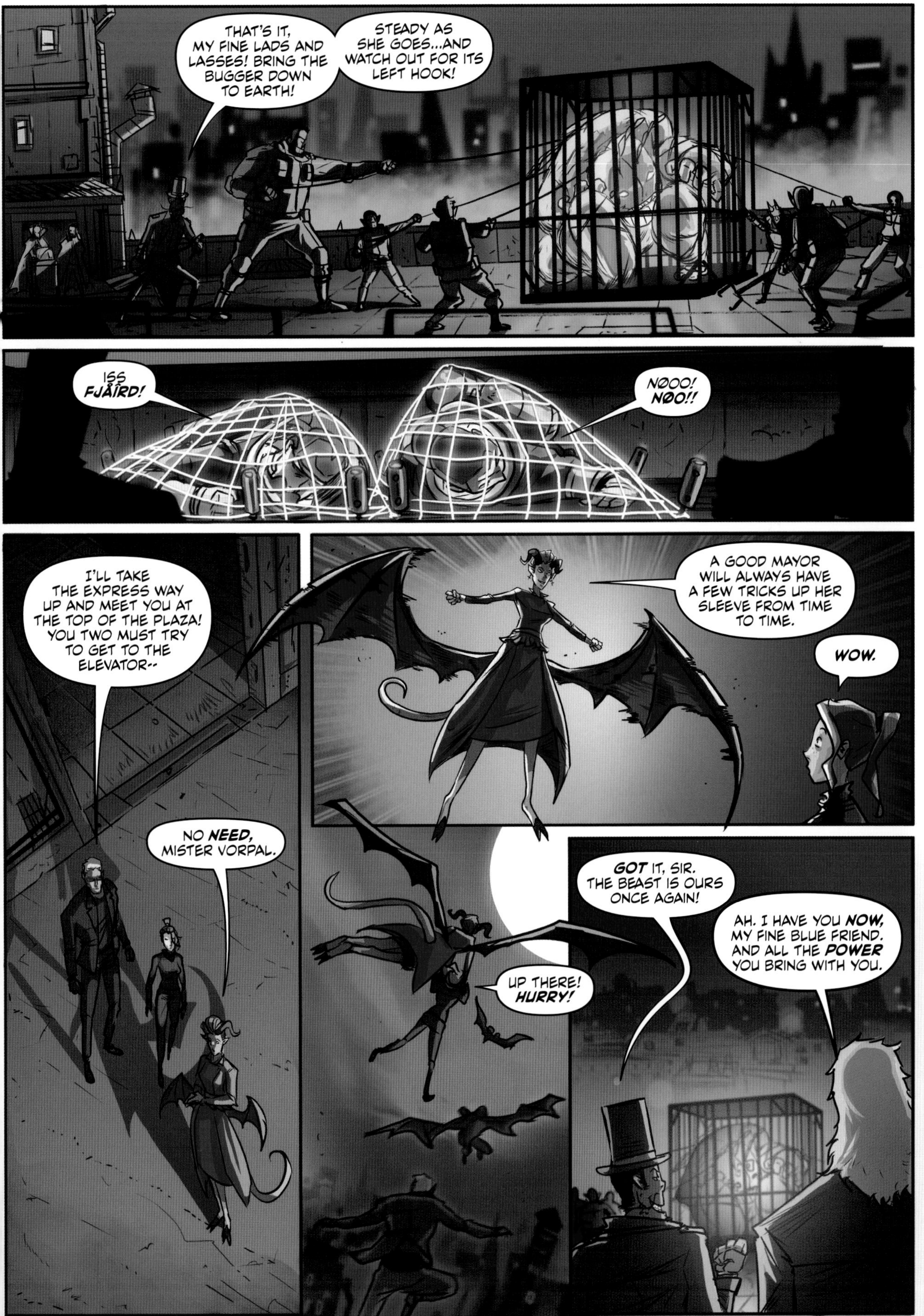
THAT'S IT, MY FINE LADS AND LASSES! BRING THE BUGGER DOWN TO EARTH!
STEADY AS SHE GOES...AND WATCH OUT FOR ITS LEFT HOOK!
ISS **FJÄIRD!**
NØOO! **NØO!!**
I'LL TAKE THE EXPRESS WAY UP AND MEET YOU AT THE TOP OF THE PLAZA! YOU TWO MUST TRY TO GET TO THE ELEVATOR--
A GOOD MAYOR WILL ALWAYS HAVE A FEW TRICKS UP HER SLEEVE FROM TIME TO TIME.
WOW.
NO **NEED,** MISTER VORPAL.
UP THERE! **HURRY!**
GOT IT, SIR. THE BEAST IS OURS ONCE AGAIN!
AH. I HAVE YOU **NOW,** MY FINE BLUE FRIEND. AND ALL THE **POWER** YOU BRING WITH YOU.

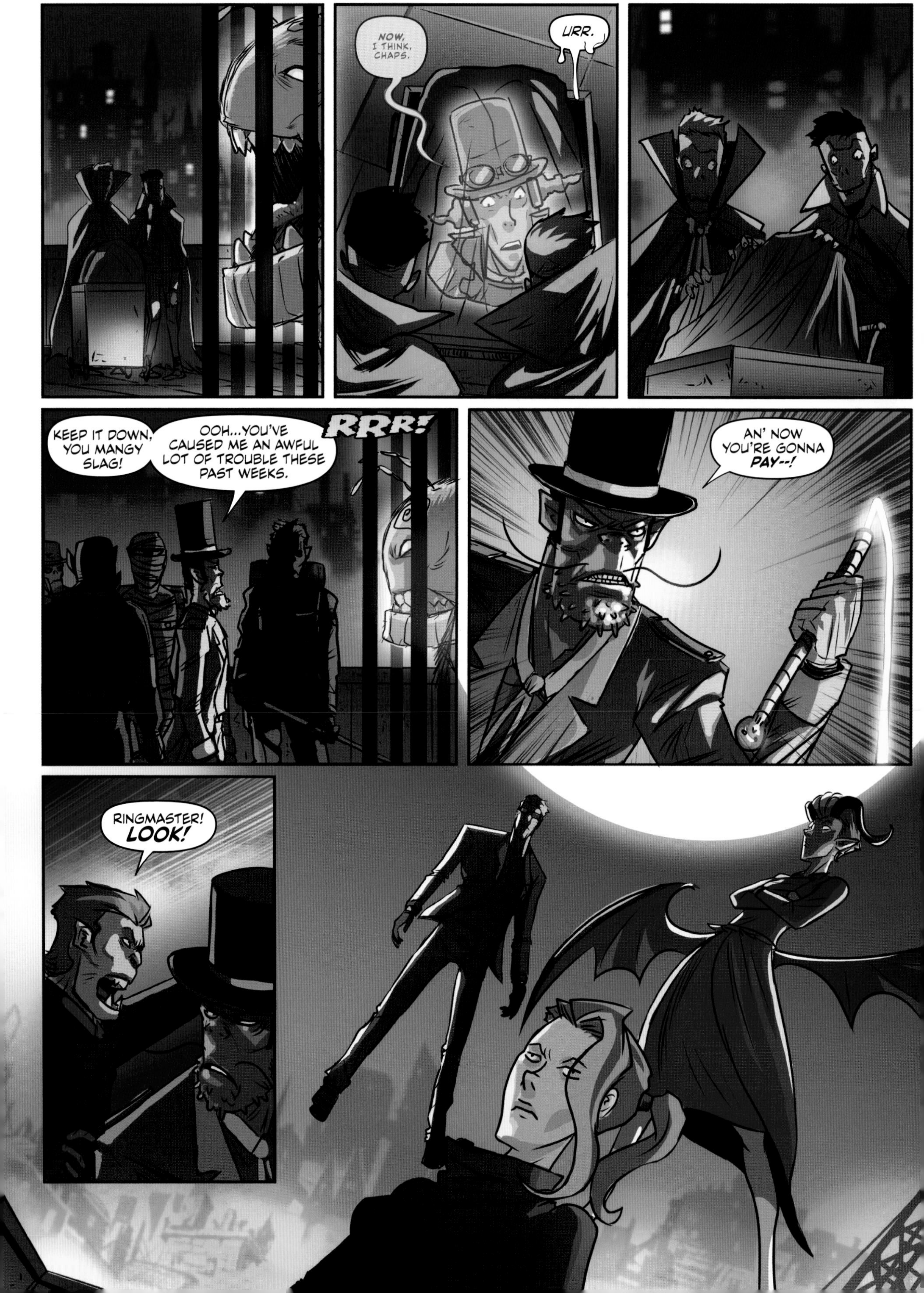
NOW. I THINK, CHAPS.
URR.
KEEP IT DOWN, YOU MANGY SLAG!
OOH...YOU'VE CAUSED ME AN AWFUL LOT OF TROUBLE THESE PAST WEEKS.
RRR!
AN' NOW YOU'RE GONNA PAY--!
RINGMASTER! LOOK!

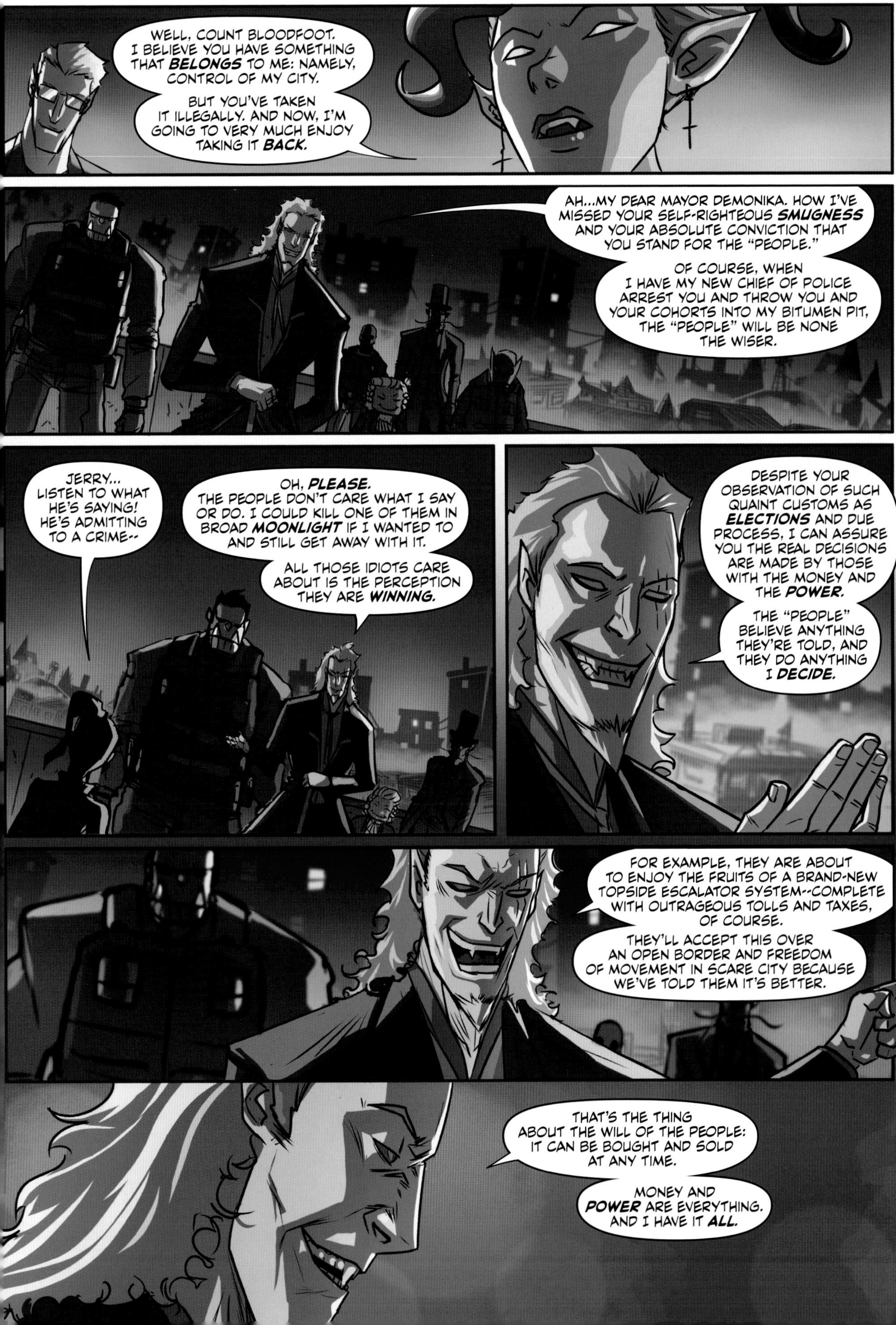
WELL, COUNT BLOODFOOT. I BELIEVE YOU HAVE SOMETHING THAT **BELONGS** TO ME: NAMELY, CONTROL OF MY CITY.
BUT YOU'VE TAKEN IT ILLEGALLY. AND NOW, I'M GOING TO VERY MUCH ENJOY TAKING IT **BACK**.
AH...MY DEAR MAYOR DEMONIKA. HOW I'VE MISSED YOUR SELF-RIGHTEOUS **SMUGNESS** AND YOUR ABSOLUTE CONVICTION THAT YOU STAND FOR THE "PEOPLE."
OF COURSE, WHEN I HAVE MY NEW CHIEF OF POLICE ARREST YOU AND THROW YOU AND YOUR COHORTS INTO MY BITUMEN PIT, THE "PEOPLE" WILL BE NONE THE WISER.
JERRY... LISTEN TO WHAT HE'S SAYING! HE'S ADMITTING TO A CRIME--
OH, ***PLEASE.*** THE PEOPLE DON'T CARE WHAT I SAY OR DO. I COULD KILL ONE OF THEM IN BROAD ***MOONLIGHT*** IF I WANTED TO AND STILL GET AWAY WITH IT.
ALL THOSE IDIOTS CARE ABOUT IS THE PERCEPTION THEY ARE ***WINNING.***
DESPITE YOUR OBSERVATION OF SUCH QUAINT CUSTOMS AS ***ELECTIONS*** AND DUE PROCESS, I CAN ASSURE YOU THE REAL DECISIONS ARE MADE BY THOSE WITH THE MONEY AND THE ***POWER.***
THE "PEOPLE" BELIEVE ANYTHING THEY'RE TOLD, AND THEY DO ANYTHING I ***DECIDE.***
FOR EXAMPLE, THEY ARE ABOUT TO ENJOY THE FRUITS OF A BRAND-NEW TOPSIDE ESCALATOR SYSTEM--COMPLETE WITH OUTRAGEOUS TOLLS AND TAXES, OF COURSE.
THEY'LL ACCEPT THIS OVER AN OPEN BORDER AND FREEDOM OF MOVEMENT IN SCARE CITY BECAUSE WE'VE TOLD THEM IT'S BETTER.
THAT'S THE THING ABOUT THE WILL OF THE PEOPLE: IT CAN BE BOUGHT AND SOLD AT ANY TIME.
MONEY AND ***POWER*** ARE EVERYTHING. AND I HAVE IT ***ALL.***

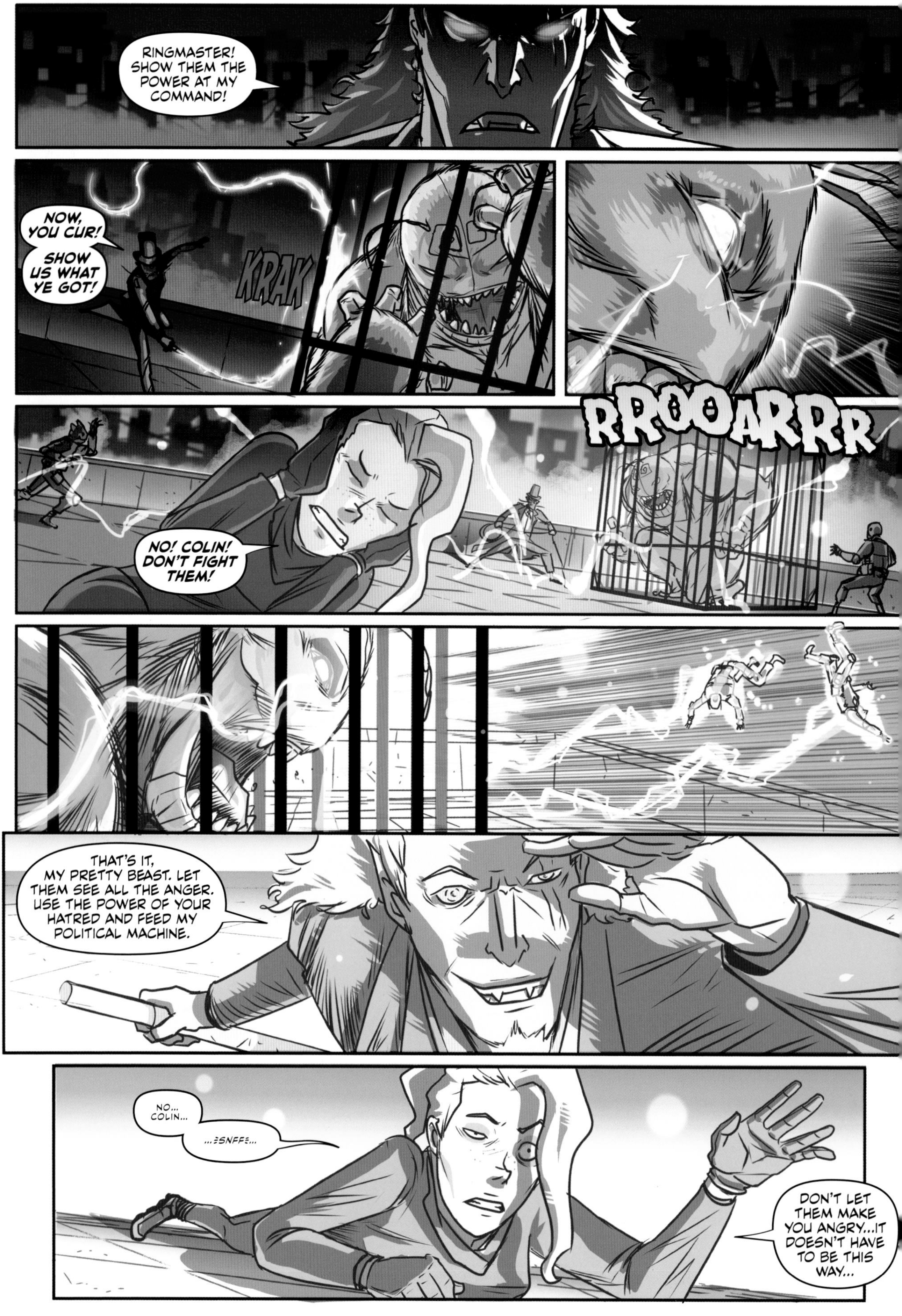
RINGMASTER! SHOW THEM THE POWER AT MY COMMAND!
NOW, YOU CUR!
SHOW US WHAT YE GOT!
KRAK
RROOARRR
NO! COLIN! DON'T FIGHT THEM!
THAT'S IT, MY PRETTY BEAST. LET THEM SEE ALL THE ANGER. USE THE POWER OF YOUR HATRED AND FEED MY POLITICAL MACHINE.
NO... COLIN...
...SNFF...
DON'T LET THEM MAKE YOU ANGRY...IT DOESN'T HAVE TO BE THIS WAY...

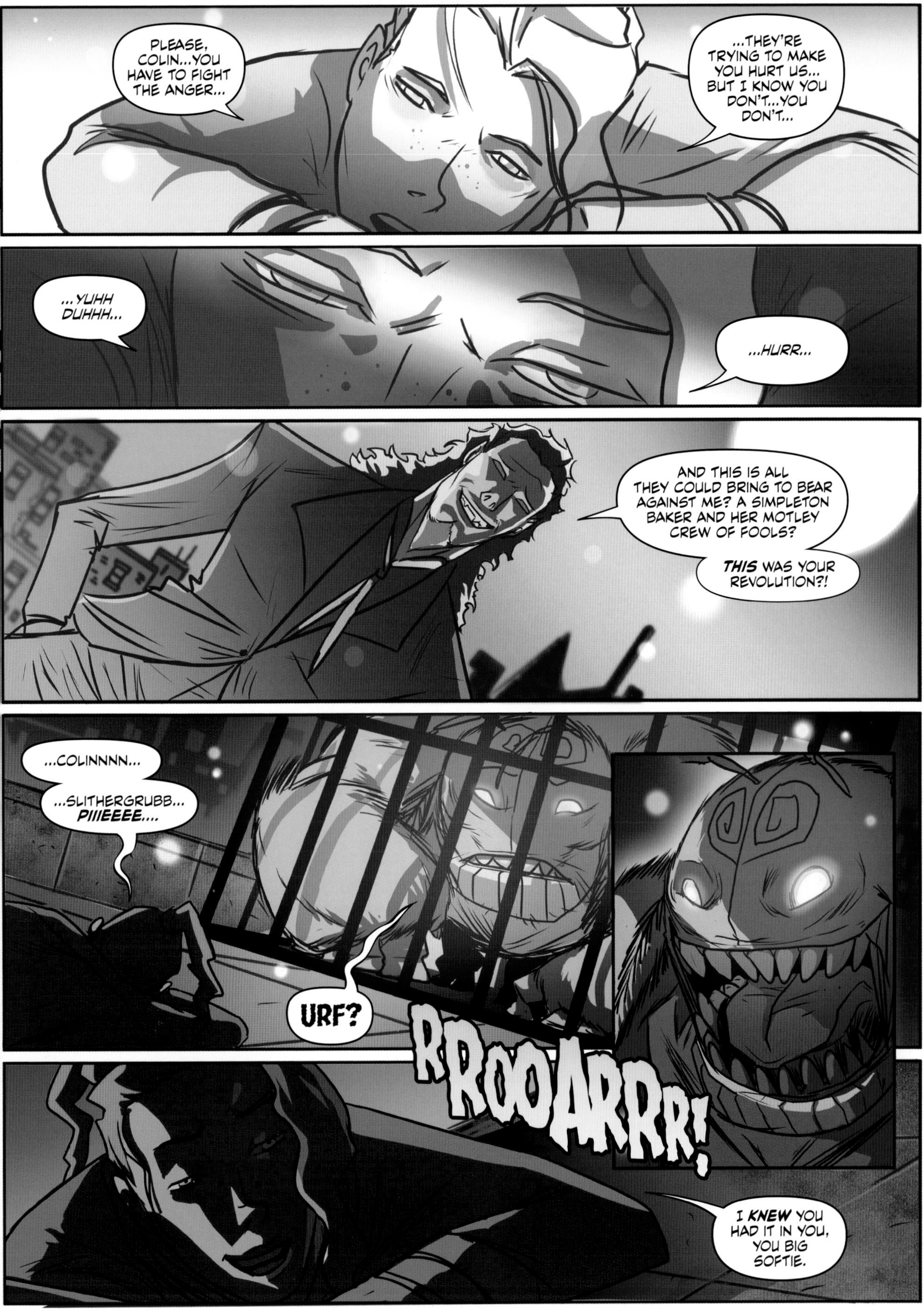
PLEASE, COLIN...YOU HAVE TO FIGHT THE ANGER...
...THEY'RE TRYING TO MAKE YOU HURT US... BUT I KNOW YOU DON'T...YOU DON'T...
...YUHH DUHHH...
...HURR...
AND THIS IS ALL THEY COULD BRING TO BEAR AGAINST ME? A SIMPLETON BAKER AND HER MOTLEY CREW OF FOOLS?
THIS WAS YOUR REVOLUTION?!
...COLINNNN...
...SLITHERGRUBB... PIIIEEEE....
URF?
RROOARRRR!
I KNEW YOU HAD IT IN YOU, YOU BIG SOFTIE.

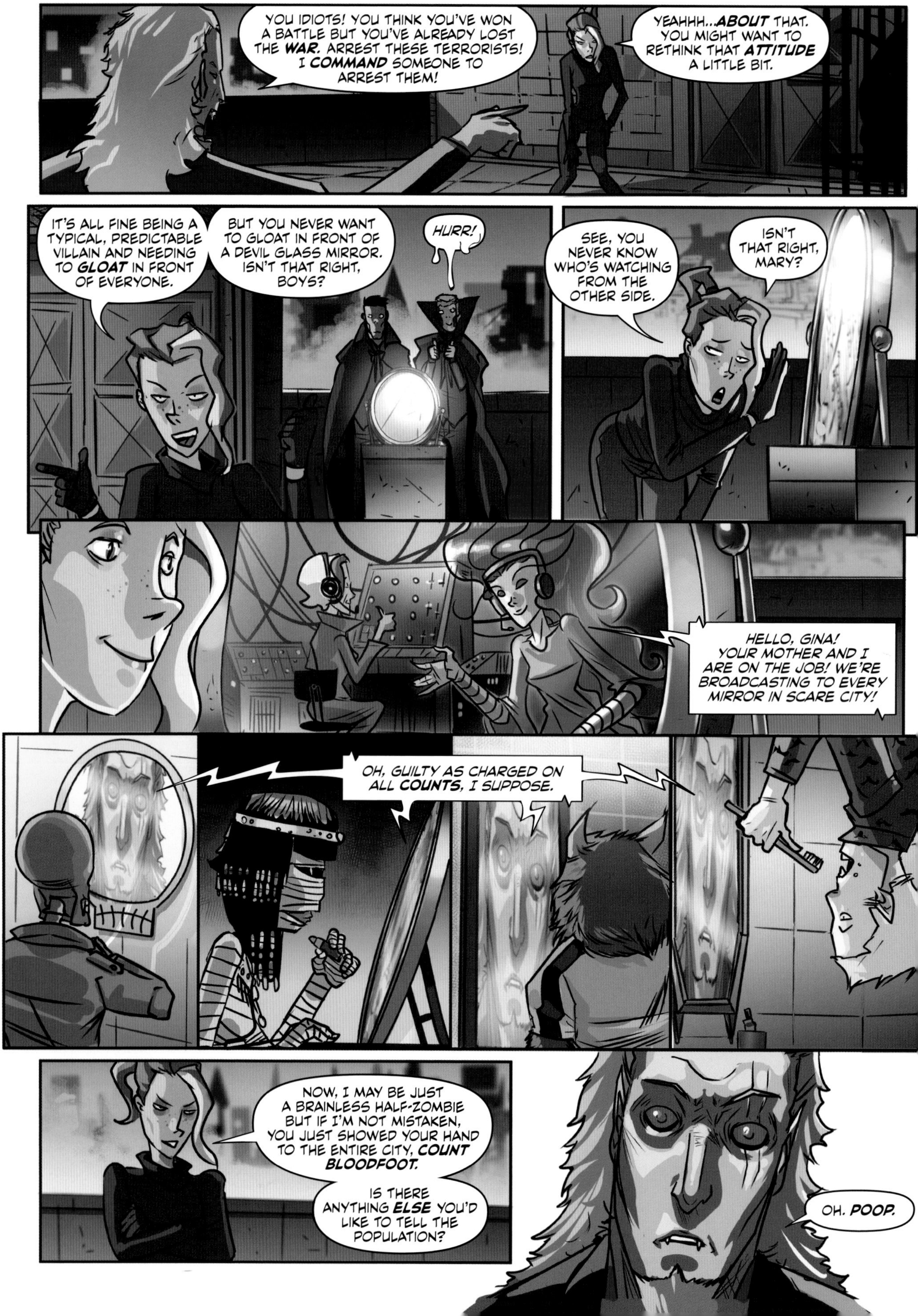

YOU IDIOTS! YOU THINK YOU'VE WON A BATTLE BUT YOU'VE ALREADY LOST THE **WAR.** ARREST THESE TERRORISTS! I **COMMAND** SOMEONE TO ARREST THEM!
YEAHHH...**ABOUT** THAT. YOU MIGHT WANT TO RETHINK THAT **ATTITUDE** A LITTLE BIT.
IT'S ALL FINE BEING A TYPICAL, PREDICTABLE VILLAIN AND NEEDING TO **GLOAT** IN FRONT OF EVERYONE.
BUT YOU NEVER WANT TO GLOAT IN FRONT OF A DEVIL GLASS MIRROR. ISN'T THAT RIGHT, BOYS?
HURR!
SEE, YOU NEVER KNOW WHO'S WATCHING FROM THE OTHER SIDE.
ISN'T THAT RIGHT, MARY?
HELLO, GINA! YOUR MOTHER AND I ARE ON THE JOB! WE'RE BROADCASTING TO EVERY MIRROR IN SCARE CITY!
*OH, GUILTY AS CHARGED ON ALL **COUNTS**, I SUPPOSE.*
NOW, I MAY BE JUST A BRAINLESS HALF-ZOMBIE BUT IF I'M NOT MISTAKEN, YOU JUST SHOWED YOUR HAND TO THE ENTIRE CITY, **COUNT BLOODFOOT.**
IS THERE ANYTHING **ELSE** YOU'D LIKE TO TELL THE POPULATION?
OH. **POOP.**

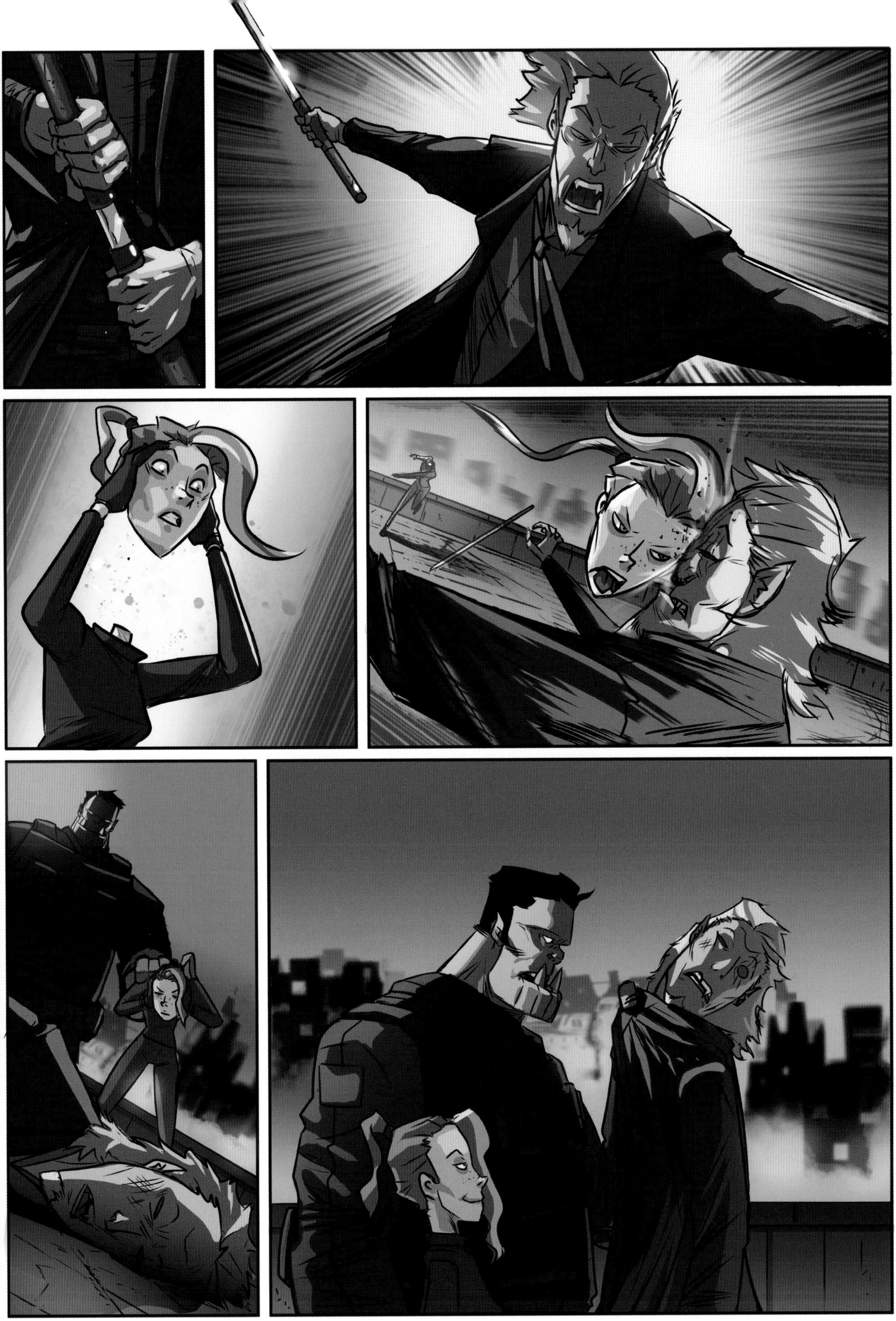

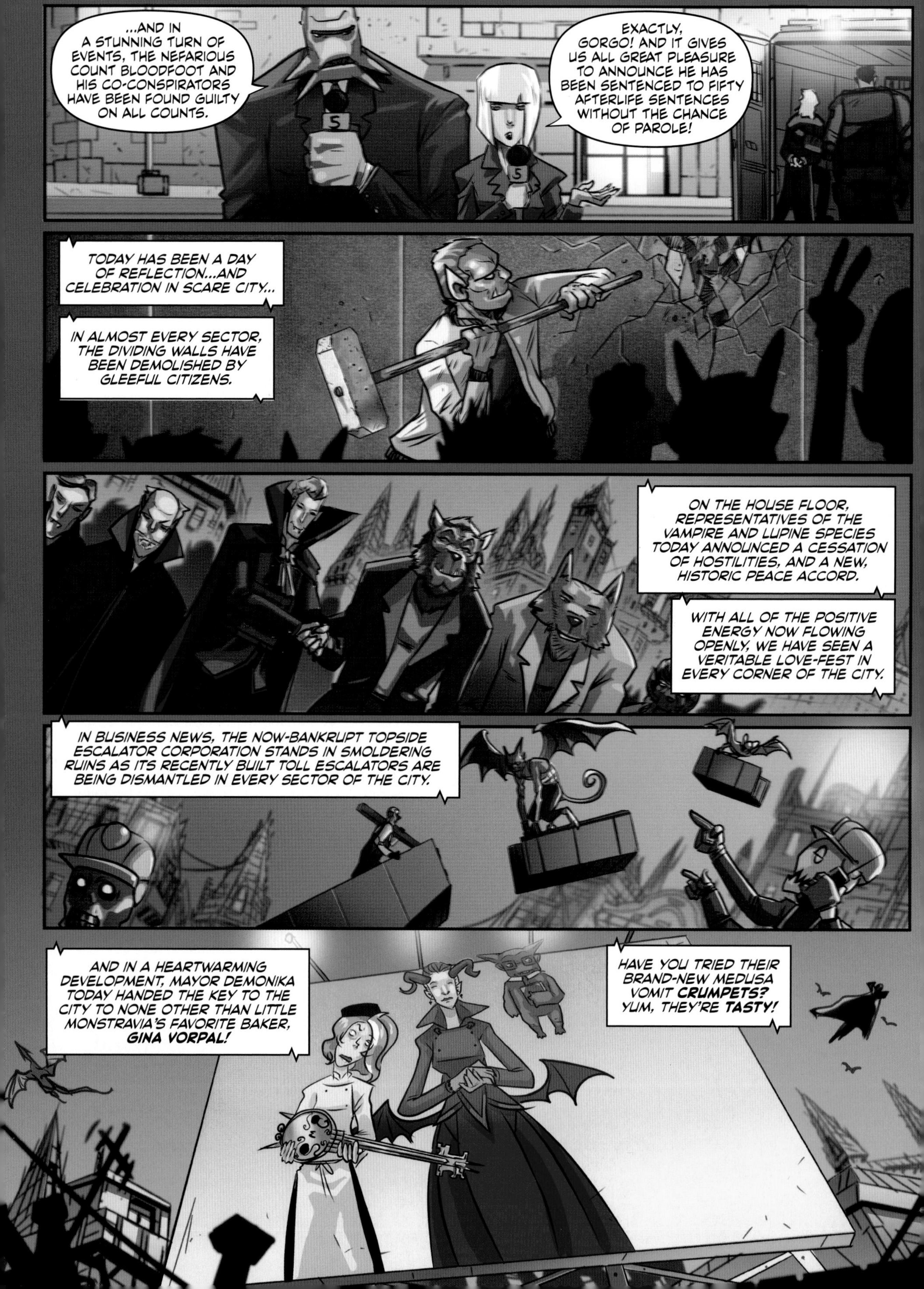
...AND IN A STUNNING TURN OF EVENTS, THE NEFARIOUS COUNT BLOODFOOT AND HIS CO-CONSPIRATORS HAVE BEEN FOUND GUILTY ON ALL COUNTS.
EXACTLY, GORGO! AND IT GIVES US ALL GREAT PLEASURE TO ANNOUNCE HE HAS BEEN SENTENCED TO FIFTY AFTERLIFE SENTENCES WITHOUT THE CHANCE OF PAROLE!
TODAY HAS BEEN A DAY OF REFLECTION...AND CELEBRATION IN SCARE CITY...
IN ALMOST EVERY SECTOR, THE DIVIDING WALLS HAVE BEEN DEMOLISHED BY GLEEFUL CITIZENS.
ON THE HOUSE FLOOR, REPRESENTATIVES OF THE VAMPIRE AND LUPINE SPECIES TODAY ANNOUNCED A CESSATION OF HOSTILITIES, AND A NEW, HISTORIC PEACE ACCORD.
WITH ALL OF THE POSITIVE ENERGY NOW FLOWING OPENLY, WE HAVE SEEN A VERITABLE LOVE-FEST IN EVERY CORNER OF THE CITY.
IN BUSINESS NEWS, THE NOW-BANKRUPT TOPSIDE ESCALATOR CORPORATION STANDS IN SMOLDERING RUINS AS ITS RECENTLY BUILT TOLL ESCALATORS ARE BEING DISMANTLED IN EVERY SECTOR OF THE CITY.
AND IN A HEARTWARMING DEVELOPMENT, MAYOR DEMONIKA TODAY HANDED THE KEY TO THE CITY TO NONE OTHER THAN LITTLE MONSTRAVIA'S FAVORITE BAKER, **GINA VORPAL!**
HAVE YOU TRIED THEIR BRAND-NEW MEDUSA VOMIT **CRUMPETS?** YUM, THEY'RE **TASTY!**

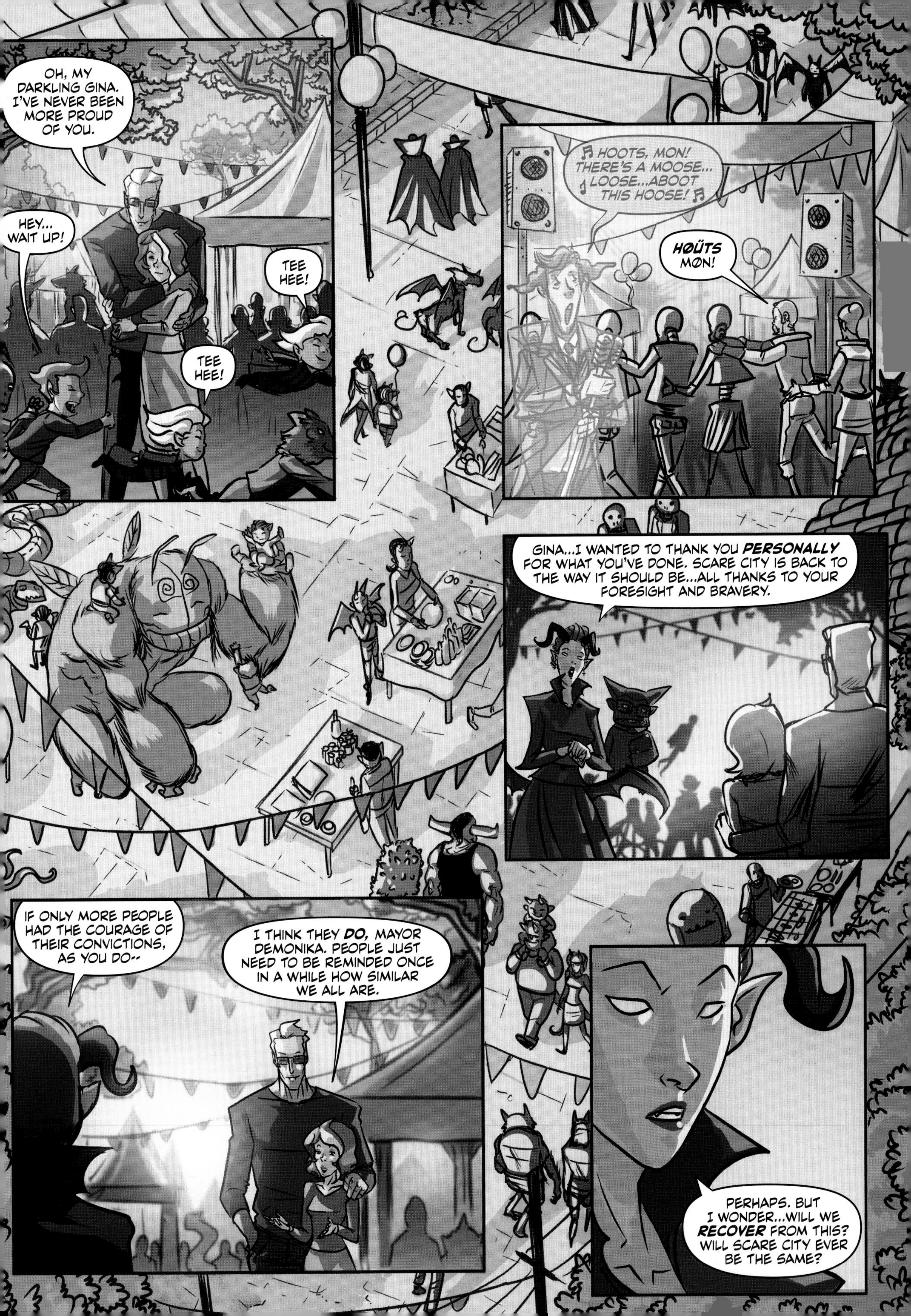

OH, MY DARLING GINA. I'VE NEVER BEEN MORE PROUD OF YOU.
HEY... WAIT UP!
TEE HEE!
TEE HEE!
HOOTS, MON! THERE'S A MOOSE... LOOSE...ABOOT THIS HOOSE!
HØÜTS MØN!
GINA...I WANTED TO THANK YOU PERSONALLY FOR WHAT YOU'VE DONE. SCARE CITY IS BACK TO THE WAY IT SHOULD BE...ALL THANKS TO YOUR FORESIGHT AND BRAVERY.
IF ONLY MORE PEOPLE HAD THE COURAGE OF THEIR CONVICTIONS, AS YOU DO--
I THINK THEY DO, MAYOR DEMONIKA. PEOPLE JUST NEED TO BE REMINDED ONCE IN A WHILE HOW SIMILAR WE ALL ARE.
PERHAPS. BUT I WONDER...WILL WE RECOVER FROM THIS? WILL SCARE CITY EVER BE THE SAME?

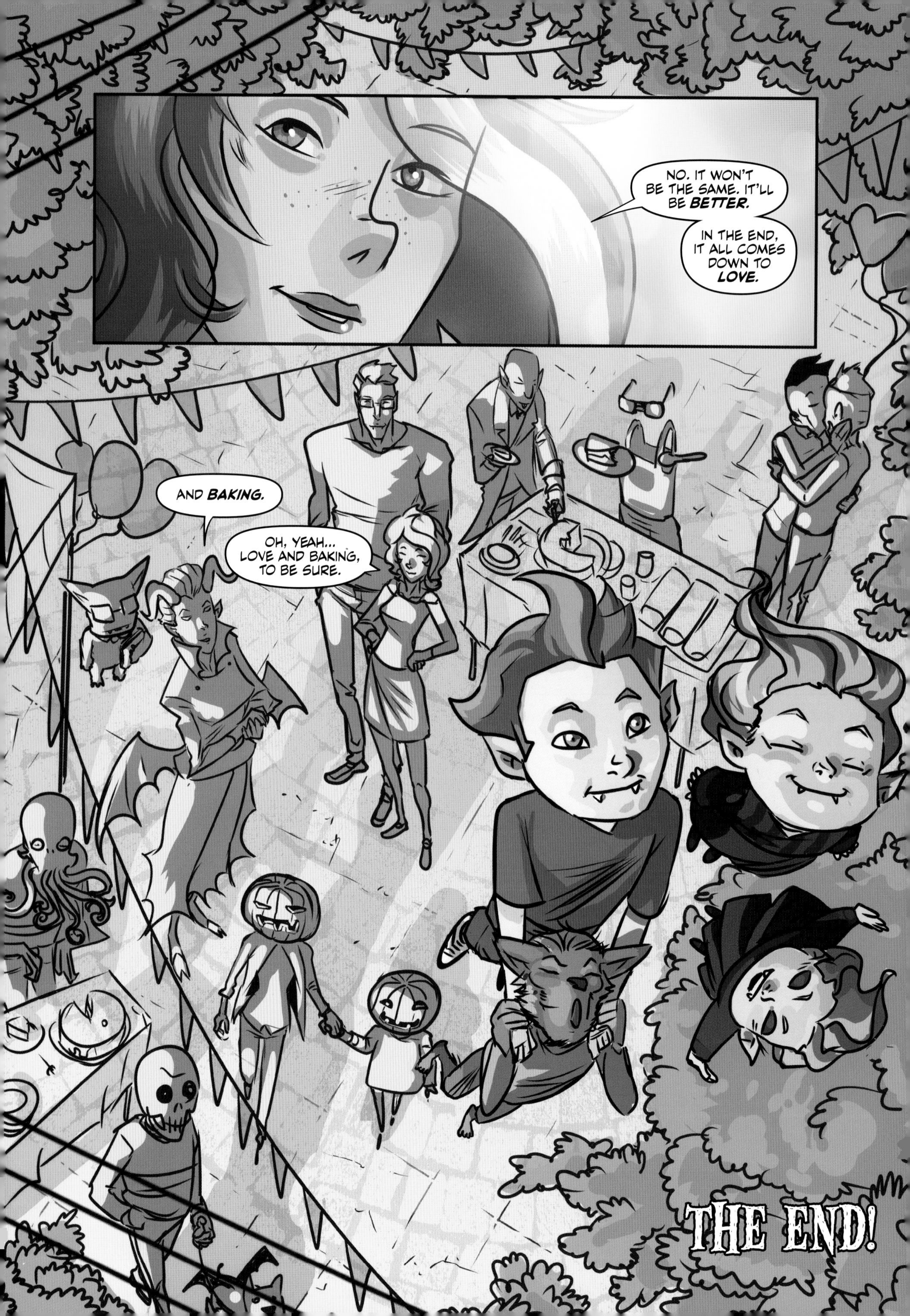
NO. IT WON'T BE THE SAME. IT'LL BE **BETTER.**
IN THE END, IT ALL COMES DOWN TO **LOVE.**
AND **BAKING.**
OH, YEAH... LOVE AND BAKING, TO BE SURE.
THE END!

SCARE CITY

MEET THE FAMILY

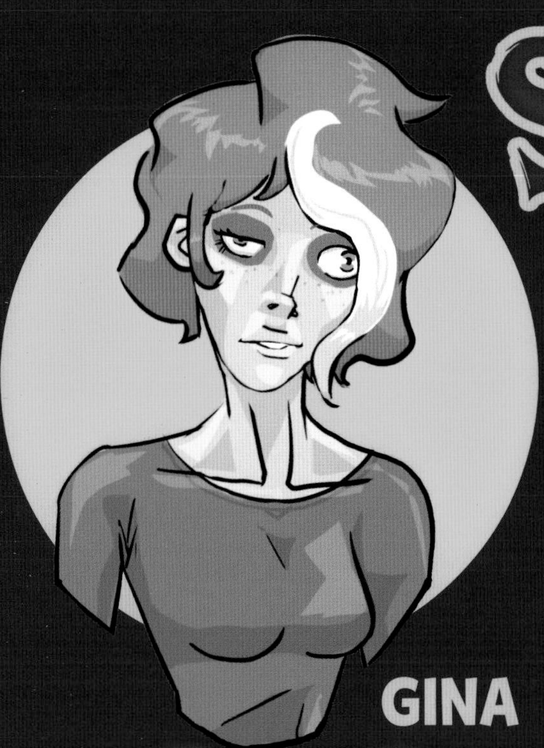

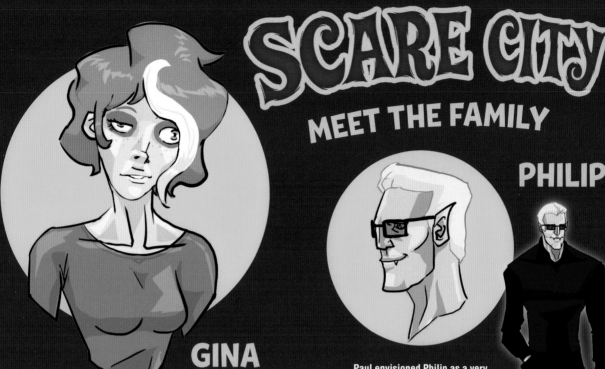

GINA

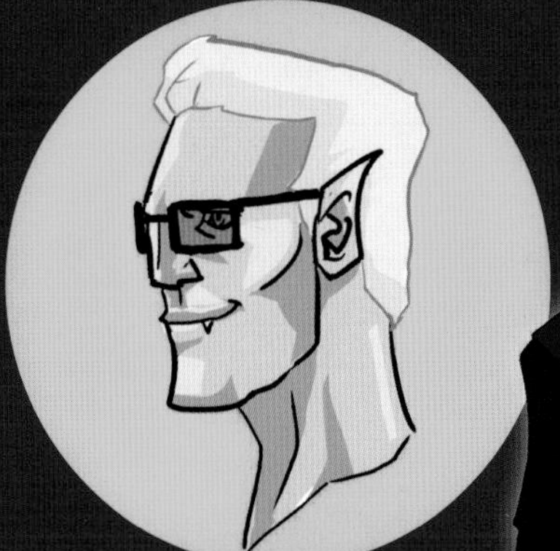

PHILIP

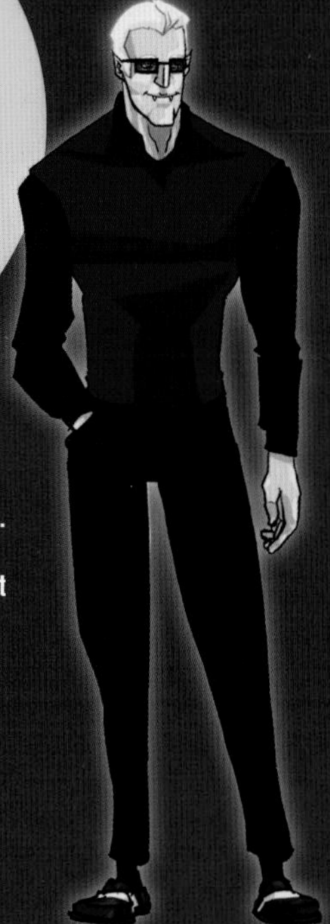

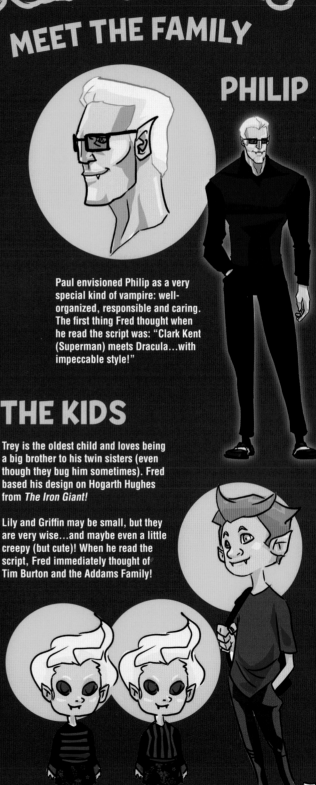

Paul envisioned Philip as a very special kind of vampire: well-organized, responsible and caring. The first thing Fred thought when he read the script was: "Clark Kent (Superman) meets Dracula...with impeccable style!"

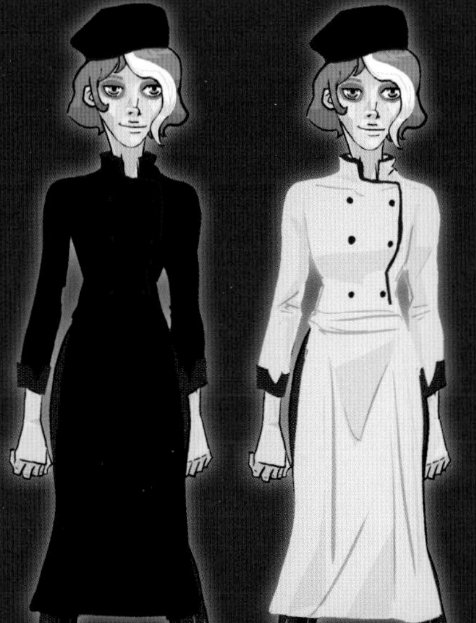

Gina is the heart of this story. Creative, compassionate, and vibrant, she would do anything for the ones she loves—and she proves it! Fred's early versions of Gina show-cased more of her zombie side, but she also needed to look like someone you'd buy treats from! Fortunately, in the past, Fred worked as a cook and knows how they dress.

THE KIDS

Trey is the oldest child and loves being a big brother to his twin sisters (even though they bug him sometimes). Fred based his design on Hogarth Hughes from *The Iron Giant!*

Lily and Griffin may be small, but they are very wise...and maybe even a little creepy (but cute)! When he read the script, Fred immediately thought of Tim Burton and the Addams Family!

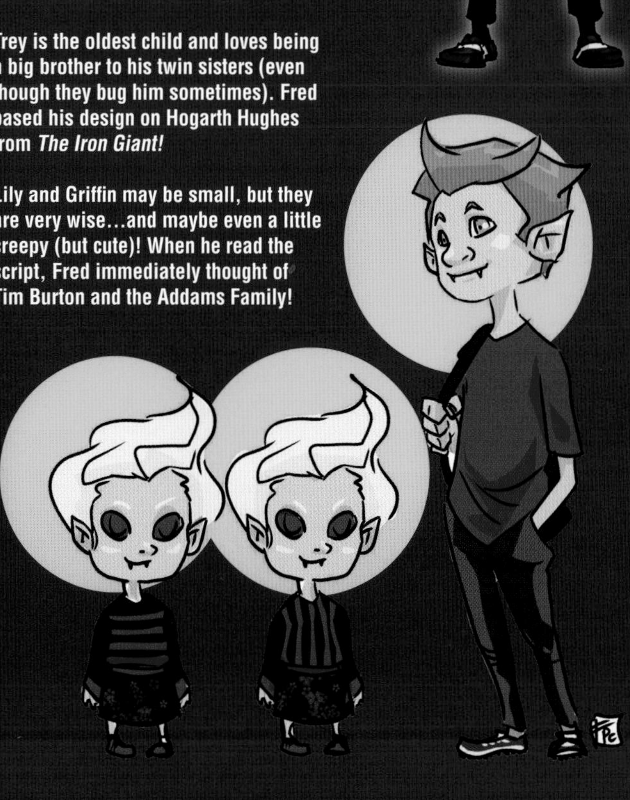

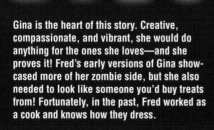

SCARE CITY

TOURIST GUIDE

① THE DEADSPACE
Home to zombies, skeletons and other undead creatures in their many forms. Deadspace residents are largely descended from ancient mummies, who occupy the very center of the Deadspace, and are greatly respected as village elders. Major exports include rotting flesh, a delicacy prized by numerous monsters in Scare City.

② DEMON DISTRICT
One of the older sections of Scare City; home to the darkest of creatures that harken back to the earliest days of human terror and evil. For practice in governing, many demons frequently journey Topside to live among us as our leaders and politicians.

③ OTHERWORLD
Home to aliens, shape shifters, and all otherworldly creatures. Otherworld houses a large population of displaced Martian invaders, as well as many hostile races from the far reaches of our universe. Since the recent easing of tensions across the city, Otherworld residents have agreed to provide Scare City with much of its technology.

④ OUTCAST ISLAND
A quiet sanctuary for those creatures who have been historically persecuted, such as Frankenstein's Monster, Medusa, and other misunderstood monsters. When visiting Outcast Island be sure to visit the Supernatural History Museum, where you can listen to cautionary tales of Topsider intolerance. All proceeds go to the Pariah Retirement Fund, a registered charity.

⑤ ANCIENT QUARTER
From the very earliest of human mythology, the Ancient Quarter houses many legendary monsters such as gorgons, fates, dragons and mountain dwellers. Stay a while at our ancient temple and gastropub, and enjoy riveting performances of spooky tales by the Time Immemorial Players (gratuity recommended).

⑥ CENTRAL SWAMP
Because all cities need a park, our city has chosen to do likewise. Home to violent offenders, swarthy criminals and generally unsavory creatures, Central Swamp has been alienating visitors and dragging unsuspecting tourists into quicksand since 1857!

⑦ SCALE LAKE
Fancy a swim with That Which Shall Not Be Named? Then head on down to Scale Lake for a once-in-an-afterlife chance to visit our friendly Cthulhu. Take to the waves with the Creature from the Black Lagoon and his Blue Lagoon cousin, Alan. Buy one of 13 disgusting flavors from our spit cream vendors, or just relax with a stroll through this terrifying collection of dead plants and trees.

⑧ LUPINE FOREST
Home to Were-men, women and children since the first Age of Change, the Lupine Forest is one of our dynamic and vibrant sections of Scare City. Since the easing of tensions between the vampires and werewolves, the Lupine Forest has become a prized tourist destination. (ATTENTION: the Lupine Forest is deemed "off-limits" during each and every full moon cycle.)

⑨ LEGAL DISTRICT
Quite possibly the single most evil place in the known universe, the Legal district is home to all of the world's lawyers, sports agents, and hedge fund managers. Enter at your own risk. (NOTE: this section is off-limits to writers, artists, actors and other creative types.)

⑩ THE 5TH MENTAL WARD
A favored tourist destination, home to many colorful individuals known as the Criminally Insane. In recent years, much of the 5th Mental Ward's abandoned tent cities have been repopulated by circus clowns and evil cosplayers. (NOTE: it is inadvisable to accept offers of food from any resident, especially candy.)

12
20
4
2
14
8
15
3
N
NW
NE
21
W
E
SW
SE
S

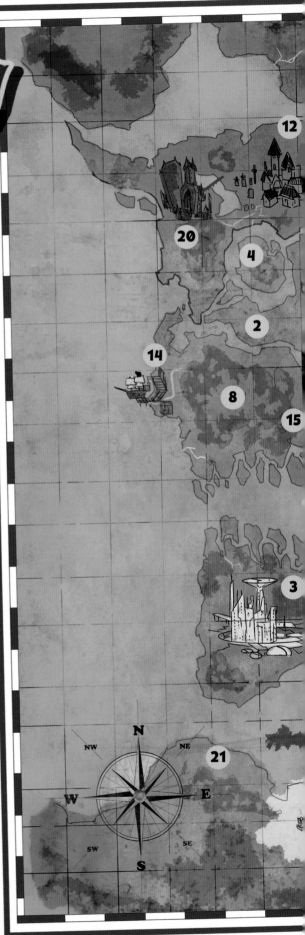

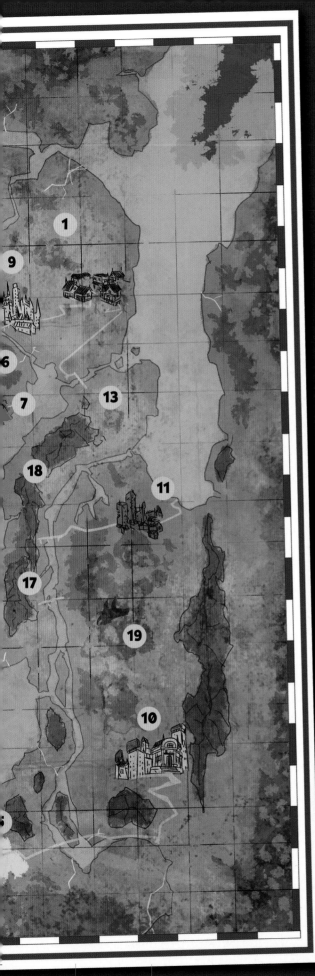

⑪ LITTLE TRANSYLVANIA
Home to many species of vampires, from the older Romanian and Hungarian tribes to the lesser-spotted fruit bat and the fabled Blood-Toothed Frenchman. Many creatures of the night can be spotted in this vibrant location, whose primary exports include everlasting hunger and genuine oak coffins. A center of fine dentistry in Scare City.

⑫ LOWER MONSTRAVIA
A center of innovation: since the easing of tensions, Lower Monstravia has housed any number of hybrid creatures, along with those wishing to integrate with other species. A melting pot of all creatures, Lower Monstravia is home to the world-famous Gina's Bakery, and welcomes each and every visitor. Except lawyers.

⑬ CENTRAL EEVILLE
Home to Scare City's insane scientists and evil villains. Much of Scare City's innovations in evil technology, evil livestock control, and evil toy and merchandise design comes to life in this stupendous section of our fair metropolis.
(NOTE: do not look any resident of this section in the eye, as there have been reports of numerous instances of accidental hypnotism.)

⑭ BONEPORT & THE SLUDGE
A number of years ago, given the popularity of Hollywood pirate movies, a group of Deadzone inhabitants (composed mostly of Skeletons and Dead Pirates) decided to break away and form their own section of society. Residents of the Sludge are now fully voting members of the city council, and enjoy widespread disdain among their fellow creatures.

⑮ SWAMPTOWN
When visiting this section, stay on the lookout for golems, Bigfoots, yetis and homunculi of all shapes and sizes (mostly large). Home to many of the world's most obnoxious creatures, Swamptown is a notorious center of all that is dangerous and violent in the world. One of our favorite tourist destinations—visit if you dare!

⑯ MUCKY COVE
Coursing through the center of our fair city, Mucky Cove is home to many unpleasant underwater creatures, such as harpies, water sprites and sirens. A vibrant and bio-diverse section of the city, Mucky Lake is also home to a number of very nervous sharks, giant squid and venomous jellyfish, which are considered delicacies by their fellow underwater denizens.

⑰ THE WITCHBACK
Home to numerous witches, wizards, warlocks, witch-doctors, and other practitioners of the Dark Arts. The Witchback is now a cultural center for most magical commerce in Scare City. Browse our marketplaces for potions and voodoo dolls, and be sure to check out our Black Cat menagerie and kitty sanctuary for pairing up with a spirit animal or familiar of your choice!

⑱ THE GOLEM TUNNEL
Designed, built and populated by goblins, orcs, immigrant mud creatures and trolls… The Golem Tunnel is a marvel of modern engineering. Building upon ancient subterranean structures, the Tunnel now houses our spanking new Terrible Trench subway system, connecting all parts of Scare City! (ATTENTION: Please do not walk on the tracks, as they are populated by giant, bloodthirsty rats.)

⑲ TASMAGORIA
A strange and wonderful section of our city, Tasmagoria houses all nightmare creatures, fever dreams and imaginary monsters. Nothing is real… and nothing here is as it seems. Described by Foodoo's Travel Guide (2001 edition) as "the most disturbing place in the entire cosmos" for six million years running. Come for the cuisine, stay because you've lost the will to live!

⑳ UPPER SPOOKHURST
Here there be ghosts and phantasms! Upper Spookhurst enjoys a special reputation as a cold, clammy, disconcerting assortment of disturbed graves and abandoned houses. Come and interact with our friendly residents, many of whom can only be seen in the corner of one's vision. For all potential future residents, make sure to visit Murder Mansion and get the job done quickly at half the price of a traditional violent death!

㉑ COLOSSUS PARK
At the far end of Scare City, a haven for enormous creatures, giants, ogres and large-scale fabulous beasts that couldn't fit into Scale Lake. While you're here, make sure to visit our Abandoned Cave of No Return. (NOTE: No refunds available.)